RAVENSCROFT

&

DARKWATER

Dorothy Eden

RAVENSCROFT
and
DARKWATER

COWARD–McCANN, Inc.
NEW YORK

RAVENSCROFT

Chapter 1

IT had begun to snow before the London coach rumbled down the narrow Windsor streets. Bella and Lally thankfully climbed aboard.

Bella had said the only thing for them to do was to go on to London. If they were set down in Piccadilly, which Papa had always said was the hub of the universe, they could surely find inexpensive lodgings for a few days until they had obtained employment.

What else was there to do? Papa's cousin, to whom he had said they must go (he remembered her as always warm-hearted and generous although he hadn't seen her for a long time), had left the small narrow Windsor house, one of a row towered over by the great castle. She had been employed as one of the laundry-maids doing the fine linen from the castle. Her work was reputed to be exquisite. She had been entrusted with the shifts and starched petticoats of the little princesses, and sometimes Queen Victoria's underwear as well. Papa had been sure that she could find work for Lally, who was a good needlewoman, and perhaps for Bella, too, although Bella was not particularly accomplished at any one task. She was too much of a dreamer, her head filled with the novels of Mr. Dickens and Mr. Thackeray.

But the stranger living in Cousin Sarah's house said that Cousin Sarah had got the rheumatism so badly that she could no longer do her work. She had moved back to Ireland, where she had lived as a child.

So Bella and Lally, in one sentence, had lost their anticipated home. They could scarcely cross the sea to Ireland to search for Cousin Sarah.

1

Lally was inclined to be tearful, and blamed Papa for his lack of foresight.

"Why couldn't he have written to her? Why couldn't he have made sure it would be all right?"

"Because he didn't know he was dying," Bella said tartly, the pain turning in her heart again. Papa had known he was dying. As a doctor, he couldn't not have known his condition, Bella realized that now. But he had wanted to protect his daughters from the knowledge. So he had behaved in his usual noisy careless way, going on his rounds, ignoring the pain in his chest, until, just a week ago today, he had dropped dead on one of his patients' doorsteps.

Later, going through his meager possessions, Bella had found the envelope containing the five sovereigns—Papa had been improvident, spendthrift, fond of his rum and whisky, and never sparing of his time for poor patients who could pay him nothing—so this money represented his entire savings. With the money was a letter telling Bella and Lally to keep the sovereigns and not use them to pay his debts—the few pieces of furniture in their cottage could be used for that. And to go at once to Cousin Sarah who was now their only living relative.

"He did what he could," Bella said stormily. She had to be angry, or she would weep, like Lally, and what was the good of that? She had wept all the tears she would ever weep over the dead when Mamma and their two little brothers had died of the cholera seven years ago, and Papa, who blamed himself for bringing home the infection, had begun to stop too frequently at the Horse and Hounds for his rum.

"Anyway," she went on, "Papa knew we were grown women and able to do something for ourselves."

Lally was nineteen, but didn't feel particularly grown, certainly not as much as Bella did at eighteen.

"Like going to London alone?" she asked with trepidation.

Bella drew her shawl more closely round her. The flecks of snow had begun to fall and it was very cold, much too cold to be uncertain where they would find a roof for their heads and a warm bed. But she was impatient, as usual, with Lally's timidity.

"Whatever can happen to us if we mind our own business? I'll ask the coachman if he knows of suitable lodgings. Or there may be a passenger who can help us. For goodness sake come, Lally, and don't look so miserable."

2

"I'm hungry," said Lally.

"Well, so am I. But we're not going to die of hunger before we reach London."

"And cold." But Lally's tears were more from fright than physical misery. She took after their mother, a gentle girl with large innocent blue eyes, a mouth given to trembling, and masses of fine fair hair. Bella had the hazel black-lashed eyes of her father, curious eyes that turned golden when she was excited or agitated. They were her best feature, for her face was pale and three-cornered, and her black hair so heavy that it constantly fell down. She also had her father's quick temper and impetuous romantic nature. When her eyes flashed stormily she no longer looked a child. Lally, although older, had always leaned on her.

It turned out that she was right once more, for before they reached London there was a passenger on the coach who could help them.

At Twickenham the old gentleman, who had stared at the two girls with unabashed curiosity, got out, and a woman, elderly, but with youthful plump pink cheeks and large pebble-grey eyes, perfectly round, like an owl's, got in. She settled herself fussily, shaking the snow off her shawl and demanding that her basket be put on the seat beside her since it contained a dozen new-laid eggs and some fresh farm butter.

Then, seeing that her companions were decently dressed young girls, she beamed upon them in the most friendly manner.

"What a nasty cold evening, my dears. Home and a good fire is the best place. And the kettle on for a nice cup of tea. My son Noah will be seeing to that for me. If he hasn't gone gadding, of course. Young men do so like to gad. I've been visiting my sister for the day. To get a breath of country air, though it was very sharp air today, I must say. We're in for a cold spell. I pity the poor folk without a roof over their heads this night. And plenty of those there'll be. You only have to walk down Fleet Street and along the Embankment to see them, poor creatures. Little children, too. The fate of poor people is monstrous. There ought to be questions in Parliament. Noah and I say that time and again."

Lally nudged Bella. Bella scarcely needed to be nudged. She was well aware of the heaven-sent opportunity. This garrulous cosy little woman was exactly the way one had imagined Cousin Sarah.

But before she could speak their talkative companion made it

3

doubly easy for her. Rocking gently to the motion of the coach, the plump little woman said in her soft voice,

"And you two sweet creatures? How do you come to be travelling alone? Or is that not my business? Noah always says I'm far too prying. But there. I'm interested in human nature. Human nature is my great study."

She fell silent, her round eyes watching the girls, waiting their reply.

Bella said, "Our father died. We're on our way to London to find employment. My sister Eulalie is very clever at needlework, and I—"

The woman leaned across to tap her with a small dimpled hand.

"No need to tell me, my dear. I can see that you would be capable at anything. You have a fine open look. Not cringing. I can't bear cringing servile young ladies. That is your upbringing, perhaps?"

"Our father kept us to our studies."

"Ah, so you can read and write. Then you can be a governess in a fine house. And your sister a milliner, or a dressmaker. You have nothing to worry about, my dears. And so healthy." The last words were said in a reflective murmur.

Bella put her chin up. She had never found it easy to ask for help.

"But we hardly know how to set about finding positions. We know nobody."

"Nobody?"

"No. The cousin we went to see in Windsor had moved. Papa didn't know. So we have no one."

Lally's lip trembled. The old lady noticed this. She pursed her little mouth and said, "Tch! Tch! Tch!" sympathetically.

"Lodgings?" she asked presently.

"We shall find some. We have money. Though if you live near Piccadilly, Mrs.—"

"Proudfoot."

"Mrs. Proudfoot. This is my sister Eulalie, and I'm Isabella McBride. If you knew of respectable lodgings near Piccadilly, Mrs. Proudfoot, we'd be very grateful."

"I live in Seven Dials. I have a smallish house. It's near the market. Covent Garden market. My son works there. He unloads cargoes of fruit from the ships coming up the river, oranges and the like from the Indies and the East, and brings them to the market. He works hard. He's a good lad. He keeps his old mother in comfort. Mind you, it's not an elegant street, and the house is smallish. Smallish but not too small. There's the attic room empty. You'd be welcome to it for a night or two until you get yourselves permanently settled. Mind you—" she silenced Bella, as Bella began to exclaim gratefully, "—I'd have to make a small charge just to keep my son happy. He has such a head for business, you see. Say a shilling a night, and a good hot meal. As for looking for lodgings, I'd say be wary, very wary. Two sweet unprotected young creatures like you. You've still to learn the wicked world, my dears. So if you're interested there's the room upstairs and a good double bed, and I'd be happy thinking I'd helped someone in need."

She clicked her tongue again as she saw Lally now weeping in earnest.

"She has too much sensibility, that one. She must grow tougher. Or find a husband to protect her, of course." Mrs. Proudfoot chuckled pleasurably. "There should be no trouble about that. Such bonny young things, both of you. Any man would be lucky to get you. I'm a widow myself. But I have my good son, Noah. He takes after his father. Strong. Black-haired. A fine young man."

It was now quite dark outside. Flakes of snow spattered on the windows of the coach. They were coming into London, for the road was lit patchily by the flaring yellow of gas lamps. There were rows of houses, low, and huddled together, and sometimes an open space with trees or bushes, as black, in the dusk, as the unknown Noah. Bella didn't know why she had had a sudden shiver of aversion about Noah. But that was purely unreasonable, and the sort of thing much more likely to happen to Lally than herself. Noah was a good son, with a head for business, and his mother was an angel in disguise.

As soon as she could interrupt the gentle monologue that was going on beneath the nodding bonnet, Bella expressed her gratitude.

"How can we thank you, Mrs. Proudfoot? We'd be so grateful to accept your offer of a room until we find positions."

"Why, isn't that nice!" Mrs. Proudfoot gave a beaming smile, disclosing the only defect in her pleasant appearance, broken and blackened teeth. It quite altered her appearance, and for one moment she seemed to be someone entirely different from the placid kind-hearted person she was. But in a moment that queer impression left Bella and she listened to Mrs. Proudfoot assuring herself and Lally that there was no need for them to be hasty about finding positions.

"Young girls can be led astray. Things are not always as they appear on the surface. Why, I heard of a sweet young creature of sixteen thinking she was going as personal maid to a lady of the aristocracy, and finding herself meant only to amuse the son of the house. And he a monster." Mrs. Proudfoot's bonnet, a gay little affair trimmed with a bunch of red cherries, nodded vigorously. "There's traps and traps for the innocent and the unwary. So I hope and pray you young ladies will allow me to be of assistance. I have acquaintances in various positions able to give advice. For instance, my great friend, Mrs. Jennings, has a sister who is housekeeper to Lord and Lady Massingham, and all of fashionable London passes through the doors of that house. I heard her mention only the other day some rich family that was looking for a governess. Who knows, we might be able to place you both in the same house, seeing you're such devoted sisters."

At that, Lally was able to speak at last.

"Oh, Mrs. Proudfoot, that would be kind."

"I can't believe how fortunate it was that we should meet you," Bella added.

Mrs. Proudfoot smiled gently, this time not parting her lips to disclose the offending teeth.

"Heaven sent me, my dears. Heaven helps the innocent."

They alighted from the coach at the stop in Piccadilly. Mrs. Proudfoot said it was but a step to her house, not far enough to take a cab.

The snow had already turned to slush beneath the hundreds of feet of passers-by, and the crowding vehicles, omnibuses, cabs, tradesmen's drays and wheelbarrows. The noise was bewildering: horses snorting and stamping, drivers' shouting, a newsboy yelling something about a great battle with the Russians at Balaclava, a skeleton-thin boy feverishly turning a barrel organ, and a ragged old woman urging passers-by in a stentorian voice, to buy her bonny heather brought all the way from the moors of Scotland by the fast Scottish express.

The gas lamps flared down on this extraordinary noisy hectic scene. Lally clutched at Bella, and Bella, giving a fleeting thought to the quiet Buckinghamshire village which they had left only that morning, resolutely followed the surprisingly nimble figure of Mrs. Proudfoot.

"Hold up your skirts, my dears," said that lady over her shoulder. "The mud's worse than ever, what with the snow and all. Keep close to me. We'll be home in a jiffy and ready for a nice cup of tea."

Lally thought the journey down darker and narrower streets and bad-smelling alleys a nightmare, but Bella was already exhilarated and excited by the strangeness of it all. She responded to new situations from which Lally, in her timidity, shrank. The bad smells, the anonymous figures huddling in doorways, sudden scurrying forms and unrepeatable shouted words of abuse, were all part of London. The same as the great houses and parks and theatres such as they would see in the next few days. They were actually going to be lodged near the wonderful Covent Garden Opera house which all the famous singers of the world visited. She had read about it, with its chandeliers and grand staircase, and red plush. One day she and Lally would go there to hear a performance. She didn't know how this would be achieved, but struggling through the evil-smelling mud after Mrs. Proudfoot's bunchy nimble figure, she knew without doubt that somehow such a thing would happen. They would wear low-cut satin dresses and jewels, and everyone would look at them, the two beautiful sisters, one fair and one dark . . . And the man who escorted them (there was only one man in Bella's dream) would be greatly envied . . .

"H-ss-t! Out of my way!"

The vicious hiss cut like a whiplash across Bella's dream. She jumped aside as a man pushing a barrow loaded with an unidentifiable mass of junk pushed by, spattering her with mud. For a moment she was as weak as Lally, tears springing to her eyes at her abrupt descent to reality. The hiss seemed to ring in her ears as, cold and hungry and now with filthy skirts and shoes, she plodded down the mean streets, with Lally's panicky grip on one arm, and Mrs. Proudfoot steering ahead indomitably.

But once within Mrs. Proudfoot's cosy parlour Bella's momentary depression vanished and even Lally's tears dried.

In the well-blacked shining grate there was a glowing fire. A kettle sang on the hob. Two wooden rocking chairs were drawn

up on the multi-coloured rag rug in front of the fire. There was a
dresser, well-stocked with platters and tankards, and a table laid
for tea. The red plush curtains were drawn across the window
making the room as cosy as could be. It was possible to forget at
once the cold muddy streets outside the front door. Here was
warmth and comfort and safety.

Mrs. Proudfoot saw the girls' expressions and nodded happily.

"You see, my dears. I spoke the truth. The kettle boiling and
a good fire, and upstairs a warm bed." She rubbed her little
plump hands, and held them out to the blaze. "Would you like
to see your room at once, and take off your wet shoes? I'll take
you up and show you where the water closet is. Oh, yes, this isn't
a grand house but that comfort I insisted on having installed. I
don't hold with ladies having to go to outdoor privies in all
weathers. Now don't be long upstairs. When you come down tea
will be ready and Noah will be home."

Upstairs, alone with Bella, Lally found her tongue.

"Oh, Bella, isn't this wonderful! I think Mamma and Papa must
be watching over us, don't you? Look, a real feather bed!" She
bounced on the bed excitedly. "And everything so spotless. See,
we have our own washstand, and there's water in the jug. Mrs.
Proudfoot must always be prepared for guests."

"Lodgers," said Bella. She was glad they were being independent and paying for their lodgings. For all Mrs. Proudfoot's kindness, she was a stranger and one couldn't accept too much
generosity from strangers. At least, one might wonder why it was
offered . . .

But there was nothing to make her uneasy here. The room was
scrupulously clean, which was probably a rare thing in this
neighbourhood, and their welcome couldn't have been more genuine had it been from the missing Cousin Sarah. Lally was right,
Mrs. Proudfoot had been heaven-sent.

"Perhaps she's looking for a wife for Noah," she said reflectively.

Lally looked startled.

"Do you suppose—oh, but she couldn't be. Noah sounds the
kind of young man to find his own wife. To tell the truth, I'm a
little scared of him."

"You're scared of everybody," Bella said, not wanting to admit
that she herself had had that strange moment of apprehension
about Noah. Strong, black-haired, Mrs. Proudfoot had said. "And

I shouldn't think there are many nice young women in these parts. Or didn't you have your eyes open as we came along?"

Lally shivered, nodding.

"Yes, I did. I kept thinking, supposing we had been alone in these streets. It is true that London's no place for unprotected girls. And that makes it so much more fortunate that we're here. Oh dear, do I look too awful? My nose always gets red from crying. Shall I change my gown, Bella? The skirt is dreadfully muddied. It wouldn't take a minute to unpack. I could put on the blue—"

"For Noah?" Bella teased. "I thought you were so scared of him."

Lally's pretty chin went up.

"Oh, Bella, you know that I can't bear not to be neat and tidy. I must wash my face and brush my hair. Oh, do look at the sweet little mirror. Bring the candle closer so that I can see. I declare, my hair is a ruin—oh, what was that?"

Her flushed face with its tangled mop of fine fair hair vanished like a ghost from the tilted mirror as she shot round.

"What was what?" To her annoyance, Bella's heart had jumped and her voice was no more than a whisper.

"I thought I heard someone moaning."

"I expect you did. In the street." Bella went and flung up the window and leaned out. "This is a horrid street," she declared vigorously, finding relief in indignation. "I had thought the centre of London would be so grand. But this! It smells of bad fish, and worse. And look, the snow's black with soot almost before it settles. What a good thing we're safe indoors. But we won't stay in these parts long, Lally. We'll get into a grand house with a hundred rooms, and staircases, and a conservatory with orange trees—"

"You're sure it was in the street?"

"What? That noise? Of course!"

"I thought for a minute it came from just under us." Lally stood uncertainly, her eyes enormous. Then she made herself laugh. "I suppose it's because I'm tired and hungry, but I'm as jumpy as a cat. Isn't it silly of me, when Mrs. Proudfoot is so kind. Help me pin up my hair, Bella, so we can go down."

Bella twisted her sister's hair deftly and impatiently.

"If you're going to be so helpless, how will you ever get a position? You need a lady's maid yourself." The brush became still

9

in Bella's hands. "But wouldn't it be fun if we did have one? Or one each."

"Now who's dreaming? A lady's maid! Us!"

"Why not? Things happen. Or if they don't you can make them. Look at how we're here safe for the night."

"Yes, I know, but this is very different from those grand houses you're dreaming about. You read too many books. Papa always said so. But I do admit it's nice to dream."

For a moment the girls stared at each other, caught up in their faith and optimism. Then suddenly Lally shivered. "O-oh, I'm cold! Don't let's be parted, Bella, wherever we go to work. I'd so hate to be parted."

"My dears! My dears!" That was Mrs. Proudfoot calling up the stairs. "Come on down. Supper's ready and Noah's home."

The tall young man dominated the room. His head with its thatch of coarse tousled black hair was only an inch or two from the ceiling. He had very broad shoulders and great hands that rested loosely on his hips. His cheeks were reddened to a holly brightness, perhaps by the cold wind off the river or perhaps simply by the health that flowed through his strong body. But his eyes, small and intense, were blacker than anything Bella had ever seen. Black and piercing beneath heavy brows. His loosely hanging hands and his negligent attitude were simply a pose. He was summing up the two girls with the most acute awareness.

"These are the young ladies, Noah," Mrs. Proudfoot said with her warm enthusiasm. "Miss Eulalie McBride and Miss Isabella McBride. Fancy two such innocent creatures abroad on a night like this. Didn't I do right to bring them home?"

Noah began to grin broadly, showing large white teeth.

"Quite a find, eh, Ma?"

Mrs. Proudfoot turned to the girls to share her delight.

"Now isn't that a clever way Noah has of talking? Quite a find. As if you are both jewels. Now sit down, my dears. Tottie, Tottie! The eggs! The bread and butter!"

A girl came hurrying in from the kitchen laden with a crock of eggs and a plate piled high with thick slices of bread and butter. Hungry as she was, Bella noticed Tottie before she was aware of the food. Her shock at Noah's size now turned to a new feeling of uneasiness. In an old brown dress, terribly shabby, with her wispy hair hanging round the white wedge of her face, Tottie looked no more than twelve years old. She had a dull daft look.

Her hands were covered in chilblains. In contrast to Mrs. Proudfoot's plump cosiness and Noah's radiant health, she was like a starved cat, all eyes and bones.

She put her burden on the table, clattering the eggs as if she were terrified.

But Mrs. Proudfoot said quite kindly, "That's a good girl, Tottie. You've counted right this time. How would you like to boil another egg for yourself?"

The child stared as if she hadn't heard correctly. Her mouth fell open in disbelief.

"Well, off you go and do it. Nobody starves in this house."

Mrs. Proudfoot flapped her hands and Tottie fled like a scared chicken.

"There's no use expecting any sense out of her," Mrs. Proudfoot explained. "She's dumb, poor soul, and I rather think half-witted as well. We've only just found her, haven't we, Noah. She was living all alone like a little rat in an old shed. Noah brought her home. We've not had time to dress her decently yet. Indeed, if Miss Eulalie's as good with her needle as she says, she may help me make the poor child a gown."

"Oh, *yes*, Mrs. Proudfoot," said Lally eagerly.

"Don't call me Mrs. Proudfoot, call me Aunt Aggie. All my girls do."

"All your girls?" Bella asked.

"Bless me, my dears, you aren't the only ones I've helped. Are they, Noah?"

Noah gave his gleaming smile.

"But they're prettier than Tottie, Ma. You had a better find than me."

"Oh, pshaw, Noah! None of your making sheep's eyes. The girls are only here for a day or two until they find positions. I'm going to send word to Mrs. Jennings tomorrow. She'll know of something, I'll be bound."

Bella knew she should have been grateful and happy for Mrs. Proudfoot's plans. But all she could think of was trying to avoid Noah's sharp black stare. He never stopped staring. He had no manners at all. Bella found herself wondering how poor little Tottie, crouching in the darkness of the tumble-down shed, had felt when she had been dragged into the light by that great hand that was now carelessly cracking an eggshell. Perhaps that was when she had been struck dumb . . .

After supper Mrs. Proudfoot, who liked to be called Aunt Aggie, sat in her rocking chair knitting. She had put on steel-rimmed spectacles, and through them her eyes were magnified until they seemed to Bella, who by now was sleep-dazed, like perfectly round grey moons. Her needles clicked and she sometimes pursed her little pink mouth and said "Tch! Tch!" reflectively. She had stopped talking and Bella had no idea at all what her thoughts were.

Noah had gone out. Bella didn't wonder what his errand was. She was only thankful he was gone. She tried not to think about him at all, because if she did she would imagine him searching derelict houses and sheds for more starved little girls.

But it was only her tiredness and the strangeness of the long day that was making her so foolishly imaginative.

At last it was Lally's head that fell forward on her chest. She jerked it up, exclaiming in confusion, "I'm sorry, Aunt Aggie! I dozed off."

Mrs. Proudfoot started up.

"Oh, my poor dear! There you are tired out and I hadn't noticed. You must go straight upstairs, both of you. Come, I'll light your candles myself."

She preceded them up the stairs, carrying the flickering candle. The girls stumbled after her, scarcely able to see their way, the frail light obscured by Mrs. Proudfoot who, with her wide skirts, completely filled the narrow stairs. The first time they had mounted the stairs they had been too intent on where they were going to notice the first landing, and now it was too dark to see what doors led into what rooms.

In the attic room Mrs. Proudfoot lit two candles on the dressing table, and made a great fuss of turning down the bed and untying the pretty blue ribbon bows of the curtains so that the night was shut out. Then she stood in her dark gown with its snowy kerchief and smiled her goodnight.

"You must sleep soundly, my dears. Tomorrow, as I said, we'll begin planning your future. I'm sure Noah will have some notions. He was very taken with you. Especially Miss Eulalie. I noticed him looking at her pretty face."

"Aunt Aggie!" Lally gasped.

The old lady chuckled, showing her shocking teeth. In the flickering light, her mouth was a dark hole, her pale eyes swallowed into the pale blur of her face. For a moment Bella had another of her disconcerting impressions—that Mrs. Proudfoot had a gargoyle head, open-mouthed and staring.

"Isn't it nice to be admired by a strong young man. But there, I won't tease. Sleep well. And don't be alarmed if you hear strange noises in the night. You little country dears. You're not accustomed to the goings-on in a city street. Such goings-on. They don't bear listening to. But you'll be safe here, my little loves."

As soon as she had gone Bella sprang to the door and shut it, then wedged a chair under the knob.

Lally watched her open-mouthed.

"Whatever's come over you, Bella? Surely you're not afraid of Noah. Not with Aunt Aggie—"

"Don't call her Aunt Aggie!" Bella said.

"But she asked us to. Everyone does, she said. You heard her."

"Who is everyone?"

"Why—girls like us, I suppose. She said she often helps girls. She must keep this room just for them, I mean with the ribbons on the curtains and that darling mirror. And this bed. Oh, this lovely bed! I can't wait to get into it. I shall sleep like a log."

"I shan't close my eyes," said Bella.

"Bella, whatever has come over you? You weren't like this before supper."

She hadn't seen Noah then, nor Tottie. Where did Tottie sleep? In a dark cupboard in the kitchen, curled up in her rags? Out of sight of Noah? Surely, if she had been in the house only a day, there would have been time for Aunt Aggie (now even she was thinking of Mrs. Proudfoot as Aunt Aggie!) to find some warmer tidier clothing for her. But she had had a freshly-laid egg for her supper. She wasn't being starved any longer. And if she were really as frightened as she looked she could run away, couldn't she? Even in the snow. Cold was better than terror. So it must be only that Mrs. Proudfoot hadn't yet had time to wash her hair and dress her decently.

Lally in her nightgown, with her hair let down, was climbing into bed.

"Do hurry, Bella. Blow out the candles and let's get some sleep. I didn't like Noah either, if the truth must be told. But we might not need to see him again. I expect he goes to work before dawn, and by night we might have positions to go to ourselves. Anyway, Aunt Aggie isn't entirely philanthropic. She's getting a shilling a night from us. So we aren't in her debt."

13

It was unusual for Lally to be the one who was calm and sensible. Bella was suddenly ashamed of her wild imagination, and began to undress quickly.

"I expect you're right, Lally. Anyway, it's only for tonight. Tomorrow we'll go out ourselves and see what can be done. It will be stopped snowing by then."

"Aunt Aggie must have found positions for those other girls," Lally murmured sleepily.

"Yes, she must. And we're in London at last. It's really very exciting. Think of all the famous people perhaps not a mile from here. Think of the great houses and the lights. Anything can happen to us now we're not in a little village any longer."

Lally was pleased to hear the familiar optimism in Bella's voice.

"There you are, dreaming as usual. Well, perhaps your dreams will come true. Perhaps you will live in a great house."

"You, too, Lally."

But when the candles were blown out the girls clung to each other in the feather bed, tense and listening, until sheer weariness overcame them and they slept.

Because they slept so soundly, the shriek that awakened them seemed doubly shocking.

Chapter 2

As Bella had surmised, not a mile away, indeed less than half a mile, there were many famous people, and they in their turn were watched over by portraits of more departed famous.

Beside a richly glowing fire in the Garrick Club, Guy Raven was entertaining his old friend, Doctor Bushey.

"Some more brandy, Daniel?"

"I will. It's excellent. It'll keep the cold out on my way home."

"I'll give you a lift."

"No, no, I prefer to walk. You fellows in carriages never see life."

"Life? What sort?"

"My dear Guy, don't raise your eyebrows like that. Not your sort of life, I grant you. It has nothing to do with smart gambling dens or restaurants or ballrooms. Or boudoirs. It bears no relation to your invented diversions."

"Invented? That's the right word at least, even if the following one hardly fits my case. I seldom feel diverted!"

Doctor Bushey's shrewd eyes were almost lost beneath the luxuriating grey lichen of his eyebrows.

"Now look here, Guy, you've indulged in enough self-pity. That's what it is, no matter what you like to call it."

Guy shrugged. "You're talking of my behaviour? I put no labels on it. My mother calls it licentious. She thinks because I no longer have a wife I also no longer have physical desires. I agree that what I do isn't related to love. But if a pretty woman's willing —who the devil cares about my reputation?"

"Don't misjudge your mother, Guy. She wants you to marry again. And rightly."

15

The young man leaned back with an exasperated sigh.

"Not you, too, Daniel. So Ravenscroft needs an heir. So I tie myself to some eager young virgin and produce one. Isn't that as licentious as sleeping with a whore? And what the devil would I talk to this young woman about for the rest of my life? Damn it, Daniel, marriage might have been invented to regularize having children, but no one said it should be a prison." His eyes went dark. "And it would be a prison for me with anyone but Caroline."

Doctor Bushey regarded his host, a young man in his late twenties, handsome with his high-browed face, his lazy blue eyes that could turn to steel, and too often did, his cool hard mouth, his air of dandyism. It was becoming difficult to remember the Guy Raven of two and three years ago, passionately in love with his delicate young wife. There had been no boredom in his eyes then. A great deal of enthusiasm for the son he hoped for, but most of all that unashamed tenderness for Caroline.

Of course Guy would be thirty on his next birthday. All this cynicism and impatience had been in him and would have come out one day, but it would have been levelled intelligently only against hypocrisies and the smug social values he hated.

Now, alone, and, Daniel guessed, appallingly lonely, he was simply letting himself go. He did need to marry again. But who? In spite of his wealth and looks the more timid eligible young women were being frightened off him—or their mothers were. He could be unforgivably rude and deliberately shocking. And the purely ambitious woman who would have been a match for him he scorned. Besides, as in a slightly drunken moment he confided to Daniel, young women were romantic and wanted some vestige of a heart. His was in the grave with Caroline and the dead baby.

But perhaps his recent plans for a political career—as another diversion?—would save him. He was standing for his own constituency in Hertfordshire, and so far was bringing a surprising amount of energy and enthusiasm to his campaign. Although that, Doctor Bushey knew, had a good deal to do with his opponent, Sir Henry Shields, being a man whom Guy disliked and despised. He could be a devilish hater, another tendency Caroline might have softened. Surely there must be some other young woman in the world who could care for this unpredictable exasperating brilliant reckless young man who was so good at making enemies.

Doctor Bushey firmly believed in the balance of good and evil. A hater could also be a lover.

After the silence that had fallen between them Doctor Bushey thought it discreet to change the subject.

"Have you decided yet on what issue you're going to fight this election?"

Guy grinned, and looked suddenly much younger.

"Chiefly the desire to do down my opponent who's a smug-faced hypocrite. He leads his wife and his five daughters to church every Sunday, and on Monday starves his employees, and uses children, babies, in his mills."

"He's a powerful man, Guy. He has the press on his side."

"I'm not frightened of the press. They could use cleaner ink, too. But of course you're right again, Daniel. Once I've trampled Sir Henry in the dust I've got to build something on top of him. There's the defence policy, of course. This expensive and exceedingly bloody and, in my opinion, quite useless war in the Crimea. There's the Irish question. There's income tax. It'll have to go up, not down."

"And there are the poor," said Doctor Bushey.

"Unpopular."

"I didn't think you were concerned with popularity. And you mentioned yourself the children in Shields' mills. Do they have to be used only as a weapon against him? He isn't the only guilty one. The whole country's guilty. Why don't you fight their cause generally?"

Guy smiled lazily at his companion's earnestness.

"You're not on an election platform, Daniel."

"Sometimes I'd like to be. Look here, come with me to one of the Ragged Schools one day. You might think, or make your constituents think, how washing facilities could be introduced into the tumbledown shed where the schools are held. Then, when the children come off the streets from selling matches or running three miles behind a cab in the hope of earning twopence for carrying baggage, or any of the other devious occupations they pursue to fill their bellies, we might be able to wash a bit of the filth off them. And perhaps even give them a bowl of hot soup to encourage their learning of the alphabet."

"What else?" said Guy, very quietly.

"Well, there are the young women, girls, mere children, forced on to the streets either by drunken parents or because they have no parents. I won't try to describe their lives, unless they're rescued pretty young. Have you noticed Betsey at my house, by the way? But of course you have. You've an eye for a pretty girl. Would you believe that two years ago she was in a brothel in Waterloo Road. She got typhoid and was thrown out into the street to die. Someone picked her up and took her to the fever hospital in Islington. I found her there. So now her story has ended happily. But for one Betsey there are hundreds less fortunate. Innocents . . . Come, Guy, there's a cause worth fighting for. Get this city cleaned up. Crush these monsters who exploit the unfortunate."

"You're on your hobby horse, Daniel."

"I'm giving you a cause."

"I admit I'm interested. Now convince me. This girl, Betsey, for instance—she's now clean and well-fed, but hasn't that experience perverted her?"

"Untouched!" Doctor Bushey declared heatedly. "Untouched! A child can have an inherent innocence that saves it. Not all, of course. But if they have, they seem to overcome even the physical degradation. Those are the ones to be saved. I'll make you a challenge, Guy. Walk with me through the streets of Soho one evening. I'd suggest tonight if it weren't snowing. What about tomorrow?"

"My mother has some affair. I'd willingly escape it, but I promised her I'd be there. Reluctantly."

"She has some young lady for you to look over?"

Guy swung round violently, beckoning to the waiter.

"Two more brandies. Doubles. Yes, you're right, Daniel. A prissy miss in a crinoline. At the moment, I assure you, I'd rather look over your Soho drabs. But I suppose I can get drunk again. Make it the following day. I'll look forward to it."

"This is hardly meant to be a pleasure."

Guy's eyes were narrowed, hiding their expression.

"I believe you think all this suffering poor stuff is a revelation to me. Have I gone about with my eyes shut?"

"Your eyes see what your mind allows them to. Like those of fashionable ladies dabbling in good works. Otherwise how could they bear it? Make your class *look* at things."

Guy's mouth quirked suddenly, without humour.

"You're an old sobersides, Daniel. Why don't we pick up a

likely looking girl and take her to the Ritz? Feed her, and pick her brains. If she has any."

"My God, I'll prove this is no amusing evening out," exclaimed Doctor Bushey, suddenly losing his temper. "If you are a specimen of the kind of man who sits in Parliament—blind, introverted, selfish, spoilt—then heaven help this country!"

Guy's mouth tightened. But he said with deliberate good humour, "You'll have me taking you seriously, Daniel. I'll find I'm using the poor as more than a stick with which to beat my dishonourable opponent."

"I'll show you. I'll prove it to you!"

"I believe you will."

But the last brandy had slightly fuddled Doctor Bushey, and his flash of anger had tired him. He didn't notice that Guy spoke seriously at last.

Chapter 3

LALLY clutched Bella in a suffocating grip. They both lay rigid, listening.

"What was it?" Lally whispered, at last.

"Some—" Bella hesitated, "—poor woman in the street. Robbed, I expect."

"No, it was in this house."

Bella had thought so herself. She was still trying not to alarm Lally who was inclined to hysterics.

"It was the same person we heard moaning this evening," Lally said with certainty. She sat up in the dark. "Who can it be? What can be the matter with her? Wouldn't Aunt Aggie have said if there were someone else here?"

The dark pressing on Bella's eyes was intolerable. She groped for matches and lit the candle. Even such a small and wavering light restored her common sense.

"I expect it was Tottie. She probably has nightmares that she's still in that dreadful shed. Perhaps with rats."

"I can hear someone walking about," Lally exclaimed, clutching Bella afresh. "Coming up the stairs," she whispered.

The footsteps, ponderous and slow, were quite distinct. The ancient stairboards creaked. A door clicked shut, softly.

Then abruptly, freezingly, the scream came again.

Without conscious thought Bella was out of bed and standing rooted to the floor.

Lally had begun to whimper, her face ash white.

"What are you going to do, Bella? Don't leave me!"

Bella picked up her shawl and flung it round her shoulders.

"I'm going to find out what's going on."

"Bella, don't! Don't! It might be Noah."

Bella looked at their feeble barricade, the chair propped beneath the doorknob.

"Noah! What would he be likely to do?" she said with a fine pretence at scorn. At the same moment the door handle turned very gently.

Lally's knuckles were in her mouth. Bella, gripping the end of the bed, was able to say in quite a loud voice.

"Who is it?"

"My dears! What's making the door stick?"

It was Aunt Aggie's voice, warm, throaty, reassuring. Bella sprang to the door to remove the chair.

"We heard someone scream. Lally—we were both nervous!"

"So you barricaded the door. In my house! My *foolish* little dears!" Aunt Aggie, in nightcap and voluminous red flannel dressing-gown, holding a candle aloft, looked the picture of cosiness and normality. "I said to Noah, those dear girls upstairs will be alarmed. I must slip up and see if they have been disturbed. I can't stay—" a deep shuddering moan from beneath her stopped Aunt Aggie for a moment. Then she went on quickly, "It's most unfortunate, my poor niece is having her baby quite six weeks too soon. She's a delicate creature. I was afraid this would happen."

"You mean she's been here all the time?" Bella exclaimed involuntarily.

"All this evening? Certainly. And for a week before that. She came to London to await her husband's return from abroad. He's a sailor. His ship's due in any day, any moment. But I fear—" Aunt Aggie chuckled cosily, "his child is going to arrive first. Now settle yourselves, my loves. I didn't tell you Mary was here for fear you'd be disturbed."

"We're doctor's daughters," Bella said, rather stiffly.

"Why, so you are. But I expect your dear Papa sheltered you, for all that." Another cry came from downstairs. "Oh dear, I must go. Mary doesn't show much fortitude. She's very young, poor dear."

"Can we help?" Bella persisted.

"By no means. I wouldn't have your young eyes distressed. Goodness me, I've brought a score of babies into the world. Noah's in the kitchen boiling water. That's all the help I need. Now pull the blankets over your ears and go back to sleep."

The door closed and Aunt Aggie had gone. Bella got back into bed, but didn't blow out the candle. The frail light was a small shield against nightmares.

"Do you know," she said at last, "I think that baby is Noah's."

"You mean Mary is his wife?"

"Well—" Bella thought nothing of the kind. "I think that's why she's here. Because the baby is Noah's."

"Oh," said Lally, shocked but satisfied. "That's why Aunt Aggie wouldn't talk about her."

It was the first light of dawn before the baby's thin feeble wail sounded.

Bella edged herself out of Lally's clutch that had scarcely slackened all night, and got out of bed to draw back the curtains. It was still snowing.

When she saw the inexorably falling flakes, making the narrow street spotless and silent, her heart sank. This meant that she and Lally would have to remain prisoners in the house for another day.

But prisoners by snow, not by any persuasion on the part of Aunt Aggie or Noah, she told herself firmly. She would pay Aunt Aggie the shilling for their night's lodging and beg her hospitality until the snow stopped. It was the only thing to do. No one could go abroad looking for work with skirts dragging in twelve inches of snow.

Anyway, her night's fears seemed foolish now. A baby had been safely born, which was a wonderful, not an alarming event. Bella only hoped that Lally would wake in a similarly calm state of mind. In this, too, her mind was soon at rest, for Lally opened her eyes and instantly exclaimed, in excited anticipation,

"I wonder what the baby is. I long to see it. Let's get dressed and go downstairs."

A newly-lit fire was burning cheerfully in the little parlour. Before it stood a wooden cradle.

Lally was beside it in a flash, and bending over its occupant.

"Oh, Bella! It's awfully tiny. Come and look. It's no bigger than a doll. It has black hair like—" She bit off her words as Noah's laugh came from the doorway.

"Were you going to say like mine, Miss Eulalie? But you'd be wrong in that. Mary's only my cousin. And I suppose that poor worm of a thing is my cousin, too. Lost me my night's sleep, it did."

But Noah didn't look as if he had lost any sleep. His huge shoulders filled the doorway, his cheeks were as healthily red as ever, his little coal-black eyes intensely alert. It was impossible to imagine him having any sympathy for the young mother upstairs, whether the child was his or not.

"Is it a boy or a girl?" was all Bella could find to say.

"A boy. If you can call it anything at all. It came too soon. Ma says it likely won't live."

Lally gave a cry of distress, and knelt beside the cradle to fondle the baby's incredibly miniature hand. The fingers curled feebly round her forefinger. She gave a softer exclamation, of pity and enchantment. It was as if the little scrap of a thing were appealing to her, asking her to help it to live.

Aunt Aggie had come in carrying steaming plates of porridge.

"Well, look at her, the daft creature," she said tolerantly. "Is your sister soft about babies, Miss Isabella?"

Lally looked up, pleading.

"Aunt Aggie, it won't die, will it? Noah says it will."

"The Lord knows, my dear. It's got a bad start, poor scrap. It won't take any food yet. I fancy it's too weak. I've seen that kind before. They just take a brief look at our sorrowful world and then off they fly to brighter climes. Now don't take on, Miss Eulalie. If the Lord had meant that little being to stay with us He wouldn't have sent it too soon. Come and sup your porridge while it's hot."

"How is its mother?" Bella asked.

"Fine. She's eaten a hearty breakfast and now she's sound asleep."

The porridge plates were liberally filled and there was a jug of milk from which Aunt Aggie urged everyone to help themselves lavishly. Tottie, still dressed in the same deplorable dress that was little better than a piece of sacking, came in to take away the empty plates, clattering them clumsily in her swollen fingers. Her face was not so much white as blue, either from cold or starvation or both. Presently she came back with bread and dripping and thick fried slices of gammon.

"Eat up," said Aunt Aggie comfortably. For all her disturbed night she looked remarkably fresh, her cheeks pink, her eyes round and benign. "Noah, don't forget that you must call on Mrs.

Jennings before you go to work. That's the lady I mentioned as might be of assistance in finding positions for you young ladies," she added to Bella and Lally. "Get her to send a message, Noah, if she has any prospects. It's no day for women to be abroad. I haven't seen so much snow in London for years. You two dears mustn't attempt to go out. You'd be mired in a few steps. I'm sorry it will be such a dull day for you," she fluttered her plump hands, "but Noah and I can't be held to blame for the snow. I think I may be right in suggesting you could find worse places to be than this fireside."

Her expression was so kind, her plump figure so attractive in its neat dark dress fastened at the neck with a jet brooch, her cap so crisply starched and snowy, and this all following a sleepless night, that Bella could only nod in helpless admiration. Her apprehensions had been completely vague and unfounded. Even Noah, by daylight, was simply a large uncouth young man with his head hung greedily over his plate.

"Can we see your niece later, Aunt Aggie?" Bella found herself automatically adopting the more intimate form of address. She had caught it from Lally.

"Well, now, that I don't know. She's shy of strangers. She's a country girl. But we'll see. We'll consult. I want her to sleep as long as possible. So as to get strong if her husband should arrive. In the meantime, if you want to be of use, I can find you plenty of needlework. If Mrs. Jennings should call it would be sensible for her to see how nicely you sew."

Noah suddenly made a stifled sound, between a grunt and a cough. He lifted his head and cleared his throat vigorously, as if a crumb had lodged inconveniently. His small eyes were shining, not with distress, but with malicious laughter.

"You're a one, Ma. Getting your mending done for free," he added.

Bella wanted to explore. Lally was content to sit by the baby's cradle, her needle half the time idle in her hand. But Bella kept listening for Aunt Aggie's whereabouts. She had the most lively curiosity about the baby's mother, and a compulsive desire to see her. Once, when she had been sure Aunt Aggie was upstairs, she went into the kitchen, a narrow dark chilly room with damp walls and a stone floor, and a tiny window looking on to a square of snowy backyard. She wanted to see Tottie, too.

She asked Tottie for a glass of water, and while the girl was getting it, said conversationally, "It's nice being here, isn't it, Tottie?"

The little unkempt head nodded warily.

"I noticed you have such bad chilblains, you poor thing. You ought to have something to put on them. My father had a very good prescription. I'll tell it to your mistress and she'll get it for you, I'm sure."

The child stared, shrunk against the wall. Bella had a queerly certain feeling that she could speak if she wanted to.

"But anyway they'll soon get better now you're in a warm house. It's better than that horrid shed, isn't it? Do you really have no mother or father, or brothers and sisters?"

Tottie shook her head violently. Bella moved nearer.

"Tottie, have you seen the lady upstairs. The sick one?"

But before Tottie could make any kind of response the ceiling above them creaked, there were steps on the stairs.

Tottie made a flapping movement with her hands. Her face was full of unreasoning terror. She seemed to be frantic for Bella to go.

Bella's swift instinct of fear had simply been caught from this child who was like a little wild animal, captured and mesmerized. She made herself say lightly, "It's only Mrs. Proudfoot, Tottie. She wouldn't hurt you. Is it Noah you're afraid of?"

But the child had fled through a doorway that led down a steep narrow flight of stairs, obviously to a cellar. Perhaps that was where she slept, down in the dark and the damp. She must have been in hiding from a hostile world for so long that she instinctively preferred the dark.

Surely, if anyone could tame her, it would be Aunt Aggie.

Resolutely reassuring herself, Bella returned to the parlour fire and Lally, with her anxious vigil over the baby.

"Bella, it never cries."

"I expect it's too weak."

"I think that's because it's hungry. It sucked my finger quite strongly."

Bella looked down at the tiny pinched face. It didn't look like the face of a newborn baby, healthily red and crumpled. It was a curious bluish-white and looked old, a miniature old old man.

But even so weak a child could be coaxed to life. Papa had used to perform miracles with delicate babies. He had insisted on constant feedings, a very little at a time.

All the same, after Tottie scuttering away into her cellar, Bella felt defeated and wasn't sure she wanted to fight for another even more pathetic scrap of humanity. She had a sudden desperate longing for their cottage in Buckinghamshire, Papa coming in smelling a little of rum but hearty and cheerful, the table laid for supper, the fire burning, Lally at the pianoforte singing in her sweet reedy voice, the present, secure and comfortable, lasting unquestioningly forever.

Nevertheless, when Aunt Aggie came in, she would have made the suggestion if Lally hadn't bravely spoken up first.

"Aunt Aggie, I think the baby's hungry. Shouldn't it go to its mother?"

Aunt Aggie bustled over with the greatest interest.

"Do you think it will drink now, the little mite? Well, there's no harm in finding out. I'll take it upstairs."

She was away for a long time. When she came back with her bundle she was doleful.

"I doubt it took much. It hasn't the strength to suck. However, we must trust in the Almighty." She laid the baby back in the cradle. "There, the little lamb. So quiet and good. Not a cry against this wicked world."

Later in the day, just before the early dusk began to fall, there was a great knocking at the street door. Aunt Aggie, for all her bulk, could move lightly and very quickly. She was out of the parlour at once, closing the door behind her. Bella could move quickly, too. Without formulating her reason she had sprung to the door and opened it a crack.

"Bella!" Lally exclaimed, horrified.

"S-sh! I want to hear."

But she couldn't hear much, only disjointed scraps of conversation. Something in a man's voice about fog and ice on the river, and Aunt Aggie oddly emphasizing one word, *awkward, awkward*. Then she said quite clearly, "Tomorrow morning at the latest, fog or not," and in reply to something the man said as he stepped away from the door out of earshot, "A great prize, you can be sure."

She gave her low throaty chuckle as she closed the door.

Bella had scarcely time to regain her seat before Aunt Aggie came back into the room.

"Now isn't that exciting! The ship is in."

"The ship?"

"Mary's husband's, of course. But it can't dock yet because of the fog."

"Then the baby will be going," Lally exclaimed.

Aunt Aggie patted her head benevolently.

"Silly child. You didn't think it could stay here, did you? Any more than you and your sister can. Poor Aunt Aggie is the one who should be sad. She is just a milestone all you young people pass. However, that's life, and we must accept it. Now do you know what Tottie and I are going to do. We're going to toast crumpets for tea. Presently Noah will be home. We'll all have a cosy evening round the fireside."

There hadn't been a sound from upstairs all day. Lately, the dreadful suspicion had been growing on Bella that the baby's mother was dead. She wasn't leaving happily with her newly-returned husband in the morning, she was going to be carried out, smuggled away before it was light. That was what the furtive conversation with the man at the door had been about. That was the thing that was so awkward. Aunt Aggie hadn't wanted to distress them by telling them the news.

Could it be true? Was it only her strained and fevered imagination? It was so uncanny that there was no sound at all from upstairs. Even when Aunt Aggie went up, there were no voices. And she still insisted that her patient wasn't well enough to be visited. Was that why the baby didn't drink—because its mother lay dead?

The same unreasoning impulse that had driven Bella to listen at the door now made her run softly up the stairs while she knew that Aunt Aggie was busy in the kitchen.

There were two open doors on the first landing. They led to small bedrooms, one obviously Aunt Aggie's and the other Noah's. The door to the third room was closed.

Bella knocked gently then, afraid to linger, turned the knob. The door was locked.

"You!" she called softly. "Mary! Are you awake?"

No one answered. There was a curious musty smell on the landing. It seemed to come from the locked room. Bella called again, more urgently,

"Are you all right in there? I'm your friend. Please speak to me."

She pressed her ear against the door, and fancied she could

hear deep breathing as of someone drowned fathoms in sleep. Yes, she was sure it was breathing. Abruptly she was filled with a wonderful sense of relief. Mary was sleeping, as Aunt Aggie had said. Once again, Aunt Aggie's actions had been perfectly innocent. Really, she was awful to have let her imagination run away with her like this. It was only because the day had seemed so long and dark, and the house so claustrophobic. Dead bodies, indeed! There was only a young girl sleeping after the ordeal of having her first baby.

Relief made her quite gay that evening. When Noah came home to say that Mrs. Jennings would be sending for Bella and Lally some time the following evening, she welcomed the news with gratitude and optimism.

"Does she know of some suitable positions? That would be wonderful."

Aunt Aggie tapped her gently with her knitting needle.

"Such impatience! She wants to be gone from us, Noah. No, my dear, Mrs. Jennings doesn't recommend young ladies to positions without having first seen them and ascertained their capabilities and character. She is the soul of integrity. She merely wishes to make yours and your sister's acquaintance. It may be she will know of something you can go to immediately. It's quite probable since it isn't every day one meets such nice refined young ladies as you two. Mrs. Jennings' complaint is the great vulgarity and bad manners of so many modern young women. Some of them without even a curtsey, if you can imagine it."

Aunt Aggie tch-tched with disapproval. Then her needles began clicking busily again and she said cosily.

"But Miss Isabella and Miss Eulalie haven't a thing to worry about, have they, Noah? They'll be taken care of."

Noah suddenly let out his choking hiccuping laughter.

"You're right, Ma. As usual."

Chapter 4

LALLY couldn't sleep that night. She turned and twisted, and resented Bella sleeping so soundly. Didn't Bella give a thought to the little baby that may not live till morning? Lally couldn't get it out of her mind. Each time she closed her eyes she saw the minute bluish-white face and the wren's claw hands. Why didn't it move more and open its eyes? Why didn't it cry? It had seemed to be starving this morning, but after it had been with its mother it had scarcely stirred again.

It wasn't natural. It should have been awake again and screaming for food. But it just slept on and on, scarcely breathing.

Now she kept listening to see if it were crying. If it were it would be a feeble whimper that perhaps no one would hear.

Bella had worried about the young mother, so mysteriously quiet all day and with her bedroom door locked. But Lally had thought that a grown-up person could speak for herself, and make demands. The baby was helpless.

The worry turned round and round in her mind until at last she did fall into a sleep that was full of fantasies. There was the sound of someone sobbing, the crack of horses being whipped up, and suddenly, quite near, Noah's snorting laugh. That last sound was so real that it brought Lally sharply awake, only to realize that the house was silent and she had been dreaming.

Although could she, very faintly, hear the baby crying? She sat up listening. Then, very cautiously so as not to wake Bella she got out of bed and crept to the door. She listened intently through a crack. No sound came up the dark stairs. This didn't reassure Lally, but rather alarmed her more. For now she was beginning to imagine the baby dead or dying. In spite of her nervousness of Noah—for supposing that laugh hadn't been in a dream at all—she knew that she had to see the baby.

Surely she could creep down the stairs without disturbing anyone. She put a shawl over her nightgown, and groped for the candlestick. She mustn't strike a match until she was outside the bedroom for if Bella woke she would forbid her going.

On the landing there was still silence. With shaking fingers, afraid she would drop candlestick and all, Lally struck a match and lit the candle. The trembling light reassured her. She began to make the journey downstairs, the violent beating of her heart seeming to make as much noise as the alarming creaking of the stairs. It surprised her that she accomplished the journey without disturbing anyone.

There was still a ghostly glow from the fire in the parlour and the warmth lingered. Holding the candle carefully, Lally darted forward and peered anxiously into the cradle.

It was empty.

The clothes were thrown back, the barest imprint of a tiny head remained in the pillow.

Lally gave a cry of loss and desolation. The baby might be with its mother. It might have been taken into Aunt Aggie's bed for warmth. She told herself this, but her sense of loss remained overpowering. Her eyes filled with tears. She had come downstairs on bare feet, and she was shivering with cold. There was nothing for it but to make the cautious journey upstairs again. She turned disconsolately to do so.

In the passage a sound caught her ears, a tap-tap-tapping that seemed to come from the cellar.

Bella had told her the stairs down to the cellar, where she thought Tottie slept, went from the kitchen. Scarcely knowing why she did so, Lally tiptoed out there, the stone floor striking ice cold on her bare feet.

The noise that sounded like nails being hammered gently into wood was louder now. The door leading downstairs to the cellar was slightly ajar, and a faint glimmer of light showed.

As Lally stood there filled with an unnameable fear there was a final sharp bang, and the noise of a hammer being thrown aside. Then there were footsteps coming fumblingly up the stone steps.

Lally looked round wildly for some place to hide. There wasn't time to do more than blow out the candle and conceal herself behind the door, praying that whoever was coming wouldn't shut it and expose her, trembling, in her nightgown.

Something bumped against the door frame. There was a brief muttered imprecation in Noah's voice. The large shape of Noah, with a candle in one hand, what looked like a shovel in the other, and with a narrow box tucked under his arm appeared. He crossed the kitchen without looking behind him, and opened the door to the backyard. His candle blew out at once. He swore again, and leaving the door open to the icy wind, disappeared.

In a flash Lally was at the window, peering out. The moon shone through torn rags of snow-cloud and lighted eerily the white ground and against it Noah's black form.

He had put the box on the ground and begun to shovel the snow away from a small area near the wall. Lally watched in fascinated horror as he dug steadily, the narrow hole becoming a black gaping wound against the white snow. He didn't waste too much time over the digging. As soon as the hole was deep enough to accommodate the box he picked it up and put it in with a contemptuous toss, and began scraping soil over it.

At that moment Lally could contain herself no longer. She gave a low whooping cry and fled for the stairs. She blundered up them in the dark, falling twice, bruising her knees and her knuckles, caring nothing for the noise she made.

"Bella!" she was gasping. "Bella! Wake up, for God's sake! Bella, we must get the police. Noah's murdered the baby. And now"—her voice choked in unutterable horror, "he's burying it!"

She was at the bedside shaking Bella violently awake.

"It's true! You can go down and see. The moon's shining. It makes the earth against the white snow look as if—as if it's bleeding! And there's Noah—he made the coffin in the cellar. I heard him. Oh, Bella, the poor little baby!"

Bella had somehow got a candle lit and was trying to calm Lally's babbling.

"Hush, love, for goodness sake! You'll have everyone awake. You've only had a nightmare."

"It's true!" Lally beat Bella with clenched fists. "It's true. It's happening now. The cradle's empty. The little b-baby—Noah's murdered it, I tell you!" she shrieked.

There was a click of a door opening and shuffling steps.

"What's the matter up there?" came Aunt Aggie's voice, strangely thick, as if she were half asleep.

"There, I told you!" Bella whispered. She raised her voice. "It's all right, Aunt Aggie. Lally's had a nightmare."

Lally ran to the top of the stairs, screaming, "It's not a nightmare! Noah's burying the baby. I saw him."

Aunt Aggie came up the stairs, slowly, each step creaking beneath her weight. She was in a voluminous flannel nightgown, with her nightcap strings tied beneath her chin. She completely filled the narrow stairway, forcing Lally back with her slow formidable approach.

But her voice was, as usual, kind and mild.

"What's this, my dear? What's this? Noah burying a baby. What nonsense! I declare, it's almost comical. My innocent Noah!"

"The cradle's empty!" Lally whispered, her strength suddenly gone.

"Of course it is. Because the baby's gone, with its mother. Not an hour since."

"In the middle of the night!" Bella exclaimed in disbelief.

"A sailor hungry for his wife and child has no heed of time, my dears. The ship had docked, a fly must be sent immediately. So it came, and the driver was in a rare bad humour, I can tell you. And baby and mother have gone, whisked into loving arms." Aunt Aggie yawned deeply. "And now, my dears, can I have some uninterrupted sleep? These nocturnal upheavals," her words were strangely slurred again, "are exhausting."

"Then what," Lally insisted faintly, "was Noah burying?"

Bella took her arm. "It was a nightmare, love. It really was."

"No." Lally shook her head stubbornly. "If you come downstairs you'll see him, dressed, with snow on his boots. Listen! There he is now."

Sure enough there were cautious footsteps on the stone floor of the kitchen. Bella's heart gave a great leap.

"He *is* there, Aunt Aggie."

Aunt Aggie breathed heavily as if she were already half asleep. Her eyes looked peculiar, very large but completely colourless, the pupils shrunk to pinheads. She shrugged suddenly, and said, "Then go downstairs, both of you. Dig up the backyard. Find your dead baby. What cruel nonsense, indeed! How you repay my kindness! Noah, Noah!"

"What's the matter, Ma?" Noah's deep voice, very alert, came up the stairs.

32

"These young ladies think you've been committing a horrid crime."

"Me? That's a joke. What sort of crime?"

"Why, burying the baby in the yard, if you can believe it!"

"Ha ha! Ha ha ha! That's a rare one. I suppose they heard those tomcats yowling. Thought it was my victim. Ha ha ha!"

Lally seized Bella's hand in her ice-cold one.

"Bella, come! You've got to come. You'll see the hole in the snow. It *is* true!"

Shivering with distaste, Bella nodded. She would go, to quieten Lally. Otherwise there would be hysterics all night. Besides . . . things happened in this house. That girl with her newly-born baby being spirited away in the night as if no one must see her go . . .

She seized her shawl.

"Come then. Excuse us, Aunt Aggie. But my sister must be humoured when she's in this state. She has a nervous temperament."

Aunt Aggie nodded sympathetically.

"I can see that, my dear. I'll come down with you, and mix her a soothing draught. She's in a state, that's clear."

"Look, Bella, look!" Lally said, at the kitchen window. "It's there—at least—"

The moonlight shone on nothing but snow. There was no dark gash in the earth. True, the snow was trampled but that, Noah explained, at their backs, was because he had gone out to throw something at the noisy cats.

"It's covered up," Lally whispered.

"Neighbourhood's full of pernickety cats," Noah said. "I'd trap 'em, shoot 'em."

"Drink this," said Aunt Aggie, holding a cup to Lally's lips. "Poor little love! You're shivering. You must go back to your warm bed. And sleep."

Lally drank without knowing what she was doing.

"And sleep sound," said Aunt Aggie, her round colourless eyes shining.

"All day, if she likes," said Noah, towering above them, the undercurrent of secret mirth in his voice.

"And some for you, too, my dear," Aunt Aggie said, holding the cup towards Bella.

Bella was about to take it, then suddenly shook her head.

"Come!" Aunt Aggie coaxed. "It'll do you good. Soothe your poor nerves."

Bella was suddenly wondering why Noah laughed at everything, even marauding tomcats. There would be nothing funny about them. Neither would there be anything funny about burying a baby, dead by natural causes or otherwise. Yet he laughed . . .

"No," she said, shaking her head impatiently. "I must stay awake to look after my sister."

The briefest flash of anger seemed to pass over Aunt Aggie's face. Then she said kindly, "But of course you must. She looks ill, poor dear. Take her up to bed. Make her rest. Otherwise Mrs. Jennings isn't going to be very favourably impressed tomorrow. She admires a sound nervous system. Doesn't she, Noah?"

Noah chuckled, softly and intolerably.

When Lally was still asleep at midday and no amount of shaking would rouse her, Bella was thoroughly alarmed.

"What did you give her to drink?" she demanded of Aunt Aggie.

"Just a few drops of laudanum, my dear. Nothing to harm her. I feared a brain fever, the way she was behaving last night. This long sleep will avert disaster and do her all the good in the world."

Papa had often prescribed laudanum for his patients. At least it was reassuring to know that Lally had swallowed nothing more dangerous. And perhaps it was wise that she was having such a long rest. She had been in a state bordering on dementia last night. Bella was too perturbed to go into the question as to whether Lally had been suffering from a fevered imagination or whether she had truly seen the horrible episode she had described. The only thing that mattered now was for Lally to wake up and for them to get out of this house. If Mrs. Jennings didn't send for them they must go of their own accord, snow or not. They might be doing Aunt Aggie an injustice, she might genuinely be the soul of kindness, but too many things had happened under her roof for Bella to be able to endure the thought of another night here.

And however simple Aunt Aggie might be, there was no doubt Noah was far from simple. Bella prayed she would never need to set eyes on him again.

The door of the third bedroom on the first floor stood wide open today. The cradle had disappeared from the hearth in the parlour and this room stood open as if to flaunt its empty bed.

Bella stepped inside, as she was sure she had been intended to. It was a mean little room with scarcely any light coming through its small window that faced the backyard. There were no ribbon bows on the curtains to impress lodgers newly arrived, no washstand with prettily decorated floral jug and basin. There was only the narrow iron bed, a bit of rag matting on the floor and a hard chair. The young woman who had been in here had not been made very welcome. Was it because she couldn't pay a shilling a night for her room, or because she was a poor relation and hadn't needed to be impressed. And have her nervous fears allayed . . .

Or was it simply that with the birth of her baby about to take place it was more practical to have a mimimum of furniture and fripperies?

Now she had gone and all that was left of her was that faint curious smell Bella had noticed yesterday. She recognized it now, for Lally's breath carried the same odour. Laudanum. That explained why the girl had been so quiet. Perhaps it also explained why the baby hadn't cried. Papa had said some lazy and unscrupulous mothers didn't hesitate to give laudanum to a fretful baby.

But if it were given to so frail a child, surely the consequences would be fatal. Perhaps they had been . . .

Bella left the horrid little room and ran upstairs for the twentieth time to see if Lally had yet stirred. When she found her lying just as inert and sunk in sleep, her pale hair spread like an elusive sunshine over the pillow, Bella gave a whimper of despair. What was to happen to them? It had stopped snowing at last, but soon it would be too dark and too late to venture out. If Mrs. Jennings sent for them they would not be able to go.

Mrs. Jennings had been like a lifeline in her mind, but now Bella was beginning to wonder about that lady. It was terrible to have to be suspicious of people's kind deeds, but why should this woman be so eager to help two complete strangers? What did she get out of it? Not many people did things for nothing. Even Aunt Aggie, was getting her shilling a day.

But she and Lally were in a desperate position. They had to trust someone.

To calm herself, Bella set about packing their bags. She made as much commotion as possible, hoping to wake Lally. It was now fourteen hours since she had fallen asleep. Bella was growing more anxious every minute.

At last she went downstairs to find Aunt Aggie who was knitting peacefully before the glowing fire. The picture of comfort she presented made Bella's wild fears subside.

"Aunt Aggie, my sister still can't be woken."

"Let her sleep, my dear. Be thankful she can. This is doing her all the good in the world."

"But isn't Mrs. Jennings arriving at any moment?"

"Not Mrs. Jennings herself. A conveyance will be sent for you."

"Supposing Lally is still asleep?"

Aunt Aggie looked at Bella blandly over the top of her spectacles.

"Then she must be carried, mustn't she? Noah will see to that. Noah's very strong."

She smiled suddenly, disclosing her broken teeth.

"Don't look so alarmed, my dear. Mrs. Jennings is a very influential woman. She's expecting you and mustn't be disappointed."

"C-carried!" Bella whispered. She ran forward to seize Aunt Aggie's arm. "Who is Mrs. Jennings? What does she want with an unconscious girl? *Tell* me!"

"Tch tch tch! I thought it was only your sister who indulged in hysterics. Mrs. Jennings has positions for you. Haven't I told you a dozen times? Doubting Aunt Aggie, indeed! There's ingratitude for you. Ah dear, it's a hard ungrateful world."

Bella drew back staring, seeing suddenly not the cosy kind old woman who had helped two strangers so astonishingly, but a mealy-mouthed hypocritical creature with unknown depths of cunning. The moment of illumination was shattering. She twisted her damp hands, praying that this was imagination, unreliable intuition.

But thinking of Lally helpless upstairs, and listening to Aunt Aggie's unperturbed plan to carry her *unconscious* to a strange house, Bella knew that she had to face this new terrifying position, and revile herself for her innocence and blindness.

Tottie's state of terror should have told her. Noah's unholy amusement should have been revealing. The disappearance of the young mother and baby should have been, not innocent but sinister. But it had taken this last desperate state of affairs, herself a prisoner here because she couldn't carry Lally bodily away, to make it plain what was happening.

How could she have been so gullible? She forgot her fear in the hot anger that swept over her.

"Mrs. Proudfoot, would you be good enough to tell me exactly what you were planning to do with Lally and me, what secret scheme you had in mind?"

"Eh? Eh, my dear?"

"Don't tell me your friend is finding positions for us, because I no longer believe you. Or perhaps I do. Only I daren't imagine what the positions are. Oh, what a fool I've been! Listening to your blandishments. But not any more. I'll pay you what we owe you and the moment Lally stirs, we're leaving this house."

"But, my dear young creature—"

"How can you sit there so calmly," Bella stormed, "while my sister may be dying from that drug you gave her? Yesterday you watched the poor little baby dying—heaven knows what you did to its mother—"

"My dear, what *fantasies*! Your sister told me about your romantic imagination. Dreaming of a rich world. I fear that isn't your destiny. But how pretty you look when you're angry. I believe you'll do very well—in your new life. You are almost my best— Where are you going?"

"To the kitchen to tell Tottie to make plenty of black coffee. And then out to find a doctor. And don't dare to stop me."

"I won't, my dear." Aunt Aggie chuckled with slow relish. "But I rather think Noah will."

"Noah!"

"He came home early today. He's been busy in the back. Shovelling snow. Snow is pretty when it first falls, but later, when cats and other animals scatter it about—" her owl's eyes were on Bella without a flicker, "then it's a nuisance. Noah is tidy-minded."

Sheer horror sucked away Bella's fine flood of anger. So what Lally had seen was true. Noah was not tidying snow. He was smoothing away all traces of a grave . . .

"And Tottie doesn't understand orders from anyone but me," said Aunt Aggie. "She's dim-witted. Besides," she went on, after a moment, "I have the key to the front door here in my pocket, and if you think to go by the back way, Noah's there."

But Noah wasn't in the backyard. His voice came from the doorway, making Bella start violently.

"What's up, Ma?" he asked, standing there swinging his large hands loosely.

37

"Miss Isabella is getting impatient to begin her new life."

Noah grinned. He opened and closed his hands slowly.

"Then she'll have to be a bit patient, won't she? The fly don't come till after dark. Didn't you tell her?"

"I must have a doctor for my sister!" Bella insisted.

"Ma knows more than any doctor. We don't need no doctor in this house." Noah had taken something out of his pocket. He now dangled it ostentatiously. It was a key. The key to the back door no doubt, since his mother had the front door one in her pocket. His bright little eyes were full of malice.

"I'll scream for help," said Bella, between tight lips.

Noah flung back his untidy black head and roared with laughter.

"Try it in this street, love. It's natural noise in these parts."

"Yes, my dear," said Aunt Aggie, knitting placidly. "No one is going to go to the help of a Soho drab."

Bella caught her breath sharply. Suddenly she flew to the door, pushing past Noah contemptuously, and ran upstairs. In the bedroom she banged the door shut, and stood against it, panting. As soon as she could listen above the sound of her harshly indrawn breaths she realized that no one had followed her. But downstairs Noah was still laughing. And on the bed Lally stirred at last.

Bella was at her side in a flash.

"Oh, Lally! Wake up! We've got to get away from here."

Lally's heavy eyelids lifted showing her eyes cloudy and unfocused. Then they fell again and she breathed in deep sleep-drugged breaths.

Bella shook her violently.

"Lally, wake up! We're in great danger."

Lally mumbled, then slept again, and Bella, dropping her limp body, wondered what was the use anyway. For the doors were locked, and Noah guarded them.

But was she to sit here helplessly until that fly came furtively in the dark to carry them away—to what? So much for being thought a Soho drab. She would scream. Noah and Aunt Aggie would hear how she could scream.

She flung up the narrow window and leaned out into the foggy yellow murk. The moment a passer-by appeared—Holy Mother, let it be someone with ears that listened—she would open her lungs.

Two ragged children huddled in a doorway opposite, their rags drawn lovingly over their bare feet. A very small boy trudged past in the snow and slush, pushing a barrow laden with a miscellany of junk. A little later a woman appeared, hurrying. Bella caught only a glimpse of her white drawn face beneath her bonnet. The street was empty for a minute, then two men appeared, and Bella's heart lifted. But they were drunk, stumbling and singing. A third companion was trying to catch them up, but he fell sprawling in the slush.

And there were footsteps on the stairs . . .

The doorknob rattled.

"What you got against the door, love?" It was Noah's voice, coaxing. "Move it, will you, or I got to use my strength."

Two more men had appeared in the gloom. There was no time to wait and see if they were drunk or sober, friends or evil-doers. Bella leaned out of the window and screamed at the top of her lungs.

"Help! Help, I beg you! I need a doctor! My sister's ill! We're in great danger!"

The men had stopped and looked up. One was short and square, one very tall. They wore top hats, Bella now observed. Thank God, they were gentry. And they had stopped to listen.

"Please help—" There was a great clatter as Noah burst into the room. In two strides he was at the window and had flung Bella away. "Little bitch!" he muttered. Then he had thrust his own head out and was saying in a blandishing voice that would have done credit to his mother.

"Take no notice, sirs. It's my wife. She's a bit weak in the head, like."

On the floor where she had fallen Bella put her head in her hands and sobbed.

Noah closed the window and turned slowly. He stood over her, enormous, menacing. His voice was very soft.

"Think you'd get away with that, did yer—"

And then there was a great thumping on the street door.

"Open up!" came a clear, arrogant, autocratic voice. "Open up. My friend is a doctor. And I intend fetching the police."

The voice brooked no refusal. It was the most heavenly sound Bella had ever heard.

39

Chapter 5

It took all Bella's strength to hold Lally upright in the coach. She concentrated on that, and nothing else. She had no idea where the gentleman who had introduced himself as Mr. Raven was taking them, but she trusted him. She had to. Anything was better than the house from which they had escaped.

The last hour had been the worst nightmare of all, and Bella was only glad that Lally had been too drowsy and stupid to take in what had happened, the stalwart police constable guarding Aunt Aggie and Noah in the parlour while a sergeant and another constable searched the house, and, on Bella's directions, since Lally was not able to give them, dug in the backyard.

The flimsy packing case was unearthed, and the lid lifted to disclose the tiny frozen body. Bella thought she would have fainted then, but that the young man in the caped greatcoat kept so firm a grip on her arm that the pain kept her conscious. His friend, the elderly doctor, examined the baby, and lifted a grim face.

"I think there could be more investigations done here, sergeant. This is a newborn infant. Its death could have been natural but its burial isn't. This yard may hold other grisly secrets. What can you hold that fine pair on?"

The sergeant had an impressive flow of legal conversation.

"Detaining young females unlawfully with intent of immoral purposes. Concealing a death and illegally disposing of the body. Smuggling away the infant's mother whose whereabouts have still to be traced. Don't you worry, sir, I'll have a charge sheet a yard long."

"Just keep them under lock and key," said the doctor. "My friend and I will see to the young ladies."

"If you can be letting me have their address, sir. Their evidence will have to be taken."

The younger man spoke authoritatively.

"They'll be my responsibility, Daniel." He handed a card to the sergeant. "You'll find my address there."

The old doctor lifted his matted brows.

"Is this wise, Guy? Wouldn't they do better with me. Betsey—"

"No, they'll come to me. You wanted me to have a crusade. I believe this is where I begin." He glanced at the mummified infant and his face had a hard look of anger and outrage. "You were right, Daniel. There are things to be uncovered in this city. Let's get out of this damned place. What about the other girl? Will she be all right?"

"She's recovering from a heavy dose of laudanum. Try and get some hot milk into her. She should do very well by morning. I'll call and take a look at her."

The last thing was Aunt Aggie's language as she was taken away. She burst into a string of vile oaths directed at Bella and Lally. Her face beneath the respectable black bonnet with its velvet ribbons was a mask of fury, her large pale eyes so full of cold malignant hate that Bella shivered. Noah was bad enough. Held between two burly police he was sullen and furious. But Aunt Aggie had let the evil show through her pink and white innocence. She was like the stinking sewers that ran beneath the city's comfortable buildings and ornamental parks and gardens. Bella prayed that neither she nor Lally would ever need to set eyes on her again.

But ten minutes later, in the jolting cab, Bella suddenly sat upright.

"Tottie!" she exclaimed.

The young man sitting opposite, his gloved hands folded over the knob of his cane, listened attentively.

"Tottie? Another waif?"

"We are not waifs, Mr. Raven," Bella said haughtily.

The young man's calm eyes went over the two girls, observing their neat but plain clothing, their obvious air of distress and dishevelment.

"Of course not, Miss McBride," he said politely. "But Tottie?"

"She was Aunt—I mean, Mrs. Proudfoot's servant girl. Noah found her living in some derelict building a few days ago and brought her home. At least he said it was a few days ago, but now I'm not sure. She might have been there much longer."

"This is interesting. Certainly she must be found. She'll be a valuable witness."

"She can't talk. She's dumb."

"Dumb? She was born dumb?"

"I don't know. I had the thought it might be from terror. She was very afraid of—that old woman—and Noah." Bella's eyes darkened. "They let her be dressed in rags and she had dreadful chilblains. She was probably hiding in the cellar."

"The police will find her," said Mr. Raven. "They'll be searching the house thoroughly. Then Daniel—my friend, Doctor Bushey, will take care of her. Rest assured."

He smiled, and Bella thought what cold eyes he had, blue and aloof, occupied with their own thoughts. He had rescued Lally and her from a fate she didn't dare to think of, and she was intensely grateful to him. But now it seemed to her that their plight had suited some private purpose of his own. She began to wonder uneasily where he was taking them, and what he intended to do with them. She wished it had been the old doctor who had taken them, with Tottie. He was bluff and kindly. She would have trusted him completely. But Mr. Raven was a swell. His clothes were exquisite, from his silk cravat to his well-polished boots. Doctor Bushey had looked at them with a gentle and fatherly eye. This haughty young man merely considered them waifs.

And perhaps, after all, Bella reflected honestly, that was unpalatable only because it was so near the truth.

The cab drew up at last outside a tall, grey, imposing house, one of a row of such houses flanking one side of the road, while on the opposite side were the trees of a broad park.

"This it, guv'nor?"

"That's right, cabby." The young man had sprung out lightly, and was looking up at Bella. "Can your sister be roused, or must she be carried?"

From that angle he looked younger, and anxious, almost boyish. Bella was suddenly ashamed of her misgivings. She shook Lally energetically.

"Come, Lally. Wake yourself up. Do you want to be lifted like a baby?"

Lally moaned and shivered, and with a great effort sat upright.

"Where are we?" She clutched Bella, memory touching her drowsy brain. "It's not—Noah?"

"It's Mr. Raven. He wants to help you out. Come along, love. You can manage very well."

Somehow Lally contrived to climb down. Mr. Raven paid the cab-driver, and with a last curious glance at Lally, the man whipped up his horse and drove off. Mr. Raven unceremoniously put his arm round Lally's waist and half carried her up the steps to the shining mahogany front door. He rang the bell vigorously, and when the door swung open, didn't seem at all perturbed that the stooping white-whiskered old man in butler's dress should see him standing there with a swooning young lady on one arm and Bella beside him laden with the bulging carpet bag which contained all hers and Lally's possessions.

"Take the young lady's bag, Doughty. Tell Mrs. Doughty to prepare—let me see—I think the blue room." He had motioned Bella in and helped Lally over the last step. Lally was now standing upright, her eyes round with amazement. She thought she was dreaming, poor creature, and who wouldn't, to find herself in this luxurious hall, with rich rugs on the floor, a shining stair-rail leading up into the gloom, and huge bowls of flowers in mid-winter scenting the air.

With calm aplomb Mr. Raven took the girls' shawls and handed them to the astonished Doughty.

"Hurry, man. Can't you see my guests are exhausted? As soon as Mrs. Doughty has the fire alight, tell her to come to us in the library."

"Yes, sir. At once, sir."

Lally gave a sudden nervous giggle, then clapped her hand to her mouth. Bella nudged her sharply to follow Mr. Raven across the hall into a large book-lined room. A fire burned invitingly, throwing its flickering light on to the leather-covered armchairs and sofa. Mr. Raven motioned the girls to sit down, and again Lally had to be nudged into obeying, she was so dazed and open-mouthed.

But Bella had kept her wits. She sat primly on the edge of the sofa, and inquired stiffly what Mr. Raven intended to do with them.

"Why, get you justice, if I can." He looked at Bella, and for the first time his mouth quirked in amusement. "What plan did you think I had?"

He was amused that Bella should be afraid he had evil designs on them, Bella thought in the greatest indignation. He might have realized she was not as naïve as that. She might be simply dressed, and Lally might at present look a bit daft, but he needn't think they were ignorant servant girls.

"I don't know what you mean by justice, sir," she answered coolly. "All my sister and I have to come to London for is to find respectable occupation. I would hardly have called that justice."

"What I meant, Miss— I'm afraid I don't even know your name."

"I am Isabella McBride and this is my sister Eulalie."

Mr. Raven bowed with a courtly air that momentarily fascinated Bella. She had a passionate admiration for good manners.

"Will you go on and explain about the question of justice, sir?"

"Certainly. I want to make the plight of young women like yourself and your sister public. I still have to hear how you fell into the clutches of that monstrous old woman, but the important thing to prove to the world is that people like that woman and situations like this exist. I tell you, I'm shocked and horrified. If it hadn't been for the happy intervention of Doctor Bushey and myself, where might you be now? I'd make a guess and say on your way to the docks to be forcibly put aboard a ship bound for some Middle Eastern port."

"W-what for?" That was Lally, sitting upright, her eyes sticking out.

"Why, to be thrown into some low brothel," replied Mr. Raven. "For the use of foreign sailors and worse."

Bella started, meaning to reprimand him for speaking so brutally to sensitive Lally, but then she realized he hadn't been thinking about delicate ears, he was so genuinely incensed about the existence of such crime and depravity.

"I will take this matter into the House," he declared. "There will have to be a complete investigation into this kind of thing. One walk through a slum area and I stumble on it. Is such a thing happening every day, every night? There'll have to be more police, new laws, greater penalties."

His words had galvanized Lally into life.

"Will Aunt Aggie go to prison?"

"Aunt Aggie? You call that old witch aunt? Certainly she'll go to prison. I hope for life."

"And—Noah?"

44

"Him, too."

Lally sighed deeply and murmured into Bella's ear, "Now we can feel safe."

The young man stopped his erratic pacing up and down. For one moment the hard anger left his face, and he was looking down at Lally's pale face with its drooping eyelids and tumbling fair hair with a detached interest. He had noticed her at last, as people always did, though most people much sooner. She was so pretty.

"Yes, you can feel safe, Miss McBride. But we shall need yours and your sister's help to put them in prison. You will both have to give evidence in court."

"We will have to be witnesses?" Bella exclaimed.

"Yes. Tomorrow you'll give statements to the police. That's the beginning. Later, when the two are tried—"

"Oh, no!" Lally cried out. She buried her face in Bella's shoulder. "I couldn't bear to see them again. I should die."

"S-sh, Lally!" said Bella absently, her mind on the more practical issue. "So you intend keeping us here, Mr. Raven, until the case is tried, and, as you say, justice obtained."

"Is that so great a hardship? Mrs. Doughty, my housekeeper, is very respectable, and quite kind."

Bella flushed. "I didn't mean that. I meant, are you asking us to represent all unfortunate young women? What is that going to do to our future?"

She saw that he had never thought of them as individuals. He had suddenly noticed that Lally was pretty, but they were still two anonymous young women to be used for a cause. Respectable servant girls, no more. And wasn't that what they were, anyway? Why had she to be so high and mighty because Papa had brought them up as ladies, and she had filled her head with romantic novels, and they had been almost within sight of Covent Garden Opera House?

She was aware of the quickly-veiled surprise in Mr. Raven's eyes when she had mentioned their future, and suddenly she saw the truth as he saw it. They would, with luck, be governesses, or perhaps assistants to a milliner or a dressmaker, so would it matter if their names had appeared briefly in the newspaper as the innocent victims of a wicked old woman and her son? If their plight could help other unfortunates, then the ordeal ahead must be faced.

45

Diamonds, operas, grand houses . . . Bella gave a little philosophic shrug, facing reality at last. Visiting London had made her grow up very quickly.

"I assure you, Miss McBride, neither your reputation nor your future will be harmed. I will guarantee you positions when this is over. In the meantime—ah, here is Mrs. Doughty. Mrs. Doughty, these two young ladies are Miss Isabella and Miss Eulalie McBride. They are to be my guests for a short time. I trust their room is ready?"

Mrs. Doughty was as short in stature as her husband, but much broader. She had a fleshy red nose and the high colour of someone who might conceivably, Bella reflected shrewdly, help herself to a little port after the dinner guests had departed. But, as Mr. Raven had said, she looked kind, if at this minute completely flabbergasted.

"Yes, sir. It's ready. The fire's alight. The beds are scarcely aired. If I'd known guests was expected—if I'd had a warning—" Her little pouched eyes rested incredulously on the two girls again.

"None of us had a warning, Mrs. Doughty. Events take charge of us. But I'm sure you'll manage. I think the young ladies would prefer a tray in their room tonight. So I will say good night."

He gave his small courtly bow again, and Bella felt a little twist of excitement in her stomach. But again it was Lally at whom he looked. No doubt he was reflecting how she would look when her hair was tidied. Perhaps he might find the little servant girl amusing . . .

The room was the most beautiful Bella had ever seen. She found herself tiptoeing across the soft carpet towards the dressing table with its gilt-framed mirror and its elaborate array of toilet necessities. There was a huge bed, covered with a snowy-white tasselled bedspread, and with mahogany steps, to make climbing into its dazzling softness the easier. There was a washstand, with jugs of steaming hot water and fleecy towels, and on the opposite side of the room, a writing desk equipped with candlesticks, a silver holder containing quill pens, and silver inkwells, pin cushions, and a blotter in an elegant red leather frame. The curtains of rich blue brocade were drawn across the windows, the walls were a paler blue damask. In the grate the fire, which was just beginning to take hold, sparkled on the shining brass fender and fire-irons. Two low chairs, in quilted white velvet, were drawn up invitingly to the blaze.

It was a room that almost brought back Bella's romantic dreams. But not quite. She and Lally were here only temporarily, while a rich young man indulged himself in his passing whim for a crusade. As he had pointed out, for the sake of other unfortunates like themselves, they must support him.

Mrs. Doughty had opened the carpet bag, and spread out their simple flannel nightgowns. No doubt she was used to handling fine lawn and linen, and this would be another reason for the perplexity in her face. But, as a well-trained servant, none of this came into her voice.

"Would you be liking your supper now, miss?" She addressed herself to Bella, for Lally was plainly now beyond speech. "A nice bowl of soup would do you both good."

"Thank you, Mrs. Doughty. That is kind of you."

The woman obviously liked the way Bella spoke, for she said briskly, "I'll bring it up myself. That stupid Annie does nothing but gawp and gape."

The moment she was out of the room Lally clutched at Bella.

"Bella, we must say our prayers!"

"Whatever for, you goose?"

"What are we doing in a place like this?" Lally looked wildly round the room. "That fine gentleman wants us for his own purposes."

The excitement turned again in Bella's stomach, a barb of mingled pleasure and apprehension. She knew exactly why Mr. Raven wanted them because he had explained his impersonal and lofty reason to her and she had believed him. She was still hearing his voice, deep, quiet, completely confident. Above all, a man should have confidence and be in command of others. That was a quality to be admired. Sentimentality was unnecessary.

She took Lally by the shoulders and swung her round to the mirror.

"There! Look at yourself! Would a fine gentleman be interested in a fright like that? Your hair coming down, your face smudged. Why, you look no better than a street girl."

Lally pushed at her hair shamefacedly.

"I didn't know. I'm so sleepy still. Why did you let me go out looking like this?" She added, with sudden defiance, "Perhaps he likes street girls."

47

"Perhaps he does. So does Noah. Would you rather be back with Noah?"

Instantly Bella was sorry for her sharpness, for the quick terror was in Lally's face again.

"Don't say his name!"

"Then be thankful to Mr. Raven for what he has saved us from." More gently she said, "Don't cry again, Lally. We're safe now. And look at this lovely bed. I'll help you undress, and you can have your supper in bed."

Lally shivered and sighed.

"You're so calm, Bella. How can you be so calm? Didn't you care at all about the little baby?"

"I care about Aunt Aggie and Noah being punished for it. Off with your boots! There! Your feet are frozen. Do you know, I think Mrs. Doughty would bring a warming pan if we asked her."

At that moment there was a knock at the door, and Mrs. Doughty was back with a laden tray. She set it on a table by the fire, and whisked the covers off steaming bowls of soup, and hot toast.

"Now, come and eat up, young ladies. You both look fair starved."

While she had been away she had obviously decided on the manner she would take to these perplexing guests. It was a nice blend of respect and equality, by no means concealing a very lively curiosity. But there was no doubt she had a warm heart. She wouldn't turn a dog from the door in this snowy weather, much less a pair of nicely-spoken young ladies fallen on bad times. If the master decided for some mysterious reason of his own to give them the best room, then obeyed he must be.

"Thank you, Mrs. Doughty." The fragrant smell of the soup had made Bella's spirits rise instantly.

"Is there anything else you might be wanting, while I'm here? Coming so sudden-like, you might have overlooked some requirements."

"All the belongings we have in the world are with us," Bella answered, with dignity. "We shall manage very well. Only my sister is very chilled. She hasn't been well. Could she have a warming pan?"

"But of course, miss. I could see at once your sister was poorly. Has she caught a chill? Perhaps she's been sleeping in a damp bed."

48

Bella smiled slightly at Mrs. Doughty's delicate way of obtaining information.

"No, the bed wasn't damp. It was a very good bed."

"But the baby was buried in the snow!" Lally cried suddenly and wildly.

Mrs. Doughty's mouth fell open. Her broad-tipped nose glowed scarlet.

"Bless me! She's wandering, poor dear!"

"No, she isn't," said Bella. "We had a terrible experience. Mr. Raven rescued us. You'll hear all about it, I expect. There's to be a court trial. Aunt Agg— . . . the people concerned are to be punished. Mr. Raven is anxious to see things like this can't happen again to unprotected females. He mentioned something about a law in Parliament."

"Why, yes, he's hoping to be elected to Parliament. Ah, so that's what it is. Doughty will understand better than me. He says it's a wonderful blessing Mr. Guy—Mr. Raven, that is, we keep calling him Mr. Guy, knowing him from a small child, you understand—it's a blessing Mr. Raven has decided to do something for his country. It takes him out of his dreadful grief."

"Grief?"

"He lost his sweet young wife two years since. Her and the baby." Lally gave a gasp. "A baby!" Bella motioned to her to be quiet. She realized that her curiosity about their host was as strong as Mrs. Doughty's about Lally and herself.

"How sad! Did he love her very much?"

"It was a marriage made in heaven. And in heaven it ended, poor souls. She was like an angel, so fair and sweet. When she died, he went wild. We all thought he'd ruin himself, gambling, drinking, taking no respect for anything, laughing. You should have heard him laughing with his friends, late at night. I used to say to Doughty, 'Listen to that. Laughing like a devil and crying inside.' But Doughty knew it would work itself out, all that wildness, and so it had."

"He's recovered from his grief?" Bella was remembering the cool emotionless eyes, and wondering suddenly what they had been like while his young wife was living.

"Never. But he's come to terms with it, like. Oh, he can still be wild, I'm telling you. But he's going to be a member of Parliament so he's got to be respectable and serious. And he will be. Whatever Mr. Guy does, he puts a great fire into it. Indeed, you might say, what he wants he intends to get. Nothing will stand in his way. Only excepting the Almighty who took Miss Caroline and the child away."

Mrs. Doughty sniffed, and touched her eyes with her apron.

"But there, I'm talking too much. I'm only telling you nice young ladies—and you do look nice, I said as much to Doughty—that now Mr. Raven's helped you from whatever this dreadful experience of yours was, it's your plain duty to help him to make a law in Parliament, if he wants to. It'll be for the good of all, I can assure you. And you can rest safe here."

Chapter 6

LALLY had a nightmare about Noah in the night, and Bella had to light the candle and soothe her. She awoke perfectly dazed, and quite unable to grasp her surroundings. At last she seemed to recognize the luxurious room, with the embers of the fire still glowing, but instead of being reassured lay quietly sobbing, "What is to happen to us, Bella? What is to happen to us?"

Finally Bella said sharply, "For goodness' sake, Lally, stop being so dreary or I'll think a ship to Marseilles the best place for you. Can't you have a little optimism?"

Lally was quiet then, but her large eyes were curiously empty, and Bella couldn't rouse her again. She decided that Lally was suffering still from the after-effects of the laudanum and she must try not to be impatient with her until she was quite recovered. By that time Bella expected her to be feeling the same growing excitement and pleasure that she herself felt. Couldn't Lally enjoy their stay in a luxurious house while it lasted, for it would be brief enough?

In the morning Bella was at the window, with the curtains pulled back, and a fascinating new world spread before her, when there was a tap at the door, and a very small maidservant struggling with a large coal bucket appeared.

"Do your fire, miss," she said, shooting an inquisitive glance at Bella, and at Lally, still submerged in the big bed.

"Thank you," said Bella. "What's that out there?"

"What, miss? Oh, you mean Hyde Park, and that's Rotten Row."

Bella gazed, entranced. She knew all about Rotten Row where the fashionable people rode and drove in their carriages and even sauntered by on summer evenings. This was very different from Seven Dials, and the mean dirty streets where screams were unanswered, and children walked barefoot in the snow. This was really the London of her dreams.

"There won't be many out in the snow, miss," the little maid-servant went on. She was using the bellows vigorously. "You need to wait till the spring."

Where would they be in the spring, when the ladies emerged from their winter hibernation and sported their new bonnets and parasols? Far from the fashionable world of Rotten Row and Hyde Park, Bella thought. But at least there it was now, beneath its glistening coverlet of snow, and one brave gentleman rider was cantering by, the snow flying off his horse's hooves. The trees spread their leafless branches in a faint lilac-coloured mist. A hackney coach clattered by on the road beneath, and already the newsboys were shouting in their cracked rasping voices. "Lord Palmerston says more troops for Crimea. Big losses in Crimea." An organ grinder had begun a turgid melody, errand boys were hurrying by. Even in this quiet part far from the incredible jostle and confusion of Piccadilly and the Strand, the city was awake.

The fire had begun to glow. The undersized maid, who must be Annie whom Mrs. Doughty had mentioned, got briskly to her feet and said she would bring hot water immediately. She opened a cupboard and brought from it a hip bath painted white and decorated with pink flowers, which she placed in front of the fire. Then she disappeared on her way for the pails of hot water.

Bella shook Lally awake.

"Do look, Lally! We're to bathe before we dress. Oh, I do enjoy luxury."

Lally sat up, blinking and rubbing her eyes. But she seemed, thank goodness, to be in possession of her senses again.

"Don't start enjoying it too much because it won't last. It'll be us lighting the fires and carrying the hot water in our next place, most likely."

Bella undid her plaits and shook her black hair in a curtain over her shoulders. She picked up a brush and sat in front of the mirror saying softly, "I wonder whose face last looked out of that glass. A rich spoiled one, I expect. But it's mine today."

She studied critically her white skin with the almond blossom tinge on the cheekbones, the slanted slender black brows, the heavily lashed topaz eyes. Her face was pleasant enough but, she decided honestly, not nearly as pretty as Lally's. Her nose was too short and had a dusting of freckles. And she had that long neck. Papa had used to say she looked like a flamingo. She took after his family, while Lally was all her mother, fair and pink and white, with her little prim mouth and innocent eyes.

All the same, Bella thought she didn't do the beautiful mirror a disservice. She looked pretty enough, with the thick shawl of her black hair.

"Bella, don't dream again! It gets you nowhere."

It was Lally's turn to be practical, and Bella reluctantly had to agree. She had forsworn dreaming since yesterday.

During the morning the nice elderly doctor, Doctor Bushey, called. The girls were asked to come down to the library to see him.

He smiled at Bella's urgent question, "Did you find Tottie? Is she all right?"

"Tottie's very well, although I didn't know her name until this minute. Betsey's pampering her in my kitchen, feeding her and warming her. But I can't get a word out of the child."

"She's dumb," said Bella. "She's been dumb ever since Noah found her."

"Not before?"

"How would I know? But I thought—Noah's a very alarming person."

"That's very intelligent of you, my dear. How did you guess there's such a thing as hysterical paralysis, sometimes of the limbs, sometimes of the vocal cords?"

"Our father was a doctor."

"Ah! So!" Doctor Bushey exchanged a glance with Mr. Raven, who was standing silently before the fire. "Well, then, I'm inclined to share your diagnosis of Tottie's condition, but I'm not prepared to say how long it will last, or indeed whether she'll ever regain her power of speech. And she doesn't appear to be able to read or write, so we'll get no help from her. Beyond exhibiting her rags or her condition of semi-starvation, of course. But the Proudfoots can swear they found her only last week, or the week before. There's nothing to prove she's been living like a rat in a hole in their house for longer than that. Though I suspect it. The poor child will take months to stop being terrified of a human being, let alone begin to talk. But I'm not here to discuss Tottie. How's the younger Miss McBride today?"

He was looking at Lally, who flushed and said, "Oh, no, Doctor, I'm the elder. Though most people don't think so. I'm not as—as advanced as Bella."

Mr. Raven was looking from one to the other, the expression of aloof interest in his face again. They were exhibits, that was all. Bella found herself flushing, too, though not with shyness but indignation.

"Well, older or younger, you seem to have thrown off the effects of the drug. Not sleepy today? Now, now, don't flinch, child. I only want to feel your pulse."

Lally submitted, her eyes wide and nervous.

"Splendid," Doctor Bushey murmured. "But I recommend rest and quiet. There's been a shock to the system. Miss Bella?"

Bella held her arms to her side, then reluctantly extended one of them.

"There's nothing the matter with me."

"No. I see that. A much stronger constitution altogether. Well, they'll do very well, Guy."

The girls were dismissed. They were not required again until a policeman who said his name was Inspector Gulley called to take a very long and complete statement of the events of the past three days, from the moment of meeting Aunt Aggie on the coach until Mr. Raven's and Doctor Bushey's arrival. He particularly wanted to know about the young woman who had had the baby, and seemed disappointed to hear that neither Bella nor Lally had set eyes on her. Bella recounted the conversation overheard at the door between Aunt Aggie and the man who had come by fly, and Lally told a confused story about hearing someone sobbing, and horses being whipped up in the night. "But I thought I dreamed it," she added.

"There's no actual proof," the Inspector said aggrievedly to Mr. Raven. "If, as we suspect, the ship concerned was the *Star of Asia*, she's well up the Channel by now, and she'll have discharged passengers at her first port before we can get word through to have her searched. Anyway, from the state of this young woman's health, drugged, and recovering from a premature birth, she'll probably be dead and dumped overboard—sorry, miss."

"There's no doubting the proof of the dead infant," Mr. Raven said crisply.

"No, sir, we'll get them on that. But if we can prove this other thing they'd be in for a life stretch."

Beside Bella on the sofa, Lally shuddered convulsively.

Bella said, "Is that all you require us for, because my sister's distressed?"

"Is that all, Inspector? Then certainly go upstairs. Ring for some tea." Mr. Raven's voice was kind, but still impersonal. He was speaking again to the Inspector before they had left the room.

Later there was a tremendous commotion outside, horses stamping, the yapping of dogs, and a high clear voice giving peremptory orders.

"Hannah, bring Loulou. You know the fuss she makes if I'm out of her sight."

Bella, who had been growing bored with their luxurious imprisonment, and who had more than her share of curiosity, had thrown up the window and was leaning out to watch a lady, elegantly dressed in a lilac-coloured crinoline, with a fur-trimmed cloak over her shoulders, sweep up the steps and ring the bell. The impatient clangour must have been audible through the entire house, for even Lally started up from her fire-drugged lethargy.

"Who is it, Bella?"

"I don't know. A lady. Her maid's carrying her dog. One of those hysterical French poodles. She seems very much at home. She's awfully fashionable. I'm going to find out who she is."

"Bella!" Lally exclaimed, shocked again at her sister's new-found shameless propensity for listening at doors.

But Bella had no time now for the niceties of etiquette. Hers and Lally's lives had suddenly become too extraordinary. One not only needed good ears but good eyes as well.

She went softly down the stairs and paused where they curved to give a view of the hall.

The visitor, with her black-clad maid holding the struggling poodle, stood in full view. Mr. Raven was out of sight but his voice perfectly distinct.

"Mamma, what brings you out in this weather?"

"Gossip spreads," said the lady tartly. "Whatever is this new indiscretion of yours?"

"Indiscretion, Mamma?"

The lady tapped a tiny extremely well-shod foot. Bella could see only half her face beneath the brim of a lacy nonsense of a bonnet, but the whole of it she judged to be exquisite. Exquisite and pampered and artfully young, as a face always sheltered from ugliness would be.

"Guy, don't hedge. You know very well what I'm talking about. This abduction of servant girls!"

"Abduction? The word's your own, I trust, Mamma."

"The word's the one being used, I regret to say."

Mr. Raven laughed softly, and with apparent enjoyment.

"Don't tell me the story's out already. Or should I say the most popular version of it? And what version have you heard?"

"Why, that you're sheltering these two creatures whom you picked up in some unmentionable slum—though for what reason I'd rather not know."

"Then you needn't know, Mamma," Mr. Raven said indulgently. "You shan't distress yourself. A little thing like cleaning up the slums—giving the submerged tenth of the population of whom you've never heard a chance to live decent lives—need hardly concern you. Take Loulou home and give her the food a starving child would sell its soul for. Leave me to my own brand of crime."

"Guy! I won't be laughed at!" Mrs. Raven's voice was sharp and angry.

"Neither will I, Mamma."

"Good heavens, I'm far from laughing at you. I've come to beg you not to ruin yourself."

"Ruin myself?"

"My darling boy, haven't you any sense? Oh, I know well enough your motives are probably quite honest. I can't see you finding a servant girl irresistible." (Bella caught her breath in quick anger. What a hateful stupid *impossible* woman!) "You've much too fastidious an eye. But what are your enemies going to make of this?"

"You mean Sir Henry Shields?"

"And others. You're like your father. You don't care two figs about making enemies and then you underestimate them. Politics can be dirty, hadn't you realized?"

"I've realized."

"This is playing into Sir Henry's hands."

56

"On the contrary. After I've finished with white slaving I shall begin on the children in mills. Sir Henry's among others."

Mrs. Raven had thrown up her gloved hands in a gesture of horror.

"White slaving!"

"What did you think, Mamma? That I was entertaining prostitutes for my private amusement?"

Mrs. Raven sucked in her breath audibly.

"Guy! I don't believe a word of your philanthropy. I give you up. White slaving, pro—" She couldn't bring herself to repeat the unforgivable word. Her lifted face was full of outrage. "I believe you're enjoying this disastrous situation."

Mr. Raven's voice was meticulously polite.

"Would you like to meet the young ladies, Mamma? I assure you, they are human beings."

"Never! This is madness. Get them out of the house. Send them to some sort of home, can't you?"

"No, I'm afraid I can't. Actually, I'd thought you might help in finding situations for them after this is over."

Mrs. Raven seemed to have difficulty in finding her voice. "You're preposterous! You've lost your senses! Can't you listen to me? What will happen isn't just my imagination. I shan't dare to look at a newspaper for weeks. They'll tear you to bits. You know what those low-class journalists can do. Your reputation—"

Mr. Raven laughed again.

"Reputation? That comes long long way after an empty belly or a raped—"

But there his mother gave a faint cry and turned swiftly to the door.

"Hannah! I apologize for you having to listen to this. Come. Loulou—my smelling salts—Guy, if your father, if Caroline—"

"This," Mr. Raven's voice cut in icily, "has nothing whatever to do with the dead. It has to do with the living. Of whom I sometimes doubt you are one."

For all her appearance of fragility, Mrs. Raven obviously was no person to swoon for anything but effect. The faintness went out of her voice. She was stung back to aggrieved life.

"How I could have such an imbecile son! What about Mademoiselle Hortense, pray? She took a fancy to you, and I rather thought you did to her."

"Mademoiselle Hortense is enchanting. But she isn't in danger from greedy and evil people. She isn't penniless and in want. She's on the right side of society. Forgive me, Mamma, but suddenly I find that impossibly tedious."

"If you must have a new fad, why do you choose one like this? The poor! So unwashed, so ignorant! You'll soon tire of this, as you do of everything else. But you'll have lost your reputation in the meantime."

"You don't begin to understand, Mamma. I'm not just pursuing a new fad. I'm deadly serious. I've found something worthwhile to do at last. I even regard it as worth losing my reputation for."

There was a brief silence, then his mother exclaimed,

"Then play with fire, you fool! Burn yourself up! But don't expect me to reverently scatter your ashes."

From nowhere Doughty appeared to open the door. With a great swishing of skirts, the lady swept out. The meek Hannah in her sober black followed. After a moment Mr. Raven sauntered across the hall. From her vantage point, still perfectly fascinated by what she had heard, Bella looked down at the sleek honey-dark head. Her cheeks burned with the unfair insulting remarks that horrible elegant alarming woman, his mother, had made about her and Lally. She wanted to rush down the stairs and beg Mr. Raven not to ruin himself for their sake. If it were likely he would be ruined. Yet she had a contrary desire, so overwhelming it made her blood grow hot to think of it, to see that well-bred face lose its slightly chilling composure and grow ardent in their defence. She could pray to see that . . . She knew she was never going to beg him to give up his quixotic crusade.

"Who was it, Bella?" Lally cried. "Could I hear someone quarrelling?"

"Mr. Raven's mother," said Bella briefly.

"Oh! Doesn't she like him?"

"I should think she adores him. It's us she doesn't like."

Lally looked perplexed.

"But she's never seen us. Oh, it's because we're here and shouldn't be. Is she very terrifying?"

"She doesn't terrify me."

That evening Mrs. Doughty came up to tell them that the master wanted to see them in the drawing-room. She scarcely gave them time to tidy their hair.

"Come along, young misses. The master doesn't like to be kept waiting. He has a rare temper at times."

58

Lally was all eyes for the beautiful room with its gold silk hangings, its chandelier with its central glowing rose of flame where the gas jets came through, its pictures and portraits. Bella looked straight at the man standing before the fire, and saw nothing else.

Had he been thinking over the wisdom of his mother's words? Was he going to send them away?

He asked them to sit down, and offered them Madeira wine. Lally took her glass because she was afraid to refuse, Bella because she had an odd idea it might give her more confidence in her prayer being answered.

He trusted that Mrs. Doughty was looking after them well, and that they were comfortable and happy. When they assented, he went on,

"I merely wanted to tell you that I'll be away for ten days or so. I have to go down to my constituency and make speeches. I'm a candidate in a by-election to be held shortly. I can't neglect the people whom I hope will vote for me."

Lally sipped her wine and murmured something inaudible. Bella said plainly, "So what are we to do, Mr. Raven?"

"Why, stay here, of course. I want you here until after the trial, which will be held in two weeks' time. You understand that, don't you? You're under subpoena as witnesses, and it would be an offence against the law if you disappeared."

"We have no intention of disappearing, Mr. Raven." (Where would they disappear to, Bella thought ironically.)

"No, I'm sure I can trust you. You're quite free to go out, of course. Only I'd suggest you don't go without Mrs. Doughty or Annie."

"W-why?" Lally gasped.

Mr. Raven looked into her huge alarmed periwinkle eyes, and again, ever so little, his face softened. She reminds him of his dead wife, Bella thought suddenly and fiercely. The fair sweet Caroline . . .

"Because it's customary for young ladies to be accompanied by chaperones. Not because the streets are full of Noah Proudfoots. Not in these parts, at least. You'll be quite safe." He was formal again, moving away to pick up the wine decanter and refill his glass. "I hope you won't find it too tedious here. You may use the house as you wish."

"The library?" Bella asked eagerly.

He did look at her this time, but not as he looked at Lally, merely with faintly lifted brows and polite interest.

"I'm afraid I have very few novels, Miss McBride. My mother is the person for those. If she should call you must ask her to lend you the latest."

"Is it likely she will call?" Bella asked.

"Most unlikely. We quarrelled today. But Mamma is a person of whims. However, that's beside the point. I merely wanted to tell you that as from tomorrow until my return you are in charge of my house."

He smiled and gave his courteous bow, dismissing them. Upstairs Lally found her tongue, and chattered without stopping.

"Isn't he kind, Bella? Isn't he a gentleman? And so good-looking, but if only he would smile more. He looks sad. Yesterday I thought he was merely scornful and superior, but now after hearing about his dead wife I know it's sadness that makes him so cold. I wonder if he will marry again. Surely he will. He must be very rich, and he has that big house in the country Mrs. Doughty told us about. Bella! Bella, aren't you listening? Aren't you interested?"

"He imagined I'd only want to read novels," Bella said resentfully. "He puts people in a category."

"In a—what are you talking about? If you ask me, you read too much."

"He'll have to learn better," Bella said.

The restlessness grew on Bella. The house was a haven, but who wanted to hide forever, smothered in richness. The next day she persuaded Mrs. Doughty to allow Annie, the sharp and alert maid, to put on her bonnet and shawl and accompany Lally and herself on a walk in the park. The snow had at last disappeared, and she was sure she could see the gold candle flames of crocuses beneath the trees. There were more riders out in the Row, too, and carriages bowled past drawn by shining and mettlesome horses. Bella longed for her first look at fashionable London.

But the outing came to nothing. The three girls had barely descended the steps of Mr. Raven's house before a man pounced on them. Lally screamed, but the man, who had a lean, hungry, avid face, said at once in quite a cultivated voice,

"Don't be alarmed, miss. I only want to ask you a question. How long is Mr. Raven intending to shelter you? What is his object? Oh, come now—" Bella was dragging at Lally, hissing, "Don't say a word, Lally. It's a newspaperman. We mustn't talk to him."

The man was pursuing them up the steps. "Come, please, miss! Just a few innocent questions. What's your occupation? Does the gentleman offer you better prospects than you had before?"

Furious at the man's growing insolence, Bella hustled Lally and Annie indoors, and said with deceptive calm,

"What is your newspaper?"

"The *London Clarion*, miss. I only want a short story about you. But I promise you headlines." His bright, avid eyes glinted unpleasantly. "You're news, miss."

"If one word about us is printed in your paper," said Bella, and now her face was blazing, "I can promise you a very great deal of trouble."

She swept in and banged the door. Old Doughty who came hurrying across the hall showed a reluctant admiration.

"You sent him packing, miss. Good riddance to him."

"I lost my temper," said Bella. Already she was uneasily suspicious that this wasn't the way to treat the press. That little rat of a man would know she couldn't make trouble for him. How could she? But he could print a malicious story if he pleased, in revenge.

She brushed away angry tears.

"We can't even have a peaceful walk. We can't see the Row. I never knew London was such a wicked city."

When the newsboys started shouting the next morning she asked Doughty to go out and buy a copy of the *London Clarion*. Surely the man wouldn't have dared to make up a story about them. They couldn't be headline news as he had suggested. Not her and Lally, two unimportant country girls.

The man had kept his promise. There were headlines.

> *Mystery in Knightsbridge. Who are Mr. Guy Raven's beautiful protégées?*
> *They were dressed for a walk in fashionable Hyde Park, these unfashionable young ladies in their unpretentious bonnets and shawls. But they were unduly modest—or had they had instructions from their host—and refused to talk to our reporter. We can, however, confirm the rumour that they are extremely comely, the one fair and the other dark. But per-*

*haps it was hardly to be expected that the aspiring candidate
for Hertfordshire would give sanctuary to any of the fair
sex less well-endowed with good looks. Would he get so heated
about the wrongs of a squint-eyed Polly or Mary Ann? Let us
leave him his foibles while he remains a private citizen, but do
we want this sort of thing intruding into the serious affairs of
Parliament?*

Bella gasped over the article. "But it's wicked! It's evil! Why,
it's suggesting—"

"What?" asked Lally nervously.

"Why, that we may be more than—" (Oh, why was Lally so
innocent!) "—than just guests."

"I don't understand, Bella."

"It's what Mrs. Raven meant when she said this would ruin
him. I thought she was just a jealous old woman, but now—"

She hadn't finished speaking before Mrs. Doughty knocked
on the door.

"Oh, miss—" even the phlegmatic Mrs. Doughty looked flustered, her nose a hot and angry scarlet, "—the master's mother
is downstairs demanding to see you both."

"Mrs. Raven!"

"Aye. And she's a character to be dealt with, for all her delicate
looks. Shall I say you're poorly?"

"Oh, yes, please!" Lally began, but Bella interrupted her with
an imperious, "You'll do nothing of the kind, Mrs. Doughty. Go
and tell her we'll be down immediately. Lally, tidy your hair!
Put on a clean fichu." Bella was at the mirror, smoothing her own
hair, noticing the flush in her cheeks and the blazing brilliance
of her eyes. Good! She could outstare Mrs. Raven. She was ready
for battle.

The lady sat very upright in the drawing-room. She had a rose-
leaf complexion, a haughty little parrot's beak nose, and sparkling dark eyes that gave her face an appearance of great
vivacity. She was very delicately made with a waist as small as
Lally's, and long fine hands that were arranged composedly in
her lap. She was dressed with a richness that Bella instantly suspected was deliberate. She intended to overawe the two servant
girls.

Lally, of course, was overawed. She curtseyed too deeply and
was then overpowered with shyness. It was left to Bella to say

politely, "You wished to see us, Mrs. Raven? I am Isabella Mc-Bride, and this is my sister Eulalie."

"I am not interested in your names," said Mrs. Raven. She looked at the girls sharply and inquisitively. If she were surprised by their neatness and good looks she concealed the fact. She sat erect like a displeased queen.

"I only want to tell you that you must leave here at once. Whatever schemes may be in your heads, I don't think either of you would want to ruin my son."

"Schemes!" Lally gasped, surprised into speech. "We have no schemes. Have we, Bella?"

"I think you're upset by the newspaper this morning, Mrs. Raven," Bella said calmly. "We are, too. We're terribly sorry such a thing happened. The man simply waylaid us. We told him nothing. I suppose he was frustrated, so this is how he has taken his revenge."

"A revenge against my son."

Bella's chin went up. "It isn't exactly flattering to my sister and myself, either."

"Then you must see it doesn't happen again, mustn't you? By packing your bags—if you have any—and leaving here at once." Her insolent tone made it difficult for Bella to keep her temper. She made herself speak reasonably,

"We can't do that, Mrs. Raven. We've promised Mr. Raven to stay until he returns from the country and the trial takes place. He has committed himself to making public this kind of crime. It's a horrible crime, Mrs. Raven. Perhaps you didn't know?" She waited a moment for Mrs. Raven to answer, but that lady merely tapped her fan restlessly, the jewels on her fingers flashing. Bella went on, "So it becomes the duty of my sister and myself to stand by him, no matter what it does to our own reputation."

"*Your* reputation!" Mrs. Raven gave a high tinkling laugh. "But, my dear young woman—" She caught the look in Bella's eye, and cleverly changed her tactics. "I think you must both be grateful to my son for what he has saved you from. A fate literally worse than death, I believe. Yes, I see your sister agrees with me. So couldn't you perhaps show your gratitude by nipping this deplorable scandal in the bud? You have only to leave here at once. I personally will find you situations in some other part of the country. I promise you shall have unsullied reputations. All I beg of you is not to ruin my foolish, impulsive boy's future. You know he's standing for Parliament, of course, and you realize that any more of this kind of publicity will be fatal to his chances. I can see you're intelligent young women. You must be sympathetic, too. Poor Guy suffered a tragedy in his marriage and it's been the greatest relief to us all that at last he's emerged from his sorrow and begun to show what he can do. He has a brilliant brain. It's our duty not to deprive his country of that."

Lally was looking intensely distressed.

"Bella, we must—"

Bella interrupted her with an impatient, "Hush, Lally! Mrs. Raven, I don't think you understand the position at all. We *are* part of all that you say about your son's future. He's making our unfortunate experience part of his electioneering campaign. So we have to be here as proof to his story. We can't disappear. It would be most ungrateful to him. I think he would be furious."

"Of course he'd be furious!" Mrs. Raven snapped. "Because he has no sense. And neither have you. Or have you—" her eyes narrowed "—a great deal of sense as to where your own fortune may lie?"

Bella bit her lip, determined to control her temper.

"We made a promise, Mrs. Raven. We don't break promises."

"Oh, tush, girl! Don't take that high-flown attitude with me. I see through you. You're nothing but an adventuress. The whole thing is a plot. You're hand in glove with that old woman in Seven Dials."

Lally was scarlet and on the verge of tears.

"Oh, no, Mrs. Raven! How can you say that! Bella, tell her it isn't true! Tell her we'll leave and not make trouble."

"What about the baby, Lally?"

"The b-baby?" Lally's eyes fell before Bella's fierce regard. "What do you mean?"

"Are you going to say that it doesn't matter that it died? Have you forgotten it already? Don't you care that other innocent babies die that way? Are you *really* going to let Aunt Aggie go free? What are you made of, you, my own sister!"

Lally was crying in earnest.

"Bella, you know I'd do anything for the baby. But this l-lady—"

"She never saw the baby," Bella said, her quiet voice belying the high points of colour in her cheeks. "It's difficult to feel for someone you've never seen. She's naturally only concerned for the good of her son. But he's a grown man and how he manages his life is his own affair. We can only do what we promised."

Mrs. Raven was snapping her fan open and shut. Her mouth was sucked into her cheeks, making her look suddenly old, but far from feeble. On the contrary, her abruptly bony face had a frightening intensity, as if hate burned beneath it. She was not used to being thwarted. She was certainly unfamiliar with such a humiliating situation as a young woman of much inferior standing defying her. She would never forget it. Beneath her own anger, Bella was soberly aware that she had made an enemy not to be underestimated.

But did it matter? When this affair was over she was unlikely ever to cross Mrs. Raven's path again. And how *dare* the old woman treat her and Lally like subhumans to be whisked out of the path of her precious son?

"I think you don't entirely understand the situation, Mrs. Raven."

"Oh, I understand it very well," Mrs. Raven said tightly.

"No, I think you don't. I think you expected to find my sister and me illiterate and common. You thought we could be patronized and intimidated. You don't like us to have a sense of honour—"

"*Bella!*" whispered Lally, scandalized.

Mrs. Raven was on her feet. She was quite small, smaller even than Lally. She stood so erect, she looked eight feet tall.

"On the contrary, Miss McBride," her voice was ice, "you're exactly what I expected you to be!"

Then she swept out. For all that Lally was still there, snuffling and drying her eyes, the room seemed extraordinarily empty. And Bella had an uncomfortable suspicion that she had had the worst of that interview.

"Bella, how could you be so rude?"

"She was ruder."

"No, she wasn't. She was only worried for her son."

"She was rude in the things she was thinking about us. I could read them if you couldn't. I'm never going to let people patronize me! Never!"

"Now she hates us."

"That's better than despising us. At least she knows we're human beings. She didn't before she came. She thought we were faceless and anonymous the way she thinks of anybody not in her own class. I can't endure snobbery. Somehow I don't think Mr. Raven can, either."

"Bella, I think you're getting above yourself," Lally said soberly.

The flame was still in Bella's cheeks.

"I'm *being* myself, that's all. I'm not going to truckle to anybody. Why, you'd have let her make us run away. You'd not even have fought for the dead baby."

Lally's fist was in her mouth. But she said stubbornly, "Suppose all this scandal does ruin Mr. Raven."

"It won't. Oh, I grant you it's true it might damage his career for a while. But don't you see, it will make his character. It wasn't after he met us, but before, that he was ruining his life. Didn't Mrs. Doughty tell us? All that idling and gambling. Now he has a cause to fight for. Haven't you noticed how he's changed already?"

"No."

"He has. He's lost that world-weary look."

"Oh, Bella, you're imagining things," Lally said uneasily. "You never saw him until two days ago."

Bella had a pang of surprise as she realized the truth of this. She had such an extraordinarily clear image of Mr. Raven when he was surrounded with fashionable young people, and bored to death. She knew exactly how he had looked, with the carved lines of weariness in his cheeks. Now he was not weary. He was cool, calculating, alert, and not to be intimidated by slanderous attacks in the press, or anywhere else.

The now familiar excitement was twisting inside Bella again. She began to smile dreamily, running her fingers caressingly over the beautifully carved mantelpiece. "Anyway," she murmured, "I confess I like being here. Ring the bell, Lally. We'll have the fire lighted in this room today."

"Bella!"

"Oh, don't be such a mouse! Didn't Mr. Raven say we were to use any room we pleased?" The smile was curving her mouth again. "I enjoy luxury. I intend making the most of it."

Chapter 7

"So you had a visit from my mother?"

Mr. Raven had arrived home long after dark. He was still in his greatcoat, and walking restlessly about the hall. Lally had retired early. She was working herself into a fever about the trial tomorrow, and Bella had been down to the kitchen to ask if she could prepare the soothing drink that Papa had always administered when Lally was in one of her states. She was carrying it upstairs now, and that was how she had encountered Mr. Raven.

"Yes. We did."

"You found her not particularly well-disposed towards you?"

"She thinks we are doing you harm."

His mouth quirked in what could have been the beginnings of a smile.

"I gather you were more than a match for her."

The humiliation of that scene, with Mrs. Raven looking down her little beaky nose with that arrogant contempt, was still too vivid.

"I was rude to her. But not as rude as she was to me." She held his gaze defiantly. "I think you should have remedied your mother's misapprehensions about Lally and me, Mr. Raven."

"Do you think she would have listened?"

Bella wanted to burst out with all her brooded-over grievances, that Mrs. Raven was arrogant, disdainful, narrow-minded, selfish, intolerably snobbish. Instead she heard herself saying, quite meekly,

"Are we doing you harm?"

He did smile then, with a kind of retrospective pleasure.

"Indeed you are. I had some stormy meetings. They were very exhilarating. Sir Henry is rubbing his hands in glee."

"Sir Henry?"

"My opponent. He boasts of influential friends in the press. I suspect he buys them. Unscrupulous reporters. Or simply editors who don't like my brand of politics. It's all in the game."

"We couldn't help it about that reporter," Bella said. "He waylaid us. We didn't tell him a thing. What he wrote was all made up. We haven't dared to go out since."

"Don't worry. There'll be much worse, especially after the trial tomorrow. What's that you have in that glass?"

"It's for Lally. She's dreading having to see Mrs. Proudfoot and Noah again. It doesn't do any good to tell her they'll be safely in the dock. She's just scared to death."

"I'm sorry to hear that." There was genuine concern in his face, the first that Bella had seen. It was because he was thinking of pretty Lally with her highly sensitive feelings. Bella unreasonably thought she would rather have him remain aloof and detached. "But she won't need to be in the witness-box long. She only needs to describe seeing the baby buried. She does understand that, doesn't she?"

"She has to re-live a nightmare," said Bella.

"Yes, yes, I know. I'm sorry. It can't be helped." He was growing impatient. "It began when you talked to a stranger in a coach. Now you have to see it through."

"Yes, Mr. Raven." Bella began to move towards the stairs. His voice called her back.

"But you, Miss Isabella. You don't share your sister's nightmare?"

He was forcing her to look inside herself again. She had an uneasy feeling that it wasn't feminine to anticipate so much satisfaction from seeing Aunt Aggie and Noah prisoners in the dock. Nor feminine to have secretly enjoyed defying Mr. Raven's mother. Nor should she be so fiercely ready to fight all the slander a hostile press may make about him as her and Lally's protector.

She should be like Lally, inconspicuous and tearful and in need of petting and sympathy.

She met Mr. Raven's inquisitive glance.

"I have a much stronger constitution than my sister," she said levelly.

The gloomy courtroom was crowded. Bella hadn't seen the newspapers that morning but Doctor Bushey, who had called to accompany them to Bow Street, admitted that there had been a great deal of publicity given both to the forthcoming trial and to Mr. Raven's so-called philanthropy.

"One or two of the papers are kind," Doctor Bushey admitted, when pressed by Bella. "They say it's important that we should have some members of Parliament who are interested in the cause of humanity. It's refreshing when a rich young man is deeply concerned for the poor."

"But the others?" Bella persisted.

"The others are the sensational press."

"What do they say? What do they call Lally and me?"

"They are very complimentary about your appearance, Miss McBride."

The old doctor, in his gruff kindly way, was so like Papa, that Bella felt completely at home with him. Mr. Raven may have been sympathetic—who knew?—but there was no doubt he was using them for his political ends. Doctor Bushey was genuinely a friend.

"You're not telling me everything, Doctor Bushey. Do they say that Mr. Raven is only pretending to care about justice, that—" Bella flushed and went resolutely on, "—he is really keeping us for immoral purposes?"

"Well—if you insist, lassie—they do suggest you might be a certain aspiring young politician's lights of love. But don't take the slander to heart. I assure you Guy isn't. He's enjoying the tussle. It's doing him all the good in the world—if that interests you." The doctor gave Bella a shrewd penetrating look, which she evaded.

"It won't do him any good if he loses the election."

"If he loses, he'll fight again. But he won't lose. Today's trial will bring out the truth. Anyone only has to look at the innocence in your two faces. Don't worry yourself, my dear. All will be well."

But Doctor Bushey's reassuring words were forgotten when Bella stood in the witness-box and looked directly at the prisoners. Noah's small coal-black eyes, smouldering with fury, his great shoulders and lounging body, and beside him the dumpy form of his mother, a humble respectable deeply distressed old woman who kept her eyes meekly downcast, and her black-gloved hands quietly clasped in front of her, brought back all the terror she and Lally had suffered.

69

Whatever it cost, hers and Lally's reputation and even Guy Raven's political future, this evil pair must be prevented from ever again exercising their designs on other innocent young women.

Neither the police nor Mr. Raven need have been afraid that she would forget her lines or be afraid to speak them. She saw no one in the stuffy crowded room but the two in the dock. She gazed unflinchingly at them and told her story. Once she noticed Noah bare his teeth and lick his lips. But Aunt Aggie never lifted her eyes. She was a wronged old woman, her only weakness her too kind heart.

Bella told how Lally had run upstairs in the early hours of the morning scarcely able to speak about the terrible thing she had seen, the tiny narrow box in the snow, the great stooping form of Noah. She said that as a doctor's daughter she had been able to identify the odour of laudanum, both on Aunt Aggie's and her sister's breath, and almost certainly from the locked room of the young mother whom she had never seen. She finished by relating how it was intended that her sister should be carried unconscious—here her voice rose with remembered incredulity— to interview a strange woman about a possible position, and how, when she had become suspicious and frightened, she had been told it would be useless to scream for help.

"I understand," the magistrate murmured, "that this is an area where screams of distress are less heeded than, let us say, birdsongs. Go on, Miss McBride."

But Bella had finished her story. The anger and indignation that had carried her along had burnt out, leaving her exhausted.

"That's all, sir. That's when Doctor Bushey and the other gentleman, Mr. Raven, happened to be passing. They did hear my cries for help, and so—" she couldn't bear to speak their names, she pointed at the pair in the dock with her accusing finger, "they were wrong when they said no one would listen."

It was then that Aunt Aggie very slowly lifted her eyes and looked at Bella. Her lips moved. Bella could hear her whispered, "Tch tch!" Her round pale eyes were sad and forgiving. She looked so neat, so round and soft and cosy, her cheeks a clear baby-pink, her expression gently disillusioned with the ingratitude of the human race, that Bella was suddenly convinced she would never be found guilty. The press, already eager to tear Mr.

Raven to bits, would find pink-cheeked Aunt Aggie a dear kind misunderstood and wrongfully accused old lady.

The policeman beside Bella was indicating that she was to step down. She ignored him and leaned forward, crying passionately to the magistrate, "You must believe me, sir. Don't let her deceive you with her look of innocence. She is a wicked old woman."

"This court is interested only in evidence, Miss McBride," the magistrate reproved, in his detached voice. "Step down, please. Call the next witness."

The next witness was Lally. Bella saw at once that she was in a fine state of terror, her cheeks blanched, her eyes dilated. She looked everywhere but at the dock. She hadn't the courage to face her nightmare again.

Her evidence had to be coaxed out of her and was almost inaudible. She stumblingly whispered about the empty cradle, the hole in the snow. Her very incoherence was, Bella realized, far more convincing than Bella's own angry story. Everyone in the room was listening with fascinated attention to poor Lally's terror.

The magistrate was gentle with her. He listened attentively, coaxing her when need be, and shortly told her kindly that she could stand down.

Mr. Raven was the next witness. In spite of having to soothe the half-fainting Lally, Bella was immediately conscious of the rustle through the court, and suddenly she realized the number of men present with notebooks and stubby pencils. One of them was looking intently at her and Lally, and obviously sketching their likeness. Bella quickly turned her head away, only to look directly into other insolent eyes. The benches at the back of the gloomy little room were crowded with people who had come to see, not a pair of evil-doers, but herself and Lally, and the man, now standing composedly in the witness-box, who had protected them.

She felt hot and angry and curiously naked. She was thankful that Lally had given way to her distress and was weeping quietly into her handkerchief. At least she needn't be aware that they had enemies other than the two in the dock. It was Bella's first experience of being a public exhibit, of knowing that the onlookers were consumed with curiosity, hostility, perhaps even a certain lewd admiration. Noah and Aunt Aggie might be found

71

guilty and sent to prison, but she and Lally were being labelled as loose young women without even a trial.

Mr. Raven was having to answer what seemed impertinent questions. Standing in the witness-box he seemed very tall, very cold, very definite.

"You say it was pure chance that took you and your companion down this particular street?"

"It was. We had been to visit a Ragged School in that area. We were already in a state of great concern and indignation about those unfortunate children."

The magistrate leaned forward.

"Keep to the point, if you please."

"Then let me say we were in the state of mind to be very conscious of distress. I merely wish to emphasize there was genuine distress in Miss McBride's calls for help. It was immeasurably shocking to stumble on such persecution in an English city."

The magistrate was becoming irascible.

"The witness stand is not a political platform, Mr. Raven. We want your evidence only."

"Doctor Bushey and I broke into the house," Mr. Raven went on. "We found these two unfortunate young women literally prisoners. I offered them the shelter of my home. I admit I wanted this particular depravity existing in our seemingly enlightened civilization to have as much publicity as possible."

The pencils wrote furiously. Mr. Raven stepped down and Doctor Bushey took the box. After his evidence the prosecuting counsel asked that the prisoner Mrs. Proudfoot be put in the witness-box.

It was growing dark and the gas had been lit. The flaring jets accompanied counsel's monotonous impersonal voice.

Was it the prisoner's habit to take as lodgers only young women obviously in trouble? Was that why she made the room disarming, with pretty furnishings, so that a suspicious young woman would be pleasantly surprised? Wasn't it strange that her friend Mrs. Jennings, who apparently was so useful in finding positions for these completely strange young women, couldn't be traced? Perhaps Mrs. Jennings didn't exist, perhaps she was, in reality, a completely different article, a ship anchored in the Thames, due to sail for distant ports?

And if the woman whose baby the prisoner had delivered—and subsequently buried—was actually her niece, as she maintained, wasn't it strange that she too couldn't be traced? Wouldn't she have been a little grateful to her "aunt" for successfully delivering her, even if, sadly, the baby hadn't survived for many hours? And wasn't it odd that a new-born baby's stomach showed traces of opium which could have come from a drug known as laudanum? Moreover when it was obvious the baby wasn't going to live wouldn't it have been natural to call a doctor, certainly to get in touch with the proper authorities about its burial?

And wasn't it a still further coincidence that a ship called the *Star of Asia* that had sailed at dawn, scarcely three hours after the baby's burial, had had on board a mysterious passenger who had had to be carried to her cabin? Perhaps the prisoner wasn't aware that the *Star of Asia* had had to put into Gravesend to shelter from high winds, and there had been searched. It might interest the prisoner to know that no young woman was found on board, but there were certain articles of women's clothing discovered hidden in a locker. Wasn't the prisoner distressed that her "niece" had obviously been put off the ship hastily? It may well be that she had not survived her son by more than a few hours, so that one lay buried in the snow and one beneath the bounding wave?

The quiet monotonous voice pounded on and on until at last Aunt Aggie's glib answers and denials became fumbling and incoherent. Finally she was silent, her mouth open helplessly showing her rotting teeth, her eyes quite empty.

Bella was tiredly exultant. She heard the magistrate saying that the prisoners would be kept in custody while awaiting trial in the central criminal court before a judge and jury. There was something about a charge of infanticide, and then suddenly it was all over. Aunt Aggie and Noah were being led away between two burly policemen. Aunt Aggie had composed herself again, her head was meekly bent, her whole posture suggesting injured innocence. But Noah threw back his wild black head, searching the courtroom until his eyes rested on Mr. Raven. Then his expression became frighteningly malevolent.

"Curse you!" he said audibly. "Curse you!"

Lally trembled and her hot hand clutched Bella's. Even Bella, confident as she was that Aunt Aggie and Noah would be safely under lock and key, felt a shiver of premonition.

The room was shuffling itself empty. Everyone could go home. Home?

Chapter 8

SONGBIRDS IN SOHO? That was the headline in the London Clarion the next morning.

With flaming cheeks Bella read the article.

"As the Magistrate aptly remarked in Bow Street courtroom yesterday, screams are more common than birdsongs in some areas of our fascinating city. But the Raven's ears were attuned to both the goldfinch and the blackbird. Obviously he found it impossible to decide which had the greater charm. The simple solution was to carry them both to his love nest. And who, whose eyes rested on the fair forms of the Misses McBride, could blame him? It is entirely right that such charming examples of our English beauty should not be criminally smuggled out of the country. We sincerely wish Mr. Guy Raven the greatest happiness in his private life. But let him now have the good sense to give up all thoughts of a public life. Or, if he fails to heed our advice, let the people of Hertfordshire think carefully before electing such a man to Parliament."

"We are notorious!" Bella exclaimed. She thrust the paper at Lally. "Read that."

Lally frowned over the small print.

"What does it mean? Are they trying to say we only pretended to need help?" Lally's eyes grew stormy. "They should have seen that poor baby for themselves. Aunt Aggie said she gave him laudanum to stop him crying, but he never cried. He never cried, Bella!"

"The baby's dead. Forget him. We have to think of ourselves now. What is to happen to us if we have no character?"

"You didn't seem to care about that when you talked to Mrs. Raven." Lally said, with unexpected sharpness.

"That was because she was patronizing us. I've told you I hate to be patronized. I don't think I could let even Queen Victoria do that to me. And I didn't think I could endure it in the courtroom yesterday when all those men stared and drew pictures of us. If only there was some way to show them how we look down on them and despise them."

"I only want to be safe," Lally murmured, her eyes dark. "Noah looked as if he would like to kill us. I keep having nightmares that we meet him again, in a dark street."

"Don't be silly, Lally. He'll be locked up for years. But we have to go on living in the world. It's all very well to have new laws made for the protection of women and children, but they're too late to help us. Who *is* going to employ us now? I can think of no one but some lecherous old man who likes to pinch servants in dark passages, and has a wife who is too timid to protest about it. Don't look so scandalized. There are plenty of those."

"Mr. Raven will look after us," Lally said uncertainly.

"I think Mr. Raven will be quite occupied in saving his own reputation."

Lally didn't seem to understand any of this. She was so unworldly and concerned only with the fundamentals. A baby had been murdered, and probably also its mother. What did reputations matter? But Mrs. Doughty was more practical. She arrived upstairs, breathless, to announce that the master wanted to see them in the library, and that he was in a fair taking.

"He's got all the morning papers, and dear to goodness, they're slandering him something cruel. There's a sketching of you two in one of them. It's wicked. It makes you look bold and sly. Doughty says politics is a dirty business, and that's true."

Mr. Raven was pacing up and down the library, frowning, his mouth hard, his eyes a wintry blue. He didn't greet the girls but said immediately.

"This is developing into a real fight, isn't it? I seem to have underestimated my opponent. Mind you, I've played right into his hands, getting involved in a scandal."

"It's only the newspapers that have made it a scandal," Bella said hotly.

"That's true. I hadn't realized I was so unpopular. I knew I wasn't approved as a Parliamentary candidate, of course. Too

75

young, too irresponsible, too lax in my morals. Now they're having a fine time proving they've been right all the time. Look at that."

He tossed the paper depicting Bella and Lally sitting on a bench in the courtroom on to the table.

"Oh, I don't look like that," Lally said indignantly. "So bold. And my nose doesn't turn up like that."

"No, it doesn't, does it," said Mr. Raven thoughtfully. "The artist wasn't very observant, or he'd have noticed you have a much prettier nose."

Lally flushed, looking pleased. This, thought Bella, was a fine time for Mr. Raven to indulge in polite flattery, even though in such a withdrawn and curiously calculating manner. She was just beginning to realize, uneasily, how little she knew him, and how lightly she had been taking this scrape into which she and Lally had got. She should never have agreed to stay in this house. She had been even more unworldly than Lally. To help Mr. Raven in his fine principles, indeed! The world had no time for fine principles. It preferred to crucify.

"What are we to do?" she asked bluntly.

"Do?" The question seemed to astonish him. "Why, fight, of course. Do you think this muck frightens me?"

"We are only women."

"Well?" A trick of the light made his eyes look silver. There would never be any warmth in them, Bella thought, angrily, hopelessly.

"A man can live down a tarnished reputation. A woman can't. Surely you must know that."

"Is your reputation of more value than your life? I don't think that was in your mind when you screamed for help."

"In this society there's almost no difference. With a ruined reputation a woman doesn't have a life. Oh, I know you saved Lally and me from a dreadful future. I'm very grateful. But how was I to know this would happen, this muck, as you call it?" She indicated the spread newspapers. "I can see only one thing for Lally and me now. We'll have to emigrate."

Mr. Raven stared at Bella's flushed and angry face. Then suddenly he began to laugh.

"Don't be a coward, Miss Isabella."

"A *coward*!" Bella's eyes sparked. "Don't dare to call me that!

I'm not being a coward. I'm being realistic. It's time someone was."

Lally was clutching Bella's arm.

"Leave England? Oh, Bella!"

"On the contrary, Miss Isabella," Mr. Raven said. "I'm being realistic, too. You're so taken up with your indignation that you haven't bothered to inquire why I wanted to see you. I was going to explain to you both that there's only one way to silence these malicious rumours."

"Can that be done?" Bella asked in surprise.

"Certainly it can be done. Very simply. By my marrying one of you."

Momentarily Bella was beyond speech. She simply stared at Mr. Raven unbelievingly. He couldn't be proposing marriage in that cool emotionless way, with nothing but calculation in his eyes. This was the greatest indignity of all.

And yet the lightning had shot through her stomach, making her feel faint.

"You don't have to emigrate, Miss Eulalie," he was going on. As he looked at Lally, his gaze had again softened, as it always did for Lally. Always! "It would be ironic if I subjected you to almost the fate from which I thought I had saved you. At least, that's how the newspapers would interpret it. So I want you to be my wife."

"Me!" Lally gasped. She had gone paper-white. "Oh, Mr. Raven, thank you, I couldn't!"

"Couldn't? Come, Miss Eulalie. You don't flatter me. I won't make pretty speeches. I won't even pretend that I love you. How can I? I scarcely know you. Besides I must tell you now—I lost my wife and I will never love again. This would be a marriage from expediency only. But you would be mistress of this house, and of Ravenscroft. We'll drive down to Ravenscroft when the weather improves. I promise you you'll find that a very beautiful house. My grandfather built it."

Lally was gazing at him with a hypnotized look, her soft mouth open, her wild childlike eyes full of a dazed terror.

"Confess," Mr. Raven went on, "that it has passed through your mind more than once since you have been here that you would like to be mistress of a house like this."

"No, no!" Lally managed to say. "That's Bella. I've had no such thoughts."

77

The cool blue eyes raked Bella.

"The realist again?"

She was furious that the blood rose in her face, furious with Lally for being so naïve, for looking so innocent and gentle and untroublesome, indeed, for promising to be the kind of wife whom a man could conveniently ignore. She was most furious of all with this man for putting them in so ignominious a position. Yet already her honesty was telling her that he had meant well from the start, and was now choosing the best method he knew to save their reputations.

She could still, by a tremendous effort, keep her voice cool.

"Who doesn't enjoy luxury?"

"Exactly. And it would, of course, be yours also after your sister and I are married."

"A *ménage à trois?*" said Bella sharply, and he put back his head and laughed delightedly.

"That's scarcely language for someone assumed by the press to be a Soho drab. I believe we can still set London by the ears. In a very different way, of course, from what we have achieved already. My mother could dress you both. Yes." Finger on lip, he surveyed them thoughtfully. Why, he even notices now that we have bosoms and waists, Bella thought in angry sarcasm. And reflected on the extreme unlikelihood of that haughty little parrot woman, Mrs. Raven, condescending to advise them on wardrobes.

"We aren't *playthings!*" she declared, and incredulously heard her voice tremble.

The laughter had gone out of Mr. Raven's face, too. He looked suddenly tired, the lines unnaturally deep in so young a face.

"I never thought you were, Miss Isabella. I assure you this isn't a joke that has gone too far. It's a deadly serious thing I set out to do, and I simply don't intend to be thwarted by a lot of vicious scandalmakers. I've explained that marriage means little to me now. But it will afford permanent protection for your sister and yourself. For myself, it may whitewash me sufficiently to scrape by with my electorate. If it does, then I can begin on the really important business of social reform. It's a barbarous thing that young women like yourselves, without family or dowry, should have no real place in our society. And even less place now that you've unfortunately been caught up in the publicity treadmill. Well, I'm offering amends. And damn it—" he said with sudden impatience, "I see no reason at all for going down on my knees to do it."

Bella gave Lally a little push.

"Go on, then."

Lally looked at her piteously.

"Go on?"

"Say you'll marry him, of course."

"But, Bella—forever?"

"Marriage is forever."

Lally twisted her fingers in the greatest distress. Her eyes were swimming in tears.

"I thought—I meant to l-love—the man I marry."

"Love?" said Bella in a high voice, as if the word were one she had never understood. "Don't be a dolt!" she said, and picking up her skirts swept out of the room.

She couldn't bring herself to speak to Lally again, even after she had heard Mr. Raven calling in a loud impatient voice to Doughty to get him a cab, and later heard him leaving the house. Lally, she knew, would be looking for her to pour out her terror and excitement, and triumph. For of course she must feel triumph. Who wouldn't? Mr. Raven was one of the most eligible men in London. Lally only had to play her cards right and she could win for herself an important place in society. It would take time, of course. People had long memories. But with her gentleness and innocence and angelic prettiness, Lally must eventually win even Mr. Raven's mother. That was, if she used her commonsense and didn't go on babbling forlornly about love. Who could expect love in this world? Only a baby or a simpleton.

As for herself, with the respectable chaperonage of her sister and new brother-in-law, and the background of rich houses, there may eventually even be someone to marry her. A music master, perhaps, or an elderly widower.

Bella paced up and down the little morning-room. She felt on fire. She couldn't sit still, she didn't want to engage in an interminable conversation with Lally, she abhorred the thought of a little soothing needlework which would only serve to remind her of all the long useless days to come, dabbling with painting, pressing wild flowers, netting purses, being neither wife nor mother nor servant. Being nothing . . .

Yet this marriage was undoubtedly the way to save all their faces. Wasn't it? Or was there any other way?

An impulse seized Bella. She flew upstairs to get her bonnet and shawl. Lally was standing at the window of their bedroom, a handkerchief to her eyes.

"Oh, Bella, there you are!" she exclaimed in relief. "Bella, I truly can't face—Bella! Where are you going? *Bella!*" Her piteous voice followed Bella down the stairs.

But Bella was in the hall asking Doughty for the address of Doctor Bushey, and would he please get her a cab.

Doughty disapproved. "There's pesky newspapermen lurking outside, miss. I don't think the master would like you to expose yourself."

"Please do as I say," Bella said haughtily.

The old man, recognizing the voice of authority, hastened to obey. But he was right about the men outside, and Bella had to hold her shawl about her face, and shake off impertinent hands.

"What about your life story, miss? We'll pay you good money."

"Can we hear your plans for the future, miss? Don't be shy, dear. Let's have a look at your lovely face."

"Then if you won't talk about yourself, how about telling us of your patron's plans?"

Scarlet with rage, Bella reached the waiting cab and clambered in. In a calmer mood she would have enjoyed the drive across the park past Tyburn Hill to the Edgware Road and then to Wigmore Street with its rows of neat respectable houses. As it was, she was scarcely aware of the lavender-coloured morning, with the mud splashing up in fine style from the wheels of passing carriages and coaches, the bustling throngs, the incredible welter of noise and vitality. By a great effort of will she composed herself, and sat still in the cab that smelled of wet straw and old tobacco smoke. But she could see nothing except Mr. Raven's stony eyes and the implacable set of his head. Perhaps Lally did well to be afraid . . .

Doctor Bushey was at home, and expressed himself astonished and delighted to have a visitor. The neatly-dressed maid who showed Bella in to the small cosy parlour smiled and bobbed when Doctor Bushey told her to fetch Tottie.

"Miss Isabella would like to see Tottie."

"That wasn't why I came."

Doctor Bushey's eyes didn't lack warmth or humanity or understanding. Indeed, they had a little too much of the last quality. Bella was very well aware he had noticed at once her flushed cheeks and distrait air. But he preferred to wait until Tottie arrived.

Her hair had been brushed and pinned back, her face was clean and her cap and apron spotless. But she still had the look of a caught animal, her eyes flying from Bella to Doctor Bushey in instant apprehension. She stood cringingly just inside the door, as if ready to fly if anyone moved.

"Don't be afraid, Tottie," Doctor Bushey said quietly. "Miss McBride is your friend. You remember her, don't you?"

Tottie nodded jerkily, but her gaze went beyond Bella, as if she expected to see Aunt Aggie or Noah spring up from behind the furniture.

"You must learn to say "How do you do" to your friends, Tottie. But all in good time, eh?"

"Her chilblains are better, I think," Bella said.

"Yes, Betsey's been treating those. Hasn't she, Tottie? All right, you can go now. But slowly, child. No one's chasing you."

Tottie's impulse to dart out of the room was overcome. Bella found her eyes tightening with sudden tears as she watched the suddenly deliberate and pathetically dignified departure of the little figure.

"She's learning," she said in amazement.

"Yes, she's learning. She hasn't spoken yet, but I'm quite sure she will, in time. We don't even know how long she was with that terrible pair, but I'd make a guess at about two years."

"Two years! A mere child, and living like that!"

"Yes, my dear. Living like that."

"Doctor Bushey, are there many Tottie's in London?" Bella asked in the greatest distress.

"I hope not. Although I fear so. But that's better, my dear."

"What's better?"

"You're looking less agitated. You've found someone with a bigger problem than your own."

"You brought Tottie in deliberately!"

"Of course. Of course. A little emotional therapy is good for everyone. Now tell me, what has my headstrong young friend, Guy Raven, been up to?"

"The newspapers, Doctor Bushey!"

"Yes, yes, I saw them. They've found a good story and they'll thrash it to death. They need boiling in oil, the lot of them. But don't tell me Guy is intimidated by this cheap sensationalism."

"No, he isn't," Bella admitted. "He has found a solution."

"So?" Doctor Bushey nodded interestedly.

"He proposes to marry my sister!"

Doctor Bushey leaned back, surveying Bella with his bright shrewd eyes. The knowledgeableness in them brought the colour to her cheeks again. She hadn't meant her voice to be so full of indignation, but it had been, and now this kindly old man who might have been her father was reading entirely the wrong meaning into it.

"Guy never does things by halves," he murmured.

"You don't seem at all surprised."

"I'm not. Except perhaps," the thick brows flickered, "by his choice."

"I think Lally reminds him a little of his first wife. Isn't it true a man always admires the same kind of woman? Though he was perfectly honest and explained he would never fall in love again. Anyway," Bella's voice grew resentful, "he has scarcely looked at us. It's all a matter of convenience only."

"And what are you asking me, my dear? Whether your sister should accept this offer of marriage?"

"Is there any other way out?" Bella said desperately. "Supposing it doesn't remedy the situation but does Mr. Raven even more harm? Frankly, Doctor Bushey, my sister hasn't the temperament to meet such a situation. She's timid and inclined to hysteria. Things must go gently and smoothly for her. For instance just having to encounter Mr. Raven's mother again would put her in a state of collapse. So if there is still persecution after the marriage, then wouldn't tarnished reputations be better for us all, after all."

"Tell me, what have you advised your sister to do?"

"Advised—"

"You haven't remained entirely silent, I take it."

Bella's eyes fell before the sharp humour in his eyes.

"If you must know, I told her to fly into his arms! The silly dolt!" She met Doctor Bushey's gaze defiantly. "Thinking tears are the answer to everything."

"And Guy thinks an advertised respectability the answer to everything. I warned him of this at the beginning."

"You knew this would happen!"

"Not perhaps this precise predicament. But some sort of one."

"Then should he do it? Should Lally do it?" Bella leaned forward earnestly. "I love my sister and want her to be happy. Is there any chance of happiness for her now?"

"Or Guy? He is *my* particular care."

"But he says he will never love again, anyway."

"Oh, come, Miss Isabella! Is someone who could act so spontaneously and generously towards two unknown young women incapable of love?"

Unconsciously, Bella pressed her hands to her heart. Why must she go on wondering whether those cold impersonal eyes could grow alight?

"He was pursuing his own ends," she muttered. "He wanted a cause. A picturesque cause, I think."

"Tottie was not so picturesque. Nor are a thousand others. Nor did you think you and your sister were at the time. My dear, be fair. Guy deserves his chance, his career. It can be a notable one."

Bella rose.

"Then he is to marry Lally."

Doctor Bushey held out his hand. His eyes twinkled kindly, conspiratorially.

"He is to marry one of you."

Chapter 9

Mrs. Doughty came hurrying downstairs when Bella arrived back.

"Thank goodness you're there, miss. Your sister's nearly out of her mind. I don't know as you shouldn't call the doctor."

"She can't be as bad as that!" Bella exclaimed in alarm.

"She is, too. Crying and sobbing. Saying she's been abandoned. You didn't ought to have gone off like that, miss."

"I had an errand," Bella said stiffly. Kind as she was, Mrs. Doughty was becoming too familiar. From now on they were no longer equals, as Mrs. Doughty imagined, but mistress and servant. This was a bridge Lally would have to learn to cross. She must understand that there was to be no more weeping on Mrs. Doughty's shoulder.

Lally, however, was in no state to understand anything. Bella found that Mrs. Doughty hadn't exaggerated her condition. She was prostrate, her eyes swollen, her little nose (which Mr. Raven had glibly admired) pink, her breath fluttering exhaustedly. When Bella, her bonnet still on, bent over her, her eyes widened in a moment of purely instinctive terror before she recognized who it was.

Then she whispered faintly, "Why did you leave me?"

"Good gracious, I've only been gone an hour. You were perfectly safe."

"Safe!"

"Oh, Lally, of course you were safe. Aunt Aggie and Noah are miles away and locked up."

"But now there's Mr. Raven."

Lally's voice was so low as to be almost inaudible. She searched Bella's face with her wide strained eyes. Her fingers, feverish and

84

alarmingly claw-like (she seemed to have lost weight overnight) were tightly wound round Bella's wrist. It was too late to be impatient with her or to attempt to scold her out of her panic. Her state of mind, Bella realized, was serious.

"When he touched me—after you had gone out of the room—" she was speaking in a low murmur, as if to herself, "—he only laid his hand on mine—but it was as if he were suddenly Noah. Or someone—as bad as Noah. I couldn't stand it. I snatched my hand away. And he—"

"Yes?" said Bella. "What did he do?"

"He smiled, I think. He said I was not to be worried, he would not be a demanding husband, but for the sake of propriety, I must sit at the head of his table, and receive guests, and—and share his room. Bella, I can't! I can't, I can't, I can't!"

Lally's voice had risen in the hiccuping cries of hysteria. Bella slapped her face and ordered her to control herself. Then, when she was silent, very white and scarcely breathing, Bella said gently,

"Lally! Sweetheart! Don't you realize how lucky you are? Why, it's like a fairy story. At one moment you were practically a waif, and now you're to be mistress of two fine houses. Think of the clothes and jewels you can have. I warrant Mr. Raven is generous. And he won't be unkind. He's a gentleman."

"It's another trap," said Lally restlessly. "We thought how kind Aunt Aggie was, too. We liked the pretty room. But see what happened. No one is to be trusted."

There was a knock at the door. Mrs. Doughty stood there with a laden tray.

"I've made some hot chocolate, miss. It's very soothing. I wouldn't let Annie bring it up. All agog she is."

"Why?" Bella asked, wondering if it were possible for Annie to be more agog than Mrs. Doughty, whose eyes were positively starting out of her head.

"All them milliners' and dressmakers' boxes arriving. The area bell's scarcely stopped ringing for the last ten minutes. What those rascally newspapermen are making of this, I'd not like to say. What is it, miss? Are you and your sister to be dressed up and flaunt the town?"

"Are the boxes addressed to us?" Bella asked faintly.

"Certainly they is." Mrs. Doughty's speech was a little garbled, as if she might have had recourse to the port decanter to fortify

85

herself against further excitements. "The Misses McBride, 16 Knightsbridge. That's no mistake."

"Then you'd better ask Annie to bring them up."

"You mean you was expecting them?" Mrs. Doughty gaped. "Surely you wasn't out shopping this morning, miss!"

"No, I wasn't." Bella had recovered her composure, and even Mrs. Doughty's goggling eyes could not see how her heart was beating. "I think they were sent to help my sister recover from her nervousness."

"Nervousness?"

"That will be all, Mrs. Doughty. Have the boxes sent up."

Lally could take no more than a sip of the chocolate. She gazed in a stupor as Bella took the lids off the exciting boxes, and displayed the ravishing contents. Bonnets, one pink and one blue, with French silk ribbons and roses as soft to the touch as real ones, two gowns, one the palest blue satin with a low-cut bodice and a gently stiffened skirt belling out from a tiny waist, the other pink, also in rich satin. The material gave Bella a sensation of sheer sensual delight. She had never seen such lovely gowns. There were evening slippers, too, and long white satin gloves, and two cashmere shawls.

Like a summer garden, the room had sprung into bloom.

Bella held the pink dress against herself and looked at her reflection in the mirror. But although it was beautiful and expensive it was too insipid a colour for her. So was the blue. Wouldn't Mr. Raven have realized that with her black hair and vivid cheeks she needed jewel colours, ruby reds and sapphires. But of course he wouldn't realize that. He had never looked at her.

"The things are for you, Lally," she said pettishly. "Can't you sit up and take an interest in them?"

Lally's eyes wandered dully over the strewn finery.

"There are two of each. One bonnet and gown must be for you. The pink, I expect."

"I detest that baby pink!"

"Then have the blue. You could have them both," Lally said longingly, "if you would have Mr. Raven, too."

Bella was suddenly very still, a tremendous excitement mushrooming inside her.

Then her mind fastened feverishly on smaller things. She noticed a letter in the bottom of one of the boxes and snatched it up. It was addressed to "Miss McBride" which, strictly speaking, meant Lally, but Lally was in no mood to make sense of the thick black writing. Bella tore open the envelope and unfolded the thick notepaper.

"My dear Eulalie,

It may lift yours and your sister's spirits to have a pretty gown and other gee-gaws. I hope that you will both do me the honour of dining with me this evening.

Your affianced husband,
Guy Raven."

"We are to have dinner with Mr. Raven tonight," she said.

"Oh, I can't, Bella. I can't, truly." Lally's lip was trembling again. "I only wish I need never face him again."

Bella lost her patience.

"Don't you want to put on that lovely gown? Don't you want to thank Mr. Raven for it? Don't you want him to see how pretty you can look?"

"I should be sick if I tried to eat. I know I should. And why does he send us these expensive things? Is it another trick?"

"Lally, nothing's a trick any more. You're to marry him. He wants you to look the way his bride should, that's all."

"That's why he rescued us!" Lally exclaimed. "I see it now. He only wanted to get one of us at his—at his mercy. The way Noah would have, too. Or any man. And then there would be another baby—to be buried in the night."

Lally was frighteningly colourless, her eyes enormous and sunken, her little hands beating at her breast.

"Lally, Lally, little love! Be quiet." Bella was genuinely alarmed. Lally seemed to be going out of her wits. The dreadful experience to which they had been subjected in Aunt Aggie's house had burnt itself too deeply into her mind. Her marriage now to a man who terrified her could complete her breakdown. Bella had sufficient medical knowledge to realize that.

And she saw that what had flashed into her mind, no, what had been there all the time, the impossible outrageous alternative, was now to be a necessity.

At once, now the decision was made, she became calm and assured.

"Lally, you shan't go down to dinner tonight. You shall rest quietly here by the fire. You shan't do anything you don't want to."

Lally's eyes took on a wild gleam of hope.

"Really, Bella? Not even marry—"

"Not even marry Mr. Raven." Bella's voice was quiet, definite, protecting. "If he still insists on having one of us, it will have to be me."

"Oh, Bella, you're so brave! I do so admire you. Mr. Raven must see you would make a much better wife than me." Lally clutched at her in a passion of gratitude. Then she said less certainly, "I don't have to tell him, do I?"

"I shall tell him myself. Tonight."

He was standing in his usual posture with his back to the fire. He looked very handsome in his black dinner-jacket and gleaming white cravat. There seemed to be a certain anticipation in his eyes as he looked up at the sound of Bella's entrance. He was no doubt curious to see how his bride to be and perhaps her sister, also, looked when dressed as elegant young ladies.

But his expression immediately changed to a polite question as he saw Bella, alone, and in her best gown of grey tarlatan which was a little dowdy and old-fashioned, since it had been made by Miss Anstruther in the village quite eighteen months ago. Miss Anstruther had never been able to achieve a clever cut, and had an obsession about what she called a ladylike neckline. Nor was grey Bella's colour, but Papa had bought the cloth when he had bought Lally's blue, and certainly, if nothing else, the grey gown was dovelike in its modesty.

It made her look like a governess.

"Didn't the dressmakers' boxes arrive?" Mr. Raven immediately inquired.

"Yes, they did. Lally and I found the contents—very extravagant. But—" Now she was faced with it, how was she to make this incredible suggestion?

"They perhaps didn't fit? I had to make a guess as to size. But where is your sister? She's coming down, I hope?"

"She asks to be excused. She has a very bad headache. She— Mr. Raven, you know us both equally little. Why did you decide it was Lally you would marry?"

She hoped she looked more composed than she felt. Her heart was pounding so violently that the lace trimming on her bodice trembled visibly. She had meant to be cool and tactful, and now she had blurted out the question like a schoolgirl.

She didn't know how she had expected him to react. Certainly she wasn't prepared for his deliberate survey of her. His gaze went assessingly from her coiled dark hair to her feet. It lingered on her throat, her bosom and her waist, and finally rested on her slippers peeping from the hem of her gown.

"Not because her charms exceed yours, Miss Isabella. Simply because she is the elder of you." He laughed. "I had to have some distinction to make."

How *could* one marry a man like that, cold, insolent, assessing one's advantages as he might an animal he wished to purchase? Lally was right to be afraid.

Then why wasn't she herself afraid? Why did she feel only this terrific sense of challenge and destiny?

Bella lifted her head proudly on her long neck.

"I thought perhaps my sister reminded you a little of your dead wife?"

He moved sharply, turning to the fire.

"That's an impossible assumption. My wife has no duplicates."

"Then, Mr. Raven—if you have no special preference for Lally, will you marry me instead?"

He swung round, staring at her.

"My sister has a much more delicate nervous system than I have. She's suffered dreadfully from shock, she has nightmares all the time about Noah and the dead baby. Now the thought of marrying someone virtually a stranger terrifies her."

"Terrifies? Not a nice word, Miss Isabella."

"It's only that you're a stranger. I'm afraid another ordeal so soon would make her brain give way. She begged me to—"

"Offer yourself instead? And doesn't the thought of such an ordeal terrify you, too?"

She hated his growing amusement.

"I've said I'm much stronger," she said tartly.

"Yes. Yes, I can see that. You'd be capable of making a sacrifice."

"A sacrifice?"

"That of a loveless marriage."

"It isn't a sacrifice but a solution. You explained that yourself."

"I did." He laughed again, suddenly looking as if he were enjoying himself. "Sit down, my dear. Let's drink to this extraordinary situation. I lose one bride and gain another in the space of twelve hours. Incredible. Damned amusing, really."

"Then—you will do this?"

"Why not? It makes no odds to me which one of you I have." His eyes met hers blandly. "The goldfinch or the blackbird, as the newspapers so cleverly put it."

Chapter 10

THE newspapers loved that catch phrase about the goldfinch and the blackbird.

They were able to use it to full effect the next day when most of them carried a discreet announcement of an impending marriage.

"All London is agog to know the identity of Miss Isabella McBride. Is she the fair beauty or the dark, the golden-feathered finch or the black songster? It is rumoured that bets are being laid in all the elite gambling houses. Indeed, it is the kind of wager that Mr. Guy Raven would have enjoyed himself in the recent past, before he became so oddly reformed a person. We feel his new personality is greatly to fashionable London's loss, and not at all to the country's gain. Sincere congratulations to clever Miss Isabella, but can a belated marriage certificate whitewash a man's reputation?"

That was the scandalous *London Clarion*. The more respectable papers confined themselves to a bare announcement, or a few lines that contained only a mild jibe.

On the whole Guy was not too dissatisfied. There was every chance now that he could weather the storm. Except as far as his mother was concerned.

She sent him a note by hand.

"Since I will never set foot in your house again while those scheming and unscrupulous creatures are there, I will expect you here at eleven."

She was waiting for him in her elegant drawing-room that looked over Chelsea embankment and the turgid yellow waters of the Thames. She was dressed entirely in black. Guy recognized the gown as the one she had had made when in mourning for Caroline. He didn't suppose she had put it on deliberately to remind him of Caroline, but because she felt this occasion required black.

She sat rigidly on a straight-backed chair, her poodles yapping and quarrelling about her feet. Hannah, the elderly maid, hovered in the background, but was immediately dismissed. Things had gone too far even for Hannah's trustworthy and sympathetic ears.

"Well, Guy! At first you were a fool, now I can only think you're a raving lunatic."

Guy kissed her on her exquisite pale pink cheek. His mother was now sixty-five. He was her only child whom she had borne at the age of thirty-five after several tortured years of thinking herself barren. She loved him with a demanding possessiveness. Even for the gentle well-bred Caroline she had not been an easy mother-in-law. Guy could only hope that, at the most, she would reluctantly acknowledge his new wife.

"I want to bring Isabella to meet you, Mamma."

"Isabella! Stuff and nonsense! That won't be her real name. It will be plain Bessie or Bridget. Can't you see the girl for the scheming hussy she is? She was only waiting for someone like you and that gullible old fool, Bushey, to come along and fall into her net. Heavens, boy, at your age to be taken in by the oldest trick in the world."

"And when you've met her, Mamma," Guy went on imperturbably, "perhaps you'll be good enough to advise her on a suitable wardrobe. Something simple to be married in, since we plan a very quiet wedding, but after that you can let yourself go. See that she's dressed the way my wife should be. Will you do that for me, Mamma?"

The sound that escaped Mrs. Raven's lips could only be described as a hiss. Her beautiful, heavy-lidded eyes blazed with outrage. She thumped her ivory-headed cane on the floor several times, and a poodle yelped.

"So the slut expects to shelter under my wing! That she should *dare!*"

"Be careful of your language, Mamma." Guy's voice was mild, but his mouth had tightened.

"I'll use exactly what language the subject deserves. The girl obviously is a slut. Both of them are. By the way, which one is this Bella, or whatever her name is?"

"Are you interested, then?"

"I met them," his mother said tightly.

"She's the dark-haired one. The younger."

"I expected it! The saucy one. At least the other might have been manageable. But you would have an eye for cheap vivacity. Don't begin to think you'll be the master with that one. Isabella, indeed! She's already been abominably rude to me, and yet now you expect me to forget her gutter manners and introduce her to society."

"Perhaps you were rude to her first."

"I merely told her the truth. In any case, I was brought up not to answer back to one's elders."

"The girls have been under considerable strain, Mamma."

"I should think so! I should think so!" the old lady crowed. "Catching a rich husband. Quite an ordeal. Oh, Guy! I'd never have thought a son of mine could be so stupid. Let your career go, if it must. What does that matter compared to a lifetime of misery. Do you realize, for one thing, you'll never see me in your house again? Neither in London nor at Ravenscroft."

"Don't be absurd! Ravenscroft is as much yours as mine. You know you love it."

"And I shall sacrifice it. Guy! My boy!"

He met the appeal in her lifted eyes, and his own hardened.

"I'm sorry, Mamma. You call me a lunatic. I'm afraid I must call you a narrow-minded, intolerant, cowardly old woman."

"You'd dare!" Her moment of softness had gone. Her beaky nose was held high, her expression that of a malevolent old parrot. "Cowardly! You think I haven't the courage to introduce that woman to society. Why, I'd introduce a worm if I felt so inclined. But not a schemer. No, not if I have to endure loneliness until my dying day."

"You should have been on the stage, Mamma."

"And you should be back in an infant school!" she screamed.

The memory of that little funereal figure like an angry wasp infuriated him, perhaps because he saw so much of himself in her. He, too, enjoyed the histrionic gesture, and the flouting of public opinion. He even had an odd satisfaction in making this improbable and wildly unsuitable marriage. He would find imposing his will on society highly stimulating. His bride would be accepted and he would make his mark as a politician. The future promised to be lively, at least, a welcome change from the dark, lonely nightmare of the last two years.

Only one small thing nagged at him. He had had to give way in his choice of his bride. It was a detail, it mattered little which of the two girls he married, it amused him more than anything that the elder should have been afraid of him. He had liked her soft prettiness. The other, Isabella, Bella, whatever he was to call her, had a tendency to dramatize things. Sauciness, his mother called it. Perhaps it was better that his wife (how he hated and resented using this word of another woman!) had spirit. Lifting herself from a nondescript background to that of wife of a rising politician would require all the skill and courage she possessed.

Would it ever work?

Well, if it didn't, she could stay down at Ravenscroft with her sister and enjoy a rural life.

In the meantime, she must be properly outfitted. She had looks and would make a presentable figure.

Yet when he tried to remember how she looked he found he could only remember that her eyes were a curious dark yellow. He remembered that because they had blazed at him, like an angry cat's.

He knew, at least, that she would not be a coward.

For the rest, as long as she behaved with discretion and cut a reasonably good figure in public, she would get by. He didn't think she would have too much trouble with the servants. If she did, they would have to go.

But he suspected she would manage them excellently, since she had already, and very definitely, got her way with him. The thought did rankle, damn it. But apart from the money and the clothes, the houses and the servants, she would find she hadn't made much of a bargain.

Probably the material things would content her very well.

But she must be dressed properly. Since Mamma wouldn't undertake this chore, he must send for Cousin Henrietta.

Lally perked up amazingly when she found that she was no longer required to go through the ordeal of marriage to a stranger. She became quite high-spirited and giggled obligingly

93

at Mrs. Doughty's sallies. Bella said Mrs. Doughty was not to be encouraged, considering their changed status in the house, but it was difficult to restrain Mrs. Doughty's exuberance. She found all weddings delightful, and this one particularly so.

"It'll make the master a human being again," she declared. "I never did like those la-di-dah young ladies who've been trying to catch him. You'll learn to understand him, miss, and make him happy. And you've class, for all the newspapers say. I've said to Doughty all along, them young ladies has class."

Bella was touched, in spite of her decision to permit no familiarity from servants.

"I hope everyone will be as kind as you, Mrs. Doughty."

"Pish to them as isn't. Warm hearts in your own home is all that's needed."

Mrs. Doughty obviously cherished the romantic notion that all marriages were made for love. If she had suspected the enforced bargain, she had as quickly put it out of her mind. She expected Bella to be blushing and starry-eyed, and it was a shame to disappoint her.

But it was Lally who did the laughing . . .

Then Cousin Henrietta arrived.

She was a dumpy plain dowdy little woman who stood in the hall surrounded by a multitude of bags and boxes and peered at Bella and Lally through a lorgnette.

"Which one is the bride, Guy? They both look remarkably young."

Guy led Bella forward and presented her.

"Ha! Well, my dear, let me congratulate you on your courage."

"Courage, Cousin Henrietta?" Guy queried good-humouredly.

"From the little you've told me, and the great deal I've gleaned from the newspapers, the situation would alarm any woman. But," the old lady peered again, "she has a good chin, I see. Well, when do we begin shopping?"

"As soon as possible. The ceremony—" (He didn't, Bella noticed, say wedding), "is to be next Wednesday. It was good of you to come, Cousin Henrietta."

"I did it to annoy Edith, if you must know." The old lady gave a loud cackling laugh. "Is she still sulking?"

"You know Mamma."

"She must be as mad as a March hare. Deliberately losing her son, losing a charming daughter, losing her grandchildren. Don't

94

blush, young lady." Cousin Henrietta poked suddenly at Bella with her stick. "You're a fine healthy-looking female. And it's time there was a filled cradle at Ravenscroft. Now, where's my room? I must take a nap before we lay our plan of campaign. I'm not as young as I was, and the roads were atrocious. By the way, Guy, any limits to expenditure?"

"None within reason."

"Good. Splendid. The sister, too?"

"Eulalie, too, naturally."

The old lady gave her hearty cackling laugh.

"It isn't naturally, at all, and you must admit it. Ha! I confess I enjoy this situation. It's titillating. Ha, ha, ha! Trust a Raven. Did you ever hear that story about your grandfather and the Maharajah's third wife? No, well, neither did I officially. But it was a rattling good one. Have my bags sent up. I've brought my own pillows."

"She's *mad!*" said Lally.

"Anyone can see that," said Bella furiously. "Does Mr. Raven really think I'll wear what a crazy old woman chooses for me. We were perfectly well able to do our shopping ourselves. I told him so. But, no, he said we must be suitably chaperoned and advised. His mother would at least have had good taste, if she had deigned to have anything to do with us. But this old frump—"

"I hope you're not referring to the Countess of Lyminster, my love," came Guy's voice.

He had followed them to the drawing-room and stood in the doorway looking at them unsmilingly. Already like a reproving husband, Bella thought, as she exclaimed, in confusion.

"Not Cousin Henrietta? Not that—"

"Frump? I'm afraid so. I apologize for not making it clear to you earlier. I thought I had."

"You never did!" Bella said indignantly. "How could you be so thoughtless! Making us look foolish. You know very well she looks exactly like a gardener's wife."

"Bella!" Lally protested.

"A gardener's wife doesn't travel with twelve pieces of luggage. You must learn to be more observant, my love. Well, can I leave you in Cousin Henrietta's capable hands? I assure you they are capable."

He wasn't angry at her outburst. Bella wished he had been. He was only faintly amused. Nothing she said or did seemed to rouse him to any emotion. It was like talking to someone through a closed door. She wanted to beat at him with her fists, and believed she would, after they were married, if he continued to behave like this. She tried one more small protest.

"If she dresses us in her own taste—"

"Trust her, Isabella my dear. You may be surprised."

"Now, if you have to curtsey to the Queen—"

"The Queen!"

"I sincerely trust you will be invited to one of Her Majesty's drawing-rooms. We might arrange later for one or two lessons in the royal curtsey. To continue. If you entertain Lord Palmerston to dinner—"

"The Prime Minister!"

"He was a friend of Guy's father. Didn't you know? Hasn't that young man told you anything?"

"He didn't even tell us you were a countess!"

The infectious high cackle broke out. The old lady's sallow, weathered face was seamed in a thousand wrinkles.

"Did he think it would alarm you?"

"He should have known better," Bella muttered.

"Yes." Cousin Henrietta's voice was suddenly absent, as she studied Bella. "Yes, I can see that. But don't give him too many surprises too quickly. You must ride him with an easy rein at first. He's been abominably spoiled by that doting mother of his. He's arrogant like all the Ravens, selfish by nature, unobservant. Remarkably unobservant. Yes." The old lady tapped one gnarled finger against her teeth. "We must do what we can to open his eyes. But where was I? Ah, yes. If the Prime Minister comes to dinner, you will place your guests so—"

"I won't wear pink," Bella said defiantly.

Cousin Henrietta poked at a roll of taffeta with her stick.

"That," she said to the salesman. "I have a camellia that colour at Lyminster. It makes me think of a rosy dawn in the East. Romantic. Full of promise. Of course you'll wear pink, my dear. The right shade of pink."

She went on buying and buying. Silk, taffeta, velvet, fine wool. Buttons, braids, exquisite hand-made lace, yards and yards of ribbon. Elegant little buttoned boots, satin slippers, silk stockings, gloves, and lengths of lawn and linen for petticoats and nightgowns. Bonnets, a fur-trimmed cloak for daytime, and a glorious Chinese-red satin for evenings.

In the middle of it all, Bella suddenly burst into tears.

"Now what? Now what?" Cousin Henrietta said impatiently.

"I keep thinking of Tottie."

"Tottie! Who has that absurd name?"

"She hadn't a dress. It was only a bit of sack somehow stitched together. It seems so wicked to want all these lovely things."

Cousin Henrietta waved to the discreetly goggling shop assistants.

"Some sal volatile, and hurry. Have you never seen a bride in tears? You!" Her expressive stick was pointing at a very young salesman. "Fetch that brocade. I think for a grand toilette—Lord Palmerston admires well-dressed women, I believe—we must find you a maid who is clever at hair dressing. Your task, my dear, is to please your husband. Let him look after the unfortunate Totties."

She was right, of course. If Bella could do her part in making Guy a successful wife it would help him enormously in his career, and ultimately Tottie and her kind would find the world a kinder place.

She crushed down her feelings of guilt that she should feel such avid delight in the luxurious clothes. Now she would be able to face the world with the greatest confidence. Now, she told herself in secret breathless joy, her husband must notice her.

He was not quite her husband yet. After an exhausting week spent almost entirely with dressmakers and milliners, her wedding day had come. She was dressed in grey with a little bonnet trimmed with modest pink roses. She hated the mousiness of the clothes, and wore them only because of Guy's insistence on extreme simplicity. Indeed, Lally looked gayer than the bride in her favourite blue. Cousin Henrietta looked a fright, and Doctor Bushey, the only other person present, did nothing to mark the special occasion except wear a rather drooping rosebud in his buttonhole.

It was a curiously furtive wedding, Bella thought resentfully, not, she sensed, because the pavement outside was crowded with inquisitive sightseers and newspaper men, but because nothing must be done to make it seem like a festive occasion. It must in no way resemble the happy and glorious occasion of Guy's wedding to his first wife three years previously. Caroline's ghost must be discouraged from attending such a modest ceremony.

Anyway, where was her good sense? They were not in love with each other. She was thankful to escape the hypocrisy of obvious festivity. She didn't tremble, though only by the exertion of tremendous will-power, when Guy slipped the ring on her finger. She noticed that his hands were square and strong. She began to think confusedly of them on her body that night, and was scarcely aware that the meager ceremony was over, and she, Bella McBride, was the wife of the most talked-of young man in London. She was suddenly wishing there had been some way of letting Cousin Sarah know. It would have made the marriage seem more real.

There was gaiety in the house that night, as it happened. Mrs. Doughty, on her own initiative, had prepared a celebration dinner. Bella had thankfully shed her grey mouse wedding gown and put on one of the new ones, the apricot silk. It bared her shoulders and set off her lovely long neck.

Her husband had not so far spared one glance for his bride, she could have been a blackamoor for all he had noticed her at the church. But he should look at her tonight.

Lally, also, took a timid pleasure in dressing in a pretty gown and twisting up her fair hair. Cousin Henrietta had not yet found them a maid who came up to her highly critical standards, but she promised to do so before leaving for the country.

Doctor Bushey had come back to dinner and when Bella went downstairs she found two strange men whom Guy introduced as political colleagues. Bella was not unaware of the startled look of admiration that came into their faces. Her heart began to bound. If she were to be actually admired by her husband's friends, things would not be too difficult after all.

But she found the dinner had not been arranged for her pleasure. The men had too many absorbing political topics to discuss, and she was too nervous and inept to get control of the conversation. Cousin Henrietta, who might have helped, chose to be silent, and Lally, unexpectedly faced with strangers, was tongue-tied.

There was champagne, certainly. Bella found it a much over-rated drink. It merely made her miserable. She had wanted to sparkle tonight. She would have sparkled if Guy (she was making herself call him Guy in her thoughts as if, by doing so, he would become less of a stranger) had so much as given her one approving glance. But for all his determination that she should be correctly dressed to sit at the head of his table, he now seemed to find her part of the furniture.

She drank her champagne rather quickly and hoped Doughty would notice and refill her glass—which he did. The second glass did make her sudden onset of misery less acute. She decided the table was much too long, Guy much too far away. When they dined alone she would insist on sitting at his side. The candlelight caught gleams in his thick dark gold hair. He was animated as she had never seen him before, but about some wretched school in the East End.

"Every boy an Oliver Twist, I swear it. You read Mr. Dickens, I take it? He doesn't exaggerate."

Cousin Henrietta was tapping Bella's arm. Bella recovered herself hazily. Was dinner over? She had almost forgotten to eat. She realized she was to rise and leave the gentlemen to their port.

Followed by a relieved Lally, she led the way to the drawing-room. Cousin Henrietta at once excused herself, saying she had had a long day and would go up immediately.

"If you ask me, you'd be wise to do the same. They'll be in there for hours."

"Hours! But—"

"Port and politics. Even a new bride provides little competition to that irresistible combination."

"You mean this new bride," Bella said with sudden bitterness. "I don't expect you faced such a situation when you married, Cousin Henrietta."

"No. I grant you the circumstances were completely conventional. A tediously dull affair, a conventional marriage. Comfort yourself with that knowledge."

"But your husband at least *looked* at you!" The champagne had made sad work of Bella's pride.

"I don't believe he really saw me once in thirty years. Not that he didn't have an eye for a pretty young woman. I was constantly dismissing maids. But I had my roses." Cousin Henrietta shrugged philosophically. "That's how it is, my dear. Marriage is a state on earth, not a state in heaven. Far from perfect. How it succeeds is largely up to oneself. Now don't ask me how to behave, child. Use your instinct."

99

Instinct was all she had to use, for she had the vaguest notion of what to expect when Guy finally came to share the room that had been hastily re-decorated and furnished for their needs.

Lally had even less, Lally was in a flutter of nervous apprehension as if it were she who had to climb into the big bed and wait. She insisted on coming up with Bella and helping her to undress and put on the snowy-white lawn nightgown with its ruffle of lace at the throat and wrists.

"Shall you braid your hair or leave it loose? Shall I brush it for you?"

"No. Yes, just a little." Bella wanted Lally to go and at the same time to stay. She felt a little calmer when her sister was there, the waves of excitement not washing so shudderingly over her.

He hadn't noticed her naked shoulders at dinner and now they were covered. But the nightgown was flimsy, easily discarded.

His body would be like his hands, strong, hard . . .

"Bella, you're trembling."

"I'm cold."

"You don't look cold. You look on fire." Lally nodded sagely. "It's the champagne."

It's the thought of my husband's naked body. I've never seen a man naked . . .

"Yes, it's the champagne. I drank two glasses."

"I didn't. The bubbles went up my nose. Get into bed and I'll brush your hair there. Don't braid it, Bella. It'll look pretty against the pillow. So black and shiny. Bella," Lally's voice came in a breathless rush, "are you afraid?"

"Afraid?"

Lally began to giggle helplessly.

"You sound so haughty, just like Cousin Henrietta. I can tell you, I'd be scared to death. I'm just so glad it isn't me. I don't think I'll ever marry."

"Of course you will."

"I'd keep seeing Noah's hands. Those big crushing hands . . . Oh, Bella!" Lally's voice quivered. "This is the first night we've ever been parted."

"By one flight of stairs," said Bella. "Goose!"

Nevertheless, she clung to Lally tightly before Lally went. She wasn't sure whether it was Lally's tears that wet her cheeks, or her own.

But when she was alone the enormous anticipation swept over

her again. She was trembling one moment, her body taut the next. She didn't know how to compose herself. She sat up primly against the plump down pillows, laying her hands flat on the counterpane and staring at her wedding ring.

Mrs. Guy Raven . . . She was that not from love or ambition, but expediency. She had to keep reminding herself of this fact, for obviously her husband needed no reminding. He was in no haste to join his bride. Far-off gusts of laughter sounded from downstairs. The port decanter must be being passed round again. And again . . .

A wind had risen and beat against the window, and presently there was the thin sound of rain flung against the panes like fine gravel. It must be late for the traffic was only spasmodic, a weary cab-horse being whipped up or a carriage rolling past. There was a little French gilt clock ticking on the mantelpiece over the embers of the dying fire. Bella lifted the candle to peer at it and saw the hands pointed to one-thirty.

Such an ardent bridegroom . . .

She got out of bed, and went and turned the clock's face to the wall. Then she was acutely conscious of its officious knowing ticking. She contemplated dashing it to the floor. But it would be like stopping a heartbeat, the only heartbeat in the room beside her own.

Suddenly she realized that Guy was not coming.

She got back into bed and blew out the candle. The rain blew in icy flurries against the window. Her body was icy, too, all its heat put out.

Chapter 11

THERE was a tap at the door and in response to Bella's sleepy "Come in," Mrs. Doughty appeared, carrying a breakfast tray.

She set it down and briskly drew back the curtains.

"The master gave orders you were to have your breakfast in bed. I'll send Annie up at once to tend the fire."

Bella frowned at the thin winter sunlight.

"Has Mr. Raven breakfasted?"

"An hour since, madam." Mrs. Doughty was remembering to be very prim and formal. But her watery eyes held a gleam, and by the look of her purplish flush the gentlemen hadn't drained the port decanter last night. "He said you weren't to be disturbed until now."

Bella suddenly thought of the unoccupied side of the bed, pristine, clearly unslept in. But it wasn't so pristine, after all. She must have tossed and turned a great deal, for the pillows were rumpled and the blankets awry. Mrs. Doughty had noticed nothing amiss. Indeed, her knowing look indicated a very mistaken interpretation of the reason for Bella's weariness. Bella supposed she would make nothing of the bed in the adjoining room also having been slept in. Ladies and gentlemen liked their occasional privacy. They were not like the lower classes who got into a double bed on their wedding night and stayed there, willy nilly, for the rest of their lives.

All at once Bella was envying them . . .

"Has Mr. Raven gone out yet, Mrs. Doughty?"

"Not yet, madam. He's in the library with his secretary."

"Tell him I'd like to see him before he goes out."

"Certainly, madam."

It was an hour before Guy came. Bella had thought to toy with her breakfast, but the coffee, the hot rolls, the lightly boiled eggs and the thin toast and marmalade were too good. She recovered her spirits by the minute, telling herself that this luxury was no longer a temporary one, to be snatched away as soon as she became a governess or a seamstress. It was hers for the rest of her life. Even alone in a double bed . . .

She had put on one of her new robes and brushed her hair, although it still hung loose to her waist, when the knock at the door announced Guy.

He came in saying in his formal voice, "Good morning, my love. You wanted to see me?"

Naturally I wanted to see you. Isn't it usual for a wife and husband to say good morning? Even to kiss?

But it was impossible to burst out with her angry and bewildered thoughts. They were exactly as they had been two days ago, two weeks ago. Strangers.

"I wondered if there were anything new in the papers?"

"Only a rumour that there will be questions in the House today."

"About us! Oh, why can't they mind their own business!"

"If I'm to be a public figure, I must accept this." He was speaking painstakingly to her as if she were a child of dim intelligence.

"But our marriage was to have solved the trouble," she said miserably.

"I hope it will have. Forgive me, but I must be off."

He had never seen her with her hair down. He didn't see her now. Bella stamped her foot softly.

"Mr. Raven! Guy—"

He turned politely.

"Yes, my dear?"

"You were very late last night. You perhaps didn't want to —disturb me?"

Now he did look at her. But his eyes hated her. He was wishing for her long black hair to be corn-coloured, her face to be gentle and aristocratic. His thoughts were as clear as if he had shouted them. And she didn't know what to do about his ravaged face, his loneliness.

"Don't let me—keep you," she managed to say, but when he had gone, willingly, she tormented herself that she had not behaved differently, made him touch her, shown him that her body, too, was soft and desirable, that all hair looked the same colour when it was entangled in one's lips and eyes.

She ached for him, and at the same time hated him for the way his cold good manners froze her. Cousin Henrietta had told her to use her instinct. But she found she had none. She had nothing when faced with that resentment. She was as inarticulate as Lally.

Lally, incidentally, had to be faced, and she was as bright-eyed with curiosity as Bella had expected.

"Bella—did you sleep well?"

It was a question her husband should have asked her. She replied coolly,

"Very well, thank you."

"Those men stayed awfully late. I heard them leave in the small hours."

"You should have been asleep yourself."

"I know. I was lonely without you." Lally's naïve eyes searched Bella's face shyly.

"Goodness!" Bella exclaimed. "You're behaving as if I'm suddenly a stranger. I'm still your sister. And today we'll order the carriage and drive down Rotten Row."

"The carriage!"

"Why not?" said Bella with asperity. "It's mine."

Guy was not home until just before dinner. Bella had been listening for him for hours. He went straight to his room. She realized, startled, that she had the right to follow him if she wished. But she deemed it wiser to wait until he came down.

When he did so, she saw that he looked tired and unapproachable. She had determined to make pleasant chatter this evening, to show him that she knew a wife's duty. But Cousin Henrietta was there, and had no similar qualms about displaying too much curiosity.

"Well, my boy, how was it in the House?"

"Impossible! They give a man no chance to prove his good intentions."

"They don't believe such a thing exists," Cousin Henrietta said dryly. "Certainly not that old money-grubber, Henry Shields. I suppose this came from his party friends."

"I imagine so. Oh, there was a great air of politeness about it all. The question was merely asked as to the suitability of an electoral candidate who has been the subject of a scandal in the newspapers. The honourable member assumed an air of innocence and asked what the House made of the fact that although the candidate—no names mentioned, mark you—had so far put a veneer of respectability on the affair by marrying one of the young women with whom he was reputed to be associated, he still kept the two women in his house, and what did everyone make of that?"

"But Lally being here is innocent!" Bella cried out. "They ought to see."

Lally had gone pale and looked extremely distressed.

"It means I should go away? Oh, Bella—"

"You'll not go away! At least, not without me."

"There's no question of anything of the kind," said Guy irritably. "The public only seems to be annoyed that I can't marry you both." Perfunctorily he added, "I'm sorry to burden you with my affairs. I hope you all spent a pleasant day."

"I shall go home tomorrow," said Cousin Henrietta. "I've had enough of London. Mucky place. I want my garden."

Bella made a sound of protest. She had grown very fond of the plain, downright, warm-hearted little countess, and she was far from ready to sail the seas of fashionable London life without the old lady's sage advice.

"I haven't deserted you, my dear. I'll be back when that cradle has an occupant. Eh? Eh, children?"

But Guy was in no mood to laugh, and Bella could only try not to let Cousin Henrietta see the hurt of her words. Already her marriage seemed to be in ruins. For the words spoken in Parliament today seemed to have made it a wasted gesture. Her husband clearly thought the same thing. He seemed to have no intention of occupying the conjugal bed.

Before Cousin Henrietta departed she finally declared herself satisfied with one of the many lady's maids she had interviewed. Louise, an angular young woman with sharp quick ways, was installed. Bella disliked her on sight, but had to admit she could create a most elegant coiffure. She also knew the powders and lotions that could completely conceal freckles and enhance one's natural colour. She was clever. She contrived immediately to put at least five years on Bella's age. There was no outward trace left of the unsophisticated country girl.

She took a pride in her work, but Bella had an uneasy conviction that curiosity and nothing more had brought her here. She wanted to see for herself the most notorious woman in London. Her respectful manner hid contempt.

And however much simple port-fuddled Mrs. Doughty might be deceived by the rumpled bed, Bella was certain Louise was not. She knew how to deal with contempt from an uppish maid, but not pity.

All the same, Cousin Henrietta's wisdom was proved by Guy announcing that Bella and Lally were to be prepared to go to the opera the next evening. He had taken a box, and they were to make a grand toilette.

Lally said it was like a dream come true.

"Do you remember, Bella, the very night we came to London, you said one day we would go to the Covent Garden opera house. Could you have thought it would happen so soon? How good and generous Mr. Raven is!"

"He wants to show us off to the world," Bella said.

"Then he must be proud of us," Lally said, pleased.

Sometimes Bella wondered how they could be sisters, Lally was so simple, where she herself always turned everything inside out, looking for the hidden motive.

"He's not proud of us in that way," she said crossly. "He only wants to defy the gossips. He intends to have us accepted. You'll have to be prepared to be stared at all the way up the grand staircase."

Lally immediately looked nervous.

"Oh, dear! I know I shall trip on my gown. Bella, do you think I must go? Won't people say again how odd it is Mr. Raven always has us both, as if—as if—" Lally couldn't bring herself to put the dreadful suggestion into words.

"Mr. Raven says we are both to go. So please don't argue. Wear your blue satin. I'll send Louise to you as soon as she has finished with me. She'll help you with your hair. And Lally, if you trip, or giggle, or do anything awkward, I'll never speak to you again."

She knew how important the occasion was from Guy's set face. It was the first time he had come to her room while she was dressing. As it happened Louise had just finished her hair, doing it very modishly on the top of her head so that she looked taller and older and with a dignity she didn't feel. She was wearing the Chinese red gown, because the colour gave her courage. No one could shrink out of sight in a colour like that, and she had no intention of shrinking.

She told Louise to go up to Lally and as the woman went couldn't resist spinning round in front of her husband, and saying breathlessly, "Will I do?"

He examined her toilette in every detail. At first she flushed with pleasure at his interest, then she began to pout as she realized she was being studied like a beribboned filly being prepared for a championship. He hadn't noticed her desire to please, not a fashionable audience at the opera, but just him, her husband. He was stupid and unimaginative and cruel.

"Haven't you a gown in quieter taste?"

"No!" she flared. "I'll wear this one."

His eyes flickered in surprise. "Keep calm, my dear. I only mean you to be looked at, not stared at."

"Is it only harlots who wear red?" Bella asked daringly. "Perhaps it's because they enjoy a little admiration."

He took a flat narrow box from his breast pocket.

"You'll enjoy plenty of admiration when you wear these."

He opened the box and the diamonds glittered like a sun dazzle. Bella gasped. She said, crazily, the first words that came into her head.

"They are your wife's!"

"Yes. Put them on." Since she stood gaping he gave her a push towards the mirror. "Or do you enjoy your role of harlot too much?"

"I meant— I didn't mean—"

Because she made no attempt to touch the glittering necklace, he picked it up and fastened it round her neck. The light touch of his fingers on her skin sent such a wave of giddiness over her that she dared not look at her face in the mirror. She kept her head down, waiting for the fire to go out of her cheeks.

"You can't be a harlot and my wife also." His composed voice came from a long way off. "The diamonds were my grandmother's, and then my mother's. Now—" he scarcely hesitated at all, "they're yours."

Suddenly she longed for Lally's ability to weep or to swoon. Then her mind could become a merciful blank and she needn't think at all of that other neck round which this necklace had once been clasped. There would have been no casual air about that ceremony. If the touch of her husband's fingers had enflamed her, Caroline could have turned and flung herself into his arms. She wouldn't have needed to sit rigid, struggling to hide her emotions. But now the stones were heavy, cold, like death.

"Well, hold up your head and look at them." Guy was being very kind and humouring the bedazzled little girl from the country.

Slowly Bella lifted her head. She had recovered her composure. The effort had left her pale and strained, but this her husband wouldn't notice any more than he had noticed her distress.

"I'm sorry if I talked foolishly. I expect it's because I still find it difficult to believe I'm your wife."

He turned away.

"What did you expect?"

Could he be so lacking in imagination that he didn't know about the long lonely hours, the ticking of the clock, the listening, the sleeplessness? She wanted to burst out that she knew very little about marriage, but she did know it shouldn't mean an empty pillow by her side. And the lonely rain on the window, and the listening . . .

Lally could have managed this situation better. It would have been what she had hoped for. And Lally would have adored these horrible diamonds. But she, impulsive hopeful fool that she was, had literally thrown herself into the arms of a stranger, confident that she could make them welcoming.

Isabella McBride, she told herself ashamedly, was a vain creature who had overestimated her desirability. Now she had had a salutary lesson.

"You have been very good to my sister and me," she said soberly.

"I told you I would never love again," he said, as if he in his turn found her lack of imagination surprising. "But you wear my wedding ring, so you will also wear the diamonds."

"To show the world?"

"Exactly. That was our bargain, don't you remember?" He put out his arm, smiling. She saw that his eyes held no hostility, after all. They held nothing. "Come! Don't let us make it an impossible one."

If she had pinched herself until she was black and blue, Bella could not have believed that this was anything but a dream, herself going to the Opera in silk and diamonds. Lally, on the other hand, seemed to have forgotten her luxurious state and as the carriage neared the Opera House she shrank closer to Bella.

"This is near it, isn't it?" she whispered.

"Near what?"

"Aunt Aggie's house. I can smell the same smell."

"This is the Strand," said Guy. "Aunt Aggie, as you will persist in calling her, lived some distance away. In a mean dark street. Look out of the window. There are lights and people everywhere."

"Aunt Aggie should see us now," Bella said.

Lally gave a forlorn giggle. "Yes, she'd be— Listen, I can hear a baby crying!"

The thin squall sounded for a moment above the medley of other sounds, and then was lost.

"It's only someone kept their child out late," Bella said impatiently. "You'd better not be thinking about babies and Aunt Aggie in the opera."

"No," Lally whispered obediently.

Her sister's temporary lapse into her state of nervous terror made Bella forget her own qualms about the ordeal ahead. She thought how handsome Guy looked in his tall opera hat and cloak as he waited outside the carriage for them to get down. Then her attention was taken by the succession of carriages drawing up and discharging their glittering passengers. The great doors of the theatre stood open before them. Guy said that as it was late they would go straight to their box.

"Come," he said, and to Lally, "Don't be afraid. No one will see you in this crush."

So it was not an ordeal after all to reach their box and settle down. They had scarcely shrugged off their wraps before the curtain rose, and in the next moment Bella, too, had forgotten her apprehensions in the magic of the scene before them.

For the next hour she was transported. She hung forward in a daze of delight as the scenes unfolded and the heavenly voices sang. When the curtain fell she had to be prodded back to reality.

"Stop star-gazing," came Guy's voice, tolerantly. "Let us go and get some refreshments."

Bella blinked at the lights that had sprung on in the vast dusky semicircle of the theatre. She was aware of the movement of people, of jewels winking, of heads turned their way. Someone, she noticed, had lifted opera glasses to look in their direction.

Her heart gave a great bound. This was the moment. This was what Guy had planned. They were to walk slowly, nonchalantly, if possible, down the grand staircase while everybody had the leisure to stare at them.

Guy had opened the door of the box and was standing as easily as if accompanying two notorious young women were a thing he frequently did. Bella, still transported by the music and magic of the opera, felt a sudden surge of overpowering excitement. She was conscious of no fear at all, only pride. She nudged Lally and hissed, "Hold your head up! If you shrink, I'll kill you!" then put her hand gracefully on her husband's arm and walked out.

Lally did stumble once on the stairs, but quickly recovered herself. Bella held her head so proudly, she had to virtually float down the carpeted steps. But it wasn't so high that she couldn't see the people moving back so as not to bar their passage, staring. Staring frankly, rudely. The women's heads moved stiffly in their direction, someone held up a lorgnette. There was a titter in the crowd. No one nodded or smiled. Then suddenly Bella saw a familiar face, exquisitely pink and white, the little arrogant beak-shaped nose lifted towards them.

Mrs. Raven! Guy's mother!

She was aware of her husband making a welcoming sound. But the lady's elegantly curled grey head turned deliberately away from them. With a vivacious movement of her fan, Mrs. Raven began an animated conversation with her companions. She had cut her son dead.

The strange stillness lasted another moment. Then it was broken by a long sound, curiously like a hiss. By some instantaneous consent, backs turned everywhere. And the long sigh, the indrawn breath, that had resolved itself into that hostile sound turned into a hubbub of noise that deliberately excluded Guy Raven and his protégées.

Just as Lally had been a little earlier, Bella was jolted back to the night of their arrival in London when, plodding after Aunt Aggie through the mean snowy streets, she had indulged in a dream of going to the Covent Garden opera. Then, as now, her dream had been rudely broken by the sound of a hiss. It was a curious little vignette come true.

"What will you take, my love?" That was Guy's voice, attentive, solicitous. "A little lemonade? Some mulled wine?"

Bella's wrap was slipping, and he adjusted it, his hands lingering on her shoulders.

"Eulalie? A little wine? Did you enjoy the first act? I can promise you fireworks in the next."

Lally's hand trembled so violently she could scarcely hold her
glass of wine. Bella slid her hand within her sister's arm, and
pinched her warningly. Lally instantly looked about to cry, but
Bella smiled sweetly and began to talk as composedly and quite
as animatedly as she had seen Mrs. Raven do.

"It's so wonderful. I adore every moment of it. Do you know
that moment when you see a Christmas tree alight? This seems
like a thousand Christmas trees, all at once."

Guy listened to her with his courtly air.

"I'm glad you enjoy it," he said, smiling, "because, as you must
be aware," he didn't bother to lower his voice, "we are being cut
by everybody, my mother included. We're being made social
pariahs. I always find new experiences amusing. I hope you do,
too, my love." His fingers again adjusted the heavy satin cloak
over Bella's shoulders. He continued to smile, but she was seeing
his eyes come alive at last. Repressed fury glittered in them. "Shall
we return to our seats? Eulalie? Did I tell you how charming you
look? Especially when you smile."

Talking easily, his hands protectingly on their elbows, he
guided them up the staircase and back to their box. There was
no hurry, no dismay. They might have been strolling alone in
a garden. Nothing in Guy's calm face showed that he knew his
death-knell had sounded. He had been rejected, not only by the
popular press, but by his own world.

Why, why, why? Bella was seething with rage and resentment.
Were she and Lally lepers? Couldn't people see that they were
ordinary decent young women undeserving of the reputation
with which they had been credited? Was Guy hated so much
because he had had the generosity to help them, and the courage
to become completely involved? Were his friends jealous of him?
Had he stirred their social conscience too uncomfortably? Or
was this exhibition just that ugly thing, mob hysteria, mob
cruelty?

Whatever it was, Bella found herself too deeply disturbed to
see or hear anything more that happened on the stage. The magic
had gone from the opera. She sat rigidly, her hand still clutching
her husband's arm. She couldn't let it go. Beneath her resentment

she was conscious of a fierce racing joy. Guy's performance of a loving husband had been irresistible. She was daring to hope that when they got home it wouldn't stop.

It stopped as soon as they were in the carriage. "I forgot to tell you," he said in his now too-familiar aloof voice, "the Proudfoot trial begins at the criminal court next week. As soon as it's over, I will take you to the country."

"For always?" Bella asked sharply.

"For the summer, at least."

Lally sighed with relief. For her London was already a terrifying place, haunted by Noah and Aunt Aggie and the ghost of the dead baby. Now, added to that, was the hostile stare of apparently civilized people. In the country she would be safe, and able to sleep without nightmares.

But Bella saw the move as a sign of defeat. She couldn't endure defeat. She wouldn't allow it, either for herself or her husband. Being linked ostentatiously with him in public had stirred her to a fierce possessiveness. His battles were now hers whether he liked it or not.

"Isn't retiring to the country running away from the problem?" she asked politely.

"My dear Isabella," his voice was as chilly as the night air, "I shall be immediately returning to London. I have no intention of running away."

So she and Lally were an embarrassment to be hidden away. The fine flamboyant gesture tonight had failed so another tactic must be tried. Retirement, oblivion, an awkward mistake kept out of sight until forgotten. For how long? Forever?

Bella fretted angrily, "It wasn't our fault tonight. None of this was our fault. We were in trouble and you were good to us, but you did it with your eyes open. Didn't you?" When Guy, sitting opposite, his face in shadow, didn't answer, she went on dangerously, "If you ask me, your mother's as much to blame as anyone. She turned her back on you tonight and set the fashion for everyone else. I think it was a wicked thing to do to her own son. How could she? She must be a monster."

"Bella!" Lally protested, shocked.

"It's true," Bella stormed. "I shall make a point of telling her so. How can she be so cruel and unnatural?"

"Be quiet!" said Guy ominously.

"Why must I be quiet? You have the courage to speak about

injustices done to Lally and me. I intend to speak to your mother about this injustice. If Lally and I have ruined your career it was unintentional. She did this tonight deliberately."

"I asked you to be quiet. Next week we go to Ravenscroft. That's final."

Bella's temper was getting out of control.

"And turn us all into gardeners like Cousin Henrietta? I have no taste for gardening."

"Then you must acquire one, my love. Just as you must acquire a taste for an absent husband." His voice was tightly controlled. He sounded as if he hated her.

It had all been too much for Lally. She was trembling with fatigue and nervous strain, and had to be helped upstairs. She needed support and encouragement, but for once Bella couldn't give it to her. She was unable to calm herself, much less her sister. Louise, who had waited up, a grudging look on her thin face, was sent to undress Lally, and then told to go to bed. Bella preferred to get out of her finery alone.

The tumult of her feelings had left her unbearably stimulated. She let her elegant gown and petticoats fall to the floor and left them there. She dropped the diamond necklace carelessly on to her bed where it lay glittering like tears. Her slippers were kicked off, and the pins tumbled out of her hair. Although the fire had been allowed to die down and the room was chilly, she felt as if the sun were inside her skin. She couldn't contemplate getting into the big bed and lying quietly. Her head was full of fragments of music, scraps of conversation, her own chaotic thoughts. To-night she had had a husband who had shown a loving care for her in public, and had hated her in private. The hate was far far more exciting than the pretended love. It was a genuine emotion, the first he had shown towards her. She had roused him out of his deliberate cool neutrality. The scene had been unplanned, she had had no idea her temper could carry her so far, but now that it had happened she was fiercely glad. If they could not love, they could quarrel. It was being alive, at least.

But she was too much alive tonight. It was past midnight and the thought of sleep was impossible. She felt as if she would never sleep again. She forced herself to sit at the mirror and brush her hair, a calming occupation if ever there was one. It failed completely to calm her. She found herself constantly stopping, the brush poised in her hand, to listen.

Her husband hadn't yet come upstairs. She would hear the carefully muted sounds in the adjoining room when he did come. The fire crackled a little and the clock ticked. Bella stared into the mirror, and saw not her cherry bright cheeks and the golden blaze of her eyes but the long sweep of the staircase in the Opera House, the white shoulders and the jewels of the women, the inquisitive stares, and then the turned backs. She hugged her own shoulders, remembering Guy's deliberate caress as he had adjusted her wrap. Were all their caresses and tender glances to be made in public? Forever? No, she wouldn't again tolerate that word!

Bella sprang up and began to walk about in her nightgown, her hair making a dark shawl over her shoulders. The clock ticked mercilessly. Suddenly she picked it up and flung it to the floor. It gave a small ping and was silent.

Now time has stopped, she thought exultantly. If I can create one miracle, I can create another. And I will . . .

Guy lingered downstairs until after one o'clock. He had yet another glass of port and decided that, a little befuddled, the world looked slightly rosier. His mother had been right, dammit. He had married the wrong girl. She was already becoming a shrew. So she wouldn't live at Ravenscroft and interest herself in the garden. Perhaps she would prefer a filthy Middle Eastern port and her body at the service of all comers.

Where would she have been—no, that wasn't fair. He had used her and her sister as much as he had been used. They had been the flame to kindle his great political career. But flames got out of control and had to be put out. The two girls could count themselves lucky to have the shelter of Ravenscroft while he returned to town and repaired the damage done. Perhaps later they could patch up some sort of a life together—if Isabella would turn herself into an obedient and unobtrusive wife. He had never wanted a wife with opinions.

She had scorned the diamonds (wasn't she feminine?) and would have had a scene in public with his mother. She held her head as high as if she had been a duchess. She dared to tell him what to do.

He should have married the sister, who could weep in private to her heart's content.

But that wasn't the point. The point was to continue the work he had begun. If he failed at the coming election, there would be another. Nothing had been irretrievably lost.

But nothing had been gained, either, except two females for whom he was forever responsible.

He had thought the solution of marriage easy. Well, so it would be when he got the girls to the country.

One more glass . . . The travesty of the evening was beginning to recede a little. It was time he went up.

The fire in his bedroom was only embers, but the light was sufficient to show him the figure sitting in the armchair before it.

She had no wrap on, only her flimsy nightgown. As she rose slowly, stretching and sighing, he could see the outline of her body.

Surprise, and the abrupt beating of a pulse in his throat, made his voice harsh.

"Why aren't you in bed?"

"I was waiting for you." Her voice was slow, husky, as if with sleep. "You were so long."

"Why are you waiting? Is there something worrying you? Can't it wait till morning?"

"No. Being my husband can't wait till morning. Can it? If you can be my husband in public, so you can in private. I don't like half measures."

There had been other women since Caroline, but never in his house, never wearing his wedding ring. He seized this stranger, for she was suddenly completely a stranger, by the arm, roughly.

"Do you know what marriage is?"

"No." Her voice was naïve, innocent. "You must teach me. I want to learn." She gave a sudden low gurgle of laughter. "I threw the clock on the floor. It was ticking away too many hours. I want to be a woman." Her arms were round his neck. "Even if I must first behave like the harlot they say I am."

"You don't love me."

"No. Perhaps I can learn that, too." Her skin was soft, her lips provocatively near his. She was still laughing a little. "I think you're a little drunk, my darling. But you must understand me. I won't be your wife to the world and not here, in your own bedroom."

He had his hand entangled in her hair, jerking her head back. The candlelight shone on her white face and the burning gold

115

of her eyes. Teach her, she said. She looked like a witch. No golden-haired angel, but a witch. He had made a mistake. He had married the wrong girl, the bold one, not the gentle one. He hated her, but now his pulses were throbbing so that he could scarcely breathe. He would teach her what she wanted to know.

Flung across the bed, and only half-undressed himself, his clothing wrenched open, he took her without patience, violently, having no thought for her virginity.

He heard her cry out. Afterwards she lay so still he thought she had fainted.

But it was the sister who would have fainted. Not Isabella who lay so motionless, her eyes glimmering through mere slits. She was reflecting on marriage, he supposed.

He remembered suddenly his long-controlled infinitely loving initiation of Caroline and got up abruptly, turning his back on the silent figure on the bed. He had not meant this to happen, and vowed it never would again.

Chapter 12

IN the morning Bella sat up in her own bed, a frivolous lacy scrap of a cap on her neatly braided hair, her arms and throat modestly covered by a fleecy bedwrap. She was tapping the top of her egg, her face expressing a healthy anticipation for her breakfast, nothing more.

"Good morning, Guy," she said composedly to her husband. "Have you brought me the papers?"

"They're downstairs. I'll have them sent up, if you wish. I don't recommend them."

Bella opened her eyes wide.

"Are they still slandering us? Didn't they admire Lally and me last night?"

She wasn't going to show a sign of her true feelings. Had she been shocked, badly hurt, resolved now that marriage must be endured, not enjoyed? Guy knew very well that neither of them were thinking of the fresh insults in the newspaper.

"They don't like people who flout conventions. It frightens them, makes them conscious of their own lack of courage. To the devil with them all!"

"Guy, this is very serious for you, isn't it?"

"I've never pretended it was anything else."

"We mustn't give in. We must fight. Do you still insist on Lally and me going to the country?"

"Yes, I do."

Bella sighed. Then she said, "I shall enjoy seeing Ravenscroft, of course. By the way, I've decided not to keep Louise."

"Louise?" He didn't know what she was talking about.

"The maid Cousin Henrietta found for me. I don't like her. I don't see why I should put up with someone I don't like. I intend to engage Tottie instead."

"Tottie?"

Bella burst out laughing.

"I believe you did drink too much last night, my love. You forget everybody. Tottie's the little dumb girl who was at Aunt Aggie's. She's been at Doctor Bushey's, as you very well know. He'll let her come to me, and I'll teach her how to be a good lady's maid. Let me do this, Guy. It will be helping with your own work. We can set an example by employing only these poor desperate people."

He had sensed her strong will and her boldness, but he could scarcely believe that she would so quickly try to run his affairs. As if that deplorable episode last night had given her unlimited confidence.

"If you want to struggle with a speechless maid, do so. That's your province."

"Thank you, my love. I'll see Doctor Bushey today. At least the country is the place for poor Tottie. And Lally, too. I wonder how Lally is this morning. I hope she didn't have a nightmare last night. I feel guilty, deserting her." She shot a look at her husband beneath her long lashes. "By the way, that pretty little clock will have to be mended. I dropped it last night. Such a pity. Are you going?"

"My secretary will be waiting."

"Oh! Of course." She lifted her face for his kiss. She was behaving as if they had been married for years. Her black hair on the pillow was an outrage. And he wouldn't endure her interference. Yet his blood was beating again, violently. He had this overpowering impulse to hurt her, punish her, because she was pretending to be his wife, to take Caroline's place. He would have to keep her out of his sight as much as possible. Leave her safely down at Ravenscroft. He had thought to get a gentle grateful self-effacing wife out of his unlucky predicament. Not this pert confident usurper . . .

When Guy had gone Bella lay back on the pillows, no longer needing to check her tears. She had made a vow to herself last night, as she lay aching and violated on the bed, that she would never cry in front of her husband. Which would mean a great many lonely tears in the privacy of her room.

Yet her life could be mended in other ways. She could order the servants to do as she wished, she could dismiss Louise because the girl displeased her, she could make herself enjoy being the mistress of a large house, no matter how much the present thought of it scared her. She could buy unlimited clothes, pamper Lally, take care of Tottie. She could hold her head as high as her mother-in-law held hers. Her life was certainly not over, even if romance had left it. Who expected love? She had scornfully asked Lally the identical question.

One thing was very sure, she would never again allow herself to lie here counting the minutes until her husband came to her bed. Nor would she ever beg him to love her. She must hope, by gathering the scraps of her pride about her, to overcome the humiliation of still wanting him. For, even as he stood conversing politely to her, a visitor scarcely within the doorway, she had ached for him to come near, to touch her. She had had to make it plain that she expected at least a formal kiss, and when he had bent over her she had had to prevent herself from flinging her arms round his neck. She would not be a beggar. She would not be humiliated twice.

The trial of Noah and Aunt Aggie before a judge and jury took place three weeks later. It went on for two days. The ordeal was almost too much for Lally. Constantly anxious for her, for she seemed at times to think she was a prisoner in the court just as they had been prisoners in the house in Seven Dials, Bella found it impossible to follow every detail of the trial. There was a great deal of wrangling between the opposing counsel about proof, proof that there had been a woman smuggled on board the *Star of Asia*, proof that there had been other young women similarly smuggled out of the country in the past, proof that the baby, being so small and delicate, had not died from natural causes, most of all proof that Aunt Aggie's intentions regarding her latest "lodgers", the Misses McBride, had been criminal.

In the end it was lack of this vital proof that went in favour of the prisoners. Their sentences were extraordinarily light, each of them getting only one year's imprisonment.

Aunt Aggie, who had maintained her air of injured innocence during the whole of the trial, kept her eyes downcast as she listened to the sentence. She was still the martyr, wrongfully accused by a thankless world. Bella was certain her drooping eyelids hid triumph.

But Noah was not going to take even so light a sentence philosophically. He smouldered with anger. When asked if he had anything to say, he lifted his shaggy black head and stared across the courtroom at Guy and Bella and Lally.

"What about them adulterers?" he shouted. "Make them pay! Prissy-mouthed bawds!" He stared back viciously at Bella and Lally as he was hustled away down the stairs out of sight. His great voice came hurling back, "A year ain't forever. Wait—"

Wait . . . Bella had no time to experience more than a momentary shiver at that threat, for Lally had slid from the bench in a dead faint.

When, an endless ten minutes later, she recovered consciousness she could only whisper frantically, "We must hide! Bella, we must hide!"

She recognized neither Guy nor Doctor Bushey. When Guy said, with unexpected gentleness, "We'll get you to Ravenscroft. You'll feel better there," she clutched Bella's hand and said fearfully, "Who is he? Where is he taking us?"

"It's Mr. Raven, Lally. You know we're safe with him. Surely you remember."

Lally frowned. For a moment she was frighteningly like a dimwitted child. Her lovely blue eyes had an empty look.

"People hissed," she said. She lifted a trembling finger to point at Guy. "Because we were with him. Oh, Bella!" She hid her face. "Can we trust him?"

Bella, very much aware now that a small group of people had gathered round, let a note of aggressive pride come into her voice. "Don't be silly, Lally! He's my husband."

Here was another scandal, she thought, and was suddenly angry with Lally for her stupid childish weakness. How dare she make things more difficult for Guy. Babbling nonsense that all the newspapers would solemnly print.

"Come, Eulalie," said Guy, the gentleness still in his voice. "We're going home now. Tomorrow we'll leave for the country."

"When she's fit to travel," said Doctor Bushey restrainingly. "I doubt that will be for a few days."

As it happened, it was another three weeks before Doctor Bushey pronounced Lally fit to travel. She had had a complete collapse, and it was several days before she recognized her surroundings or people, except Bella, again. After that she began to mend slowly, and seemed to forget a little of her fear about Noah and Aunt Aggie. She allowed herself to be convinced that she would be safe in the country, that people like Noah and Aunt Aggie didn't leave their city haunts, and that anyway they were now safely behind bars.

Her illness was not the only event during those three weeks. The worst was the Prime Minister's action. He had a long private talk with Guy, and advised him to postpone his political career. The scandal about the two women had now reached major proportions and threatened to damage not only Guy but the party. This came well from a man whose own private life would scarcely bear looking into, Guy thought bitterly. But for all that Lord Palmerston was a personal friend, and his advice could not be ignored. Indeed, it was the only advice that Guy was prepared to accept.

He could stand again at the next election, when all this would have blown over.

"Get the other sister married," Lord Palmerston urged him. "Have children yourself. Become an exemplary family man, and there'll never be another murmur against you. Bless you, my boy, I understand. I'd have done the same in your shoes. Two attractive young women in distress. An irresistible combination. But these impetuous actions have to be paid for. What did your criminal, the Proudfoot fellow, get? A year? Then you have approximately the same, before we set a date for the next election. Perverted justice, eh? But you'll be all the better for being a little older, and I must say," the glint of the roué shone an instant in the older man's eyes, "from the glimpse I've caught of your wife, a year's private life shouldn't be any great hardship."

So the two young women with their impeccable names, their innocent eyes and their pitiably distressed faces, had ruined him after all. And now he had to live with them.

An exemplary family life? Lord Palmerston, the old dog, had been rather more than a trifle optimistic when he gave that advice. Did he really think Guy Raven the type to vegetate in the country? With a wife for whom he felt nothing but resentment? She had deliberately misunderstood his lofty interpretation of their marriage and had already tricked him into a physical indiscretion for which he loathed himself. He had nothing whatever about which to talk to her. Her very existence did nothing but anger him, for the sight of her constantly reminded him of his lost career and the disillusionment to which ideals could be brought.

But if she thought he were a martyr to be comforted, she was very wrong. His whitewash had come off. Now he would show her his other side. Or rather, he would show her very little of himself at all. He would establish the girls at Ravenscroft and then return to London to resume his bachelor life.

Bella, it seemed, had no thought of martyrdom. She expressed anger and indignation, and then the calm assumption that of course this damage was not permanent.

"You'll stand again, as Lord Palmerston advises. On the whole this may be a good thing. You've already created an enormous impression on the public, I shouldn't be surprised if in two years they don't come to think of you as a hero. And this will give you time to really study politics. After all, one shouldn't take up so important a career on an impulse. Don't you agree?"

Guy agreed with nothing. He was speechless at her impertinence. She, a little nobody, sitting calmly at her embroidery as if she had lived in this style all her life, daring to give him advice, and behaving as if the great sacrifice of his marriage were her due!

"I should be obliged, my dear Isabella, if you would keep your opinions to yourself. They don't interest me. Anyway, they are entirely wrong."

Her eyelids fell. She seemed to be taking great care over a stitch in her embroidery.

"You still blame Lally and me," she said in a low voice.

"Of course I don't blame you. You were fate, Nemesis if you like, but that was hardly your fault. I was the one to be a fool."

"For saving us? For marrying me? For obeying your good instincts? For making all those grand gestures? If you regret all that where are we? What has been accomplished?"

Her face was lifted now, and no longer calm. The quick colour had flooded her cheeks, her eyes had darkened to that curious golden tinge that he had never seen in the eyes of any well-bred woman. Her little pert nose was lifted as high as his mother ever lifted her much more aristocratic one. She was behaving once more as his equal. And the unforgiveable thing was that he wanted to make love to her violently, at that moment, not caring that it was mid-afternoon, and someone likely to come in at any moment.

But he had determined not to give in to that weakness again. He could not treat his wife like a street girl, nor, contrarily, this woman as a wife.

"You can't answer me," she said sadly.

"Oh, yes, I can. We're exactly where we were when I explained to you what our marriage would be."

"Except that now you don't have a career to compensate for it. So you're always going to blame me and Lally. But as I've said before, it's your mother who's to blame. If she'd had the courage to take your side from the beginning, supported you instead of turning her back on you at the opera, and made her friends rally to you, it would have turned the scales. But she chose not to, and that was just the extra thing that made the world turn against you. So you blame me instead, and that isn't fair."

"I'm amazed at your impertinence!"

"No, no, what you can't believe is the truth."

"You're illogical, like all women. My mother, indeed!"

"Even now, I believe it isn't too late to make amends, if she would," Bella persisted. "If she made it public that she has become reconciled to me as your wife it would make a great difference."

"She hasn't a nature that is easily reconciled," Guy said shortly.

"Oh, I know that. She wanted you to make a better match. Some dull débutante. I believe she's only sulking at not getting her own way."

"*You* dare to say that!"

The scorn in his voice made Bella's colour flame.

"Yes, and I refuse to apologize. Perhaps you deserve a dull wife, but at least you haven't got one." She met his gaze with angry defiance. "If you had married Lally you would very soon have got tired of her vapours. And the empty chatter of a débutante—"

"You can scarcely know what débutantes chatter about," he interrupted.

"I think I'm not too unintelligent to guess." Bella had flung her sewing aside and was standing. "Believe me, you haven't made such a bad bargain. The situation is—" He had turned away sharply, and didn't seem to have heard the break in her voice. His answer came over his shoulder, flatly, bleakly.

"Unremediable," he said.

"No, no," she whispered. "Don't let us hate each other."

But he had gone, banging the door behind him, and she could tell him no more.

She had done very badly. Instead of comforting him for his lost ambitions, she had quarrelled with him. She had tried at the beginning to be wise, but he had resented the words he would have gladly accepted from Caroline. That was what had made her angry. He wanted her speechless and invisible, not a wife at all but a nonentity. He hadn't begun to know her.

Nor had his mother.

Bella put on her bonnet and cloak and asked Doughty to get her a cab. She sat in the hall tapping her feet impatiently while waiting for it to come.

Her husband came out of the library and saw her.

"Where are you going?"

Did he think she intended to vanish out of his life? She had to disappoint him.

"To get Tottie. She was to be prepared to come today, before we left for the country."

"Tottie? Oh, the deaf and dumb girl."

"She is only dumb, not deaf. It should please you to have someone who can't answer back." The childish retort escaped her before she could prevent it.

"I hardly expect a servant to do that."

"You hardly expect your wife to, either."

"No. Frankly I don't."

The now frequent feeling of sickness was coming over her again. She swallowed, praying she could conquer it. She had planned to tell him her news this afternoon, not knowing of the unfortunate interview with the Prime Minister. But she couldn't tell him, in this mood. She doubted now if she could ever tell him quietly and happily, as she had planned.

But if only he would kiss her, her lips would stop trembling.

"I don't think you would care for a wife who has no opinions of her own."

"How can you possibly know my tastes?" he said coldly, finally.

Doughty was coming in to say that a cab was waiting. His old rheumy eyes looked curiously from his master to his new mistress. At least, if Bella were not the débutante she had talked of, she knew one didn't exhibit one's quarrels to servants.

She sprang up. "Then I must go. Goodbye, my love. I won't be above an hour." She lifted her face innocently for her husband's kiss. She knew it was a trick, not to deceive Doughty, but to have his lips on hers, after all. And although he merely touched her cheek, the treacherous excitement shot through her again, making her forget her anger and her sickness and leaving her with scarcely strength to walk out of the house.

She gave the cabman the address on the Chelsea Embankment, one she had acquainted herself with some time ago, climbed into the cab and, as the door shut on her, as weakly as Lally, dissolved into tears.

There were no signs of her tears, however, when the cab stopped at the tall red brick house overlooking the muddy river. She alighted, and asked the driver to wait, as she would be only ten or fifteen minutes. After that, he was to take her to Wigmore Street.

The white door, surmounted by its beautiful Georgian fan of glass, was opened by a stiff elderly maid in a very correctly starched cap and apron. She didn't know who Bella was, and obviously impressed by her rich appearance—Bella did not intend her mother-in-law to be dressed more grandly than herself—respectfully asked her to come in while she ascertained if her mistress were at home.

"What name shall I say, madam?"

"Mrs. Guy Raven," Bella answered, carelessly removing her gloves to display her wedding ring. "Tell my mother-in-law I'm sorry to arrive unannounced, but it's important I see her."

The maid was flustered now. She left Bella in the hall as she hurried up the stairs. Bella sat composedly in one of the carved and very uncomfortable chairs. Her heart was beating rapidly. She realized she was looking forward to this encounter.

She didn't dream for a moment that Mrs. Raven would refuse to see her.

A sudden yapping of dogs came from upstairs. A door closed. The elderly maid came hurrying downstairs, more than ever discomposed.

"I'm sorry, madam, my mistress isn't at all well. She says she can't see callers. She asked me to see that you have a cab."

Bella sat very upright, unmoving.

"I don't think your mistress could have understood. It's quite vital that I see her. Tell her so, pray."

"But, madam—"

The poor faded creature was terrified of Mrs. Raven, as everyone seemed to be.

"Just tell her," said Bella gently. "I mean to stay here until you do."

There was nothing for it but to return upstairs. The woman did so, with a backward glance at Bella that expressed resentment, but also a reluctant respect.

This time there was the sound of that now familiar overbearing high-pitched voice. The words were intended, Bella realized, for her ears.

"Doesn't she understand the English language, Martha? Didn't you tell her I was ill? In any case, she must know I don't receive women off the streets. Well, go along, woman, go along."

Bella rose. Before the pitiably embarrassed Martha was halfway down the stairs, she had begun to mount them.

"I'm so sorry, Martha. You shouldn't have had to do so difficult an errand. I'll do it myself."

"Madam! You mustn't! Didn't you hear—"

"I hear what I choose to hear, just as my mother-in-law does." Bella swept on up the stairs and reached the door at the top. Without knocking, she flung it open. Then she stood within it and made an elaborate curtsey to the little upright figure in the chair by the fire.

"Good evening, Mrs. Raven," she said. "I'm sorry you're indisposed. I promise not to disturb you for more than a few minutes."

Mrs. Raven had got to her feet; two poodle puppies scattered from her lap, yapping excitedly.

"How *dare* you!" she hissed. "You hussy! Bursting in here with no manners—" She poked angrily with her stick at the yapping dogs. "Be quiet! Be quiet! Hannah! Where are you? Show this—person out."

The meek Hannah, even more intimidated than Martha, made a movement towards Bella, but was defeated by the impossibility of the task. A lady could not be shown out if she refused to go.

"Forgive my bad manners, Mrs. Raven, but I can't go until I've said what I must. You won't know what has happened to my husband today. He has been asked by the Prime Minister to postpone his political career."

"Ha! I guessed as much! And serve him right!"

"I don't think you mean that, Mrs. Raven. I think you love your

126

son very much, and would like to help him. I know that if you intervened for him, showed the world that you were on his side—"

She was interrupted by Mrs. Raven's outraged voice, "On *his* side! You mean on your side, you conscienceless fortune hunter! Have you no pride?"

"No," said Bella, and realized with wonder that she was speaking the truth. "Not where the good of my husband is concerned. I would have thought a mother would feel the same."

Mrs. Raven swung her stick dangerously. Her face was mottled with rage.

"How dare you tell me how a mother feels! Seeing you and your sister parading at the Opera, dressed up like strumpets, wearing *my* diamonds—oh, yes, mine, until my son went mad— and you dare to tell me how a mother should feel. All I ask is that you stay out of my sight. The damage is done. But I, an old woman, expect peace. Now go."

"Mrs. Raven—"

"Hush! You won't get round me with any mealy-mouthed talk. If you must know, I feel only pity for you. It can't be very amusing living with a man who will already have begun to hate you."

"Hate—" It was one thing to suspect it herself, but quite another to hear it put into words. A stone was in her heart, weighing it down. She had lost her fine anger.

"I'm glad to see you have some vestige of feeling," Mrs. Raven observed dryly. "I'd advise you to conquer it. You didn't marry into a forgiving family. But that's your mistake. Now I ask you again to go. We have nothing more to say."

Hannah was holding the door open and urging Bella out. She was on the threshold before the momentary black misery lifted and she recovered her wits.

"Mrs. Raven—"

The door had slammed in her face. There was the unmistakable sound of a key turning in the lock.

Nothing could have roused her fury more. To be locked out! And that old woman talked to her of manners!

She banged on the door, not caring now if the whole street heard her.

"If you lock me out, you lock your grandson out, too. Don't you want to see your grandson?"

There was a moment of complete silence. Bella leaned her hot forehead against the door, reflecting miserably that this was a fine way to tell her news, shouting it out to a hostile silence. But perhaps it was fitting. It was the way, after all, in which the baby had been conceived, in hostility and without love.

She whipped up her defiance.

"If you want to see him, Mrs. Raven, you must be the one to come to me. I shan't come to you again."

After a long silence the answer came, "I am afraid your cab driver is getting tired of waiting."

Chapter 13

BELLA said levelly, "Will you please ask Davis to stop?"

Guy looked at her in surprise. "What's the matter, my dear?"

Lally leaned forward. "Bella, are you ill? You look very pale."

Bella took a deep breath and controlled her mounting sickness. For a moment the landscape stopped tilting, and she could see the newly-budded trees and the green fields. She had expected to enjoy the twenty-mile journey into Hertfordshire, but the rocking of the carriage, and the closeness, with the four of them in so small a space was too much for her. She sat in rigid silence while Guy tapped on the window and asked Davis to stop the horses, then tumbled out hastily, ignoring Guy's proffered help.

"Turn your back!" she gasped. "Please!"

When the spasm was over and she was able to lift her head and gratefully breathe the sweet air, she was aware of her husband's critical gaze.

"You didn't tell me you were a bad traveller."

"I'm not, usually. I think I must have caught a chill. But I'm quite recovered now. Shall we go on?"

He had his hand on her arm, delaying her return to the stuffy carriage.

"Are you going to have a baby?"

"Yes. Yes, if you must know."

"If I must know! I should imagine it's my business, as well as yours. A fine time you choose to tell me, on the roadside in the middle of a journey."

"I hadn't meant it to be like this," she pleaded. The air was so sweet after the tainted London mist, the country so beautiful. And Guy standing there hatless, the wind lifting his dark gold hair, looked so handsome, it would really have been a romantic place after all in which to tell her news. Except that the horses were fidgeting, and Lally was looking out anxiously, and there was Tottie crouched in her corner, not once daring to lift her head, through which who knew what terrors were racing. There was no trace of tenderness in Guy's face. He looked instead as if he had been unfairly deceived, as if, indeed, she had become pregnant only to annoy him.

But of course his first thought would be of the child and the wife he had lost. That was natural. He perhaps had a horror of childbirth. It would be nice to think his stern expression was caused by anxiety for the ordeal ahead of her.

"I would have told you yesterday, only you had had the upset of your meeting with Lord Palmerston. So I intended waiting until we were at Ravenscroft."

"You needn't have subjected yourself to this journey at such a time."

She seized on his concern, and exclaimed light-heartedly,

"Poof! This is nothing. Papa used to say the more tasks a woman did, the better. Besides, I did ask Doctor Bushey's advice, and he assured me it would be perfectly safe. There's no danger of harming the baby. Truly."

Guy glanced towards Davis on the box who was staring rigidly ahead.

"Well, now you have broadcast your news, perhaps we can continue on our way."

He hadn't expressed pleasure, but after his first reaction of stiff shock, he had behaved quite courteously. He would quickly grow used to the idea and like it, Bella told herself optimistically. What man wouldn't want a son, even under these circumstances. She would promise not to be like that poor delicate Caroline and keep everyone on tenterhooks for months beforehand. And surely, when the baby was born, Guy could not go on hating its mother.

"Bella, are you really—I mean, are you recovered now?" Lally's face was quivering with excitement. Lally at least, with her passion for babies, would not let this one arrive unwelcomed.

Bella squeezed her hand gratefully, and said blithely, "I am, as well as I shall be for quite some time. You must help me with my sewing, Lally. I'm afraid we're going to be poor company for some time," she added to her husband.

But he was suddenly lost in thought, and gave no more sign of hearing her happy chatter than Tottie did. Tottie hadn't lifted her head, but Bella did think she caught a flicker of her eyes, and once she let the little pink tip of her tongue run round her lips. Poor Tottie, in her neat dark poplin dress and shawl and shiny new buttoned boots, would soon realize that she was not going to her doom. She would grow interested in the arrival of the baby. It really seemed that the baby might solve a lot of problems. Bella herself was almost able to forget her two humiliations, the way she couldn't stop herself turning to fire at her husband's touch, and the way his mother had turned her out, like some sort of vermin.

She had been a little scared and not very pleased when Doctor Bushey had confirmed her suspicions about her pregnancy. But now she was glad. The baby would change everything.

Lally exclaimed in admiration at the first glimpse of the long white house lying in a green hollow round the curve of the drive. It was not large like some of the great country houses, but Bella saw at once that it had great elegance. Guy's grandfather must have been a man of taste. Perhaps, in the arid dusty heat of India he had dreamed of this cool oasis, green lawns, yew trees, the glimmer of water, and the cool, white pillared house.

Lally's wide eyes indicated that she thought the whole thing a dream, but Bella clung to reality. It was true that she was going to be mistress of this mansion, and her baby would be born here, but she knew she would never truly belong until she and Guy had established some genuine contact, friendship at least. She refused to go on being considered a usurper.

Actually there was more to overcome than her husband's hostility. The first shock was to find that half the servants had left, influenced, it seemed, by the elderly housekeeper who had been greatly devoted to both Guy's mother and his first wife.

"Why wasn't I informed?" Guy asked, his brows tight.

Broome, the butler, replied that it had happened with great suddenness, and there had been time only to find a substitute housekeeper. He hoped to replace the maids, the boot-boy and the the under-gardeners shortly.

He introduced the new housekeeper, a Mrs. Walter. She was a neat person, middle-aged, with grey-streaked black hair drawn tightly back from a long sallow face. She scarcely lifted her eyes to look at Bella, which was a pleasant change from the rude staring to which Bella had become accustomed. She curtseyed and her mouth was prim.

Broome, like Doughty in London, was elderly, a fringe of white whiskers framing his chin. He looked at his new mistress quite frankly, but with respect. Bella liked him at once. Mrs. Walter was not so easy to know.

Although she was dropping with fatigue from the long journey Bella refused to rest until she had seen the house. She took Guy's arm and insisted that he show her every room. Lally and Tottie were sent upstairs with Mrs. Walter while they walked alone through the sunny rooms.

The sun was the first thing Bella noticed, streaming through all the long windows, filling the rooms with golden light. Here was none of the claustrophobic gloom that people nowadays loved. The curtains were drawn back, the furnishings were in delightful colours, gold, crimson and turquoise. The Indian influence predominated in the carpets, the bronze ornaments, the yellow silk curtains, and the cabinets full of old India china. There were English things, too, fine old mahogany and walnut, Chippendale chairs and mirrors, but the general effect was of tropical gaiety.

Bella found it utterly delightful.

"How could one be gloomy in a place like this."

"I told you you would like it. I believe your reply was that you refused to become a gardener like Cousin Henrietta."

Bella giggled, very youthfully.

"In this garden, I may be tempted."

"Not until after your baby is born."

She was glad for his concern, but wished he had referred to the baby as theirs, not hers alone. She bit her lip, refusing to let her thoughts grow carping.

"You are pleased about the baby?" She caught his arm. "Tell me."

"My dear Isabella, I couldn't honestly say I was pleased about anything in the present situation. I don't think you would expect me to be. But if the child amuses you, I am glad."

"*Amuses* me! Is that all you can say about your son! That he is to be a toy to keep me distracted, and therefore less of a burden to you!"

He frowned wearily.

"Please! Do you want me to be less than honest? Very well,

then," he bent to kiss her brow, "I will look forward to the child, too."

Bella turned away, blinking back tears. The lovely rooms, the sunlight, the feeling of light and warmth and happiness, was ruined by her husband's utter indifference about a child that was to be hers, and not Caroline's. She believed he wouldn't even care if this one also failed to live and its mother, too.

She would make him care!

Upstairs, the only room that interested her was the master-bedroom. Strangely enough, this was the one gloomy room in the house. It was not that it didn't get plenty of light, but simply that the decorations were too subdued, all greens and blues that gave a curious under-water effect. Not that they were not modern. They looked as if they had been done quite recently, and of course they would have been. By Caroline. No doubt she fancied the cool subtlety of the blending of colours. But to Bella the effect was extremely depressing. She resolved to make alterations as soon as she could do so.

Guy's reluctance to linger in the room was marked. He said he would leave her, as she would no doubt want to rest after the long journey.

"But there's so much more to see. The other bedrooms, the garden." Bella found herself as reluctant as he to be in this room alone.

"You have all the summer in which to see everything."

That was a reasonable remark. But all at once Bella was not in a reasonable state. This cool submarine room was doing strange things to her.

She tugged fretfully at the bed hangings.

"I shall have these changed to a more cheerful colour. I have a great dislike for green."

"I would prefer it if you didn't."

She was uncertain, looking at his suddenly ravaged face. The knowledge came to her that this must be the room not only where he had loved Caroline but where she had died. For a moment her courage deserted her. There was too much to fight.

There were plenty of bedrooms in the house. She would choose another. This one could be closed, left to gather dust and cob-webs, like an old tomb.

But no, that would only preserve the unwelcome ghost. And

she herself would remain an intruder. In this room Guy must learn to know his new wife.

So she ignored his private torment and said reflectively, regarding the bed hangings, "Yellow, I think. And white curtains at the windows. And the walls with a crimson and gold design. You won't believe the difference. Let me amuse myself in this way."

His wintry eyes met hers. She knew he read exactly what was in her mind and was astonished at her lack of tact. But some madness had seized her. If she couldn't take him in her arms, cradling that tormented face against her breasts, then she must stir him to anger, anything rather than this morbid remembering.

"You would find my scheme very much to your liking when it is complete. A turkey carpet, I think. So warm."

"Don't waste your time trying to change me, Isabella."

She deliberately misunderstood him and cried gaily, "Not you! The room! The bed, those silly spindly chairs which I am sure would collapse if you sat on them, everything. Oh, I promise not to change other things in the house. But this room where I will spend a great deal of time, surely that's my domain."

His frozen face drove her to add, crazily, "I won't sleep in the bed where your wife died!"

"I forbid you to touch a thing," he said, and turned on his heel and left.

But I will touch everything! If your first wife was allowed to decorate her bedroom why shouldn't your second have equal rights? Bella kicked childishly at one of the spindly chairs hoping one of its elegant legs would break off.

A tap at the door stopped her angry muttering. She hastily smoothed her hair and put her hands to her hot cheeks, summoning back the dignity she had lost. At her bidding the housekeeper, Mrs. Walter, appeared.

The woman stood meekly, her hands clasped over her apron, her eyes resting anxiously on Bella's face.

"Is everything in order, madam? Can I be of help to you?"

Bella saw that the woman fortunately was more concerned with making a good impression than in noticing her new mistress's discomposure. Sadly, she found herself appreciating civility after her husband's harsh treatment.

"Thank you, Mrs. Walter, but Tottie will unpack for me."

It was only a flash in her mind that this woman seemed a little too servile. That wouldn't be true, for Mrs. Walter, gathering confidence, was already expressing an opinion.

"Please don't think me forward, madam, but your sister tells me the girl you brought with you is to be your maid. She seems so young and untrained, and besides not being able to speak. Please forgive me, madam, for presuming like this—I am sure you have performed the kindest action—but I would be so happy to find you a capable maid while the child learns."

"The child is learning, Mrs. Walter. I am teaching her."

"I realize that, madam. It's most kind of madam. But supposing a grand toilette is required—"

Bella's eyes darkened. She remembered the occasion of her one and only grand toilette.

"Tottie will manage very well, Mrs. Walter. I want her with me. We won't speak of it again."

The woman's eyes were downcast, hiding their expression.

"As madam wishes."

A suspicion came into Bella's head. "Perhaps you had someone in mind?"

"Oh, no, madam. But I have experience in engaging maids."

"Of course. I am sure you have the highest credentials. It was fortunate you were able to come to us at practically a moment's notice. What was your last position?"

"It was in London, madam. With Lady Merriweather of Eaton Square. But the fogs didn't agree with me. I had to come to the country. I'd given my notice when I saw Broome's advertisement, so it was lucky I could come immediately. That's how it was, madam. I'd like to say I'm very happy to be here."

"Well, it seems fortunate for us, too," said Bella briskly, and wondered if Lady Merriweather were missing her neat, quiet, and observant housekeeper, and what had been the true circumstances of Mrs. Walter's departure. For she doubted that Broome, in his thankfulness to get a decent respectable person at such short notice, had asked many questions.

But Mrs. Walter seemed to have fallen on her feet, too. She had done well enough for herself, without getting her niece, or whatever young woman she had in mind, into the house as well. For all her meekness, she didn't lack initiative.

When she had gone Lally came bursting in.

"Oh, Bella, is it really true about the baby?"

Bella nodded, and Lally flung her arms round her, the ready tears filling her eyes.

"You should have told me! You should never have set out on that long journey without even telling Mr. Raven."

"You must learn to call him Guy, Lally."

"Yes. I suppose so. But he still frightens me. I know I'm silly, with this lovely place and all. But I just can't think how we can be here. Us, Bella! We're only used to living in a cottage. I keep being afraid there's a trick in it all." She hurried on, ignoring Bella's disapproval. "You must admit Mr. Raven's heart isn't with us. And that Mrs. Walter—"

"Snooping Susie!"

Lally's changeable little face sparkled with laughter.

"Is that what you call her? It suits her admirably. You think she's not noticing things, but she is, under her eyelids. She stared at poor Tottie." Lally clasped her arms round herself apprehensively. "There will be all the other strangers here to stare at us."

"There'll only be the servants, Lally."

"Yes. Only servants," said Lally uncertainly, and suddenly, the shadow of Seven Dials seemed to be there. It hadn't bothered Bella at all while they stayed in Knightsbridge, she had pushed the murky evil-smelling city streets out of her mind, but here, many miles away in the safety of the peaceful country, the shadow was as sharp and clear as a thundercloud.

"They won't like us. They'll think we should be one of them," Lally went on.

"They'll do nothing of the kind. I dare you to let them do so."

"I do so hate people staring," Lally muttered.

"Oh, for goodness sake, be more cheerful," Bella said briskly. "You'll love being here. And you are looking forward to the baby, aren't you?"

"Oh, yes, the baby!" Again Lally's face brightened. "I can hardly believe that. I can hardly wait. You will let me help care for it, won't you, Bella?"

"Of course I will, goose."

"And it won't die?"

"I don't intend going through all this discomfort just to have a child that dies."

Lally began to giggle. "You're so outspoken, Bella, really. How you stand up to Mr. Ra— Guy, I'll never know. Tell me—is he kind to you?"

"He's as all husbands are," said Bella, shrugging indifferently. "I'm going to do this room over. I told Guy I didn't care for green as a colour."

"Already!" Lally squeaked.

"It must be done at once."

"Because it was Caroline's?" Lally looked soberly at her sister. "How brave you are, Bella. I should just have said I liked green and been miserable. But I suppose with the baby coming, Mr. Raven won't refuse you anything. Oh, isn't it exciting! It will make him forget Caroline, and perhaps I'll forget that poor little angel in the snow. I don't dream so much of it now. Only when I'm very tired. Bella—Noah couldn't find us here, could he?"

"Lally, once and for all, Noah is in Newgate prison. And even if he weren't, he couldn't do anything to us now. We're safe. Mr. Raven has made us safe. You should be grateful to him, not afraid of him. And now, where's Tottie?"

"I told her to unpack for me, but every time she heard a footstep she wanted to hide."

Bella sighed. "Really, you and Tottie are a fine pair. And now I've got to make her a good maid or Mrs. Walter will laugh at me."

"Mrs. Walter?"

"She's already told me she could find someone better."

The quick apprehension was in Lally's face.

"I told you she stared."

"Oh, for goodness sake, she only wants to get a good position for a relation, I should think. Don't fret. I can manage Mrs. Walter."

But so far she hadn't been able to manage Tottie, who had quite disappeared, and was discovered at last crouching in the corner of the large wardrobe in Lally's room.

"Tottie, for goodness sake, come out at once."

The girl crept out shamefacedly, her shoulders drooping, her head bent.

Bella lifted her chin.

"Look at me, Tottie!"

Tottie obeyed, her dark eyes still as wary as a wild creature's.

"Now do I look the kind of person who would allow anything bad to happen to you? Or does my sister look unkind? I know this house is big and strange, but it's beautiful. You're a very lucky girl to be here. Whatever are you afraid of? That someone will eat you?"

Lally giggled obligingly. The merest twitch passed over Tottie's dull face. But Bella recognized it for what it was. The child had almost smiled. It must be something she had forgotten how to do long long ago.

She swallowed the foolish lump in her throat, and made herself speak briskly,

"Now finish Miss Eulalie's unpacking, then come at once to me. I want a change of clothes put out, and my hair brushed. Do you know, Lally, now I'm expecting a baby I find the most soothing thing of all having my hair brushed. Tottie has a very nice touch. But she must learn to be quicker about her work."

Then the small miracle happened. Tottie came to life. Nodding vigorously, and going down on her knees, she began tumbling the remainder of the articles out of Lally's bag. Her little head, with its tufted, straw-coloured hair still short from its drastic clipping by Doctor Bushey, was tousled and would have to be covered neatly with a cap, her dress was rumpled already, and her reddened hands clumsy. But all her actions suddenly spoke of willingness and hope. Bella knew the battle to win her trust was over and won. Trainable or not, Tottie was going to be a loyal servant.

If she could tame a wild creature like Tottie, surely she need not fail too badly with other people.

Chapter 14

BELLA was trying to induce some intelligible sound from Tottie when Guy paid his first visit to the disputed green and blue bedroom. It was Sunday morning, three days after their arrival at Ravenscroft. During the days Guy had been courteous and thoughtful, showing Bella the gardens, strolling with her down the long shadowed yew walk where even the quarrelling of the rooks seemed muted, displaying the rose garden and the kitchen garden, and the slope of the lawn that led to the gently flowing river, the water as green as the willows that bent over it.

There was a ballroom and an orangery, a croquet lawn and an archery. Bella had to cling again to reality. She could scarcely believe that an ill-considered acquaintance made on the London coach could have led to her becoming the mistress of this beautiful estate. She began to catch Lally's fear that they would both have to wake up. There must be a trick in all of this.

The only flaw was the lonely nights in the hated bedroom. But these she could endure at present. She had resolved to be patient. She didn't think her husband a too patient man. Her baby had not yet begun to spoil her figure. Guy must notice soon that it was charming. She couldn't believe that he would hate her forever.

"Open your mouth wider, Tottie. That's better. Now say o-oh, o-ooh."

Tottie's familiar grunt, the only sound she ever made, was cut off at Guy's entrance. She shrank back, hanging her head.

"Good morning, my love," Bella said brightly. "I was just giving Tottie her daily lesson in speech. Tottie, you may go now."

"Have you made any progress?" Guy asked, as the girl hurriedly retreated.

"Not yet. But it's too soon to form an opinion."

"How do you know she could ever speak?"

"She must have been able to, to understand everything we say. Words are familiar to her. Doctor Bushey says this. Her development has been arrested and her vocal cords paralysed by her dreadful experience. He says she is also older than she appears, at least sixteen or seventeen. If ever she is to recover it will be here, in this peaceful place."

"Perhaps. You're optimistic, I think. But I didn't come to discuss Tottie. I want you to be ready to go to church at eleven o'clock."

"Of course," Bella said placidly. "Lally, too?"

"It would be wise."

"Wise? I had hoped to go to church to worship, not to be shown off to the villagers."

Would she never learn to control her tongue? Now the friendliness had gone out of his face.

"For whatever reason, you will come."

It was only while entering and leaving the church that people had the opportunity to stare. During the service Bella, Lally and Guy sat in the boxed-in pew, its walls too high for the rest of the congregation to see over. The villagers from the little village of Underwood, and the servants, Broome, Mrs. Walter, two maids, and the shrinking Tottie, sat at the back of the church. Mrs. Walter was being kind to Tottie after all, and today had taken her under her wing, seeing that she had a posy of flowers to carry with her clean handkerchief and her prayer book, and shepherding her safely into the church.

It was a beautiful little church. Bella felt herself in a placid enough mood to enjoy its peace, and it was only when they stood to sing the first hymn that she saw the Raven pew was directly opposite the neat, square, painfully-new tablet set in the wall to the memory of Caroline Charlotte Raven, aged twenty-two years, also her son, stillborn.

Guy stood with his head held high, his profile calm and austere. Although Bella watched him surreptitiously for the whole of the service she never once saw him turn his head to the ghost on his other side.

It was left to Bella to have the tightened throat and pricking eyelids. Poor Caroline gone from the bright day. And lucky, lucky Bella to be alive.

Her mingled pity and exultation enabled Bella to walk with

easy dignity out of the church after the service, smiling a little at the frankly-staring villagers, responding graciously to the vicar's welcome. She hoped that she was behaving as her husband wished. It was so wonderful to come out into the spring sunshine, to smell the may flowers and the lime blossom. They would return home as they had come, by the short cut across the path through the fields that led to the long yew walk and the house. Already she was enjoying the thought of the stroll in the sunlight.

She was happy, she realized. She had so much. She would never complain about anything again.

The next morning Guy left for London, and refused to say when he would be back, if ever.

Once more it was Lally who took Bella's mind off herself. It really seemed as if Lally would never again be able to face the world with ease. Even going to church had proved to be a tremendous ordeal. She hadn't been conscious of anything the vicar had said, but only of the people staring. She had been so sure that they were not all innocent and friendly. An enemy could lurk behind the bluest and gentlest of eyes. Didn't Bella remember how innocent Aunt Aggie had seemed?

She had nightmares again that night, and the next day refused to leave her room. She felt safe only within those four walls. It took three days to coax her to go into the garden, and another week before she could be persuaded to accompany Bella to the village. Indeed, then it was only when Bella said she wanted to shop for materials with which to make baby clothes that Lally consented to go.

This outing, accomplished without any untoward event, seemed to restore Lally's confidence, and after that she became quite cheerful, sewing the tiny garments with her exquisite stitching. One would have thought it was her own baby for which she was preparing.

Guy, it seemed, had left instructions with Broome and Mrs. Walter that they were not to engage any more staff. He would attend to the matter himself.

A few days after his departure a letter arrived for Bella. She made herself crush down any expectancy that its contents would express affection. It was as well she did so for the letter was scarcely more than a note which advised that two servants, a young woman and a boy, named Molly Hancock and Joseph Smith respectively, would be arriving by the London coach the following day. Perhaps Bella would be good enough to arrange for them to be met at the coach stop in the village.

The brief chilly note ended, "I hope you and your sister are well."

Mrs. Walter, in spite of her meek air, somehow managed to express disapproval of the new arrivals, particularly the girl. Molly had no idea how to set about cleaning a room or laying a table and must have lied to the master about her credentials. However, Mrs. Walter said with resignation, she would personally supervise the girl's work and keep her out of trouble with Broome. The lad was a strong young fellow and would be useful for carrying scuttles of coal and other heavy work.

Bella was intensely curious about these two young people. She suspected that they had both been in some kind of trouble and that Guy, in spite of his intention to go back to the idle life of a rich man, was still making investigations among the poor.

It wasn't difficult to get Joseph's story from him. For all his large frame he was little more than a bag of bones. He had been attempting to support a sick mother and five young brothers and sisters by running errands or begging for jobs at the doors of rich houses. But mostly he had been driven off because of his rags and his unkempt appearance.

"I seemed to fritten them mostly," he said cheerfully. "They'd throw up their hands and bang the door in me face."

But somehow he had managed until it seemed as if his mother was dying. Then he had begun to steal. It was mostly food, a string of sausages snatched from a butcher's, an orange from a coster's barrow, a loaf of bread, once a blanket hung out to dry in a back garden.

He had got caught for stealing a bun out of a bakeshop the day his mother died.

"They buried her in the new plague cemetery," he said. That was the thing that lay heavily on his mind, a far worse grief than his brothers and sisters being sent to an orphanage and himself to court. "She didn't have the plague. She shouldn't have to lay there among the plague."

Joseph said he thought he was fifteen.

Bella asked him how it had happened he wasn't sent to prison, and he said that was because of the master.

"He promised to see I kept out of trouble. Then he told me

that he'd give his word I wouldn't do nothing bad so now I'd have to give mine to him. It was a new experiment, kind of."

"So of course you gave your word," said Bella.

The boy looked at her with his great hollowed eyes.

"I'd die as soon as let him down," he said.

Molly Hancock was another matter. She was a pretty creature with melting dark eyes and pouting lips. At first she would say nothing at all about her past, but finally, it was Lally in whom she confided. She had discovered Lally's intense interest in Bella's coming baby, and one day it had slipped from her that she, too, had had a baby. That was why she had been dismissed from the dressmaker's where she had worked.

"Old Miss Fairbrother, you should of seen her face. You'd of thought babies were some kind of foreign animal."

Of course, Molly explained, hers hadn't got a father, at least not one who would take responsibility. So she had had it in a charity home, a nightmare place, she said, and left it there to get adopted or put in an orphanage.

Lally was horrified. How could she bear to part with the baby? Molly tossed her head and said it was an ugly little thing. Anyway, wasn't it better that one should starve instead of two?

"Starve?" said Lally.

"How was I to get another job with a brat in my arms? I couldn't even have gone on the streets."

"You didn't do that!" Lally gasped.

"I would have if it hadn't been for that old doctor."

"Doctor Bushey?"

"Yes. He got me this place. I had to go and see Mr. Raven first and he said I could come down here. I'd rather have stayed in London, all the same. It's awful quiet in the country."

"It's safer," said Lally, with a shiver.

"Safer?"

"Terrible things happen in London. Look at what happened to you, having to part with your baby." Lally stopped her sewing to ponder on the terror in the world. "And us. My sister and me. If it hadn't been for Mr. Raven— Tell me," Lally knew she shouldn't be talking like this to a servant, but it was such a relief to air her feelings, "what did you think of Mr. Raven?"

Molly's eyes glinted.

"He was ever so handsome. I wouldn't mind being in the country so much if he was here." Seeing Lally's shocked expression she added, "You know what I mean. A house isn't alive without its master."

Lally repeated this conversation, or most of it, to Bella. Bella had to approve again her husband's good intentions, but she was afraid they might have been wasted on a lively piece like Molly Hancock. All the same, Molly was a cheerful good-natured creature, and she wasn't likely to repeat her lapse at Ravenscroft where the only men were old Broome, the gawky Joseph, and two gardeners, both elderly. Lally had taken a fancy to her, and, when Molly was with her, seemed to throw off her fear of meeting strangers or being stared at. In Molly's company she ventured again into the village on shopping expeditions.

Bella was glad to see Lally so much brighter, but she felt lonelier than ever herself.

She had written to Guy telling him that Molly and Joseph had settled down, and that she fully approved what he had done. No answer came for three weeks. Then there was a brief note saying that he hoped all was well. She was to communicate with him if anything worried her. He hoped her health remained good. He was afraid he would be detained in London for most of the summer. That was all. She had to remind herself that he hadn't lied to her. He had told her at the beginning how their marriage would be.

All the same, Cousin Henrietta's letter some weeks later made bitter reading.

"My dear Isabella,

I expected better of you. Haven't you learnt how to keep your husband at home? I hear disturbing rumours about his behaviour in London. They are disturbing, or I hardly need to tell you I wouldn't behave like a busybody and pass this news on. I think myself he is doing this deliberately from some peculiar kind of cussedness which runs in the family; since he has to suffer from that wicked gossip in the press he will prove it true. He must be stopped before he entirely ruins all prospect of a career or happiness. If you can't give him love, child, and God knows that can't be given at will, give him friendship. He needs true friends. I don't know how you can get him out of London, but get him out. Use your instinct."

Bella's first instinct, and not one she was proud of, was to sit down and weep. Her next was much more creative. She rang for

Mrs. Walter and asked for one of the guest-rooms to be prepared for her temporary occupation. She was planning to have the master-bedroom redecorated.

So Guy could console himself with cheap women, could he? That was what Cousin Henrietta's letter had been meant to convey to her. Caroline's ghost didn't intrude when his surroundings were some overdecorated boudoir and the arms about him strange ones. Therefore, every trace of Caroline should be removed from this house. The morbid blue and green furnishings should go. Bella had obeyed his order not to touch them until now. But no longer. In future, if the room reminded him of anyone, it would be of his present wife, Isabella.

This was not the act of friendship Cousin Henrietta begged. But it was the way her instinct worked.

Those shameless women in London! Bella could scarcely control her fury at the thought of them. She kept calm only by plunging herself into activity, ordering the carriage every day and driving into the neighbouring towns to look at brocades, wallpapers, carpets. Workmen were hired. The transformation began.

When it was completed three weeks later she sent the bills to Guy, with an apology that tradesmen nowadays always seemed to cost more than anticipated, but she was sure he would be as delighted as she was with the result. "After all," she wrote unabashedly, "it is important to have surroundings to one's taste when one has to spend a good deal of time in bed. Unfortunately, the doctor has ordered me to do this as my health," she stole a look at her blooming face in the mirror, "is not at present what it should be."

Which emotion would bring him back? Anger with her for her disobedience and extravagance? Or anxiety for the safety of his coming child?

Would his imagination show him a picture of her lying in the big bed with its new drapes, "48 yards Italian brocade, cutting, sewing and hanging . . ."

At least he would be reminded sharply of her existence.

But she had no opportunity, after all, to see if her ruse would succeed. For something else happened.

Lally had gone with Molly on one of their expeditions to the village. After they had completed their shopping they went, as usual, to have tea at Mrs. Bunt's tearooms. Mrs. Bunt served hot scones with whipped cream which Molly particularly liked. Lally enjoyed giving her this small pleasure, but enjoyed more sitting in the cosy low-ceilinged room with its dark rafters and gleaming copper and brass. Curiously enough, she didn't feel stared at here. The two girls always had the table in the darkest corner where they could watch people coming in and scarcely be noticed themselves.

It was a very simple diversion, and Molly thought Lally a bit simple to find it so absorbing. What did she care who groups of people off the London coach which stopped at the inn next door were? Passers-by, people you would never see again. Lally made up their histories, pondered where they had come from, discussed their clothes. Daft, Molly thought. She herself would rather be in the inn parlour, hoping for a glimpse of the men at the bar. She had struck up a close friendship with a young man, Tom Field.

But today there was someone sitting at their corner table, a little round teacosy of a woman wrapped in a woolly shawl, with a neat black bonnet trimmed with cherries framing her plump pink and white face.

Seeing her there Lally exclaimed first in annoyance, then, as her eyes accustomed themselves to the gloom, she gripped Molly's arm so hard that Molly cried, "Ouch! What's the matter, miss?"

"It's Aunt Aggie!" Lally said in a strangled whisper. "Oh, dear God, it's Aunt Aggie!" She dragged at Molly. "We must fly. Quickly!"

Molly stood her ground. She wasn't flying from anybody, least of all a harmless, plump, elderly woman. Besides, people were beginning to look now, and it was embarrassing.

She said sensibly, "If that's your aunt, you ought to speak to her, miss. Come on."

Lally gasped and looked as if she would faint, and at that moment the old lady, who wore spectacles and seemed to be short-sighted, saw them.

"Is something wrong with the young lady?" she asked in a concerned voice.

"I think she's mistaking you for someone else," Molly said, for if Lally thought this woman her aunt, the woman obviously hadn't the slightest recollection of her niece.

"You're Aunt Aggie!" Lally managed to say at last. "You must be."

The old lady shook her head.

"I'm sorry to disappoint you, my dear. I've never heard of your Aunt Aggie. Not that I wouldn't mind having a pretty niece like you. I'm a lonely old widow."

The soft insinuating voice was the same. And yet how could it be? Aunt Aggie was in jail. Lally's head spun.

"Perhaps you'd do me the honour of taking tea with me, anyway," said the old woman.

Molly made a move forward, but Lally was in a panic. "No, no, no!" she cried. "It isn't safe!" She literally ran out of the room into the street, followed by Molly who now made no effort to hide her dudgeon.

"You did make us look fools, miss. Running away like that from a nice old lady."

"She isn't a nice old lady, she's a monster! Let us go home quickly. I must tell Bella."

Bella didn't know what to make of it. She had to admit a shaft of fear touched her as she listened to Lally's incoherent story, but it was obvious that Molly had the true state of affairs. The old lady must have borne a remarkable resemblance to Aunt Aggie, that was all. After all, she had denied recognition of Lally. It must have been pure chance that she had sat at their table. She could never have done it deliberately to be sure of catching the girls' notice, for how could she know they usually sat there? She was probably a coach traveller passing through the village.

To satisfy herself, Bella immediately paid a visit to Mrs. Bunt. Needless to say, Mrs. Bunt was agog with curiosity as to what had caused Lally's strange behaviour.

"Looked as if she'd seen a ghost, poor child. And it was only the lady from Southampton breaking her journey. Coach travel didn't agree with her, she said. She had to go by easy stages."

"My sister thought she was someone we once knew," Bella murmured. "It gave her a shock to find she was speaking to a stranger. The lady's name—what did you say it was?"

"That I can't tell you, Mrs. Raven. She was a widow on a visit to her daughter in Twickenham. A pleasant-spoken body. She's staying at The Feathers."

A pleasant-spoken body . . . That description fitted Aunt Aggie exactly.

Bella knew there was only one thing to do and that was to go to The Feathers and interview the mysterious old woman.

This was not at all difficult, for the lady in question was sitting alone in the inn parlour.

Bella's heart gave a great jump. She did look remarkably like Aunt Aggie, the round body in the neat dark dress with its voluminous skirts, the short plump neck and the upswept grey hair beneath the frilled cap were an exact replica. But when the woman turned her head the resemblance ended. For one thing, she had clear penetrating eyes that needed no spectacles. (Lally must have imagined the spectacles beneath the bonnet in the dim corner of Mrs. Bunt's tearoom.) And her expression was not bland like Aunt Aggie's, but petulant and forbidding.

The truth was, a great many stout elderly women looked alike, and poor Lally's fear-clouded eyes had led her to wrong conclusions.

For this definitely was not Aunt Aggie.

"I think you were the lady having tea at Mrs. Bunt's this afternoon," Bella said. "I came to apologize for my sister's behaviour. She mistook you for someone else."

The woman nodded affably.

"That's very civil of you, my dear. I was quite distressed for your sister. She seemed to sustain a shock."

"She's in poor health."

"That was very evident. She seemed afraid I would do her some harm. Dear me, a simple old woman like me! I would consult a doctor about her."

"Yes, I intend to."

"Has she had some shock recently?"

"I'm afraid so."

"Tch! Tch!" Bella's heart stood still. The voice and the expression were Aunt Aggie's exactly. Yet she was looking into a perfectly strange face.

"Such a pretty child. You must take good care of her . . ."

The whole thing was a remarkable coincidence, and a highly unfortunate one, for, in spite of Bella's assurance, Lally could not be convinced that the innocent stranger hadn't been Aunt Aggie. Hadn't she even worn the familiar cherry-trimmed bonnet? Bella hadn't seen the lady's bonnet. But cherries were not an unfamiliar trimming on bonnets. That proved nothing.

Nevertheless, Lally shut herself in her room again and refused to have the curtains drawn back even at midday. Like a pale flower she wilted in the gloom, starting at every sound.

"She's heard about your baby, Bella," she kept saying. "That's why she's come."

Chapter 15

THE next day—or night—Molly disappeared.

Mrs. Walter discovered her absence when she went up to the servants' rooms in the attics to find out why Molly hadn't come down to help with the breakfast.

Her bed hadn't been slept in and her outdoor things were gone.

She came at once to report to Bella who was still in bed. At the urgent knocking on her door Bella started up in absurd anticipation that it might be Guy. Mrs. Walter's knock was usually much more discreet.

But the woman seemed to have caught something of Lally's uneasiness. She kept saying, "Where can the girl have got to? Out all night. It isn't right, madam."

Bella had never thought Molly a pillar of virtue, but she was a kind-hearted girl, and had been particularly understanding with Lally. It would be a pity if she had to be dismissed.

"She hasn't taken all her things, surely?"

"No, madam. But she hadn't much of anything. She was wearing her good dress and petticoats and outdoor boots. Her bonnet and shawl have gone. If she was running away, I don't suppose she'd set much store on the trifles left. I don't like saying it, madam, but if she was running off with a man, he'd no doubt be promising her better than she had. She wouldn't want to be bothering with her old things."

All that Mrs. Walter said made good sense. Molly was flighty, easy-going. She had a weakness for men. She even had a friend in the village, Lally had said. Someone she had talked to in the inn. If she didn't come back before the morning was over, it was the most likely thing in the world that she had run off with him.

It was quite unreasonable of Bella to think that Molly's disappearance was a significant happening so soon after Lally imagining she had seen Aunt Aggie.

Yet she did not think so. She gave orders that Lally was not to be told of this new event, then sent Broome to the village to make discreet inquiries as to whether Molly had been seen there last evening.

Broome came back to report that Molly hadn't been seen at all. Indeed, the young man she had favoured, Tom Field, had waited all evening for her to meet him as she had promised to do. When she hadn't come, he had gone home in disgust. He vowed he would have nothing more to do with her. She had roving eyes, he said. He had always noticed her casting sly glances at the travellers by coach. She'd be easy enough to pick up. Look for her in London, he said.

The elderly widow who had spent a night at the inn had continued her journey to Twickenham. This Broome had discovered, as Bella had asked him to. She had been travelling alone.

Bella forced herself to think coolly and logically. Molly had found life too dull in the country, and had run off the first opportunity that had offered. A letter would have to be written to Guy telling him to be more careful about the kind of servant he engaged. In the meantime Mrs. Walter had better find someone to take Molly's place.

Bella made this last decision deliberately. Mrs. Walter was proving a splendid housekeeper, unobtrusive and efficient. But Bella had never quite got over her faint distrust of the woman, and Lally disliked her. Now let her prove her honesty by the kind of girl she engaged.

Surprisingly enough, she did, that very day. The farmer who supplied the big house with milk and eggs had a daughter needing a position. Her name was Norah, she was just sixteen, a pleasant, fresh-faced country girl full of eagerness and good intentions.

Bella liked her immediately. She decided at once that Norah was the kind of girl she would like to look after her baby. And she would get on with Tottie. Tottie had been in awe of the sophisticated Molly, which wasn't surprising, since Molly considered her quite daft. But Norah would be sympathetic and kind. Bella was so satisfied with the arrangement that she began to think Molly's flight providential, and almost didn't notice the look of sly satisfaction on Mrs. Walter's face. It was a very fleeting look. It vanished at once. Bella was annoyed that it even perturbed her.

That seemed to be the end of the matter, except for Lally having to be told that Molly had gone. Bella waited until the following day, to make quite sure the errant girl didn't intend returning. Then she went to Lally and broke the news.

Lally gave a great gasp and exclaimed, "Aunt Aggie's got her!"

"Oh, Lally, how can you be so stupid!" The whole dreary story would have to be gone over again. "Aunt Aggie's locked up in jail. That wasn't her you saw. And Molly's run off with a man. She's a bad girl, I'm afraid. And Lally dear, you mustn't sit here in the dark. I'm going to draw the curtains back. It's a lovely day and you should be out in the garden. Let us take a walk before lunch. The doctor said I was to take a little exercise every day."

If she hoped a reference to her condition would rouse Lally, she was wrong, for the girl hunched closer into her chair. With her shawl drawn tightly round her thin shoulders she looked like an old woman, the gloom of the curtained room making her fair hair silver. Her hair was dishevelled, Bella noticed, and she was dressed carelessly, some buttons undone in her bodice and her skirts crumpled. It wasn't like Lally to be careless of her appearance. Her nervousness had worried Bella for a long time, but this strangely apathetic condition was much more disturbing. She needed rousing now, not soothing.

"Lally, do tidy yourself. I'll send Tottie to brush your hair and help you change your dress. Put on the sprigged lawn. It's so pretty."

Lally spoke slowly, in a slurred voice, as if she were half asleep. "Molly will be in that bedroom now. Do you remember the blue bows on the curtains? We thought Aunt Aggie must be nice because she bothered about bows on the curtains for her lodgers. I expect Molly thinks she's nice, too." Lally started up, her eyes suddenly imploring. "Bella, she must be warned."

"Lally, once and for all—" Bella stopped as the peremptory knock came on the door. Not Mrs. Walter's knock, not Tottie's, not— But it was!

"May I come in, Isabella?"

Guy's voice was as peremptory as his knock. He didn't wait to be bidden to enter. He was standing in front of them dressed

in riding clothes, and looking dusty and worn, as if he had galloped hard all the way from London.

Bella's heart beat in her throat. She had a longing to run into
his arms, to lift her face to be kissed, to tell him he looked thinner
but otherwise exactly as she remembered him.

She stood quite still and said in a faint voice, "You came? Are
you very angry?"

"Who wouldn't be? What's this new trouble? Is it manufac-
tured or real?"

"I assure you—the bills are quite real."

"The bills?" He looked as if he didn't know what she was talking about.

"For the materials and the work. There was a lot of work."

He stared at her in disbelief.

"Do you seriously think I've ridden since dawn because of a
handful of bills?"

"Then what—"

"The morning newspapers. I suppose you haven't seen them.
We have headlines again. I'm accused of abducting another
young woman. Tell me, what is all this? Where is that wretched
girl?"

So it was Molly about whom he had come. Bella couldn't begin
to wonder how the news had reached the morning papers. She
was too deflated. He seemed indifferent to her disobedience, even
to her having laid her hands on the sacred work of Caroline. Indeed, it seemed that it was only the silly feather-brained Molly
who was responsible for her ever setting eyes on her husband
again.

"I haven't any idea where the girl is," she said shortly. "And I
simply don't understand how the papers have got hold of the
story."

"I know where she is," said Lally.

"Lally—"

"She's with Aunt Aggie."

Guy made an impatient gesture. "Is she on that again?"

Bella nodded and said in a low voice, "She has been ever since
she thought she saw Aunt Aggie in the village. There was a
woman who resembled her, but she was just someone on a visit
to her daughter in Twickenham. It was only coincidence that
Molly disappeared the night she stayed in the village."

Guy was frowning in bewilderment.

"I never heard anything so improbable. The old b—I mean, Mrs. Proudfoot, is in Newgate, so how could she be in the village? Although I must say—"

Bella's heart missed a beat. Surely he wasn't going to fan that little flame of fear that never quite left her.

"What is it, Guy?"

"The newspapers were onto this story with suspicious quickness. Did you report Molly's absence to the police?"

"No, I didn't, though everyone in the village would be talking. The story was no secret. Mrs. Walter says you can't reform the kind of girl Molly is. Perhaps your good intentions were a mistake."

"It certainly seems so. I'll have to take old Bushey to task for this. He convinced me the girl only needed a new start. Though I think we ought to be sure Molly has run off with a man before we condemn her."

"And if she hasn't?" Bella breathed the words.

"Then we must make every effort to find her, if only to save the dregs of my own reputation." Guy smiled wryly. "It's being hinted now that I might be indulging in a little of the white slave traffic myself. You and your sister have disappeared from the scene, and now a servant girl."

"Guy! How appalling!"

"Hiding behind Aunt Aggie's ample skirts, eh? But the thing can bear looking into." Guy's keen eyes were on Lally. "What's wrong with her?"

"She's upset about all this."

"Is that all? Just upset?"

He had noticed Lally's strange vacancy, her dishevelled appearance. Bella put a protective arm round her sister's shoulders.

"That's all. You know how sensitive she is."

"And you, my love? I must say, for someone who has been advised to rest in bed, you look remarkably well."

Bella flushed. "I can only tell you what the doctor said."

"Then he must think husbands shouldn't be worried by their wives' delicate state of health. He said in his letter to me that your condition couldn't be improved on."

"He wrote to you! Why?"

"I imagine in answer to my letter to him. I did take the trouble to assure myself that you were not in any imminent danger."

Bella met his ironic gaze. She thought dolefully that she had meant to be reclining in bed when he arrived, wearing her new wrapper with the swansdown trimming, and looking fragile and in need of cherishing. Instead she stood here, flushed and plump and abounding in health. And Doctor Frobisher, for whom she had developed a prejudice because he had also been Caroline's doctor, had given away her foolish ruse.

But Guy had bothered to inquire about her. She supposed her small flicker of joy about that was legitimate.

"It would be too much to expect a man to understand how a woman feels," she said defensively.

"I expect it would. Well, let us get all the bad things over at once. Let me see what your efforts at interior decorating have achieved."

It was odd how her confidence in the room ebbed away when he stood at her side. Had so much red been wise? She had thought it so warm and comforting. Was the wallpaper with its cabbage roses a little overpowering? Should there have been fewer velvet drapes over mantlepiece, tables and stools? And the beautiful golden brocade bed curtains looped back—were they a little bizarre?

Guy suddenly shouted with laughter.

"It's like an Eastern bazaar."

"You don't like it?" Bella's voice was edged with ice. That laughter hurt more than his anger would have done.

"Can you sleep among so much grandeur?"

"It had to be *warm!*" Bella burst out.

"Well, now you've practically lit a fire."

She realized that he was determined not to take her changes too seriously, in case he let his guard break down in front of her again. He would find the room amusingly preposterous, nothing else. In that way he made her harmless.

Harmless! She would show him.

"Doesn't it compare favourably with the rooms you have been visiting in London?"

For a long minute their gaze locked.

"So you too join the scandal-mongers," he said at last. His colour had heightened. "I believe you're as mad as your sister."

Long afterwards a candle flared beside her bed.

"Why didn't you come down to dinner?"

Bella wanted to bury herself deep in the pillows, unwilling to face even the frail light of the candle. Why must he choose this time to come, when she had been weeping for hours, and then, worn out, had not been able to endure even having her hair brushed. She had let Tottie undress her and had tumbled into bed, aching-eyed and wan. The weeks and months of strain had culminated in that torrent of tears. She had felt unable to face life any more. It was all too much, the anxiety about Lally, the nameless threat that seemed to hang over them all the time, the baby her husband didn't care about growing heavy and tiresome within her, and last of all, Guy's accusation that she was mad. As mad as poor darling Lally.

"Are you ill?" the voice at her bedside persisted.

"No," she muttered into the pillow.

"Are you sulking?"

That roused her momentarily, and she turned, pushing back her heavy hair from her tear-stained face.

"I'm not a child!"

"But you've been crying."

"Is that—so extraordinary?"

"Only that I've never seen you cry before."

He sat on the side of the bed and looked down at her.

"What is it you cried for? Something I said? Or the state Lally is in?"

His voice was quite gentle and he had stopped calling Lally Eulalie, as if he accepted her at last. All the same his attitude resembled that of a kind uncle. Bella thought she preferred his hostility. But at least in this mood he could be talked to.

"You called me mad, too," she said.

"You provoked me."

"Do you really think Lally—out of her senses?"

"She doesn't improve, does she?"

"No," Bella had to agree. "Every time she gets a new fright she's worse. It's as if someone knows they can do this to her, and takes pleasure in it. Just as the news about Molly is already in the newspapers so that it will do you harm. Guy—" unconsciously she had taken his hand and was holding it tightly, "do you think Noah can be carrying out his threat already?"

"From Newgate prison? That would be an impossibility."

"He wouldn't want to wait a whole year," Bella said instinctively. "Yes, I suppose it is an impossible idea. We'll find out where Molly is, and all will be well. If only Lally would get better. I've asked Norah to sleep with her tonight."

"Norah?"

"She's a nice reliable girl. Mrs. Walter found her to take Molly's place. Later I want her to be the baby's nurse. And Tottie—" Bella was growing more animated, "you'd be surprised. Actually, I think Joseph has taken a fancy to her. Or else he's good at protecting people the way he did his poor sick mother. I've seen him smiling at her, and there's nothing like a man's interest to perk up a girl. Though they're neither of them more than elderly children, poor things." Bella caught Guy's expression and said apologetically, "I'm chattering. We should be talking about more serious things."

He stood up.

"In the morning."

"Are you returning to London—immediately?"

"To make certain inquiries. But not for long."

Her heart leaped. She had the courage to say, "I'm sorry if I distressed you about this room."

"Distressed me? I think you overestimate your abilities."

"No!" she said passionately. "I'm flesh and blood. Feel me! Feel my hand, my arm."

His kindly mood had gone. His eyes glinted steel.

"Let that poor ghost go, Guy. Only you keep her here."

"You're shameless!"

"I have to be! You can go to other women. Why not me? If I were a woman in the street—"

His fingers cut into her wrist.

"You're my wife."

"Your *wife!*"

"According to our agreement."

"Unwanted, unloved," she said bitterly.

"You should have thought of that when you begged to take your sister's place."

"You would rather have poor Lally without her wits!"

"I would infinitely rather have neither of you," he said brutally, and turning abruptly left the room.

Bella lay back against the pillows. An occasional dry sob escaped her. Why couldn't she be tranquil, disciplined? Why couldn't she enjoy being treated like a tearful child? All this emotion was bad for the baby.

But she couldn't help it. The truth had come to her inexorably in the last few minutes. He might never stop hating and resenting her for being his wife, but she loved him. She loved him terribly and forlornly and forever.

Early in the morning a different crisis was precipitated. Lally was found wandering downstairs in her nightgown. She didn't seem to know where she was, and when Mrs. Walter tried to take her back to her room she thought she was being attacked, and screamed that she would not be put aboard a ship, or buried in the snow. Doctor Frobisher had to be sent for post-haste. He prescribed sedatives, but viewed the situation with the utmost gravity.

"I'm afraid she'll have to be taken away for a time," he told Bella. "I know of a very reputable home that takes cases like this. There's no use my concealing facts, Mrs. Raven. Your sister's mind is temporarily unhinged."

"Don't send her away!" Bella begged. "Guy! Poor Lally! I can't bear to have her sent away."

"Is there any alternative?" Guy asked the doctor.

"You could have a reliable woman to look after her, I suppose. Someone who can be trusted never to leave her. I'd much prefer that she was in a proper establishment for this kind of illness."

"Surrounded by others worse than herself?" Bella cried. "Then she'd never get better."

"I'll find a suitable woman when I return to London," said Guy. He didn't speak to Bella but to Doctor Frobisher, who hummed and hawed, and said that he could only give advice. Nevertheless, if that was the way they preferred it, he would take his leave. The patient had better be kept under sedatives until the nurse arrived.

"Thank you, Guy," said Bella fervently. "That was good of you. I know Lally will get better when the baby comes. That's what she's waiting for."

"You'll keep her away from the baby," Guy said sharply.

In spite of her gratitude, Bella's quick temper flared.

"As if Lally would hurt my baby! She'll be as gentle as an angel."

"How can you tell, with this obsession she has about infants? She must be watched all the time."

Obsession—it was not a nice word. It was what the scurrilous papers said Guy had for young women in distress. . . .

"This woman who is to watch Lally—she had better be elderly, or middle-aged at least. And plain."

Guy's voice was hard. "Why?"

"You know very well there wouldn't have been anything to base a scandal on if that wretched Molly hadn't been pretty. I suppose there might not have been any scandal at all if Lally and I had been homely."

She wasn't crying now, so he didn't have to be gentle. He could give her that long cool rakish look, that might very well justify the stories circulated about him, and say,

"Oh, indeed! For then it's most unlikely I would have come to your help. But I saw you leaning out of the window, beauty in distress."

"Guy, don't joke!"

"Why? Must we be deadly serious for the rest of our lives? Or must we speak the unpalatable truth as we did last night? Anyway, you wouldn't want your sister frightened out of her remaining wits by some old crone. Would you?"

Chapter 16

THE wrinkled monkeyish face looked up at Guy questioningly and with servility. Finely dressed gentlemen like this seldom visited Newgate prison.

"Did you want to visit the prisoners, sir?"

"No. I'm merely inquiring about their welfare."

"Oh, they're well, sir. Very well. Not a trace of jail fever."

"They haven't attempted to escape?"

"Ha ha! Ha ha ha! They may have attempted, sir, but they haven't succeeded."

"And they're due to be released when?"

"On the twelfth of December, sir. Nicely in time for Christmas. The old lady may go earlier for good conduct. She's been quite an example, clean, tidy, helpful to others. Has a Bible reading every evening to those who will listen."

"That doesn't surprise me," said Guy distastefully.

"You know her, sir? Did you think her wrongfully accused?"

"I accused her," said Guy harshly. "Her sentence was too light by ten years. Thank you and good day."

His next visit was to the house in Seven Dials.

He went on foot so as not to arouse too much notice. For all that, the ragged children and the women in doorways, brought out by the warm summer day, stared at the fine gentleman venturing into their territory. He soon had a clutch of skinny barefoot children, like a flock of moulting chickens, at his heels. The sun had not only brought out the inhabitants but the smells of the narrow airless streets. The dust underfoot reeked. A child whose entire clothing seemed to be a torn newspaper thrust a skeleton claw at him. He peered into the matted curtain of hair to see if it were a boy or a girl and failed to decide.

This blighted street was England, he thought. Just as much England as the smooth rich lawns and sweet air of Ravenscroft. No wonder vice flourished and crafty opportunists like Mrs. Proudfoot and her villainous son battened on the weakness and desperation of misery.

Aunt Aggie's modest house with its soot-grimed bricks certainly looked empty, its windows closed and the lace curtains drawn. Nevertheless, Guy rapped on the low door and impatiently motioned to the clustering urchins to be quiet while he listened. Was that a shuffling footstep inside?

An old woman stuck her head out of a window opposite. Her frizzed hair was like grey lichen.

"There's no one home there. They be in prison." She cackled maliciously. "Serve the old 'ooman right, with her stuck-up airs."

"Does no one live here now?" Guy asked.

"'s' all locked up. There be nobody there. In spite of what my old man says."

"What does he say?"

"Swears he saw a light two, three nights ago. I tell him it come out of a pint mug." The old crone with her broken teeth cackled again. "Who's to light a candle, I ask him? They's in prison, where they ought to be."

"Did anyone else see this light, or hear anything?"

"Naw. Not my old man neither. We sees nothin' and hears nothin' at nights. 's' only way."

Guy nodded. It was the only way. But he wasn't satisfied. He tossed the persistent children some coins and left them scuffling and fighting in the dust.

By a little reconnoitering he found he could reach the backyard of the house from a narrow and particularly evil-smelling alley. There didn't seem to be anybody about. He vaulted the tumbledown wall easily and found himself in the tiny yard. There was no snow now. The sour black earth kicked up in a fine dust. The small excavation where the baby had lain was still exposed. A broken-handled shovel lay nearby. Someone had broken the kitchen window. The gaping hold made it easy to peer into the bleak strip of room where Tottie had had her uneasy domain. Something scuttered and rustled. A rat probably. These old houses so near the Fleet river crawled with rats.

But a rat couldn't have lit a candle.

Guy found that by reaching through the hole in the window-pane he could turn the lock and push up the window. He smiled wryly as he stepped into the dubious room. He wasn't dressed for breaking into empty houses.

The place was familiar enough to him after his first visit there. He remembered the little parlour, its antimacassars and bobbled velvet covered now with a filter of dust. Without the warmth of firelight and lamplight and Aunt Aggie herself, whose cosiness couldn't be denied, it was a dreary little room, smelling musty and damp.

The stairs creaked with a painful protest beneath his weight. He wasn't going to search the whole house. His main objective was the bedroom at the top. The last time he had seen it, Lally had been sprawled in her deep sleep across the bed, and the girl who was now so improbably his wife had been shaking her sister and lifting her own distraught face to her rescuers. It seemed strange now to find the room completely empty. He scarcely knew what he had expected to find. Strewn garments? A dishevelled bed? Signs of a struggle?

There were certainly marks in the dust on the dressing-table, but they could have been made by rats. There was also a little water filmed with dust in the washbasin. Beyond that, nothing.

He had never believed Lally's fantasy about Aunt Aggie in the village, and even less had he thought the missing Molly a victim of these people who could just possibly have tentacles stretching out from Newgate prison. He had felt impelled to explore these possibilities and although he hadn't believed in them he felt a curious lift of spirits to find himself right. He hadn't realized that Noah's threat had weighed on him.

All the same, there were strange aspects. The speed with which the newspapers had had the story of Molly's disappearance, as if they had been fed with private information, and this surely not from Sir Henry Shields, who was no longer his rival. There was a personal touch to this new persecution which disturbed him.

But this drab little house was innocent. Or was it? Guy's eyes caught a dark gleam in a corner of the kitchen. For a moment he thought it a drop of blood. He stooped to pick up the object. It was an artificial cherry such as a woman might wear on her bonnet. One side was pitted with tiny teethmarks, which had obviously been made by a rat. The rat would have carried its disappointing trophy here from where it had been dropped.

Who wore a bonnet trimmed with a cluster of cherries?

Mrs. Proudfoot? Isabella or her sister? Molly? Or one of the faceless stream of young women whom he was certain had passed through this house?

How was he to know? But the small object lying in the palm of his hand was almost free of dust. It seemed very unlikely it had lain there all the months Aunt Aggie had been in prison.

Guy was glad to find Doctor Bushey at home. There was a great deal to talk about.

The doctor was inclined to view Molly's disappearance with nothing but indignation.

"The ungrateful wretch! Now there I thought was a young woman anxious to turn over a new leaf. She had a chance to become respectable, get herself a husband, perhaps. But she's thrown it all away. Well, you can never tell. You have to give them a chance. I'm sorry I let you in for this new trouble. But it'll blow over."

"I wonder."

"Eh? You think it's not all cut and dried?"

"I'm not sure. Two hours ago I'd have agreed with you. But since then I've found this."

He exhibited the cherry and described how he had found it. He said, "I'm going to the police. I want this girl's disappearance thoroughly investigated. I know it's a hundred chances to one she has gone off with a man, she was apt to make friendships easily, I'm told. But the one odd chance she hasn't must be investigated. You see, if it should prove true, this can happen again. From my house. A war of attrition, so to speak."

Doctor Bushey regarded Guy with astonishment.

"My boy, what you're suggesting is fantastic."

"Don't you come across fantastic happenings every day in your round?"

"Oh, aye. That's human nature. But you're endowing this old woman with diabolical powers. Do you think she projected herself from Newgate into the village of Underwood as a sort of apparition? Or more likely, though still improbable, that she had a double? And if she had, and if Molly were lured away by some rich promises, would they do something so foolish as to take her to that same house?"

"It might be their only headquarters—I mean, they might not have had time to advise their contact from the ship due in port of a new address. In any case, that street, as you must realize, tells no tales."

"Fantastic!" muttered Doctor Bushey.

"I expect you're right. I expect the whole thing's on my nerves. On top of it all, my wretched sister-in-law seems to have gone out of her mind. That won't surprise you, perhaps."

"I'm very sorry to hear it. She has an unstable personality. It's her method of escape from reality."

"Who wouldn't escape from reality. Poverty, disease, death." Guy was thinking of the children with the grey ancient faces, the desiccated hands.

Doctor Bushey shot him a shrewd glance. "At least you made the right choice when you married."

Guy's mouth twisted.

"You think so?"

"Good heavens, boy, would you have wanted an hysteric the mother of your child? I warrant Isabella isn't out of her mind."

"Far from it. At least, not in the same way."

"You haven't really seen her yet, have you?" the doctor murmured, his eyes bland.

"Seen her! I am supposed to be the father of her child!"

Doctor Bushey began to chuckle maddeningly.

"Why, I believe she tricked you! Did she trick you, boy?"

"If you ask me," Guy said, his temper rising, "I've been tricked all round. Caroline dead, my mother alienated, my career gone, married to a shrew!"

"And able to see only an inch in front of you. Poor boy, poor boy! Let's have some brandy. It won't give you long sight, you've got to develop that yourself, but it might help to clear the way slightly."

"Oh, stop your damned riddles! I can manage my own affairs. When the child's born I shall come back to London permanently." Guy took the proffered glass, his eyes still smouldering. "And I'll get a bill through Parliament on slum clearance if it kills me."

"In the meantime?" Doctor Bushey prodded.

"In the meantime I need a woman, someone with some nursing experience, to take care of this mad creature I have foisted on me. She'll have to be watched all the time. My wife doesn't seem to realize the danger of letting her near the baby. She'll most likely smother it when she thinks she's only showing it affection."

Doctor Bushey nodded gravely.

"I see you understand her condition. She has a fixation on infants since her unfortunate experience. You're quite right, she shouldn't be left alone with the child. But certainly let her share it a little."

"Oh, my wife will see to that, you can be sure."

"Your wife shows a warm devotion to her sister. Well, then, we must find a suitable woman. I'd suggest someone young and kind to appeal to Miss Lally."

"That's exactly my own idea."

"But not Miss Isabella's?"

"My wife is suspicious of everyone, even, if you can believe it, of Caroline."

"Women!" said Doctor Bushey shaking his head. "Unpredictable creatures! Have another brandy, my boy. And did you know your mother has been ill?"

"How should I? She refuses to see me."

"You mustn't take women entirely at their word. They don't expect you to. Anyway," Doctor Bushey twirled the liquid in his glass. "She's well on the way to recovery now. She had a slight lung infection. Nothing more."

His mother's illness may have been slight, but it was enough to send Guy hurrying to visit her. He only half expected to be admitted, and was surprised when he was bidden to her bedroom. Perhaps her illness had softened her attitude, although it did not appear so by her outward appearance. Propped against pillows, a ridiculously befrilled cap obscuring almost everything but her sharp nose and the inquisitive glitter of her eyes, she gave no sign of pleasure at her son's visit.

"You come with your tail between your legs, I hope," she said in her rasping voice. "A fine mess you've made of your life. What's this new scandal about a housemaid?"

"The scandal is in the minds of news-mongers. How are you, Mamma? I'm sorry to see you ill. Why wasn't I informed?"

"Because I wasn't dying. I have absolutely no intention of sending for you except to attend my deathbed."

Guy's lips twitched. He was feeling a great deal better already. He had hated the breach with his mother. She was the most exasperating person in the world, but an incomparable wit sharpener. He was in need of having his wits sharpened.

"Then I'm glad I came while you can still hold a conversation. What does Doctor Bushey say?"

"What does that old fool ever say? Rest, physic, a melancholy reminder of one's age. I have had a small chill, nothing more. I'm getting rid of my nurse next week. I never did need the woman. Hannah could have managed very well."

"Your nurse? What's she like? Old? Young?"

"Good gracious, boy, what's that to do with you? Have you an obsession about servant girls? What did happen to this silly creature at Ravenscroft? Did she run away to you, or from you?"

"My God, Mamma, if you were a man I'd call you out for that."

Mrs. Raven sighed deeply. A tinge of colour had come into her parchment cheeks.

"Thank heaven, this impossible wife hasn't made you lose your spirit."

"Did you think she could?"

"I'd have denied you were my son if that had happened. But you're breeding from her!"

"So you know that, too."

"Of course I know it. The girl came and shouted the news at me like some gipsy shouting her wares."

"Hardly, Mamma," Guy murmured, but he was suddenly amused, seeing Bella with her blazing eyes and her indignation. And remembering with sudden violence the way her body had showed through her thin nightgown that night. That memory had been deliberately crushed for a long time.

"She's healthy?" Mrs. Raven's voice was casual, intended to disguise anxiety.

"Extremely."

"Then why the interest in my nurse?"

"A woman's required for the sister. She's had some kind of a breakdown. The doctor recommended a nursing home, but Isabella prefers her to remain at home."

"You mean she's out of her mind? Then I'd get rid of her. Immediately. But I suppose you can refuse your wife nothing in her condition."

His mother's sarcasm stung. "She has little enough!" he retorted.

"Little enough! A rich husband, a mansion, a child. And you call that little enough. How does she assess her possessions, this nobody from the gutter?"

"She has a half-witted sister and a dumb maidservant. Otherwise, nothing but enemies."

"Faugh! Melodrama!"

"She needs friends," Guy heard himself saying. It was his mother's implacable antagonism that made him defend his wife. "There seems to be some kind of conspiracy. I don't think I imagine it. That servant girl disappearing . . . I admit I engaged her hastily and perhaps too trustingly. That comes from old Bushey's sentimentality. But from now on I intend to exercise the greatest care. That's why I asked about your nurse. Would she be a suitable woman?"

"I'm glad to hear you've learnt your lesson about picking up people off the street. The poor aren't all deserving. Nor are they unfortunate innocents. You'll find that missing girl completely corrupted—if she ever turns up again. I hope for your sake she doesn't. But Miss Thompson isn't that type. Doctor Bushey knew better than to foist any of his converts on to me. She's a genteel person, has pleasant manners. Interview her, if you like. She can give you her own references." Mrs. Raven's colour was parchment again, her eyelids drooping.

"You're tired, Mamma. I'll leave you. Will you come down to Ravenscroft to convalesce?"

The befrilled head sank deeper into the soft pillow. Only the old lady's nose was visible.

"And forgive that little upstart for wearing the Raven diamonds. Her chin in the air—imagining herself a queen! And I expected not to turn my back! Forget! Forgive!" The rasping voice was only a mutter in the snowy pillow. "I've never heard the words."

Chapter 17

So Miss Clara Thompson arrived at Ravenscroft. She had smooth dark hair parted in the middle and drawn down primly over her ears, black cherry eyes and a small curved mouth that seemed to be always smiling. She was smiling into Guy's eyes as he handed her out of the carriage—he had brought her down from London himself—and she continued to smile, but in a subtly different way, at Bella when they met.

This was no flighty Molly nor yet a young woman who had been in distressed circumstances. For Miss Thompson had a rounded well-nourished look about her, as if she had never been hungry or afraid or in need of help. Guy said little about her except that she had been nursing his mother and had frequently nursed cases for Doctor Bushey.

"That silly old man!" Bella exclaimed unfairly. "His heart's too soft for his head."

"But my mother's isn't."

Bella had to agree to that, although she added that Mrs. Raven would hardly put herself out to send someone whom she and Lally would like.

"Don't you like Miss Thompson?" Guy asked patiently.

What was it she didn't like about the woman? She was soft-voiced, clever with Lally who had to be coaxed and humoured. Although she took her meals with Guy and Bella she didn't obtrude, speaking only when spoken to and then with impeccable politeness. She must have known Bella's history—who didn't?—but there was no sign of scorn or patronage in her manner.

Yet all the time there was something, a subtle confidence, almost a veiled amusement. And she got on too well with the other servants, even Mrs. Walter who might have been expected to feel some rivalry. It seemed odd that she should set out so deliberately to be liked, as if it mattered that old Broome or the awkward tongue-tied Joseph should be her admirers.

That was, she got on with all the servants except Tottie.

But perhaps she felt that Tottie was too unimportant and miniscule to bother about. And harmless because of her lack of speech?

That thought only came to Bella after she noticed Tottie try to shrink out of sight when Miss Thompson came into the room. It was months now since Tottie had reverted to that old instinctive fear. Was it fear or rather just an enormous shyness in the presence of someone so brisk and confident as Miss Thompson. Bella didn't know. She had never been able to persuade any intelligible sound from Tottie's lips, but it did seem that the girl was increasing her efforts to make herself understood, even in her happy good-morning bob and mumble with which she greeted Bella each morning. Her face had grown round and rosy and her starved flat child's body had softened into a definite shape beneath her neat poplin gowns. She blushed easily, and sometimes unmistakably giggled. She had learned to launder and iron even to Mrs. Walter's satisfaction, and her now chubby and healthy hands had become adept at twisting Bella's hair into fashionable styles. It was nice to have someone so quiet and willing and adoring. It was nice to be adored, Bella added honestly to herself. It wasn't an emotion she had much of in this house.

But Tottie definitely wasn't the same girl since Miss Thompson's arrival.

When Bella suggested this to Guy she thought she caught a flicker of some deeper interest in his eye before he said easily,

"Pooh! She's shy about being teased. We caught her making daisy chains with Joseph in the orchard."

"We?"

"I met Miss Thompson strolling in the garden last evening."

"Oh," said Bella, remembering quite distinctly what Miss Thompson had worn at dinner last night, a grey silk gown, perfectly suitable for someone in her position, but with a fichu of very beautiful lace that could hardly have been bought out of her wages as a nurse. She had touched it and said that it had belonged to her grandmother, making Bella inevitably conjure up the picture of some aristocratic old lady with plenty of servants of her own. Which no doubt was exactly what Miss Thompson had intended her to think, and perhaps it was true. Although Bella was more inclined to think the lace had been the gift of some grateful patient. Or perhaps something the sly creature had helped herself to while a patient lay dying.

Her thoughts were uncharitable, but she meant them to be so. She and Lally had sat in the drawing-room after dinner last night, she with a piece of embroidery that bored her unendurably, Lally with knitting that lay idle in fingers no longer able to work with precision. The evenings were always like this, long, monotonous, the light never seeming quite to die. It was only fair that Miss Thompson should have a little relief from her care of Lally. And Bella herself had grown too cumbersome to walk far.

But it would have been more thoughtful of Guy to entertain his wife and sister-in-law than to walk in the garden with Miss Thompson. Bella found herself unable to believe that their meeting had been accidental. She had thought that Guy was staying at Ravenscroft only to await the birth of the baby. But then she had seen him lighting Miss Thompson's candle at night and handing it to her with a courteous little bow, twice they had been laughing together in the drawing-room before dinner. Once he had drawn back a little too abruptly when Bella had come into the room.

And Miss Thompson's black cherry eyes had a secret gleam. She seemed to take especial care with her appearance.

"You never did tell me about Miss Thompson's background," Bella said to Guy.

"Didn't I? I'm sure I did. I told you she is alone in the world, like you and Eulalie. Her parents are dead and her only brother was killed in the fighting at Sebastopol. She decided to emulate Miss Nightingale in a nursing career, but to do it at home where she feels nurses are needed just as much as they are in theatres of war."

"Why hasn't she married?"

Guy gave her his cool glance.

"I've hardly presumed to inquire into her private affairs."

"She's good-looking. She must have had opportunities. Is she too ambitious?"

"My love, aren't you being a little carping? Miss Thompson is doing the job she came here to do. Your sister likes her and is much more docile with her. Isn't that the beginning and end of

170

the matter? We don't have to inquire into her ambitions or emotions. They're her affair."

"They're not if they lead to trouble as Molly's did."

"Oh, come, my dear, Miss Thompson isn't the kind to have assignations in the village with yokels like Tom Field."

No, thought Bella. Miss Thompson cast her net for bigger fish. The master of the house, no less. A careful toilette, strolls in the dusky garden, whispers over lit candles . . .

Or was her mind growing unhinged like Lally's, so that she turned every trifle into a dark shadow, a significant happening.

Even the cherry off Aunt Aggie's bonnet. But it was Guy who had thought that significant. He had asked her if Molly had had a bonnet trimmed with artificial cherries, and she had said no, that was Aunt Aggie.

How could she forget? Both she and Lally had admired the nodding luscious bunch of them on Aunt Aggie's bonnet in the coach that very first day. And later Lally had insisted that the woman in the teashop had had cherries on her bonnet, which had seemed to Lally irrefutable confirmation that she had been Aunt Aggie. But Doctor Frobisher said that must have been an hallucination. Lally had thought the woman Aunt Aggie. So she had dressed her as her mind remembered her.

Guy had thought the information important enough to have the police pay a special visit to the house in Seven Dials and search the cupboards and wardrobes to find the cherry-trimmed bonnet. But it hadn't been there. And Aunt Aggie hadn't worn it to prison. She had sat in the dock in a humble black bonnet trimmed with nothing more frivolous than a few jet beads.

So where was the famous cherry-trimmed creation? Had the rats eaten it all except one last cherry?

And where was Molly? Guy's influence in the county had caused a widespread police search which so far had yielded no clues whatever. The girl had disappeared without trace.

Then something did turn up. A small boy had picked up a mesh reticule such as ladies wore on their wrists in the evenings. It had been run over by the wheel of a vehicle and ground into the mud. The boy had found it contained, together with a handkerchief and a muddied scrap of paper, a shilling, so he had kept the shilling and hidden the purse. The visit of the police, a routine one they were making to each cottage in the vicinity, had scared the child and he had confessed his discovery.

The muddied scrap of paper was found to be a note. It said, "Instead of coming to The Feathers tonight meet me at crossroads, same time. Have made arrangements. T."

The initial T of course indicated Tom. Tom Field. And there was no doubt that that was how Molly had interpreted it. When Tom was interviewed he admitted that he and Molly had talked of running off, but they had never fixed it finally, and how could the note be his since he couldn't read or write?

So Molly had obviously been lured into a trap. Someone had been at the crossroads that night with a vehicle of some kind, and she had been spirited away. To where?

How had Molly got the note? No one knew. Perhaps it had been slipped into her hand that afternoon when she had been in the village with Lally. Nobody knew anything. All the servants at Ravenscroft were questioned. Tottie was the only one who had no answers but then poor Tottie couldn't speak. All that happened was that she got back her look of slack-mouthed stupidity which Bella knew was caused by terror. Bella understood the terror well enough, for she was beginning to feel it herself.

The safe world had vanished. It never had been safe. The shadow of Seven Dials was back, and overpoweringly threatening. No one could be trusted.

That night Bella had one of Lally's nightmares about the dead baby. She thought she had it in her arms, its tiny frozen face against her breast. She woke screaming, and Guy came hurrying in from the adjoining bedroom.

"What is it? Are you ill? Is the baby coming?"

The shreds of terror were still round her and she couldn't even take satisfaction in his very evident concern.

"Do they have designs on my baby?" she whispered. "I'm so afraid."

"You've had a nightmare," said Guy in relief.

The wavering candle flame seemed only to accentuate the shadows. Bella's arm still felt curiously the weight of that weightless infant.

"Lally said they would come for it."

"Lally's mad."

"She has intuitions which are true. She knew they'd never forgive us for digging up that baby—not letting it stay hidden. They'll bury mine instead."

"What nonsense! What utter nonsense! Do I have to remind you again that they're in prison?"

"They'll be out soon."

"Not until December."

"For Christmas. Do you think they'll have Christmas dinner in the parlour? There'll be the fire burning and the lamp lit and the curtains drawn. It's a very cosy room. And the cradle on the hearth. I can't see that room without the cradle on the hearth, although I know it won't be there. Oh, Guy!" her voice held entreaty, "I'm talking like Lally."

"You've had a nightmare. I'll ring for Norah to make you a hot drink."

"Our baby will be exactly eight weeks old then."

"When?"

"When they come out of prison."

"Stop thinking of it. You're perfectly safe." In the dim light Guy's face had grim lines. "I'll see that you're safe."

"Guy, Molly must be found."

"She will be found. Don't doubt it."

Guy was right, Molly was found, though not until six weeks later and then in a not unexpected fashion. A young woman arrested in Piccadilly for being drunk and disorderly gave her name as Molly Hancock and, recognizing that she might be the missing maidservant from Ravenscroft, the police sent for Guy to identify her.

He not only identified Molly, but Molly, brazen and impertinent, identified him as the gentleman who had kidnapped her that night at the crossroads.

Nothing would shake her from that story. Although it was pointed out to her that Guy had been in London that night, she swore he had been the gentleman in the carriage waiting at the crossroads.

She said she had thought at first it was Tom Field, who had written her the letter, and had begun to climb in eagerly. Then she realized she had been mistaken, and dropped her reticule in the ensuing struggle.

But Mr. Raven, she said, staring boldly at Guy, had been too strong and had overpowered her. She admitted that after the initial struggle she had gone willingly enough.

"But he soon got tired of me," she complained. "He turned me out without a penny. It's through him I had to go on the streets."

Guy could scarcely believe the change in the neat and self-respecting young woman whom he had sent down to Ravenscroft. Molly's hair was tangled and lank, her gown dirty, her face hectically flushed, and with that look of almost frenzied boldness. He had no notion of what she had gone through since her departure from Ravenscroft but he did guess now that beneath her brazen demeanour she was terrified. Scared to death.

The young police inspector, scenting duplicity, questioned the girl remorselessly.

If Mr. Raven had her in this house in the country why should he use such elaborate means to abduct her?

He'd hardly keep her side by side with his wife, would he, said Molly insolently. He wanted her to himself, hidden away, secret. He took her to a house near the river. No, she didn't think she could identify it again. It was dark when she arrived and dark the night she left. She knew it was near the river because she could smell the mud when the tide went out, and hear foghorns. She thought the two rooms in which she was confined, the outside door always locked, were rented from a woman who lived downstairs. The windows faced a brick wall. She couldn't look out to see where she was, nor was there any way to escape.

If she had wanted to, she added slyly.

Mr. Raven's wife was in a certain condition and it was well known that that was a time for husbands to be unfaithful. She gave this information gratuitously. In any case, everyone knew what sort of a marriage it was. Mr. Raven had been caught in his own snare that time.

Here Guy interrupted the girl's bitter invective.

"Someone has made you say all this, haven't they?" He spoke quite gently. "I don't know what you've been threatened with. But these people aren't all powerful. You're quite safe now. Just tell the truth and you'll be protected."

The girl looked at him with her sunken sullen eyes.

"I am telling the truth. Every word of what I said is true. I'll swear it to my dying day."

Bella said, with dry lips, "What are you going to do now?"

"What can I do? It's my word against hers, and unfortunately, with the sort of popularity I'm enjoying at present, the world prefers to believe the girl."

"It's outrageous!"

Guy gave a wry smile.

"Thank you, my dear, for believing me. You have little enough reason to."

"That little slut! She's quite without conscience."

"No. She's frightened. That's all."

They were all frightened—except perhaps Guy who was looking quite calm and unruffled and pretending that this new persecution was trifling and would be forgotten in a day. Perhaps it would be. But what would happen next?

"Guy, that old woman was visiting her daughter in Twickenham. That's near the river, isn't it?"

"What old woman?"

"The one Lally thought was Aunt Aggie. Though she wasn't, of course. But Molly did say the house was near the river."

"Molly has been rehearsed in a story that is nothing but a malicious fabrication. There was no house, no river, no foghorns."

"Then it was the house in Seven Dials," Bella said, in a whisper. She added helplessly, "Poor Molly. No wonder she's frightened."

Chapter 18

In exactly her old sane voice Lally said, "I think you ought to know, Bella, I saw Mr. Raven kissing Miss Thompson last night."

Bella had intended never to speak sharply to poor Lally again. But her retort leaped out. "Don't be absurd! You must have dreamed it. You know you're always having nightmares."

Lally shook her head slowly. Her eyes were wide, serious, alarmingly sober. "It wasn't a dream, Bella. It was just before we went upstairs. Mr. Raven lit a candle from the hall stand, and then as he handed it to Miss Thompson he kissed her on the cheek. She stood and stared. She looked quite embarrassed. But pleased."

By enormous self-control Bella kept her voice calm.

"I expect you did dream it, Lally dear. But if you didn't Miss Thompson will have to go."

"She looked pleased," Lally repeated.

A little later her slow wits reminded her what Bella had said.

"Don't send her away, Bella. I wouldn't have told you if I thought you would send her away. She's kind to me. She doesn't scold. Last night—"

"What about last night?"

Lally frowned, her lovely eyes going blank.

"I can't remember. I find it so hard to remember things."

"You said Miss Thompson had been kissing my husband."

"No, no I didn't. It wasn't like that. It was him kissing her. He was holding the candle crooked, spilling grease. Bella! Bella, don't look so angry! I don't like you looking angry! After all, it's nice that people should be kind and loving." Lally turned her large imploring eyes on Bella. "Don't send her away. She doesn't stare at me. She says "What a baby you are!" and helps me dress, and doesn't laugh when I can't do up the buttons. I don't know why I can no longer do up buttons. And my knitting gets into such a snarl. Look! Why is it so snarled?"

Bella gently took the knitting away from Lally's clumsy and fumbling fingers.

"I'll untangle it, love. I expect you're tired."

"You won't send Miss Thompson away, will you, Bella?"

What could she do? Lally was making encouraging progress, Doctor Frobisher said. One couldn't risk her having a relapse.

"Not if you insist."

"Oh, thank you, Bella. You're so good to me." Lally, with her swift changes of mood, suddenly began to titter. "After all, Mr. Raven has a weakness for women, hasn't he? Remember, he wanted to marry both of us."

Bella soberly studied her reflection in the mirror in her bedroom. Not even a crinoline concealed her condition now. She was as big as an elephant. It wasn't to be wondered at that Guy sought more attractive companionship. She would bide her time until the baby was born and she had got back her slim figure. Then that sneaking cat Clara Thompson would get her deserts.

At least Guy was staying at Ravenscroft, and even if it seemed much more likely that Miss Thompson, rather than his coming child, kept him there, Bella was infinitely glad to have him. The fear that hung over her like a shadow, growing a little darker with each falling rose and yellowing leaf remained in control while he was near. But one day he would laugh at her fancies and go back to London and it would be winter, and Aunt Aggie and Noah would be free.

It must be her condition that made her so easy a prey to her imagination. She had faced things blithely enough before. It was the long dull days of waiting. She hated inactivity and the harmless indoor pursuits with which ladies passed their time bored her to distraction. Letter writing—she had no one to write to. Embroidery—she hadn't the patience for it, nor for sewing the minute garments for her baby. Lally, when she was in one of her good moods, and Norah, were so much better at the cross stitching and the tiny embroidered flowers on bibs and bonnets. Pressing flowers in an album or painting in water-colours she regarded as quite useless occupations. There really seemed to be nothing to do except sit at the window and watch the autumn mists turning the air smoky blue beneath the trees in the park, and count the leaves falling.

Besides, from this vantage point, she could see Guy when he rode back from some activity of his own. He was perfectly polite to her nowadays, they hadn't quarrelled for a long time, but he never told her where he was going or what he was doing. There was no more news of the treacherous Molly in London, poor Molly who had come to a bad end. That sharp short scandal had blown over and Guy's name, mercifully, was no longer in the newspapers. Indeed, the last few weeks had been remarkably peaceful with Guy as courteous to her as if she were a visiting cousin or the sister of a friend, and Lally improving encouragingly.

But it was a spurious peace. For Miss Thompson, for all her appearance of being constantly attentive to Lally, watched the window, too, and more often than not happened to be crossing the hall, or just about to go upstairs, when Guy came in. Or she would shiver at dinner because she had left her shawl in the drawing-room, and Guy would fetch it, draping it over her white shoulders. Bella's self-control was strained to breaking point. For Lally's sake she somehow kept her temper. Also, she knew it would be a weakness to have Miss Thompson dismissed from jealousy. It would only accentuate all those stories about her husband's vulnerability for women. Miss Thompson must be found out in some other misdemeanour.

But all her wisdom was discarded the day she heard Mrs. Walter and Miss Thompson whispering together.

They must have thought she was still in the morning-room with Lally. They wouldn't know that she had grown so intolerably restless she had to walk about the house, since the early mist had turned to drizzle and it was too wet to stroll in the garden. She had crossed the ballroom, and wandered through the orangery, and was about to enter the drawing-room when she heard the low voices.

"You'd better be careful, my girl. Don't lose your head." That was Mrs. Walter, brusque and unsentimental. Mrs. Walter had never been over-friendly with Miss Thompson, probably because she resented her superiority.

"I'm not losing my head."

"What makes you think he'll fall in love with you? He's as cold and calculating as the devil."

"He wasn't always, I'm told."

"You're thinking of his first wife. That's why he's as he is now. I don't see why you think you can change him if his new wife can't."

"Her!" Miss Thompson gave an intolerable snicker. "You know *her* story. Naturally he wouldn't love her."

"No, nor anyone else. Not even his lights of love."

"I have no intention of being his light of love."

There was a hiss of indrawn breath.

"Save us, you wouldn't—"

Miss Thompson gave a little trill of laughter. The blood bursting in her head, Bella flung open the door. There was a whisk of skirts as Mrs. Walter moved swiftly to gather up fallen rose petals from a polished table, muttering something about careless maids. Miss Thompson didn't move. She lifted her little pointed chin and looked inquiringly at Bella.

"Oh dear, is Miss Eulalie needing me? I'm so sorry, I'll go at once."

She had gone, composedly, before Bella could speak. She seemed quite unashamed, almost glad that Bella might have overheard that outrageous conversation.

"Mrs. Walter," Bella said icily, "I don't approve of servants gossiping."

She had never seen Mrs. Walter in any state but her prim docile one. Even now, after the briefest flicker of fury in her eyes, she had herself in hand, and said quietly, "If you're referring to me and Miss Thompson, madam, we weren't gossiping. I was merely attempting to give Miss Thompson some advice on a foolish attachment she has formed."

Was the woman being insolent? It didn't seem so, but how could one read beneath her servility?

"Miss Thompson's moral life doesn't come within your duties, Mrs. Walter. I'd advise you to get on with your legitimate tasks. You may go."

After that it was a matter of waiting until the evening when Guy came in. She could have ordered Miss Thompson to pack her bags and be out of the house before Guy returned. She was pretty certain if she did that the woman would find some means of communicating with him, and making herself out to be the injured innocent. No, she must somehow provoke Miss Thompson into admitting her ambitious plan to Guy himself.

What would she say? "I think Miss Thompson is planning to run off with you, my love . . ." "I think Miss Thompson is waiting for me to die in childbirth . . ."

At least the dinner-table conversation would be enlivened tonight, she thought grimly. No more inventing polite comments to break the long silences. No more pretending she found Miss Thompson's replies interesting.

The afternoon must be spent preparing Lally for the shock of Miss Thompson's departure.

It was true that Lally was so much better she didn't require constant supervision. But by some freak of fate a storm blew up that afternoon and Lally hated storms. The wild wind and the sudden showers of leaves and the black clouds bringing dusk far too early filled the house with uneasiness. Doors banged and curtains billowed. A great cloud of smoke and soot came down the chimney in the morning-room, so they had to retire to the drawing-room where a fresh fire was lit. But the lamps were not enough to brighten the long room, and Lally, crouched over the fire, abruptly reverted to one of her worst moods.

"It's going to snow, Bella. Where will you hide the baby?"

"Lally dearest, the baby hasn't come yet."

"But it has! I saw it in the cradle. It was so tiny . . ." Lally began to walk about the room in distress, as if she no longer recognized her surroundings. Then suddenly, with her nose pressed against the window, she cried loudly, "Bella, there's Noah! Look! Over there under the copper beech!"

Bella flew to the window, unable to stop herself. Sure enough, in the premature dusk, she could make out a figure under the great spreading beech tree. For a moment it looked a wild sinister figure, wearing a cloak billowing in the breeze. But almost immediately she burst out laughing, saying that it was Joseph sheltering from a shower, a sack wrapped round his cowering shoulders.

At that moment Miss Thompson came in, and Lally exclaimed in exactly Bella's tone of asperity, "Don't be silly, Bella. He intends you to think he's Joseph. But he's Noah. Isn't he, Miss Thompson?"

"No!" cried Miss Thompson, her hand at her throat.

Bella looked at her curiously.

"Do you know Noah, too?"

"No, no, of course I don't. It's only that Miss Eulalie's talked so much about him. I felt startled—"

She was startled enough for the colour to have left her face. But she recovered quickly when she saw that the sheltering figure was indeed Joseph.

"I was foolish. It couldn't have been the terrible Noah. Come, Miss Eulalie—"

"I think you'd better take her to her room," said Bella. "Give her some of her sedative. The storm's upset her."

"Yes, Mrs. Raven. I will, at once. But what about you, Mrs. Raven?"

All at once, she seemed very anxious to please. But no doubt she was thinking of the episode that morning, not of the fright she had just had . . .

The wind was still battering against the walls when they sat down to dinner, the three of them. In spite of the well built house, somehow the draughts came in, and the candle flames in branching silver candlesticks flickered constantly. Miss Thompson, no doubt deliberately, was wearing her plainest gown, and for once looked dowdy and pale. She kept her eyes downcast, not responding even to Guy's attentiveness. There was no doubt she had had a fright. The last thing she would want would be to be dismissed.

So much for that, thought Bella, and opened her mouth to speak.

Her words were unrehearsed and surprised even herself.

"Don't worry Miss Thompson, Guy. She had a bad fright this afternoon. She thought she saw Noah on the lawn sheltering under the copper beech."

"Noah?" said Guy sharply, looking at Miss Thompson. "Do you know our archfiend, too? My wife and her sister constantly think they are being persecuted, by his ghost presumably, since he himself is still in prison. But I didn't know you subscribed to this fantasy."

"It's only that Miss Eulalie talks of him a great deal." Miss Thompson's voice was low and calm but she didn't look up and she was still very pale. "From her description of him, I hope never to set eyes on him."

"Oh, he's quite a good-looking fellow in his way," Guy said easily. "I can imagine some women admiring that black visage."

"Not Miss Thompson," said Bella. "She admires an entirely different type of man. Don't you, Miss Thompson?"

She hardly knew what response to expect from that remark, certainly not the quick intimate glance that passed between Miss Thompson and Guy. For a moment it was as if she were not there. Or did they think her blind? Couldn't she interpret the adoring light in that shameless creature's eyes, and the tenderness—a tenderness he had never shown to her—in her husband's?

In the next moment they were both looking at her, two pairs of eyes, polite, disinterested, as if she were no more than a shadow and deserved as little notice.

"What were you about to say, my love?" Guy inquired courteously.

The sheer blatancy of it was beyond endurance. Bella was on her feet and hardly knowing what she did, leaned forward to snatch a candle from the candlestick.

"I wouldn't dream of boring you with my trivial remarks. Continue your conversation with Miss Thompson. She knows a better and quicker way to ruin your career than I ever did. I am going upstairs."

"Bella—"

The intimate shortened version of her name caught her ear as she flung round to go. She couldn't help turning back, and it was then that the candle, held in her violently trembling hand, caught the ruffled lace of her gown. She screamed as the hot flame scorched her face. A violent pain shot through her body. She seemed to be consumed with fire. She was aware of falling, then of being held tightly, swaddled in something, and the room going dark.

When it grew light again there seemed to be a great many faces bending over her. She could hear Guy's voice from a long way off, "Not burnt, thank God! We got the flames out in time. But the doctor had better be sent for."

Bella tried to speak. She wanted to say that she must be burnt badly, otherwise why should this pain be wrenching her. She saw Miss Thompson's pale face bending too close, the black eyes full of triumph. Miss Thompson would have liked to see her burnt to charred ash. Even the baby— Oh, it was the baby giving her the pain . . .

Someone was lifting her. She could smell scorched clothing,

182

and through that the faint pleasant eau de cologne her husband used. She had so longed to be held like this in his arms, and now it was spoilt by the pain and her faintness and shock. Everything was always spoilt . . .

She must have fainted again, for somehow she was in bed and the lamp lit at her side. Now it was Mrs. Walter's face bending over her, and beyond it Norah's frightened one.

"Don't leave her—with him," she muttered.

"Who, madam? Who are you talking about?"

She shuddered as a new wave of pain poured over her. She was gripping something. A hand. Guy's hand. It must be, for now his face was there, shadowed, grim. Her enemy. Why had he smothered the flames when he like Miss Thompson must hope that she would die? He had sworn to her that he would never love again, that dead Caroline had his heart for ever. But that was before he had known how susceptible he could be to black cherry eyes and a secret smile.

Poor Guy, she suddenly thought. It wasn't his fault that she and Lally were round his neck like millstones. She must summon up enough magnanimity to set him free. Now, before she died . . .

"I shall do—exactly the same again—if you look at her like you did." Again her words bore no relation to her intentions. But she doubted if he had heard. His face remained there, just as lined and grim. Suddenly she remembered how he had looked at her the night she had asked him to marry her instead of Lally. He had wondered then if he could find her desirable. But there had been too much to overcome, his dead love, his feeling of being trapped, his resentment. Even the baby was an accident, a mistake he was determined not to repeat. Now there was nothing between them but their gripped hands, wet with perspiration.

"Are you always going to hate me? Will you never have any regard for me?" Her words were cut off by the pain, inexorable now, beyond bearing. The light faded. She was dimly conscious of a flurry of movement. Her clinging fingers were wrenched open and left empty. Someone far away said, "Of course I have regard for you."

Or did she imagine that?

"Now, Mrs. Raven, grip this. Scream as loud as you like. The little one's chosen a fine stormy night. There now. Thank you, Mrs. Walter. Oh, shock, certainly. For once all those fiddling faddling clothes women wear were a blessing. There seem to be

183

no burns. And your prompt action, Mr. Raven. I think you'd better leave us now. Mrs. Walter and I—"

"No!" shrieked Bella. "Don't let her touch my baby!"

"Decidedly shock," came Doctor Frobisher's voice from far far away. "Pity. Unfortunate. Now, my dear . . ."

Chapter 19

"Oh dear, madam, you screamed and said I wasn't to touch your baby!" Mrs. Walter, fussing by the bedside, was almost human, her long face creased in the beginnings of a benevolent smile.

Bella stirred sleepily, reluctant to come back from oblivion. Then a little pang of pleasure struck her as she remembered the snuffling, whimpering bundle that had been laid in her arms, and the blissful end of pain.

"My baby—"

"The sweetest little girl, madam."

"I promised him a boy. I always disappoint—" She stopped abruptly, on guard again.

"If you mean the master, madam, he's ever so pleased with his little daughter."

My husband has very good manners, Bella thought. Except when he forgets me altogether and gazes across the candlelight into another pair of eyes . . .

"I'll tell the nurse you're awake, madam."

"Nurse?"

"Oh dear, yes, Doctor Frobisher sent for one in a great hurry. You gave us all a fright, madam. But all's well that ends well."

Bella looked into Mrs. Walter's familiar dour face, unreadable as always, although it did seem that the woman had been moved to a little warmth by the arrival of the baby.

"And by the way, madam, if I may say something."

"Go on, Mrs. Walter."

"I think you misunderstood what you overheard between me and Miss Thompson yesterday. She's a designing creature, but the gentleman she's interested in is a stranger to you. Begging your pardon for taking this liberty, madam—"

Could she have heard wrongly? Could her suspicions have put imaginary words in Miss Thompson's mouth? Bella longed to believe Mrs. Walter. And really the overheard conversation, and the exchanged glances over the dinner-table last night seemed an awfully long time ago, divided forever by the world of pain and darkness she had since gone through. Just now, the baby, her little daughter, was the only reality.

"We won't discuss the matter, Mrs. Walter. Ask the nurse to bring me my baby. And is Mr. Raven in?"

"He went out riding, madam. I don't think he's back."

But he had seen her immediately after the baby's birth. She remembered him standing at her bedside just before exhaustion overcame her and she slept. It wasn't to be expected that he would linger indoors until she woke again. Nor should she imagine that he would be thinking too bitterly that the wrong people died in childbirth, the wrong ones lived . . .

She hoped the nurse, with her kind strange face, would think her tears were from joy as the baby was put in her arms.

"Has my sister seen the baby?" she asked.

"Only for a minute, Mrs. Raven. It was done to calm her. She was very upset last night. She kept saying it was snowing, I don't know why, because the storm had died down long since. But seeing the baby seemed to quieten her, poor soul."

"Bring her in now," said Bella.

"Oh, but, Mrs. Raven, the doctor said—"

"Never mind the doctor. I can see my own sister, surely."

Lally came in hesitantly, her huge eyes dominating her little so white face. But when she saw Bella lying with the small bundle in her arms her uncertainty left her and she flew to the bedside.

"Oh, Bella, it's alive."

"Of course it's alive. What did you think?"

"It's a girl. Does Mr. Raven mind?"

"Of course he doesn't mind. To tell the truth he was only concerned that I was all right."

Lally's eyes were shining. "Then he really does love you?"

Bella's arm tightened round the baby.

"A man always loves the mother of his child. It's only natural."

"I suppose so," said Lally humbly. "Bella—couldn't we take off the shawl and look at her properly."

"To see if she has the right number of fingers and toes?" Bella

186

laughed but she was just as curious as Lally. Together they un-wound the swaddled clothing to expose the pink crumpled face and the tiny new hands and feet.

"I think she's like Papa," Lally said.

Bella traced the shadow of honey-coloured eyebrows.

"Her eyes are blue. She's like her father."

"Is she? Oh, imagine—"

"Imagine what?"

"Why, she'll have all the things we never had. Carriages and jewels and balls. She's born to it. Isn't it strange. If we'd never met Aunt Aggie, we'd never be here now with this sweetest little treasure."

The baby stirred against her, and Bella gave a little half sob. It was perfectly true what Lally said, the baby was a tiny pre-carious blessing, snatched from disaster.

Lally's apprehension was never far away.

"Bella, we must guard her. Aunt Aggie and Noah mustn't find out about her."

"Hush, Lally! None of that talk!" To banish the shadow from Lally's eyes Bella went on quickly, "I've already decided her name."

"Oh, yes! What is it?"

"After Mamma, of course. Kate. Kate Eulalie."

Lally clasped her hands ecstatically.

"After me, too?"

"Yes. And I think Henrietta for a third name, because Cousin Henrietta was kind."

"Does Mr. Raven agree?"

"It's my right to choose my daughter's names. If it had been a son, it would be different."

"She's just ours," Lally crooned.

"Well," came Guy's voice from the door. "Baby worship already, I see."

The two heads, Lally's fair one and Bella's dark one, sprang apart.

"Oh, Mr. Raven, Bella has named the baby. Kate Eulalie! You did say that, Bella, didn't you? The baby was to be named after me?" Guy's presence had disturbed Lally and already she was fluttering and uncertain, fearful.

"Yes, I did say it, Lally," Bella answered.

"I think Miss Thompson is looking for you," said Guy to Lally.

"Oh dear, is she? I must go." But Lally's nervousness was overcome by her longing. She darted back to the bedside, her face avid. "Bella, can I hold the baby? Just for a minute?"

"Of course you can." Bella began to lift the baby, but Guy's hand on Lally's shoulder made her stiffen and gasp.

"No," he said.

"Oh, Guy—"

Bella's protest was too late, for Lally's vulnerable face had crumpled into desolation. She ran out of the room, crying.

"Did you need to do that?" Bella exclaimed. "She wouldn't have hurt the baby."

"She might have crushed it. Smothered it. She's unbalanced. Good heavens, don't you know it already?"

Bella tried not to think of Lally's face, avid with longing, her hungry hands. "She wouldn't have done anything while we watched."

"How can you tell? Mad people act in a moment."

"Mad?" Bella's voice faltered. "But she's so much better."

"Not if she still sees Noah in the garden."

"That was Joseph. It was an understandable mistake. Miss Thompson was mistaken, as well."

"How could Miss Thompson be mistaken when she's never seen Noah in her life?"

"She could be frightened on seeing him for the first time, couldn't she? I was, and so was Lally. Miss Thompson certainly looked frightened. And while we're on the subject of Miss Thompson, she'll have to go."

"Oh! Why?"

"I don't trust her," said Bella briefly.

"You don't trust her! But, my dear child, don't you see how good she's been for your sister? The improvement you mention is entirely due to Miss Thompson."

"Then Lally must go on improving without her. And don't ask me to explain the reason for my not trusting her."

"If you're referring to that ridiculous scene you made at dinner last night, I think the less said about it the better."

Bella looked at the stranger with the glittering eyes standing at the foot of the bed. She tried to speak calmly, and could not.

"Do you think I will sit meekly while you make sheep's eyes at that woman? You're my husband—no matter what the circumstances, you're my husband. I simply won't endure it. And the woman has ambitions, you don't know what ambitions. I over-heard her and Mrs. Walter talking. Mrs. Walter tries to excuse Miss Thompson now, but I know better. She must go."

"No!"

The baby, perhaps even at such a tender age sensing its mother's distress, began to wail. Bella clucked at it distractedly. She longed for the peace of a few minutes ago when she and Lally had pored over their miraculous treasure. But there would never be peace when Guy Raven was near, nor could she give her full attention to anyone else, even her newborn child.

"She shall stay for exactly as long as she's needed," Guy went on. "I understand you want Norah to be the child's nurse. So who does that leave to watch your sister? Tottie, perhaps? And how do you know what moment Eulalie will pick the baby up and love it to death?"

"Oh, Guy! You make her sound like a monster!"

"And so she could be, all unwittingly. Miss Thompson under-stands. I'm afraid you'll have to be grateful to Miss Thompson, whatever confused interpretation you put on her actions."

Bella blinked rapidly. She wasn't going to have her tears mingle with the baby's. She would never admit the good sense of Guy's argument. It was too high a price to pay for sense. And yet—if anything happened to little Kate, if Lally's obsessive love or her instinct for over-protecting, harmed the baby, she would have to blame her own selfishness for the rest of her life.

Beneath the blankets, she ran her hand over her flattened stomach. In a few days she would get up, she would be able to wear her prettier dresses, no longer hampered by pregnancy she could match Clara Thompson any day.

"You only want to keep her here," she muttered.

"I make no secret of that. The child is mine, too. I would re-mind you. She has my eyes."

"You'd noticed that?" Bella said involuntarily.

"They're certainly not yours. She's no little wildcat."

"Me?"

"Last night, without a doubt."

He was speaking with amusement now, and almost with gentle-ness, because he had got his own way. Miss Thompson would still move softly about the house, turning up miraculously at the right place to have a whispered conversation, exchange an inti-mate glance, call "Good night" in her low caressing voice.

It was outrageous and unendurable. It was marriage. That was what Cousin Henrietta would say.

"You don't mind that she isn't a boy?"

"That was an unavoidable mistake. Perhaps not a mistake." He put his finger beneath the baby's chin. "She's very sweet. I have something for you."

He took from his pocket a small morocco box and opened it. The diamonds blazed and sparkled.

"Ear-rings to match your necklace," he said in his formal voice. "I had the design copied exactly."

"They're for me!" Bella couldn't keep the pleasure out of her voice.

He smiled. "I thought you didn't care for diamonds."

"These are different."

"I defy you to recognize the technical difference."

"Oh, technical—what is that?" Bella's fingers lingered over the gems. She knew that they were the conventional gift of a rich husband to his wife after she had borne him a child, but there was still that vital difference between them and the necklace. They were entirely hers. In years to come they would be labelled "Isabella Raven's ear-rings, given to her by her husband on the occasion of the birth of their first child." Nothing could alter that. Caroline's shadowy fingers were not on these. Nor would Clara Thompson's or any other woman's be. They were uniquely hers. They didn't represent wealth or opulence, but a small bright moment of happiness. Hers alone.

"Do you like the baby, Tottie?"

Tottie nodded violently, her rosy face one broad, delighted smile.

"You will help Norah to care for her, won't you? She has to be cared for very well. You'll come to me at once if you ever see anything that worries you, won't you?"

Involuntarily Tottie glanced out of the window. Bella followed her glance, reading her thoughts. The November mists had begun and it grew dark far too early. It would be very easy for anyone to lurk in the garden unseen. Soon it would be December, and if Lally thought she saw Noah, Bella could no longer reassure her by insisting that he was safely behind bars.

Little Kate had been born into a world of obscure menace. She was surrounded by adoring servants, even to old Broome who hopefully waggled his long white moustache for her, young Norah was proving a gifted nurse and Joseph would have stood on his head for "the babby" if she would smile for him. Tottie liked nothing better than to be allowed to rock the cradle, even Mrs. Walter was not above a little baby talk.

Yet Bella could never completely relax. Guy's orders that Lally was never to be left alone with the baby seemed justified, for although mostly she was touchingly gentle and loving, she had a few wild moments when she was convinced Kate was that other frail infant whose life had flickered out so quickly, and she would cry that Kate must be hidden before Noah came up with the coffin. Any sudden footstep would throw her into that nightmare, and Miss Thompson would hurry her from the nursery and lock her in her own room until the mood passed.

This was a danger that could be controlled. The other one, the one Guy scarcely listened to or recognized, existed in the foggy garden, the dark evenings, the creepers that gave access to windows for some strong agile climber. Noah and Aunt Aggie had a debt to be satisfied. They would be content with nothing less than Guy's ruin, and her own lasting hurt.

Perhaps she had caught something of Lally's haunted imagination, but Bella was convinced little Kate would be their target.

With Lally's health ruined, her own happiness shattered and Guy without a career or a reputation, perhaps they would be satisfied.

Those things must never be allowed to happen.

Bella begged Guy to go back to London. She felt safer in the Knightsbridge house. The noisy bustle of the great city, the cabs and the drays and barrows, the shouting newsboys and vendors of other wares, the chattering, screaming, vociferous populace drowned other sounds. She wouldn't start at the rustle of a leaf blown against the window, the bark of a dog or even the innocent melancholy hooting of the white owls.

Guy laughed at her fears.

"I had never imagined you to be the nervous type. I thought you left that to your sister. London is no place for a young baby, especially in the winter. The air is almost unbreathable. We shall stay here over Christmas. Besides, didn't I tell you, Cousin Henrietta is coming."

"Cousin Henrietta!" Bella was pleased. "No, you didn't tell me. You tell me nothing."

"I'm sorry. The letter only arrived this morning. She wants to attend the christening. I believe she made us this promise before the baby was ever thought of."

"The baby was never thought of," Bella said coldly. "Cousin Henrietta has a better memory than you."

His face darkened. She knew that he hated to be reminded of that night, the disastrous visit to the Opera, and then she, unexpected and shameless, in her nightgown. He had meant to punish her forever for being his wife, and had never meant to be trapped, seduced by his own wife! No wonder the memory rankled. His pride was so enormous and so stupid. There would be successors to Miss Thompson, she supposed wearily. She clenched her hands, feeling utterly defeated. And yet she was sure he already loved the baby.

"And your mother?" she went on, making her voice cool and polite.

"My mother doesn't care to travel in the cold weather."

"Is she *never* going to see her grandchild?" Bella burst out. "Really, as a stubborn stiff-necked family, you must have no equal. I tremble to think what my daughter has inherited."

"My temper and yours, my love," Guy said. He seemed suddenly cheerful. "I agree that she's to be pitied. I expect London will rock with scandals in about seventeen years' time. But you'll be tolerably used to them by then, I daresay. In the meantime, shall we plan Kate's christening for Christmas day? And it's customary to have a servants' party in the evening. I'd like you to arrange that. Cousin Henrietta will help. Well—will all that keep your mind off the melancholy country?"

"I'd be happier if we were in London," Bella said stubbornly.

"Oh, forget this melodramatic nonsense. The Proudfoots will have too much sense not to keep well away from us in future."

"What about Molly?"

"Molly's digging her own grave."

"But you said—you thought her intimidated by somebody."

Guy frowned. "That all led to nothing, as you know. It's best forgotten."

"Forgotten! With your character deliberately blackened!"

He shrugged.

"What has happened has happened. Be content with things as they are. You probe too much. It isn't feminine."

As always, he had sparked her inflammable temper.

"But you don't want me to be feminine, do you? You give me diamonds as a polite thank you for Kate, and imagine that matter is finished, too. Don't I begin to look presentable again?"

She stood up, holding herself proudly. She knew her dress becoming, and her waist very slim. He could, if he would, put his arms round her now, pull her to him, kiss her until her lips bruised, tell her that all the hating was a lie.

A tap sounded on the door and Miss Thompson came in.

"Oh, I'm sorry," she exclaimed, in pretty confusion. "I thought you were alone, Mrs. Raven."

Guy's hand dropped to his side. It had been reached towards her, Bella could swear. She was cold with anger. She was quite certain Miss Thompson had been listening at the door.

"Perhaps it would be wise to wait until you're bidden to come in, Miss Thompson. If the matter isn't urgent I'll attend to it later."

"No, no, attend to it now, my love," Guy said easily. "I'm off to the stables, anyway. Besides, Miss Thompson doesn't worry you about unimportant matters."

No, thought Bella furiously. She didn't. She would regard the possibility of Bella being in her husband's arms as very important indeed.

Chapter 20

Cousin Henrietta arrived two days before Christmas. It was astonishing how one dumpy dowdy old lady could make the house spring to life, but this was so from the moment she stood among her usual mountain of boxes and bags in the hall.

"Bella, my dear!" She was muffled in a heavy cloak topped by a shawl, her bonnet was pushed awry, her weatherbeaten face sallow and lined from the cold and fatigue of the long journey. But her familiar grating voice was full of warmth. She was suddenly an old and dear friend. "You're looking extraordinarily pretty," she said, eyeing Bella up and down. "Didn't I say maternity would suit you? I'm sure Guy agrees. Now where's the baby? I must see her immediately."

Norah was sent to bring in Kate who was sleep-flushed and adorable. She was put in Cousin Henrietta's arms and the two surveyed one another, with the greatest interest. Finally little Kate's rosebud mouth twitched in one of her early tentative smiles and Cousin Henrietta exclaimed triumphantly, "We approve of one another. How very excellent. Has her grandmother seen her?"

Bella shook her head.

"The old fool. She must be gnashing her teeth. Well, when is the christening, and how are we celebrating Christmas? Have you worn all those extravagant clothes? No, I suppose you haven't, pregnant and buried in the country. Never mind, the opportunities will come. Guy says your sister has gone out of her senses. Poor child, it will pass. The thing is to keep occupied. Take me, I'm never idle for a moment. I can't do much outdoors—it's going to snow, mark my words, the sky's grey goose feathers from here to the Hebrides—but there's plenty to be done making the house look festive. The tree must go in the ballroom. And we shall need holly, fir branches, ribbons—have you plenty of ribbons? Candles? I shall want a strong lad to come with me to cut the holly . . ."

The shadows receded while Cousin Henrietta was there. The house was filled with bustle and gaiety. Even Lally was infected with the general light-heartedness and for the first time since the beginning of her illness was persuaded to go with Bella and Miss Thompson to the village to do Christmas shopping. She refused to go into Mrs. Bunt's to drink hot chocolate against the cold, but she succeeded in making intelligent choices for her gifts, and never once complained that she was being stared at.

At little Kate's christening, too, she looked animated and happy, her childish face framed by her blue velvet bonnet quite adorable. Indeed, it compared more than favourably with Miss Thompson's, for lately Miss Thompson had lost her colour and looked particularly pinched and cold as she stood in the small semicircle listening to the baby being formally named. Bella was almost sorry for her. Being an unloved wife was not an enviable state, but perhaps loving a married man was even less so. For Miss Thompson had no longer that barely-concealed audacity and triumph. For the most part her eyes were downcast, but once she cast a look towards Guy and Bella thought that it looked unhappy and despairing.

For her own part, she took deep pleasure in holding this small creature with the honey-coloured eyebrows who was her daughter. If there was to be nothing else for her, she could make herself content with her baby. Nevertheless, the old uncontrollable excitement was stirring in her again. Would she never stop being optimistic? Just because her husband stood at her side in church, and seemed not to notice Miss Thompson's unhappy glance, did that make him a loving husband, and Miss Thompson a harmless enemy?

As they came out of the church Bella saw that the threatened snow was beginning at last. So far there was only a frosty rime of it on the grass, but the flakes were growing thicker and the wind rising. Bella bundled Cousin Henrietta, who was carrying the baby, into the carriage immediately, and Lally after her. Guy had already announced his intention of walking, leaving the women the carriage. But Miss Thompson seemed to be missing. Bella looked for her impatiently among the little crowd of spectators, then saw her hurrying round the side of the church. In her haste she tripped on a grass-obscured gravestone and almost fell. The shock took the remaining colour out of her face and she was quite white as she approached.

"Am I keeping you, Mrs. Raven? I'm so sorry. I took a short walk, I felt a little faint." Her voice was breathless, as if she hadn't yet recovered. And her eyelids were slightly reddened, whether from tears or the biting wind, Bella couldn't decide. However, she climbed in the carriage without more ado, although, the foolish creature, she couldn't resist a backward and plainly appealing glance at Guy. Bella found herself feeling a new and unwanted emotion for the woman—pity. If she had realized the ordeal it would be for Miss Thompson to watch Guy's child christened she would not have allowed her to come.

But what else could she have expected but pain when she allowed herself to become involved with a married man? She had most deliberately and shamelessly set out to fascinate him. Bella suddenly wondered what Guy's expression was as he stood watching the carriage leave, and she lost her pity for Miss Thompson, huddled in her pretty green cloak. She was too afraid that Guy's face might have been just as despairing.

Back in the house Cousin Henrietta said bluntly, "Get rid of that woman."

"Miss Thompson?"

"Who else? She's sly and scheming."

"I know. I haven't been blind. I've wanted to dismiss her but Guy won't allow it. He says she's too important for Lally."

"She's too important for him, if you ask me. Haven't you learned to manage him yet?"

"I've tried. I always lose my temper."

"If he must have intrigues, he should keep them out of his home. A clever woman—" Cousin Henrietta had to stop as Bella interrupted her heatedly.

"What can you expect from such an extraordinary marriage as ours? Guy has protected Lally and me most honourably and unselfishly. He could have had Lally sent away. What other man wouldn't have? But he allowed her to remain here so long and she was adequately watched—poor Lally! He hasn't refused anything we have wanted. I was quite wickedly extravagant over—some furnishings, and he said hardly a word. He has hated bitterly my being here in Caroline's place. How must he have felt today in the church with my child, instead of hers? Imagine! If he felt it easier to look at Miss Thompson to whom he isn't forever tied, then I don't blame him. And yet you speak as if by being clever I can solve all these things. I can only be as I am, and mostly that's angry and bad-tempered and jealous. I've tried to be meek and patient and bide my time. Some day, I tell myself, he must see me without all that horrid resentment. But will he ever, Cousin Henrietta? Will he ever?"

"Bless me," said Cousin Henrietta, "you love him."

"From the beginning," Bella admitted.

"Then I am a foolish old woman, and perhaps you are doing very well."

"I get frightened," Bella said, with shame. "Not just of Miss Thompson, but of other things. I get like Lally, I'm afraid all this will disappear like a dream, my husband, my beautiful home, little Kate."

Cousin Henrietta gave her a hoot of derision.

"Now what? Do you think that evil couple can still do you harm? Has the country no laws?"

Involuntarily Bella looked out of the window at the darkening day and the falling snow. She couldn't rid herself of the feeling that the snow was a bad omen.

"They're still trying to revenge themselves on Guy, I'm sure. There was Molly—"

"Nonsense, Molly simply wanted to go back on the streets. Some women, once begun on that life, can never stop. They resent help."

"You mean she resented Guy for bringing her here to live respectably?"

"And that foolish idealist, Doctor Bushey, with his head in the clouds."

This was a view that had never occurred to Bella. She suddenly felt much happier.

"It wasn't true what they said of Guy in the newspapers. That was more wicked slander. Do newspapers never stop hating once they begin?"

"If it makes a good story, they'll malign their own mother," Cousin Henrietta said briskly. "That's a sad fact, but I'm sure I'm not going to let it trouble me on Christmas Eve. Are you?"

Bella jumped up, thinking that she would wear her sapphire-coloured velvet and her new ear-rings. Let Miss Thompson feast her eyes on those.

"Certainly not, Cousin Henrietta."

"You're thinking some malice, I can see. Splendid! We shall have a fine party."

Tottie had laid out the sapphire velvet, as she had been told, with Bella's satin slippers and white silk stockings, her gloves, her lace fan, her silver mesh reticule, and her six crisp white petticoats. But when Bella rang for Tottie to come and help her dress, the girl was slow in answering the bell, and then seemed extraordinarily jumpy and nervous.

"Whatever's the matter?" Bella asked impatiently, as her hair was tugged for the tenth time. "Surely you're not scared of the party tonight, Tottie? You couldn't be scared? With everyone here being your friends?"

Tottie's small bright alarmed eyes stared back at her. She moved her lips, desperately trying to say something. Nothing but the familiar unintelligible grunts came forth, but Tottie had never seemed so angry and frustrated with her lack of speech. She kept glancing towards the windows, although the curtains were drawn, and the bedroom, with its glowing fire and lamplight, very cosy.

"Oh, I know," Bella exclaimed. "You're like Lally, you're afraid of the snow. It reminds you of Aunt Aggie's and that terrible cellar where you lived, poor child. It's a wonder you weren't frozen to death. But it isn't cold in this house, is it? So you don't need to be afraid of a little snow. There, that's better. You've done those curls beautifully." The glossy curls, tied with small velvet bows over her ears, and falling in two luxuriant bunches to her shoulders were a credit to Tottie's growing skill, and at last Tottie's stiff little face relaxed into a look of pride.

"Now just hook me into my dress, and then you must run off and get ready yourself. You're to put on your best dress, remember? And your lightest boots so you can dance. Don't look so alarmed, I'm sure Joseph is looking forward to teaching you the polka."

Tottie blushed furiously, and Bella, satisfied that she had banished the child's nervousness, told her to run along, but to send Lally in before she went up to the attics to change.

This injunction wasn't necessary, however, for at that moment Lally came bursting in unceremoniously. She was still in her day dress, and her hair was dishevelled, a sure indication that she was in one of her distressed states.

"Bella, where's Miss Thompson? Why doesn't she come to help me to dress? I've waited and waited." She darted to the window and flung back a curtain to peer out. "Is she lost in the snow?"

"Hasn't she been with you all afternoon?" Bella exclaimed.

"She was there at first." Lally looked uncertain. "Then she told me I must rest if I was to be up late tonight. I didn't want to rest, I wasn't in the least tired, but she was cross about it. She said 'Do as I tell you!' and then we both cried."

"Cried! Miss Thompson cried?"

"She told me not to be a baby, but there were tears in her eyes, and her nose was quite red. I said we were both babies, and she was cross again. She pushed me on to the bed and told me to behave myself and then she went out and I haven't seen her since."

Was that what Tottie had been trying to tell her, that Miss Thompson had gone out, and, like Molly, hadn't come back? Bella crushed down her sudden feeling of apprehension. She tugged back the curtains that Lally had pulled aside, unwilling to look out at the white night.

"Go back to your room, Lally. I'll come presently and help you dress. I expect Miss Thompson's in her own room lying down. Don't you remember, she wasn't feeling well in church this morning?"

"You'll come soon, Bella? You won't leave me all alone?" Like Tottie's, Lally's eyes were bright and alarmed. But fears chased themselves through Lally's head like mice. With the onset of snow, she would be particularly tense, which made it all the more remiss of Miss Thompson to neglect her. If the woman were ill, she should have told somebody.

But the strange thing was, Miss Thompson did not appear to be anywhere in the house. Bella tried not to think of Molly, as Mrs. Walter checked that Miss Thompson's cloak and outdoor boots were gone, but nothing else.

Then Norah reported that immediately after luncheon she had gone into the nursery to find Miss Thompson bending over the baby.

"I asked her what she was doing, ma'am, and she said the baby had been crying. But I didn't believe her. I couldn't, because the little angel was sound asleep."

199

"Did she say anything else?" Bella asked tensely.

"No, ma'am. Oh, yes, only that she thought she'd go for a walk because she had a headache. And then—" Norah stopped, hanging her head and looking embarrassed.

"Then what?" Bella insisted.

"Well, later, I saw her and the master going towards the yew walk."

Bella's heart jumped and was still.

"All right, Norah. That will be all. But stay with the baby. Don't leave her."

Norah bobbed and withdrew. Bella looked at Mrs. Walter whose long face was carefully expressionless.

"Is Mr. Raven in?"

"Yes, madam. He's in the library."

Guy was sitting at the table in the library, busily writing. He threw down his pen as Bella came in.

"Well, my love! You're very grand."

"Guy, Miss Thompson's disappeared! And you were out walking with her!"

Guy's eyes narrowed. "And what do you think I have done with her? Thrown her in the river? Strangled her?"

"Don't joke, please!"

"Then don't make statements with so much innuendo. If you must know, I walked to the top of the yew walk and back with Miss Thompson. We were both feeling in need of fresh air. Then we came in."

"Both of you?"

"Come, Isabella! I told you I didn't leave her unconscious in the snow."

Bella shivered irrepressibly. She couldn't get over the feeling that he hadn't been surprised by her news. He was too calm.

"Then where can she be? She's not in her room or apparently in the house."

"Are you sure?"

"As sure as anyone can be. Lally's been waiting this last half-hour to be dressed. She must be out because her cloak and boots are gone."

"Then she's gone into the village for something."

"In the snow? And without telling anyone? Did she say anything to you about her intentions?"

He began to frown. "I'm not her confidante, whatever you may think. If you must have those suspicions, keep them to yourself. And I'm sure there's no need to raise a hue and cry. Miss Thompson will be back. She's much too sensible—"

"To share Molly's fate?" Bella said swiftly.

"Exactly."

"Then you were thinking of the possibility of her being kidnapped."

"My dear Isabella, the way you feel about the lady, wouldn't you be glad if such a thing happened?" But for all his facetiousness he was behaving as Lally had done, going to the window to lift the curtain and peer out. "Is Kate all right?" he asked.

"Yes. I've told Norah not to leave her. Then you do think—you are afraid—"

He came towards her and quite unexpectedly lifted her hand and kissed it with a courtly gesture.

"You're looking very charming. Which reminds me, I must go and dress. I think Kate must share the party, since it's her first Christmas. Let's see if she has the party spirit, or simply sleeps like a mole."

The colour that had flown to Bella's cheeks at his kiss retreated.

"Then you do think she must be watched?"

"I merely think it a pity to keep Norah a prisoner upstairs for the entire evening."

"And Miss Thompson?"

"She must make her explanations when she turns up. We can't allow her to wreck our Christmas."

Nevertheless, Bella knew that Guy was disturbed. There was a curious glint in his eyes as if he felt some secret excitement. His sudden formal kiss, so uncharacteristic of him, had been meant to allay her suspicions.

But what suspicions? He had walked with Miss Thompson briefly and come home, for here he was to prove it. No one had seen Miss Thompson leave the house a second time, but a little later Broome discovered the orangery door open and the snow blowing in. The young trees would be killed, he fretted. How could anyone be so careless?

A young woman going to a secret assignation might be careless. But as an assignation with whom?

Lally suddenly remembered that when she had woken from a nap she had heard someone saying, "No, no, no!" But then she wasn't sure that the voice hadn't been part of a dream. She enjoyed Bella helping her to dress, and for the first time for months took pleasure in what she wore.

"I do think this lilac silk becoming, don't you, Bella? I promise not to spill anything on it, or forget things. Miss Thompson says I'm not nearly so forgetful nowadays. It's so exciting to be going to a party. Will Mamma and Papa be there? Oh, no, how could I forget? Dear Mamma's in heaven. There'll be only Papa."

A gust of wind struck the windows, the curtains billowed, and some snowflakes falling down the chimney hissed on the fire. Lally shivered violently.

"O-oh! A goose walked over my grave. Bella, where's the baby?"

"In the nursery with Norah. She's coming to the party."

"Little Kate?" Lally clapped her hands with pleasure. "How perfectly sweet. She'll see the Christmas tree, and the candles lighted."

"She'll sleep in her cradle."

"Then I shan't stir an inch from it. Not an inch."

As Lally happily prattled, Bella had a curious little memory of Miss Thompson hurrying round the church that morning, very white, and more than a little distracted. She was sure now that the woman hadn't been feeling faint, but had been meeting someone. Whom?

Cousin Henrietta, who was most grandly attired in black velvet with a great deal of beautiful old lace, completely agreed with Guy that that tiresome young woman shouldn't be allowed to spoil the party. She pooh-poohed Bella's suggestion that Miss Thompson might have been forcibly persuaded to go on some journey with the comment that no one could force such a strong-minded person to do anything against her will.

"We'll do very nicely without her. I think Eulalie long past the need for a nurse. The girl grows better every day. Of course she's a little forgetful, but no more than I am, I assure you. I shall take her under my wing this evening, so you have no need to fret. Mind you," her old eyes twinkled wickedly, "I shall be as interested as the rest of you in the young woman's story when she returns. You can warn her to see that it's a good one."

"Cousin Henrietta, supposing she doesn't come back?"

"Eh?" For an infinitesimal moment the old lady's eyes flickered. Then she said loudly and enjoyably, "Then good riddance! You shall have your desire and believe it or not, I think Guy would be relieved, too."

Bella found that supposition impossible to believe, for Guy, dressed in evening clothes, was suddenly full of a heartiness she had never seen him display before, and which was quite false. She began to wonder if he knew all the time where Miss Thompson was, and was planning to meet her later. Then reason told her that he was assuming jollity for the sake of the servants. They mustn't suspect that there was any significance to Miss Thompson's absence. The party must go on.

The tree, with all its candles lit, sparkled very prettily. The servants, awkward and self-conscious in their best clothes, took a little thawing, but with the help of steaming rum punch, the music of the two young men engaged to play the piano and the violin, and Cousin Henrietta's raucous leading of Christmas carols, their constraint soon broke down. Baby Kate woke once and waved an uncertain fist at the lights and the people, then slept again, with Lally her devoted guardian. Guy danced a sober polka with Mrs. Walter, then a spirited one with Norah. After that he danced dutifully with each maid in turn, even Tottie who stumbled unhappily, and refused to lose her look of apprehension. But now she was probably only worrying about treading on the master's toe.

And all the time Bella expected the door to be flung open and Miss Thompson to appear, making a calculated dramatic entry, beautiful and aggressive and insolent in her most fetching gown. Or would she stumble in through the orangery door, covered in snow, frozen and exhausted from whatever mysterious errand she had been on. In spite of the noise and merriment, Bella kept thinking of the rest of the house, dark and silent. She kept thinking of the snow brushed away and a face pressed against a window. It was morbid imagining. She quickly drank more of the hot punch, hoping to catch the mood of gaiety. She remembered suddenly the champagne she had drunk on her wedding night, and how melancholy it had made her feel. This was only a servant's party, but it was the first she had shared with her husband as master and mistress. She should be gay. Even Lally had lost her apprehensiveness. Only Tottie and herself were haunted by the shadows. That wretched Miss Thompson! It would be better if she were here shamelessly flirting with Guy. Bella was used to that situation. It was much better than the curious image she had of a bedraggled desperate creature out in the snow.

"I think you need another drink, my love," came Guy's voice.

He handed her a steaming glass and said under his breath, "Smile!"

"Oh—I'm sorry. Aren't I doing well?"

"You're looking like the snow queen. Drink that and come and dance."

The warming drink, and then his arms about her changed her mood miraculously. A flood of hot recklessness swept through her. She began to laugh, her head thrown back displaying her long throat, the diamonds glittering from her ears.

"Do you realize, we've been married almost a year and this is the first time we've danced together?"

"Ours isn't an ordinary marriage. Must I tell you again?"

"It's a quite extraordinary one. I have to wear my diamonds to a servants' party. Perhaps you think that fitting!"

"It was a nice gesture towards the servants," Guy replied imperturbably.

"Do they look well?" she asked in a low voice.

"You have pretty ears. I expect you know that."

"Prettier than Clara Thompson's?"

"Please!"

"Do I get the diamonds and she the kisses?"

"Don't let us quarrel. Where are your good manners?"

"I suppose I haven't got any. I was rescued from the streets, remember?"

"Bella!" She could feel the savage grip of his hands on her arms. The pain sent a fierce joy through her. She danced lightly, impeccably, smiling at the other incongruous couples, Broome with Mrs. Walter, Joseph trying to steer poor Tottie, Cousin Henrietta swaying with surprising grace in the arms of Thomas, the head gardener. Guy had complained that she looked like the snow queen. Well, now she did no longer, so surely he must approve.

"Are we to give Kate a brother?" she demanded.

Again his fingers bit into her flesh. She almost cried out. She looked him fully in the eyes, seeing the shine in his, as hard as diamonds. No tenderness, no warmth, and yet suddenly her heart was beating suffocatingly. She was thinking that she would wear her lawn nightgown with the Nottingham lace in spite of the coldness of the night. She would send Tottie away early, and leave only the candle at her bedside alight. She had forgotten Miss Thompson.

Chapter 21

At the end of the party Guy stood up to make a special announcement. He said that he intended keeping a book, a "commonplace book" he called it, of events at Ravenscroft, that would interest his wife and himself in later years, and after that their children.

He proposed that everyone present at this party sign their names. Those who could not write were to make a cross, and he would mark it with their name. The page was headed Christmas 1856, and Guy suggested that the first to sign should be Cousin Henrietta. After that came Bella and himself, and Lally, and following that the servants headed by Mrs. Walter.

There was a great deal of giggling and embarrassment, and some pride among those who could write their names. Tottie was last, poor Tottie who scarcely understood what was happening and had to be persuaded to hold the pen in her hand and make her mark.

Then the party was over. From a little too much of the hot punch Bella was in a pleasantly dazed state. She sent Tottie off to bed, hardly noticing the child's reluctance, as if she were afraid to leave the lighted room and make the journey up to the attics. Kate had been carried up to the nursery without waking, and Lally, too, had tumbled into bed and slept almost at once. Cousin Henrietta, still singing *O, come all ye faithful* in a slightly tipsy voice, had departed to her room, and Miss Thompson was still out in the snow, or wherever she was. Bella found herself suddenly quite indifferent to the whereabouts of that scheming young woman who could so obviously look after herself. Her senses were lulled and drowsy and she cared nothing at this moment for mysteries. Her world was within this warm lighted room, to which presently Guy would come.

She sat waiting for his knock. All other sounds were shut from her ears, the faint moan of the wind, the flutter of the dying fire and from somewhere in the distance the persistent barking of a dog.

But the knock which eventually came wasn't on her bedroom door. It was on the front door directly beneath her windows. A thunderous urgent knocking, followed by the clangour of the bell pulled again and again.

It roused Bella from her dreamy state as completely as if the fire had sparked a live coal at her. She flew to the window to throw back the curtains and peer down.

What she could see was like a scene out of a nightmare. A burly man stood leaning backwards from the weight of his burden, the indescribably rigid form of a woman whose skirts fell in a cumbersome bundle but whose face was thrown back to catch the snowflakes—a face as white as the snow.

It was Miss Thompson.

Swallowing her sickness and trying to gather courage to go downstairs, Bella told herself frantically that it did not need to be Miss Thompson. The poor white face was quite anonymous.

But she knew it was. She knew it had to be. Tragedy had come once more with the falling snow.

Someone had opened the front door and the man had edged his way stiffly into the hall. Bella drew her head in, her face frozen. She threw off the flimsy beribboned wrap in which, a few minutes ago, she had felt suitably attired, and substituted a practical heavy woollen one. But she was still shivering violently as she made her way downstairs. The reluctant dread she felt overcame her so severely as she reached the last steps that she stood a moment unseen staring at the little group, Guy in an elegant quilted silk dressing-gown (had he been about to come to her? she wondered agonizedly), old Broome, stooped and muttering, Mrs. Walter, and the stranger who had laid his burden on the floor.

She couldn't see it from where she stood. The little group seemed to have been affected by paralysis as much as she. A dog suddenly ran in through the open door, and the stranger—no, it was no stranger, it was Norah's father, Mr. Jones, whose farm lay beyond the Ravenscroft woods—roared, "Get out!" His voice was shockingly loud, but it broke the inactivity. Guy said in a hard harsh voice, "Get blankets and brandy!" Little Broome scuttered off to obey, and Mrs. Walter dropped on her knees to chafe the cold hands of the figure on the floor.

"It's no use to do that," said the farmer. "She be gone. It's easy to see."

"Mrs. Walter! Wake Joseph and send him for Doctor Frobisher."

"It be too late," Norah's father repeated. "But I reckon the doctor should see her. I'll fetch him. It's a bad night to send the lad out." He turned back to say what he must already have said before, "She must have been lying there hours. 'Twas my old dog barking that brought me out. I thought it must be a ewe on her back. So I come out with a lantern, and found the poor lady. Right at the end of the yew walk, sir. Just at the edge of the woods. I can show you the spot in the morning."

"Yes," said Guy in his hard emotionless voice. "The police will need to see that."

Mrs. Walter's face was lifted. "The police?" she hissed on an indrawn breath.

"Certainly the police. Hadn't you noticed the poor girl's neck? She's been strangled."

Miss Thompson was walking in the yew walk with the master . . . I saw them, I saw them, I saw them . . .

Norah's voice was screaming in Bella's head. With a soundless cry, as if she too were having the breath strangled out of her, Bella flew to Guy's side. Gripping his arm tightly she made herself look down on the poor ruined face. The black cherry eyes looked back at her. They seemed to start out of the still face in loathing. You've won, Mrs. Raven, they were saying.

What bitter victory had she won? And would it in the end be a victory?

"Bella, my love! You shouldn't be here."

"Why not? Isn't my place at your side? Didn't we say 'for better, for worse'?" But this was worse than anything any bishop or parson, mouthing the marriage service, could have imagined. It was so bad that, strangely, Bella's courage grew out of it.

"We'll find out who did it. We'll settle this thing. We're not going to live the rest of our lives with a menace hanging over us. First Molly, now Miss Thompson, who next? Fetch the police, Mr. Jones."

"And cover this poor creature up," she added. "Carry her into the library. She can't lie here in all the drafts."

"Yes. My wife is quite right," said Guy, with sudden briskness. "Can you help me, Broome? She—was only a little thing."

She was only a little thing . . . Was that his epitaph for the young woman he had admired, spoken in a brisk practical voice, as if it might have been a dead bird or some other unfeeling wild creature whom he carried out of the drafts from the front door.

The library door was locked on its secret. None of the maids, especially Tottie, must come on it unawares. Guy took Bella to wait by the replenished fire in the drawing-room until the police came. He insisted on her drinking a stiff brandy, instructing Broome, who stood with the useless blankets in his arms, to have one himself and give one to Mrs. Walter.

Then, when he and Bella were alone, he said without preamble, "You know that I'll be suspected of this crime."

"Yes. I know."

"But you don't believe me guilty?"

"Never say that again!" said Bella in a low passionate voice.

He gave a wry half smile.

"You're very trusting."

"Oh, Mr. Raven! Spare me such idle talk. I know you commit sins. A great many. But strangling unfortunate women isn't one of them."

"Why aren't you in hysterics?" He regarded her under his eyelids.

"Because it would be a waste of time. Now tell me what that foolish girl said to you when you walked with her this afternoon."

"She said—heaven help her—that she had fallen in love with me."

"And you?"

"Me? What could I say but that she had been misled? She had wrongly interpreted certain actions of mine. Women are too susceptible, I fear. She was distressed in church this morning, and this afternoon her emotions carried her away. I said that under the circumstances she had better give in her notice. We came back to the house together—"

"Together?"

"Why, of course we did." His eyes, regarding Bella, hadn't a flicker of warmth. They were simply amazed that a female, a mere servant, had presumed to take his advances seriously. Yet Bella was sure there was more to it. Although she was convinced that he was telling her the truth, as it was on the surface. "If she went out again, it was later. To be quite candid, I wasn't surprised when you told me she had gone. I imagined she had left in a pique, hoping to create a little trouble and mystery. That's all there was to it, I assure you. Do you believe me?"

"I believe you."

He took her hand, just for a moment, then dropped it.

"Then why are you calling me Mr. Raven? When I call you Bella?"

Bella rubbed her cold hands.

"I can think of nothing but her. It's so horrible." After a long silence she added, fearfully, "What will happen now? There will be more headlines. You can scarcely survive these. Is that what they intend?"

"They?"

"The Proudfoots," said Bella tiredly. "Noah and Aunt Aggie."

Guy stared at her silently. Then he gave a loud cracked laugh. "Try telling that to the police. The honest unimaginative police who don't believe in wars of attrition. Much less in curses." He pressed Bella's shoulder briefly. "I'm going to wake Cousin Henrietta. You'll need her."

It was true that she would need Cousin Henrietta, for after the police had questioned Guy for an interminable time they asked him to accompany them to the police station.

Everybody was up now, for all the servants had had to be questioned. The unfortunate thing was that although Norah had seen Guy and Miss Thompson leave the house ("at least I think it was the master—it always was the master with her," she said and then turned scarlet with embarrassment), no one had seen them return. No one could swear that Miss Thompson had ever returned. There was only Lally's evidence that could have been a dream, of Miss Thompson's voice saying "No, no, no!" and the open door of the orangery to suggest that she might have gone out again later, and alone.

Guy was allowed to have an overnight bag packed for him.

"But they won't be keeping you!" Bella exclaimed.

He answered quite calmly, "The law can be very slow. I prefer my own nightshirt to a prison one."

Lally promptly gave a strangled cry and fainted. Guy looked down at Bella on her knees beside her sister.

"I believe there's nothing wrong with that young woman but a constant desire for attention," he said critically.

"She's unconscious!" Bella declared indignantly.

He smiled. He seemed grateful for the familiar diversion of Lally's distress. Broome had come in with his bag, and the police, two of them, burly, red-faced, impossibly stupid in Bella's eyes, were impatient to leave.

"Come along, if you please, sir."

"I shall be back as soon as possible," said Guy.

The fantastic enormity of what was happening left Bella suddenly faint herself.

"But, Guy—"

"We merely have a great many things to discuss and investigate. Isn't that so, sergeant?"

The sergeant grew slightly more human.

"Your husband can help us with inquiries into this shocking affair, ma'am."

"Don't fret," said Guy.

"But he can't be arrested!" Bella whispered, as the men left.

"Of course not," said Cousin Henrietta briskly. "He's not in handcuffs, is he?" But she looked very old, nevertheless. Everyone looked older and sleepless. Lally was sitting up weakly with Tottie holding her hand. Tottie was like an aged monkey, all her youthful colour gone. Mrs. Walter looked feverish, a purplish flush in her cheeks and her eyes overbright. She was giving orders to the maids in a low abrupt voice. Someone was to make hot chocolate immediately, someone else to sweep the snow from the library floor.

Miss Thompson had left some little time ago . . .

It was midday the next day that the incredible happened. Tottie opened her mouth and spoke an intelligible word. She said in a thick triumphant voice, "Clarrie!"

Bella and Lally had been sitting huddled over the morning-room fire. In spite of the dreadful shock Bella was thankful to see that Lally's condition had not deteriorated and she was talking quite lucidly, although she dwelt intolerably on Guy's behaviour.

"He really did flirt quite shamelessly with that poor creature, Bella. It isn't surprising that she took him seriously."

"He must have had motives," Bella said stiffly.

"Oh, yes, motives. To make another conquest. He's like all men, wanting as much amusement as possible without obligations. Supposing Miss Thompson had suddenly begun to make demands."

"What demands?" Bella said coldly.

"Oh, I don't know, Bella." Lally twisted her hands feverishly. "I can't help wondering—well, Molly had a baby without a father, and there was the poor darling mite at Aunt Aggie's. I never believed its father was a sailor. Some young women are very ignorant and frivolous—" Lally's voice died away as she saw Bella's icy anger.

"Are you suggesting Miss Thompson was ignorant enough or frivolous enough to become—for my husband to—oh, no, I can't even put such a thing into words. I declare, if ever you make such a suggestion again, I'll never speak to you for the rest of my life. I can only think that it's the weak state of your mind that puts such thoughts in your head. You have an obsession about babies. Miss Thompson—that sneaking creature—even though she's dead I must say it. Whatever happened to her is entirely her own fault. Oh, Lally!" Bella's voice rose exasperatedly. "Don't cry! You deserved that scolding for saying such a monstrous thing."

But Lally's reproachful tear-drowned eyes were hard to face, for her wild imagining could make dreadful sense. Guy was a healthy young man and he hadn't been sharing her bed. Nor was he any longer having anonymous adventures in London. His own words about Miss Thompson were seared into her mind. *Heaven help her, she had fallen in love with me* . . .

It was then that Tottie, sitting in the background with some sewing idle in her hands, had produced her strange hoarse word, "Clarrie!"

Bella spun round.

"Tottie! You spoke!"

In spite of her terrible anxiety, she couldn't help excitement and pleasure. They had all tried for so long to coax speech from Tottie's silent lips.

Tottie herself didn't look excited. She still had her look of shrinking alarm, and now that the word was out she was trying passionately to say more.

Mrs. Walter had come in at that moment with a tray.

"I've brought coffee, madam, thinking you might care for some. I've brought it myself because those foolish maids are all thumbs this morning, dropping everything."

"Mrs. Walter! Tottie spoke. Say that word again, Tottie. Now don't get excited. Take a deep breath and try to explain what you meant. Clarrie. Oh—it's somebody's name!"

Tottie nodded violently, her face scarlet with effort.

"A woman's name. Clarrie—Clara—" Bella went white. *"Miss Thompson!"*

Tottie nodded again, and Bella exclaimed excitedly, "But why do you call her Clarrie? Have you heard somebody else do that? Tottie—*who* have you heard call her Clarrie?"

The girl sat rigidly, her mouth open, the words refusing to come. Bella knelt beside her, holding her hot damp hands.

"Now listen, Tottie—" It was surprising how quiet her voice was when her heart was beating so hard that it was difficult to breathe. "Have you seen Miss Thompson before she came to Ravenscroft?"

Tottie nodded again, pleased that Bella was beginning to understand.

"Somewhere where she was called Clarrie. At Aunt Aggie's?"

Lally drew in her breath sharply, and looked as if she might faint again. Mrs. Walter stood listening irresistibly. Tottie made an emphatic motion of her head, several times, and Bella felt the familiar dread, like a cold stone, in her heart.

"Tottie, was she the niece who had the baby? The one who disappeared?"

"The mother of that poor little angel!" Lally exclaimed.

But Tottie shook her head this time. She was moving her lips again. After several unintelligible sounds the second word came out triumphantly. "Noah." When she found that at last she could say it she said it over and over like an idiot. "Noah, Noah, Noah!"

"Noah's wife!" Bella whispered, with certainty, and didn't need to watch for Tottie's assent.

The picture was falling into place. Tottie's fear, from the beginning, of Miss Thompson, whom she recognized, Miss Thompson's startled exclamation the day Lally had imagined she saw Noah under the copper beech, her deliberate attempt to estrange Guy even more completely from a wife he didn't love, her disappearance at church yesterday which suggested she might have been meeting Noah, her bending over little Kate, obviously debating whether to obey Noah's instructions and kidnap her, then later the distressed whisper Lally had heard, as if the woman were fighting a battle with herself.

In her attempt to make Guy fall in love with her at Noah's injunction in order to create another scandal, she had got burnt herself. She had done what no one had anticipated, she had fallen in love with her prey. This had put her in a terrible dilemma. She must have gone out in the snow to meet Noah as arranged, but without Kate. And Noah's terrible black temper had possessed him . . .

Bella sprang up, saying urgently, "The police must be told this at once. I must go to my husband. Mrs. Walter, help me to get ready."

"But I don't think you can go to the master, madam. He's been taken to London."

"To London! How do you know? Why wasn't I told?"

"I didn't want to upset you more, madam. Mr. Jones brought the news. The matter was too important for the police here. The master was taken to headquarters in London."

"Then that's where I shall go," Bella declared. "Send someone to find out what time the London train stops at Underwood, Mrs. Walter."

She was quite calm now, and full of hope.

"Tottie had better come, too, so that she can tell them what she's just told us. And I shall take the baby."

"Kate?" Lally faltered.

"She has to be fed," Bella said simply. "Anyway, do you think I would let her out of my sight after this? With Noah making his fiendish plans. Tell Norah to get her ready, Mrs. Walter."

"If you would allow me, madam," said Mrs. Walter, "I would like to come with you. You'll need help."

"But I'll have Tottie."

"Tottie! The girl's in such a dither she'll be worse than useless. Is she to hold the baby while you buy train tickets and can she find you a cab in all the hustle and bustle of Waterloo station? If she saw anything to startle her she'd fly to hide. That's her instinct."

"Yes, you're right, Mrs. Walter. She certainly has a habit of hiding in cupboards, or any dark spot. Then perhaps it would be as well if you came. Only don't let us waste time. Order the carriage to take us to the railway station. The snow isn't too deep for the horses, is it? It stopped falling some time ago. And Lally dear, Cousin Henrietta will be here with you. You'll be perfectly all right. I'll give orders for Norah to sleep in your room."

Lally's little face was pinched and fearful.

"Supposing Noah is still here looking for his—for Miss Thompson."

"I have more than a feeling that Noah knows very well what has happened to his Clarrie. He won't be here any more. You'll have to be brave, Lally."

"I can't be! It won't be safe! Nothing's ever safe!"

"Lally, please! Try to be brave!"

But Lally was well embarked on her perpetual nightmare.

"Noah will wait until he sees you leave and then he'll take his revenge on me. Oh, Bella! I can't stay here. Take me with you. Let us remain together."

"Don't you think what Miss Eulalie says might be wisest?" Mrs. Walter put in in her dry, quiet voice. "Leaving her might bring on a relapse. She'll be a prey to her fears. I gather there's a capable housekeeper in the London house."

"Oh, yes. Mrs. Doughty. She would be pleased to see us again."

"Then let us all go. It would be best, madam."

"Perhaps you're right, Mrs. Walter. Very well, we'll all go. How quickly can our bags be packed? And Cousin Henrietta is resting in her room. She must be told."

Fifteen minutes later, when Lally and Bella were both dressed warmly in bonnets and cloaks and stout boots, Mrs. Walter came hurrying downstairs to say that her ladyship was sound asleep and it did seem a pity to wake her, considering the night she had had, and her age.

"Could you just write a note for her, madam, and I'll put it by her bedside."

Bella was too impatient to be on the way to argue. Besides, it was perfectly true that Cousin Henrietta had looked alarmingly exhausted after her sleepless night. She went to her desk and hastily scribbled a note.

"We are going to London at once to see Guy. Tottie has spoken at last and been able to give us valuable information. It will completely exonerate Guy, and finish Noah and that terrible old mother of his forever. Can you imagine, Miss Thompson was Noah's *wife*. It has all been a diabolical plot. I hope we will be back tomorrow, Guy as well. I was reluctant to wake you before we left." She hesitated, and added, "Please, dear Cousin Henrietta, have the fires alight for us tomorrow, and we will begin Christmas all over again."

214

Chapter 22

THE first thing Bella was aware of as she climbed out of the train at Waterloo station was the raucous words of the newsboy at the barrier. "Murder charge! Guy Raven charged with murder!"

The words jolted her awake. She realized that she had been in a curiously sleepy dreamlike state ever since Mrs. Walter, in the train, had opened her carpet bag and taken out a bottle and persuaded each of them, Bella, Lally and Tottie, to drink a little. It was blackcurrant wine, just the kind of stimulant they needed after the strain they had all been through. Besides, it was warming in this intense cold.

Bella had obeyed, because she was so tired, and yet must remain alert. The wine was sweet and pleasant-tasting. Lally had enjoyed it, and so had Tottie. After that, since they had the compartment to themselves, Bella had unfastened her gown and fed the baby, and replaced her, drowsy and contented, in her basket. Then everybody had seemed to get drowsy. Except Mrs. Walter who didn't seem to need sleep. She had sat very upright in her corner, her arms folded, her face wearing its habitual prim forbidding expression. Bella was glad now that she had come. She was capable and unshakeable. In her care they would undoubtedly arrive safely at their destination.

Although those horrifying words the newsboy hurled at her gave her a moment of pure terror, she suddenly had a desire to laugh scornfully and shout back that it was all a lie. This was what Noah had wanted, not only to ruin Guy's career and marriage (for what it was), but to get him standing in the dock, accused, facing long imprisonment or death. He would have gone to any lengths to achieve such an event, even to sacrificing his own wife.

215

But he had failed. And now, thinking himself safe, he would be easy to track down.

Carrying the baby, Bella followed Mrs. Walter who had gone off in her capable way to get a cab. It was strange how her legs stumbled, as if they had not wakened with the rest of her body. Lally and Tottie were making slow progress, too, although Lally was trying to hold her head up and not wince away from the idle glances of passers-by. It was a long time since she had faced strangers, and the noisiness and steam and belching smoke of this vast station was confusing enough to one in the best of health.

"Bella," she panted. "Where are we going?"

"To the house in Knightsbridge. Doughty will know, or Doctor Bushey will know, where Guy has been taken. Then I will go there immediately. You and Mrs. Walter and Mrs. Doughty must look after Kate while I am gone."

"Mr. Raven won't let me touch her."

"Lally, you know that isn't true. It was only true at the very beginning when she was so tiny. He thought you might love her too much. But now it's different. You may hold her if you like. I say so."

"Oh, thank you!" Lally said fervently. A little feeble gaiety seized her. "Bella, isn't this different from our first coming to London? We are rich, we have Kate." Uncertainly she added, "If only we were safe."

"We are safe," Bella said impatiently.

"People do stare." Lally was looking round furtively. "I'm sure they all know who we are. Murderers and adulterers."

"Lally, what *are* you saying!"

"That's what it's come to. Oh, not us. But poor Miss Thompson—loved and murdered. Isn't it true? Look, there's Mrs. Walter beckoning to us. I think she has a cab. Where's Tottie? Bella, Tottie—Oh, there she is. She's so slow. Tottie, why can't you hurry? You're not the only one who's tired. I scarcely know what I'm doing. My eyes won't stay open."

"Come along," said Mrs. Walter, giving her tight smile. "There's room for us all. If you will allow me, madam, I will sit with my back to the driver and hold the baby."

"Have you given him the address?" Bella fussed, rubbing her eyes. Really, they were all in a poor state after their sleepless night. Except Mrs. Walter who was remarkably calm and wide awake.

"Indeed, yes, madam. If you would just hold the baby while I get in. There! All safe." She gave another of her rare grudging smiles, and the driver whipped up his horse which set off at a smart pace.

They were back in London. The cab smelt of wet straw, it was bitterly cold, and outside the streets were freckled with snow. The year between might never have happened. Except that there was Mrs. Walter's long sallow face opposite, not Aunt Aggie's, and Mrs. Walter held little Kate, tangible proof that a great deal had happened since their last arrival in London. And they were not on their way to the slums but to a comfortable house in a fashionable area.

The jolting of the cab increased the girls' drowsiness. Lally's and Tottie's heads lolled together, their heavy eyelids closing. Bella was glad of this, for wide awake, both girls could have got into a state of nervous terror. She herself fought with her sleepiness, and tried to take interest in what she could see through the grimy window. Snow and slush, a sky as grey as pewter, dingy buildings, a mass of vehicles, some hurtling by drawn by high-spirited horses, some moving at a snail's pace. They had crossed the river, and soon should be coming into an area she recognized, the broad Strand and Trafalgar Square, and after that the Mall that led to Buckingham Palace, then turned off to Constitution Hill and Knightsbridge, their destination.

In spite of her determination to keep awake her eyelids did droop and she started up at what seemed a long time later to find they were still jogging along, but that instead of the broad streets of the West End they seemed to have got into a narrow street bordered by small mean houses.

At first she thought she was dreaming. She peered again into the early darkness, seeing the low huddled houses and hearing the cries of ragged children. It was all too dreadfully familiar. She shot an apprehensive glance at Mrs. Walter who was still sitting upright nursing the peacefully sleeping baby, and seeming not at all alarmed by the route the cab-driver was taking.

"Mrs. Walter, I think the man's made a mistake. We're going the wrong way."

Strangely, Mrs. Walter didn't look out of the window to confirm her fears. She just gave a strange half-smile and said in her flat voice, "I think the driver knows where he's going, madam."

"But these streets—they must be a very long way round. The man's cheating. Wait till I tell him so."

She made a move to open the flap behind Mrs. Walter in order to call to the driver. Mrs. Walter's arm barred her.

"The man knows his business, madam."

"He certainly does not. None of these roads lead to Knightsbridge. Even the little I know of London tells me that. Why, we must be miles from the city." The never far absent fear was stirring in Bella again. The little dark streets were so oppressive, so reminiscent of that other evil-smelling street shrouded in darkness and snow where the nightmare existed. "Mrs. Walter, please move aside. I must speak to the driver."

"I think not, madam."

The woman's voice was still polite, but subtly not that of a servant any longer. Her smile had gone, her eyes had a narrowed secretive triumphant look.

"You see, I gave the man his orders, madam. He is taking the way he was bidden."

"You mean—" Even then Bella tried not to believe what she was being told. "You mean we're not going to Knightsbridge."

"No, madam."

"But Mrs. Walter—how dare you do this! I must stop the cab immediately. Driver!"

"I think you won't, madam."

"But I will!" Bella declared vigorously, and dragging open the window at her side she stuck her head out. "Driver! Stop at once! We're going the wrong way."

The man on the box, muffled in a greatcoat and stove-pipe hat, slowed his horse to a walk. He turned his head.

"Ma'am? You said something?"

His voice was grotesquely familiar. So was his face. Dark, grinning, evil, it looked down at Bella. The cab driver was Noah.

Bella sank back, breathless and faint.

"It's a plot! You're in it, Mrs. Walter. You! And I trusted you!" She looked frantically at Lally and Tottie, huddled together, deep in slumber. There was no help there.

Mrs. Walter read her thoughts and nodded slowly, smiling her infuriating sour smile.

"It wasn't wise to drink the blackcurrant wine, madam. Such young things, they haven't heads for wine."

"You put something in it," Bella whispered. "What was it? Laudanum?"

"Wine's an overpowering drink, madam."

"I shall put out my head and scream for help," Bella announced tightly.

"I wouldn't do that, madam. Really I wouldn't." An indescribable coarseness had come into Mrs. Walter's voice. "If you was to do so I only have to put my hand over your child's face."

Bella stared in mounting horror. The cab was jolting again as the horse was whipped up.

"A baby smothers easy," said Mrs. Walter.

Chapter 23

GUY RAVEN shut the book with a bang.

"Does that convince you the case must be reopened?"

The Inspector nodded slowly.

"We'll try to locate this young woman. It shouldn't be too difficult. She has a regular beat, I understand. She'll have to be made to talk, of course."

"It's urgent," said Guy.

"I agree with that. Things look black for you, I may say, if it can't be proved that Molly Hancock and Clara Thompson are part of the same plot."

"You've got to lay this crime at Noah Proudfoot's door."

"I hope we can, sir. Now let's just go over this again. Why didn't you suspect sooner that someone in your own household might be involved? Apart from the dead woman, of course."

"Because it was only yesterday that I persuaded Clara Thompson to talk. I'd always had suspicions about her. She'd seemed to arrive in my mother's household out of the blue, and to be remarkably anxious to come to Ravenscroft. She was to nurse my sister-in-law who had had a mental breakdown. Not the most appealing occupation for an attractive young woman. However, it took all this time to get beneath her guard. I had to resort to somewhat despicable means that only bore results yesterday afternoon when she told me that she couldn't go on with what she was doing."

"She had become emotionally involved with you, I gather?" the Inspector said pompously.

Guy bowed his head. "It was a course I had to pursue and I succeeded all too well. Although, even then, I couldn't get the woman to divulge her secrets. She did tell me she had 'had enough'—those were her words—and that she intended starting a new life. But she would like to warn me about traitors in my own household. She was in a state of great emotion. I thought she was being a bit melodramatic. But after she had left the house, for London, I presumed, I took this method of getting specimens of handwriting."

He reopened the book and stabbed his finger at the first signature.

"You agree that there's no mistake. My housekeeper's handwriting exactly corresponds with that in the note to Molly making an assignment at the crossroads."

"It does, it does."

"And of course that explains how the note was delivered to Molly. It was easy enough for Mrs. Walter to slip it to her saying Tom Field had brought it. Probably giving the girl a scolding for receiving notes from young men." Guy sprang up restlessly. "But surely we're wasting time. Can't Noah be apprehended at once?"

"Not without grounds, sir. After all, the Thompson woman didn't at any stage acknowledge any connection with him."

"No. I couldn't get her to do that. But I told you of the episode when my sister-in-law imagined she saw Noah in the garden. The woman gave herself away then. She knew Noah, there was some connection between them."

The Inspector nodded.

"But unfortunately Miss Clara Thompson is now beyond telling us anything. So we'll have to depend on the girl Molly for evidence. Don't be impatient, sir. My men are out. I haven't been wasting time, as you suggest."

"Then I hope your men make haste. I don't think even yet you realize how dangerous this black villain is. He'll strike again, at any moment. I'm worried about my wife and child. I trust I'm free to go home."

"No, sir. That's where you're wrong. So long as you appear to be in custody Noah will hold his hand. You see," the Inspector smiled grimly, "I do believe your story. What's more, I believe the black villain, as you call him, has one object, and that is to get you hanged."

Chapter 24

THE room was exactly the same, the bobbled red plush curtains drawn against the dark and the inquisitive eyes of neighbours, the lamp lit, the fire burning cosily, the cradle on the hearth, and Aunt Aggie rocking gently in her chair.

"Well, my dears, you've had a long journey. It couldn't be helped. Noah had to drive you about until dark. Wasn't it a stroke of fortune that he happened to see you catching the same London train as he was catching himself? He was only anxious to be of service when he bribed the cabby—handsomely, I can tell you—to borrow his cab. But he couldn't bring you here until after dark because we're so troubled with unmannerly neighbours in this street since we've come home from prison. All our comings and goings are watched as if we were criminals! It's quite distressing. But never fear. You won't be stared at. You'll be up and away before the birds."

She smiled affably, her large pale eyes looking over the top of her spectacles.

"Was it quite a surprise to come here again? But a pleasure, I'm sure. *I* find it a pleasure to see your pretty faces once more. And you both so richly dressed, too. Such clothes! Such jewels! See what good fortune I brought you!"

"Mrs. Proudfoot, why have you brought us here?"

Once again anger was overcoming Bella's fear. The shock of returning to this house had brought back Tottie's look of animal fear and Lally's blank-eyed apprehension. The two girls crouched on the small sofa, holding hands, dazed and uncomprehending. They were useless, puppets in Aunt Aggie's plump white fingers. Bella had to fight alone. How could she, against so many enemies?

"I don't know what you're planning to do," she went on vehemently, "but you won't succeed. I left a letter for Cousin Henrietta telling her exactly what had happened. She will get the police immediately."

Aunt Aggie put her hand in her apron pocket and drew out a folded sheet of paper.

"Is this the letter, my dear?"

Bella's mouth went dry. "Mrs. Walter didn't leave it!"

"Naturally. She wouldn't be so foolish. Oh, but you don't really know Mrs. Walter, do you?" Aunt Aggie raised her voice calling, "Lily! Come here, will you, my dear."

In a moment Mrs. Walter had appeared. Her long face wore its look of guarded triumph. As Aunt Aggie said, "This is Mrs. Jennings, my dear," Mrs. Walter dropped a mocking curtsey. Aunt Aggie went on, "The lady everyone decided didn't exist. So foolish of them. The only person who didn't exist was Lady Merriweather, her supposed mistress." Aunt Aggie chuckled comfortably. "Your grand husband was careless there, Miss Isabella. He went to such trouble to find out what he could about poor Clarrie, and quite ignored Mrs. Jennings, who is a great deal more clever and trustworthy. Aren't you, Lily, my dear? And I believe you still have those nice positions for these young ladies?"

Mrs. Walter nodded, her mouth hard.

"Ready and waiting. The parties concerned are getting impatient, I may say."

"Yes, we know. They'll be satisfied before morning. Tch, tch, Miss Isabella! You're looking alarmed. I wouldn't hurt you. Not a hair of your pretty head. I have a most sensitive nature. But Noah—he's another matter. He's very upset about Clarrie. He trusted her and it wasn't nice to find she wasn't trustworthy. Indeed, I've never known him so upset, and I fear he hasn't my sensitive nature. He's revengeful. If I know him he won't rest until someone has paid for Clarrie, and everything else."

"You mean he killed his wife because he found her—" Bella couldn't go on.

"Unfaithful," said Aunt Aggie sadly. "Untrustworthy and unfaithful. She refused to do as he told her. Now you as a married woman will understand, Miss Isabella, that it's a wife's duty to obey her husband. She even threatened to leave him, no less! And he still has not recovered in health after that terrible year in prison. Small wonder he—well, no matter. But you may be sure he is clever enough not to have the crime laid at his door."

"My husband is to be accused!"

"And has been," said Aunt Aggie, her sausage curls nodding gently beneath her spotless white cap. "So now there is only the little matter of you and your sister. And Mrs. Jennings is seeing to that."

"You're monstrous!" Bella whispered.

Although Aunt Aggie still smiled blandly, a subtle change had come over her face. Her eyes had turned as cold as stone.

"Monstrous, you say! And who wouldn't be after the year Noah and I have lived through. Stink, squalor, corruption! Rats running over our faces at night. Food not fit for a pig to eat. Lice, fleas. Filthy straw, damp, jail fever. The poor dregs of humanity, the rakings of the gutter, as companions. Ah, if you'd heard the screams, the despair, the dreadful language. Night after night, day after day, and you, Miss Isabella, you and your sister, living in luxury, pampered, petted, never giving a thought to the ones responsible for your blessings. Never a thought for Noah and me. Oh, no. My sister told me that."

"Your sister!"

"She reported faithfully on your doings. She had great amusement from wearing my best bonnet—you will remember the one with the cherries—and frightening Miss Eulalie out of her wits."

"The woman in Mrs. Bunt's teashop!" Bella exclaimed. "Then she *did* lure Molly away."

"That was a trifle. A mere preliminary skirmish. Not a tenth of the debt your husband still has to pay."

"She took her to her house. The house by the river that Molly talked about."

"In Twickenham, my dear. Where I go once a week to get fresh eggs and butter. She has a nice little farm. Only a few acres, but well-tended. Why, you'll remember sampling her eggs yourself. And talking of food, why don't we all have a nice cup of tea? Tottie! Tottie, wake up, girl!"

Tottie started up, her poor little face a mask of terror.

"Go into the kitchen and get out the tea things. Make haste now, or Noah will be up the stairs to hurry you up."

"Mrs. Proudfoot! Tottie isn't your servant any longer."

"You mean, she is too grand, also? I think not. I think not, Miss Isabella."

Tottie slunk out of the door. If Bella had had hopes that she might have the sense to escape out of the kitchen door and try to get help they quickly died. A persistent hammering was coming from the cellar. It indicated Noah's whereabouts, and Bella knew Tottie's meagre courage unequal to defying Noah. She herself didn't dare to leave the room because of the baby asleep in the cradle on the hearth. She had already heard Mrs. Walter's dreadful threat, and she was all too sure that that woman or Aunt Aggie would not hesitate to carry it out.

Besides, with Tottie's departure, Lally had suddenly roused herself and gone down on her knees beside the cradle. Her face was full of the utmost anxiety. One finger very gently touched Kate's chubby cheek.

"It's so small and weak. Aunt Aggie, will it live?"

Aunt Aggie shook her head concernedly, and gave her "Tch! Tch!" Her concern was not for the baby but for Lally.

"Dear me, she thinks it's that other baby. It's true she's lost her wits."

Bella sprang up furiously.

"If she has, it's all due to you! Are you a woman or a fiend? Let us go! Please let us go! We'll go on foot in the snow. Anything! Please let us go!"

The slow bland smile showed Aunt Aggie's black rotting teeth.

"You were thankful enough to shelter under my roof the last time it snowed. Shame on you, my pretty child, where's your gratitude?"

"If my sister and I disappear like this how do you think you can escape suspicion?" Bella cried passionately.

"Now who in the wide world is going to worry about two young women picked up out of the gutter returning to it again? With your grand husband discredited and hanged—oh, hanged, indeed, don't wince, my dear!—who is going to trouble? Certainly not your mother-in-law, eh?" Aunt Aggie chuckled obscenely. "Nature will out, you know. It was proved with Molly. She wanted only to get back on the streets. Why not you and your sister, too? Oh, the world won't fret about you. It doesn't care for upstarts. If Noah and I and Mrs. Jennings can't make up a pretty enough story to explain your disappearance then we're poor creatures, indeed. As dim-witted as your sister."

"And—my baby?" Bella gasped.

"As sweet an infant as you'd ever set eyes on. I'll take care of her, you may be sure. Calm yourself, my dear. Would Aunt Aggie harm an innocent child?"

After a long time Bella managed to say, "Molly will be found and made to tell the truth."

"Molly? Oh dear, oh dear! You don't know about Molly, of course. You'd better come and see for yourself. And Noah's downstairs, too. He'll want to see you. He's hard at work, as you can hear. Bang, bang, bang, from the moment he arrived home. I declare it splits my poor head." She gave a glance at Lally who was sitting on the hearthrug crooning wordlessly to the baby. "Leave her there, poor child. Let her be happy in her world of fancy. She's fortunate, if only she knew it."

The cellar stairs were steep and dark. Bella wanted to refuse to go down them, but a dreadful fascination forced her on. The tap of Noah's hammer ceased as first Aunt Aggie, and then Bella, stumbling after her, reached the cellar.

In the guttering light of two candles, Bella saw him towering in the dank room, his black tousled head all but touching the ceiling. His great hands hung at his side in their familiar posture, she saw that his face was stubbled with a half-grown beard, his eyes red-rimmed.

Yet the only impression that remained in her mind was his teeth gleaming in a grimace that wasn't so much a smile as an expression of derision and triumph.

"So here she is, Ma, the delicate lady of fashion. What has she come to see?"

"Why, your work, of course. Show her your clever work. You didn't know Noah was so handy with carpenter's tools, did you, my dear?"

"It's not exactly a piece of furniture I'm making," Noah said, with his sudden coarse laugh. "Perhaps the lady would like to look closer at it. I'll hold the candle."

The room was damp and chilly enough, but it wasn't that that made Bella freeze with horror. It was the shape of the box that the wavering light showed. A long narrow box made out of rough planks of wood. There was an identical one beside it, obviously finished, for it had the lid on.

They were coffins.

"Not a baby's size this time," Noah said in his indescribably gleeful voice, and behind him his mother gave her cosy chuckle.

"See, isn't Noah versatile! Of course, the wood isn't of the best

226

quality. I'm afraid it's only what they use for paupers and plague victims. But, even so, Noah doesn't spare his workmanship."

Bella was clinging hard to self-possession and sanity.

"You—told me—I would see Molly."

"And so you shall, my dear. So you shall. Show her, Noah."

Noah moved the candle so abruptly that the flame wavered wildly.

"I'll show her."

He tipped the lid of the second box back. Bella's hand went to her mouth, strangling a scream.

She wouldn't scream, she wouldn't faint. That would please these two monsters too much. She would somehow look at Molly's ivory face and remain calm.

"Murder!" she whispered. "You think you can escape with murder?"

"Bless you, you pretty innocent," cried Aunt Aggie. "She isn't dead. She's only asleep. There!" She stooped over the still form. "Feel her heart. She's quite safe. It's only more convenient to have her this way. It stops her tongue from wagging. Doesn't it, Noah? We'd prefer Miss Isabella and Miss Eulalie to be quiet, too, wouldn't we?"

"I'd have them quieter than that," said Noah, with ferocity. "I'd have them as quiet as Clarrie." He swung round on Bella. "Did you know your swell husband wasn't content with you, but he had to have my wife, too? I had to kill her, the bitch. That's women for you. You all deserve to go the same way." He gave a kick at the box he had been hammering, sending it slithering towards Bella. "Get in it and see if it'll fit. There's another for your precious sister. Where's the sister, Ma?"

"With the baby, poor wandering creature."

"Then fetch her. We haven't got all night. We've got to get going. A brougham to fetch and three coffins—I *beg* your pardon, ma'am—" he sketched a low satirical bow to Bella, "three boxes to load, and then the drive to the docks."

"Get the girl," Aunt Aggie said briefly to Mrs. Jennings.

Mrs. Jennings hastened to obey, her skirts rustling up the narrow stairs.

Bella clenched her frozen hands. "My baby?" she managed to say. "Tottie?"

"Now never you fret, my dear. They'll both be cared for. Tottie will learn to be grateful for the good home she scorned, and as for the baby—a foundling home, perhaps. What do you think, Noah? Is a foundling home too good for Guy Raven's daughter?"

"Well, now, Ma, that will have our consideration." Noah spoke with exaggerated gentility. "Perhaps the dear little mite would be happier in the gutter. One thing's certain, she can't go with her ma. Oh no, that would be no good at all. Unhampered, they likes them. Buxom and healthy and unhampered."

"How can you carry—these things," Bella couldn't bring herself to call the boxes by the grisly name, "on board a ship? You'll be stopped and questioned."

"That's where you're wrong. No one interferes with the dead, especially dead Chinese liking to be buried in their own country. I'll have names put on these. Lee Wang, Lee Hong, Lee Ching. Three brothers. Very sad." Noah gave his great laugh, but it was cut off sharply as Mrs. Walter's voice came hissing down the stairs.

"Mrs. Proudfoot! I believe the girl's gone!"

"Who? Tottie?" Aunt Aggie had darted towards the stairs.

"No. The mad one. You did say you left her with the baby. The baby's gone, too. The cradle's empty."

The stairs shook as Aunt Aggie's ample form catapulted up them. She was followed by Noah who reached the top in three strides.

Left in the cold dark cellar, Bella stood rooted to the floor. She didn't dare to hope. Had Lally miraculously had the sense to take the opportunity to fly? Had Aunt Aggie trusted her weak mental state too much? She had forgotten Lally's obsession about harm coming to the baby, any baby, either Kate or the other long-dead mite. If Lally had snatched up Kate and fled, she would hardly know which infant it was, only that it was alive and must be kept that way.

There was the sound of doors banging. This was followed by a long silence. After an interminable time footsteps came back. Bella heard Noah's furious voice,

"You left her alone! Knowing she could run off!"

"But her senses had gone. She didn't know what went on round her. Mrs. Jennings! You knew that?"

"I must say I didn't expect her to have the spirit, any more than the dumb one."

"Never mind about spirit!" Noah said savagely. "She's gone.

She's nowhere in sight and I'm not going knocking on doors, looking for her. You two muddling fools! You lunatics! I'm off!"

"Noah! Where are you going?" For the first time Bella heard an uncertain quaver in Aunt Aggie's voice. It gave her an exultant vindictive delight. Darling Lally, flying like that to save Kate!

"To save my skin. Where do you think?"

"But who's going to take in a crazed creature like that with a baby and listen to her? She'll be turned out in the snow."

"With her fine clothes? Anyone'll tell she isn't off the street. And what about the brat, dressed like a lord's daughter? And knowing how the neighbours is full of Christian charity and love for us! You stay and face them if you like, and serve you right for muddling fools. But I'm off!"

Aunt Aggie's voice had risen in panic. "What about the other one with her educated tongue? Are you going to let her go free?"

"I won't touch her, Ma!" Noah's voice was suddenly vicious. "Not that I don't want to. What I'd give to get my fingers round her pretty white throat. I'd like to see her without a breath in her body. I'd make her pay for Clarrie. But I won't swing for her! I've got enough sense for that. Kick her out in the snow. Let her freeze. If you know what's healthy, you'll come with me. Only I ain't hanging around waiting. So make up your mind quick. Are you going to wait to be strung up, or coming with me?"

After a long moment Aunt Aggie's voice was slow, faltering, the voice of an old woman.

"Where?" she asked.

Chapter 25

THE little erect figure in the elegant bonnet and lavender gown sat before the fire dandling Kate on her lap. She paid no attention to Bella's tumultuous entrance. She appeared to be fully engrossed with the baby, talking and cooing to her, and then laughing with surprised delight at Kate's tentative response.

Bella's first instinct was to snatch Kate from her. How dare she think she could behave in such an icily, bitterly hostile way, and then walk in and take possession of her grandchild, as if the baby belonged to nobody else.

But all at once Bella found she had been too near too many ugly tragic things to have any more hate.

"Her name is Kate," she said. "Do you like her?"

As if just that moment aware of Bella's presence, Mrs. Raven lifted her eyes.

"She resembles her father, although she has my hands. I confess I don't care for the name Kate, but I wasn't consulted so I suppose I must put up with it. Good gracious, child, you're shockingly dishevelled. Let Hannah—where is Hannah? Find her and ask her to attend to you."

"Why did you come here?" asked Bella curiously.

"To defend my son, of course. Why else? I draw the line at murder. Other indiscretions, perhaps, but murder is absurd. I'm very glad the whole nasty affair is cleared up. If you ask me, your sister has been the only one to keep her senses."

"Lally!" Bella said, giving a high-pitched laugh at the absurdity. "Where is Lally, anyway?"

"Here I am!" Lally cried, at that moment flying into the room. "Oh, Bella, how did you escape?"

Bella thought of the interminable time that had elapsed after Noah, Aunt Aggie and Mrs. Walter had fled. The house had been so eerily silent. She had sat in the cellar in the flickering candle-light straining her eyes to hear that Molly still breathed. She had been obsessed with the fear that if she went for help Molly would die. She had told Tottie to fly to open the door immediately any-one came, but Tottie had crouched half-way down the cellar stairs, paralysed with fear. It had been a time when all will had left Bella. She had sat chafing Molly's cold hands, sure only that Lally would send help.

"I saved the baby!" Lally was saying. "Bella, do you hear? I saved the baby!"

"How you can say your sister is crazy when she seems to be the only one who kept her head, I don't know," Mrs. Raven observed, rocking Kate in her arms. "It seems a very unfair and damaging statement to make."

But Bella knew Lally was unaware it was Kate whom she had saved. She thought the other forlorn baby was alive again, and the knowledge seemed to have brought back her sanity. Her face was white and intolerably strained, but it had none of its old wildness. Instead it had a sad sweetness that made Bella put her arms round the slight figure and draw her close.

"You were so brave. How can I thank you?"

"I wasn't brave at all. I was scared to death. That's why I took the baby before Noah could get a chance to bury it. I could hear him hammering a coffin, couldn't you?"

"Yes," Bella said, shuddering. "And where did you take the baby, Lally?" Noah and Aunt Aggie hadn't known much about human nature or they would have realized that that sinister sound would have penetrated even Lally's dazed wits.

"To the house across the street. I banged on the door and made the old woman who lived there let me in. She called her husband and said he must go off at once to Bow Street to fetch the police. She said that he was not to stare at me and think I'd made up a tale, he knew well enough queer things went on in that house. So presently the police came, and there was a nice sergeant who said I must take the baby home and wait for you because you wouldn't leave Molly. I didn't know Molly was there. Bella—" the flicker of fear touched Lally's eyes again, "she wasn't dead?"

"No. And she won't die, never fear. But Doctor Bushey says it will take her several hours to wake up."

"Is that all the old fool can do?" Mrs. Raven demanded. "Predict the effects of laudanum on young girls. Why isn't he here seeing that my granddaughter has taken no ill effects from this dreadful affair? Or me, having had not a wink of sleep all night?"

Bella was suddenly almost collapsing from weariness herself. With the greatest effort she said, "Doctor Bushey and Guy have gone with the police to search for the Proudfoots. They may not be back for some time. If you will excuse me, Mrs. Raven, I must tidy myself. I'm scarcely fit to be seen."

"Didn't I tell you to ring for Hannah?"

But Bella had a childish longing for familiar faces and reassurance.

"I would rather have Mrs. Doughty, thank you."

It was curious what a feeling she had of being home at last when she was upstairs in her bedroom with Mrs. Doughty fussing and clucking in her motherly way.

"Dear, dear!" she kept saying. "Dear, dear, dear! And Doughty says the predictions are for a new comet in the sky and terrible storms. What a dreadful world, to be sure. And there was the master fretting in town half the summer. Never going anywhere or seeing anybody."

"He must have had some diversions," Bella said.

"Not a one," Mrs. Doughty lied loyally. "There now, madam, your bath's ready. And what gown will you wear? The wine velvet perhaps? A nice cheerful colour for this bitter weather."

Bella knew the dress had been decided on, so made no protest. In any case, Mrs. Doughty's choice was right. The rich colour took away her wan look. Her eyes were quite bright by the time she had finished dressing and drunk the inevitable hot chocolate. She found she was listening intently for the return of the men.

"Aye, fretted all summer," said Mrs. Doughty, her eyes bright, too, and her nose the colour of Bella's gown.

Yet when, a half-hour later, there was the unmistakable sound of arrivals downstairs, Bella found herself leaving her room slowly, and descending the stairs with dignity.

She was not going to fly into her husband's arms. Oh, no! Though she hadn't known the strength of will-power she possessed to prevent it.

She was aware of Guy standing in the middle of the hall looking up at her. There were two ghosts between them now, she thought, Caroline and Clara Thompson.

She could hear Doctor Bushey's voice telling Mrs. Raven what had happened.

"We caught up with Noah just as he was about to board a steamship bound for the Far East. Presumably the vessel that would have carried the girls away."

"And the old woman? Don't tell me she escaped?"

"No, oh, no. It appears she had fallen on a patch of ice and twisted her ankle. She couldn't keep up with Noah so he callously deserted her. We found her in a public house with her evil companion, Mrs. Jennings, both of them more than a little tipsy. I make a prediction there'll be no Bible readings in Newgate prison this time, judging by the obscenities used. But I won't distress your ears, dear lady."

"My ears can stand a little of my son's voice. Where is he?"

Bella's feet took her down the remaining stairs, almost reluctantly. By the look in her husband's eyes, there didn't seem, at that moment, to be ghosts between them. Or perhaps the way he must be so dazzled with the snow, and exhaustion, he couldn't see them.

"Guy, can't you spare me a moment of your time?" came his mother's querulous voice.

Guy held out his hand.

"Come," he said to Bella.

They stood side by side before the old lady as if Bella were being presented to her for the first time. Mrs. Raven held her head high, looking down her little haughty nose. At last she said,

"I hope now you will begin work on your career again, Guy. The Prime Minister wishes you to. He meant you only to stay in the background temporarily, not to disappear out of sight. And don't keep your wife buried in the country, either. I make no predictions, but it's possible she may be no great hindrance to you. She has a passable appearance, and at least she can fight. If you'd heard her shouting at me once through a locked door—" The old lady's head dipped, her bonnet deliberately hiding her face. She seemed to be intent on the baby. Her shoulders shook very slightly. "I confess I laughed for hours. Never enjoyed anything so much. My son has met his match, I told Hannah."

Guy scowled, dropping Bella's hand.

"Mamma, you're impossible. First you won't speak to us, then you laugh at us."

"Yes, I surprise myself. I must be growing old. What's all that commotion in the hall?"

The commotion was the arrival of Cousin Henrietta. A cab was at the door, and Doughty was unloading the familiar endless number of boxes and bags. Cousin Henrietta, hopelessly dowdy in her sturdy country clothes, took one look at Bella and Guy, murmured, "Thank God!" under her breath, and then turned her bright saturnine gaze on Mrs. Raven.

"Good gracious, Edith, you look very old!"

Mrs. Raven inclined her head. "Thank you, Henrietta. I return the compliment."

"But I see you've made the acquaintance of your grandchild."

"And not before time! Do you agree that she has my hands? Her father's eyes perhaps, but definitely my hands."

The two bonneted heads bent over Kate. Bella found she had slipped her arm through Guy's, and it was held there, firmly tucked against his side. Neither of them spoke. It was enough, at present, that they could smile together at two sentimental old women. It was Cousin Henrietta who had said that marriages were made on earth, and Bella had never lacked determination or optimism.

Perhaps it was her optimism that made her suddenly so certain the ghosts had departed.

DARKWATER

Chapter 1

As the swirling smoke of the engine cleared, the little group was etched forever in Fanny's brain—the outlandish figure of the Chinese woman in her black trousers and high-collared smock, and the two children in their quaintly old-fashioned clothes, the girl with black hair, stick legs emerging from her pantaloons, and tense eyes staring unwinkingly, the boy smaller, unexpectedly fair, his eyes dreamy and lost.

And the smoke clouding over, then clearing again to show the tall dark figure of the man.

She had known at once that the man belonged, although he stood a little distance away. He was watching her too hard, seeing the effect that the sad wrinkled alien face of the amah and the two waif-like children had on a young lady of obvious wealth and fashion.

In her mind, for a moment, like a view enclosed inside a bubble, bright and impermanent, was a picture of Darkwater, the faded rose many-chimneyed house, the lawns, the trees heavy with summer, the strutting peacocks, the distant flicker of the lake. Nowhere into the picture came this little trio. Instinctively she knew that they would be forever strange and unwelcome.

Yet her immediate impulse was to sweep the children into her arms and say, "Don't be afraid. You're safe with me."

Safe . . . It was true that the chilly grey summer day, the hissing of steam, the shouting and bustle of a busy London railway terminal, and the constantly belching smoke, did constitute a menacing atmosphere to such new arrivals from another world.

She couldn't be sure whether the watching man was part of the menace.

She only knew, with frustrated anger and bitter grievance, that from this moment her life had to be changed, that it must follow a very different course than the one she had planned so hopefully when she had packed her bag at Darkwater.

Chapter 2

AT the bottom of her bag Fanny laid her modest pieces of jewellery, the silver locket which sprang open to hold a miniature or a lock of cherished hair—it was empty, and Fanny scarcely knew why she kept it since it was unlikely ever to contain anything—the seed pearl necklace, the ring set with garnets and seed pearls, the gold brooch that had been her mother's. She had never known what had happened to the rest of her mother's jewellery, unless, more than likely, she had been too poor to have any.

She had come from Ireland, and the Irish were not renowned for their wealth. She had been beautiful, they said, but it had been a foolish marriage for Papa to make. He should have married an heiress. Not only had she been poor, but also too delicate to survive childbirth. Her name had been Francesca. That had been given to Fanny—that and her deep blue eyes and black hair. And her life. So great a gift as the last was the main reason for Fanny's secret plans at this moment. She must make the most of something so dearly given.

Over the shabby morocco jewel box in her travelling bag she laid her underclothing, two sets of everything.

Dora would have done her packing for her. Fanny was not encouraged to give the servants orders. This was a tacit understanding between Aunt Louisa and herself. But Dora, recently promoted to the upstairs, adored Miss Fanny and would even have risked Hannah's disapproval to do her behests.

As it happened, Fanny preferred to do this task alone. She couldn't let even loyal Dora see that for one night in London she was taking two of everything, and her summer as well as her winter gowns.

She was on fire with excitement. Ever since her cousin George had come home wounded from the Crimea she had been waiting for this opportunity. She had made and rejected a dozen plans, but this chance had been handed to her out of the blue. It was meant to be taken.

The only way she could explain her suppressed excitement, at breakfast that morning when she could eat nothing, and it was left for the rest of the family to eat heartily from the array of dishes on the sideboard, was to say that the train journey and the visit to London were such an adventure. Not to mention meeting the new cousins, poor babies, who had travelled so far.

Uncle Edgar had smiled indulgently, but Aunt Louisa had compressed her lips, not with scorn for Fanny's naïve excitement, but with the thought of the new arrivals. Aunt Louisa had never cared for children who were not her own. At the tender and vulnerable age of three Fanny herself had made that discovery.

It was left for George to say to the table at large, "Fanny looks deuced pretty when she's excited. Doesn't she? Deuced pretty."

His eyes, ever so slightly vacant, rested for an embarrassingly long time on her face.

Aunt Louisa said sharply, "Don't forget the time, George. Mr Maggs comes to give you your treatment at nine."

"Yes, Mamma," said George mildly. He still stared at Fanny. The doctors said he would eventually recover from the head wound he had received at Balaclava—perhaps they didn't care to tell his parents otherwise. All Fanny knew was that the lofty scorn and small sadistic cruelties with which her cousin George had been accustomed to treat her had been metamorphised into this distressing and embarrassing affection. Where once she had defied him, she was now ever so slightly frightened of him.

It was one more reason for her desire to escape. Long ago she had begged Uncle Edgar to let her take some employment, she was young and active, she hadn't Amelia's chances of making a good marriage, if indeed she made any at all, and above all, she was bored. She refused to be content with a life full of trivialities and invented occupations.

Uncle Edgar was shocked and adamant. A Davenport to go into service! Besides, above all, she was his ward, a sacred trust to him from his poor cousin Edward. He would carry out that trust to his dying day.

"There are plenty of ways of occupying yourself in this house," he had said repressively.

Fanny knew all about that. Running errands for Aunt Louisa and Amelia, stitching at the household linen with Hannah, because she sewed so neatly, reading to old Lady Arabella, feeding the screeching peacocks, playing and singing to Uncle Edgar in the evening when he was in the mood for a little music. She was a puppet pulled this way and that. A puppet everlastingly dependent, everlastingly grateful . . .

Gratitude could turn sour, Fanny thought, as she folded her last garment. Indeed, she was unnatural enough to feel none at all. It hadn't been her fault that her mother had died at her birth nor that her father had contracted a consumption that carried him off before she was three. And Uncle Edgar and Aunt Louisa had so much. This enormous house, the gardens, the lake and the parkland, the little village where the villagers doffed their caps deferentially, the church and even the parson.

One small bewildered child, arriving from the hot sun of the Italian Riviera where her father had gone to die, should not have had to feel gratitude.

Perhaps it was her look of defiant independence that most antagonised Aunt Louisa. Fanny looked at herself in the tilted mirror on her dressing table. At this moment excitement had heightened her colour and her dark blue eyes were brilliant. In spite of the drabness of her grey poplin gown she looked very pretty. She had a long slender neck and a waist that Amelia bitterly envied. Her blue-black hair, smooth and luxuriant, made her look foreign, Amelia said. English men like fair-haired women. And Aunt Louisa considered that Fanny had too bold and direct a way of looking at them. Amelia knew how to lay her thick fair lashes prettily on her cheeks. Not that Fanny hadn't long lashes, too. She must remember to use them modestly. She must remember her position . . .

While she stayed at Darkwater, she could never forget her position. But she would go on looking directly at people, too. It had never amused her to flirt. She ran rings round giggling Amelia when it pleased her to do so, but in the end the young men discovered that it was Amelia who was the heiress, and the slow significant coolness came into their manner.

Fanny despised all of them. Some day she would meet a man to whom money was of minor importance. But not, intuition told her, while she stayed at Darkwater . . .

There was a knock at her door, and before she could speak Amelia came bursting in.

"I say, Fanny, have you packed? Papa wants to see you in the library when you're ready. I really do think he could have let me come with you."

"Perhaps you'd like to go instead of me?" Fanny said coolly.

Amelia flung herself into a chair, pouting.

"What, and be nursemaid to two children!"

"That's what I'm to be."

Amelia's round pink and white face, too plump and already uncannily like her father's, remained unconcerned. She never saw any point of view but her own.

"Oh well, that's different, isn't it? But we could have gone shopping. Will you bring me some French ribbon, anyway. To match my pink bonnet."

"If I have time, and you give me the money."

"Oh dear! I've overspent my allowance. I shall have to ask Papa."

"He won't refuse you."

"Well, after all, he is my Papa," Amelia pointed out. "If yours had remained alive, I expect he'd have been glad to buy French ribbons for you, and seen that you had a respectable dowry. Fanny, who do you think will marry you?"

The question stung.

"Someone who loves me," Fanny replied calmly.

"But who will that be? I mean, without a dowry—"

"I don't intend to sell myself."

Amelia sprang up, her cheeks pink.

"What a revolting thing to say. You mean that men prefer me to you just because I'm rich. In other words, that I'm selling myself."

Fanny gave her direct gaze, without speaking. Amelia's eyes glinted with anger and hurt pride.

"Very well, you have an eighteen inch waist, but Mamma says men prefer women not to be too thin." Her eyes went to the lovely curve of Fanny's bosom, and fell. She stamped her foot childishly.

"Fanny, you are exasperating. All right, I'm sorry I asked who would marry you. It must be a question that hurts. You can't change customs, and it *is* important to have a dowry, whatever you say. But I'm sure you'll find someone suitable. Only there isn't that much time, is there?"

Amelia was referring to the fact that Fanny was in her twenty-first year. Fanny chose to misunderstand her.

"No, there isn't, and if I'm to see Uncle Edgar in the library before I leave—"

"I didn't mean that sort of time, but never mind." Amelia had recovered her good nature. "Do you think having these children in the house is going to make much difference? Mamma says it will, but Papa says if they're kept out of sight we'll hardly know they're there. And anyway how could he refuse to have his own brother's children. It's awfully lucky Papa's so generous, isn't it? First having you as a ward, and now these two. And coming all the way from China. Mamma's afraid—"

"Afraid of what?" Fanny asked, as Amelia hesitated.

"We just don't know who Uncle Oliver married in Shanghai. Wouldn't it be terrible—"

"If the children were Chinese?"

Amelia's eyes were round and shocked.

"They couldn't be completely because Uncle Oliver wasn't. But they could be—sort of half—and even if they are Mamma says Papa will insist on their coming to church with us on Sundays. Imagine us with ivory-coloured cousins!"

Amelia began to giggle, but she was still anxious. It was easy enough to read her thoughts. She was wondering if even a substantial dowry would tide her over that sort of scandal.

"Mamma thinks it was awfully inconvenient of both Uncle Oliver and his wife to die in that typhus epidemic," Amelia went on. "But Uncle Oliver always was in trouble, and I suppose this was his climax, so to speak."

"Your father must have been glad when he decided to go out to the East twenty years ago, and didn't come back."

"He must have," Amelia said in a heartfelt voice. "Dear Papa, who's so respectable. I believe it wasn't only money with Uncle Oliver, but—" she lowered her voice "—women! That's why Mamma says these children could be anybody."

Fanny tried to remember the distant day when she, a mere baby, had made the long terrifying journey to Darkwater. She remembered the dark muffling folds of a blanket, and much later, the strange strident noise which sent her into floods of tears, but which proved to be only the elegant and haughty peacocks on the lawn. She could have been anybody, too.

"They're your own flesh and blood, Amelia," she said reprovingly. "Your father sees that. He's the only one, it seems to me, who does see it."

Amelia flounced across the room. She had still to learn to move gracefully.

"Oh, Fanny, don't be so righteous. I know what one's duty is, as well as Papa, and as well as you. But it's an awful bore having to explain about infant cousins all the way from China. And if they should have slant eyes—well, I don't care, I'm not going to let them interfere with my life."

Poor babies, Fanny was thinking. No one wanted them. Not even Uncle Edgar, really. And she was callously planning to run away, and let Hannah, who would accompany her to London, bring them home.

But she had to seize this opportunity! If she didn't do it now, the war in the Crimea would be over, Miss Nightingale wouldn't require any more volunteers, she would have no alternative but to apply for a position as a governess or a companion, both impossible without references, and both nauseating to think about. At least, in the Crimea, one would be doing a worthwhile task, and probably meeting at last a man to whom integrity, a warm heart, and a little beauty, too, meant more than landed property or stocks and shares.

The children were travelling with their Chinese amah who would remain with them. They would be adequately cared for.

"Fanny, you're not even listening to me!" Amelia said peevishly.

"Yes, I was. I was thinking how we all try to protect our own lives."

Amelia's pale blue eyes, a little prominent, like her father's, widened.

"But what have *you* to protect?"

"My heart beats, the same as yours," Fanny said dryly. Then, because she was fond enough of Amelia, who was selfish and undiscerning and remarkably empty-headed, but who did not, at least, have her brother's sadistic qualities, she said reassuringly, "I'm sure you're worrying unnecessarily. The children will stay upstairs in the nursery and the schoolroom, and you'll hardly see them."

Amelia shrugged. "Yes, I expect so. After all, what are servants for? But don't stay in London a minute longer than you need to.

I shall have to read to Grandmamma while you're away. You know I can't endure that."

Both Aunt Louisa and Uncle Edgar were in the library. Aunt Louisa was walking up and down as if this were the end of an argument, and one which, as usual, she had lost, for her lips were compressed, and the tip of her large nose flushed. Uncle Edgar was watching her with benevolence. Arguments seemed to amuse rather than anger him. He rarely lost his temper, a fact which drove his wife to fury. She could have coped with a hot temper, she couldn't cope with the unbendable unbreakable iron beneath her husband's soft, plump, pleasant, facetious and good-natured exterior.

When Fanny came in they both turned.

Uncle Edgar said at once, in surprise, "My dear child, why are you looking so shabby? You're not proposing to travel in those clothes?"

Fanny had meant to scrupulously leave behind her fur-trimmed coat, her striped silk gown and her dark blue bonnet with the velvet ribbons. They were her best clothes and as good as anything that Amelia or Aunt Louisa wore. She considered that they still belonged to Uncle Edgar, and anyway, in her new circumstances, she would have no use for them.

"I thought, for a train journey, with the dust and smuts—"

"Which is very sensible and prudent," said Aunt Louisa.

Uncle Edgar shook his head.

"On the contrary, Louisa my dear, that's quite wrong. Fanny is representing me. She must look her best. In any case, we always like her to look her best."

When he noticed her, Fanny thought privately. For he had a curious trick of seeing her, and probably his own family, too, only through the eyes of outsiders. She could wear a faded and shabby house gown the entire week, without comment, but as soon as visitors were expected, or, more particularly, when she followed the family procession into church on Sunday mornings, she had to be expensively and fashionably dressed so as to do him credit. So that people could say that Edgar Davenport was remarkably generous to his penniless niece?

It was only in her darker moments that Fanny believed that last assumption. Uncle Edgar was a fair and kindly man. He was absent-minded at home. He truly didn't notice what his family

245

was doing or wearing unless they drew attention to themselves. He spent a great part of the day in the library with his stamp collection, his erudite books, his correspondence on charitable affairs which he meticulously looked after himself, and his committees. He looked just a little eccentric, with his high domed balding head with its ruff of hair that would one day be a saintly shining silver, his prominent mild blue eyes, his full-lipped mouth. In the house he liked to wear a shabby wine-coloured velvet smoking jacket, and was given to extravagantly-coloured waistcoats. A heavy gold watch chain lay across his chest. The watch concealed in his pocket was a chiming one. He had used to make it chime for the children when he was in a jovial mood. It had often stopped tears and tantrums. Fanny wondered if its magic would be called upon for the new children. She hoped it would, for if Uncle Edgar were not kind to them, who would be?

"You will go upstairs and change," Uncle Edgar was saying. "You have plenty of time. The carriage has been ordered for half past eleven. The train leaves at twelve. Now repeat to me again exactly what you have to do."

"Yes, Uncle Edgar. I'm to take a cab from the station to the shipping office to make enquiries as to whether the *China Star* has arrived, as expected, and which train the children will be on. I'm also to ask if an official has been sent to meet them and escort them to London, and later to suitably reimburse him."

"What is suitably?"

"A guinea as you suggested, Uncle Edgar."

"Correct, my dear. What next?"

"After we've been to the shipping office and ascertained our time-tables Hannah and I are to go to our hotel and wait."

"Correct again. You see, Louisa, Fanny is quite capable of taking charge of this business. It saves you a journey which I'm sure you don't want, and it's quite impossible for me to get away. I'm far too busy. I'm a man of many affairs."

"Too many," said Aunt Louisa tartly. "If you'd taken a little more interest in your brother when you were both young, we might never have been in this contretemps."

"I don't think my influence would have stopped Oliver going to the bad," Uncle Edgar said seriously. "He was always uncontrollable, even as a small boy. Anyway, I wouldn't refer to this matter as a contretemps. It merely means our family is a little larger.

What of that? There are enough empty rooms in this house. It will keep the servants up to the mark."

"The children will have to be taught."

"Ah, yes. You mean the problem of a governess." Uncle Edgar's eyes flicked to Fanny and away so quickly that she couldn't be sure he had looked at her. "Well, we don't need to take all our fences at once. And anyway, my dear, we've been over this matter often enough. Oliver has made the children my wards. I have no alternative, have I, even had I wanted one. Which naturally I don't. I shall enjoy the little beggars."

He gave his wide beaming smile. And Fanny knew that he didn't want these strange children any more than, seventeen years ago, he had wanted her. But he was a man of principle and it worried him that he should have uncharitable thoughts. He was busily convincing himself and his wife that he hadn't.

Aunt Louisa got up, in her fussy bossing manner.

"I won't have Amelia's chances ruined."

"My dear, whatever do you mean?"

"You've promised her a dowry of ten thousand."

"Did I suggest reducing it?"

"No, but you frequently talk as if money is short, and now there will be extra expense. You can't deny that. And the other thing is—" Aunt Louisa hesitated, biting her lip—"must we let it be known the children are coming until we see what they look like, I mean, supposing—"

Uncle Edgar threw back his head, guffawing heartily.

"You mean, supposing the little beggars are yellow? There's not a chance. Oliver was a fool, but not that much of a fool."

"How do you know?" Aunt Louisa said tightly.

"Why, the devil take it, because he was a Davenport."

Uncle Edgar was feeling in his breast pocket. His expression had changed. His brother Oliver's undisciplined life and inconvenient demise had been put out of his mind, and he was smiling with anticipatory pleasure.

"Come here, Fanny. Your aunt and I thought we would like to make you a small gift. You've been with us a long time now and you've given us a great deal of help, not to say pleasure."

Fanny looked swiftly from one to the other. Aunt Louisa's expression had not changed. She was still thinking petulantly of the awkwardness and inconvenience of having to give a home to the strange children arriving from Shanghai—or was she thinking of the unsuitability of giving Fanny a gift?

But Uncle Edgar was smiling and waiting for Fanny's response.

She bit her lips. Whatever the gift was, she wasn't sure she could accept it gracefully.

"Look," said Uncle Edgar, opening a small red morocco box.

The jewel gleamed on the red velvet. Fanny's self-possession left her and she gasped.

"But Uncle Edgar! Aunt Louisa! It's too valuable!"

Uncle Edgar picked up the pendant and swung it from his plump forefinger. It was a dark blue sapphire set in diamonds and gold filigree.

"It belonged to an aunt of mine," said Uncle Edgar. "A great-aunt of yours. So you're entitled to it just as much as Amelia would be. That's what you're thinking, isn't it?"

Fanny looked again mutely at Aunt Louisa. Aunt Louisa said in her tart voice, "Don't thank me. I personally think your uncle is spoiling you. Just because you're going on a short journey which is no doubt a great excitement and pleasure to you."

So she was expected to take charge of the children when they had settled down at Darkwater. Aunt Louisa could not have told her more plainly. She was full of indignation and confusion, for she didn't mean to come back, anyway. So how could she accept so valuable a present?

Fanny had inherited from her Irish mother not only her luxuriant dark hair, but a mobile mouth whose lower lip protruded when she was hurt or angry. It was something she couldn't control.

"Why are you giving it to me, Uncle Edgar?" she asked aggressively.

Uncle Edgar's expression remained amused, benevolent, just a little unreadable.

"Because it pleases me to. It's as simple as that. Your aunt thought we should have waited until your twenty-first birthday. She didn't agree that this was the right occasion on which to make you a gift of this kind. Why not, I said? Fanny's like a daughter to us. We must do all we can for her. After all, she has only her looks to get her a husband. I've no doubt they're more than sufficient, but a bauble or two may help. Come here, my dear. Let me put it on you."

Some people, Fanny thought, were born to be givers and some

248

takers. Neither appreciated the other. She must accept this gift gracefully, although it couldn't have been made at a worse time. This was not the moment to begin feeling grateful, otherwise her strength of purpose would weaken. After all, she could leave the jewel behind. Amelia would eventually pounce on it greedily and claim it as her own.

Uncle Edgar's plump hands, remarkably soft, on the back of her neck made her flesh prickle. Once before she had felt them there. It was a long time ago. She was dripping wet from her fall into the lake, and he was caressing her beneath her soaking hair, reassuring her. She remembered that she had been still trembling with fear and shock.

The sapphire lay like the touch of a cool finger-tip against her throat.

Aunt Louisa had thawed sufficiently to give a frosty smile and said, "It's very becoming, Fanny. You must wear it at Amelia's coming-out ball."

"Yes, Aunt Louisa. Thank you very much. Thank you, Uncle Edgar."

(And people would say, Where did you get that magnificent pendant? Your uncle? Isn't he the most generous person in the world! . . .) But she wouldn't be there. She would be far far away in the Crimea, in a useful world she had found for herself. Fanny's lashes fluttered, and Uncle Edgar cried joyously, "There! She's looking delighted. Aren't you, my love?"

He gave his throaty chuckle and patted his wife's cheek.

"I hope you will look as delighted the next time I give you a piece of jewellery. Eh, my dearest?" He was using his playful tone, which meant he was in a high good humour. "But of course you will. You always do. That's one of the most charmingly predictable characteristics of the fair sex. Now, Fanny," his voice changed to his brisk business-like one. "You have only fifteen minutes in which to change before Trumble will be waiting. So run along, and see that Hannah is ready, too."

Chapter 3

DARKWATER . . . The name had come from the peculiarly dark colour of the water in the moat that had surrounded the house until the last century. The brown soil and the frequently lowering grey sky had made the water look black. Now the moat had been drained and the sloping lawn was green and innocent, but the lake glittering beyond the yews and chestnuts had the same tendency to turn into black marble on a dark day.

The drawbridge had gone, the Elizabethan façade of time-mellowed brick, diamond-paned windows, and rows of tortuously shaped chimneys, remained. Extensive restoration work had been done at the beginning of the century, but there were still the cavernous fireplaces, the winding stairways, the elaborately carved oak ceilings, darkened with time, and the tiny minstrels' gallery hanging over the long dining room.

There were twenty bedrooms, as well as those of the servants in the attics. The house and parkland lay in a gentle fold of the hills. Only from the upstairs windows were the moors visible. The wind blew across them and into the house which was always full of draughts and ancient creaking noises.

It was only in the summer that the place was innocent. Then the tattered and writhing shapes of the oaks were concealed beneath green leaves, the yellow flag irises swayed on the edge of the lake, and the water reflected the passing clouds. Sun shone through the diamond-paned windows of the house, and the whining edge had gone out of the wind. In the downstairs rooms there was an old old smell, impregnated in the walls, of pot pourri, beeswax, woodsmoke and roses. The warmth of the sun brought it out.

In summer Darkwater was beautiful. It was as if its happier ghosts—perhaps there were summertime ghosts—lived then.

But in winter the picture was entirely different. The gardens and parkland were desolate, leafless and stricken. Clouds and mist hung close to the ground. The Chinese pavilion by the lake, built by the same Davenport who had restored the house, its red and gold paint flaked and faded with the years, looked barbaric and completely alien. The wind battered on the windows and the heavy draperies made slow deliberate movements. Logs smouldered in the great fireplace in the hall day and night and fires had to be maintained in the living rooms and bedrooms. With the curtains drawn and the lamps lit the rooms took on a cosiness that deceived all but the most sensitive. These might be nervous maids who spilt hot water or a scuttle of coals in the passage because a curtain billowed out, or a voice cried. Or it was more likely to be the children who didn't care for the long passages at dusk and screamed if a draught blew out the candle. Amelia used to cling to Fanny's skirts. Fanny remembered once taking a wrong turning and instead of opening her bedroom door finding herself in a completely strange room, with a fourposter, and the dark shape of a form in the bed.

She had been sobbing with fright when the maid found her.

"It's your own fault, Miss Fanny! Running ahead like that, thinking to be so clever."

"There's s-someone in the bed!" Fanny stuttered.

The maid held the candle high. Its flickering light fell on the plump coverlet and the long shape of the bolster. The bed was empty.

"You see! There's no one there. This room hasn't been used for ages. Not since my time here, anyway. You're a silly girl to be frightened."

But the little maid, not much taller than Fanny, was frightened, too. Fanny knew that by the way the candlestick shook in her hand. They had scurried back down the passage, round the right turning, and safely to Fanny's room, the little narrow one next to Amelia's and the nursery.

That was when Fanny first began to hear sounds in the wind, voices, laughter and sometimes footsteps.

But that was partly Lady Arabella's fault for the unsuitable stories she had used to tell the children before their bedtime. She would begin an innocent fairy tale, and then, when the three children's attention was completely engaged, the tale would become subtly and indescribably sinister, this somehow made worse by Lady Arabella's own plump kindly and cosy appearance. Only her eyes showed a curious glee. They were the wolf's eyes looking out of the amiable sheep's head.

Amelia used to burst into sobs and have to be comforted with sugar plums. Fanny had never cried. Once she had put her fingers in her ears, and Lady Arabella had chuckled with what seemed to be gentle satisfaction. But mostly she had been driven to listening with a terrible fascination. She was not always able to eat her sugar plum afterwards, but put it in the pocket of her apron to be enjoyed in a calmer moment. George, of course, the eldest and a boy, never showed any nervousness or fear, but it was significant that now, in his delicate state of health as the result of his war wound, he frequently had nightmares and cried out, not about the charging Cossacks, but about the human head beneath the innocent piecrust, or the clothes in the wardrobe that came out and walked about in the dusk.

George was too old now to be comforted with sugar plums. He kept a bottle of brandy beside his bed instead. It was on the doctor's recommendation.

When Edgar Davenport had bought Darkwater some three years after his marriage, Lady Arabella had come to make her home there. She hadn't been interested in sharing the young couple's quite modest manor house in Dorset, she had bitterly opposed her daughter's marriage to a young man whom she had considered a nobody. She was the daughter of an earl herself, and had thought that Louisa could have done a great deal better for herself. But Louisa hadn't any great beauty and since Lady Arabella's husband had squandered her own fortune, and then drunk himself to death, Louisa's chances were considerably marred. At the age of twenty-three, she had been very glad to take Edgar, as perhaps her only chance. And anyway, if he was a quietish sort with no dashing looks, he was still a pleasant and amusing young man, with none of his young brother's tendencies towards wildness. As it turned out, he was a very good catch, for when the ancient great uncle in Devon died, and Darkwater came on the market, it appeared that Edgar had more resources than he had divulged.

Darkwater, he said, must not be allowed to go out of the family. He would buy it himself, even if it meant economising for years to come. His wife demurred, it was late autumn when she saw Darkwater for the first time and it depressed and vaguely frightened her. The leaves were falling and the clouds hanging low. The house indoors had the shabbiness to be expected after the eighty year occupation of a bookish and solitary bachelor. It made Louisa shiver. Or perhaps this was only because she was at that time expecting Amelia, and pregnancies didn't agree with her.

But Edgar had no intention of asking his wife's opinion. He was the master and the decision was his. He had made up his mind the moment he had heard of his great uncle's death.

So, just before Amelia's birth, the family moved to Devon, and Lady Arabella accompanied them. It was necessary for a mother to be near her daughter at such a time, she said. Her innocent myopic eyes told nothing, but it was clear enough from the start that she considered Darkwater a fitting residence for herself, the descendant of a noble family. She meant to spend the rest of her life there.

She had no patience with Louisa's fancies about the place. Anyway, Louisa's blood had been considerably watered down by the unfortunate father she had had, and one wouldn't expect her to fit so easily into this environment.

Edgar took immediately to the life of lord of the manor, with his stable well-stocked with good hunters and his house with servants, his tenants eagerly welcoming a landlord who was interested in their welfare, the village church no less, for it needed restoration and a vicar less old and doddering, and the sparse social life of the moors desperately wanted an infusion of new blood. Lady Arabella also took to the mingled charm and desolation of Darkwater. She found that it suited her temperament. The closing down of the mist filled her with excitement, she adored the wind-petrified shapes of the leafless trees, she simply put on another shawl if the draughts were too bad.

She selected two large rooms on the first floor and made them uniquely hers. As the years went by the rooms shrank, for they were so cluttered with her possessions. These included a life size marble statue of her mother, the Countess of Dalston in Grecian robes which stood imposingly in a corner. At dusk, before the maids had brought in the lamps, it looked terrifyingly like another person in the room. Even more so when Lady Arabella had negligently tossed one of her shawls, or perhaps her garden hat, on to it. But this was strictly her privilege. No servant or child was allowed to take such liberties.

For the rest, there were innumerable small tables, knick-knacks, paintings, low chairs with uncomfortably sloping backs, an astonishing edifice of seashells and fishes beneath a glass dome, an enormous globe on which she was wont to make the children trace all the countries of the British Empire, a birdcage empty and a little morbid since her parrot had died, heavy plush curtains heavily ornamented with bobbles, gilt-framed mirrors, cupboards filled to overflowing with a hotchpotch of stuff, and in the centre of the room the chaise-longe on which Lady Arabella spent a great deal of her time, doing her needlework or pursuing what she called her historical readings. She was deeply interested in history and folklore, particularly regarding the part of the country in which she lived.

Or she might simply sit idle with her cat Ludwig in her lap.

"Do you know why he is called Ludwig?" she used to ask the unwillingly enthralled children. "Because once I was in love with someone called Ludwig. Oh, yes, stare if you like, but it's true. He was a German prince. He had moustaches, so!" Lady Arabella puffed her cheeks and caressed imaginary moustaches. She was a born story-teller. "But he wasn't permitted by his parents, or protocol, call it what you will, to return your Grandmamma's love. And anyway I was only sixteen, which was much too young even in those days, when we were all wearing muslin dresses that looked like nightgowns and pretending to be afraid of Napoleon Buonaparte. So now I have only a cat to love me. Unless by some chance any of you children do."

She stared at them so hard with her round short-sighted eyes that they murmured affirmatives, Amelia going so far as to cry, "I do, Grandmamma. I do."

It was always George, her favourite, to whom Lady Arabella looked for a display of affection.

But it was only Ludwig, the big dark tabby with the flat supercilious face who sat on her lap and rubbed his head insinuatingly against her. Fanny was sure he was the German prince reincarnated.

Those two rooms were a small world within a world. As a child Fanny had felt as if she had been on a nerve-wracking journey when she had had to visit Lady Arabella. It was only when she was grown-up and read to Lady Arabella daily that she lost her fear of the old lady. Or thought she did.

Louisa had grumbled continuously after the move to Darkwater. Finally her husband, in spite of his constant talk of economy, found enough money to buy her an elegant sable cape and muff. So Louisa made the discovery that an expensive gift could do a great deal towards mending hurt feelings. She never let her husband forget that again.

When Fanny, the difficult precocious three year old, who already showed that she was going to have more looks than Amelia, arrived, Louisa found that a diamond brooch made her more tolerant towards the child. During the years, various crises were suitably marked by trinkets, a new bonnet, silk for a gown. Edgar Davenport was an indulgent husband. Or perhaps he just liked peace.

Needless to say, Louisa was already debating the price of the orphans from Shanghai. This could be a high one, because the situation was getting ridiculous. Edgar's relatives seemed to have a habit of dying like flies and leaving their offspring in his devoted care. To have three penniless children foisted on one was not amusing during the course of one's marriage. Not to say that Fanny wasn't quite useful now, so long as she kept her place. But with the worry of George's health and the launching of Amelia into society, there was just no time or place in Louisa Davenport's life for small foreign children.

George was waiting at the turn of the stairs when Fanny, dressed now in her best, came down. He sprang out at her and seized her hand. She started violently. She hadn't seen him there in the shadows. He was always doing this sort of thing now, lying in wait for her, and then laughing immoderately, especially if she screamed.

He wasn't laughing today. Instead he put her hand to his lips, pressing a passionate kiss on it.

Fanny tried to snatch it away. She couldn't until he chose to let it go. He had a frighteningly strong grasp.

"I wish you wouldn't do that, George. It's absurd, and I don't like it."

"Absurd?" The word faltered. He was hurt, his confidence ebbing. He was such a good-looking young man, tall, broad-shouldered, a high glow in his cheeks. When he had joined the

27th Lancers he had looked so proud and arrogant in his uniform. But now, although he had suffered no physical disfigurement, his long body had that vaguely shambling look, his eyes changed too quickly from uncertainty and hurt to intense excitement. His actions, too, were unpredictable. He would want the groom to saddle his horse at midnight so that he could ride over the moors, or he would walk about the house calling out softly to see who was awake and would talk to him.

All the doctors said that a long period of rest and quiet was essential. After that he should be able to lead a normal life, not too strenuous, perhaps. His army career was certainly over. But there seemed no reason why he shouldn't eventually marry.

"George!" That was his mother's voice from the foot of the stairs. It was sharp. Although it was addressed to George, the sharpness was for Fanny. She was annoyed by this attachment her son had formed for Fanny, and blamed Fanny for it. It was easy enough to cool a young man's ardour if one wanted to. Fanny obviously didn't want to. After all, George was quite a catch.

"George, Tomkins has been walking up and down with your horse for half an hour. He said you wanted it by eleven. Don't keep the poor beast waiting any longer."

"Oh, lord, I forgot." George was an abashed schoolboy, the passionate lover gone. "Well, good-bye, Fanny. Have a good time. Don't stay away long. We'll miss you."

Why, this might be the last time she ever saw him! The knowledge swept over Fanny, making her forget George's recently developed disturbing habits, and remembering only that he had always seemed to be her brother.

"Good-bye, George," she called fondly. "Take care of yourself."

George turned to give a gratified wave. His mother said tartly, "Since you'll be gone no more than two nights, Fanny, nothing much can happen to George or any of us in that time."

"Things can happen to people all the time," Lady Arabella was shuffling down the passage from her room. "I fancy I heard the bird last night."

Once, only once, long ago, when she had been less than ten years old, Fanny, too, had heard the bird. She had lain petrified for hours after the scuffling noise had stopped. The legendary bird was reputed to be imprisoned in one of the many chimneys, though in which one no one was ever quite sure. It had been a white bird, the legend said, though when finally it fell lifeless into the hearth it was pitifully soot-streaked. It could have been a white barn owl, people said, or a dove. Or there was the fantastic story that it had been a white heron, its long legs hopelessly entangled in the narrow space. That had been why the fluttering and screeching had been so loud. Its imprisonment had coincided with the death of the young mistress of Darkwater at that time. When the dishevelled creature had fallen into the hearth, her young face had lain like snow on her pillow.

As the years and then the centuries passed, the struggling bird was heard again and again. It always portended disaster.

"Mamma, there was a gale blowing last night," Aunt Louisa said. "That's all you heard."

"That's what you'd like to think," said the old lady portentously. "But remember the last time I heard it. We had news about George soon after."

Aunt Louisa clucked impatiently.

"Goodness me, it's a good thing we haven't all got your imagination. If I'd listened to all your omens I'd have been frightened out of my life years ago. Now watch your step. Where are you going?"

The old lady lifted her voluminous skirts an inch or two and peered short-sightedly at the stairs.

"To say good-bye to Fanny, of course. Should I be left out of the farewells?"

"First George, and now you. Anyone would think Fanny was going on a long journey and not coming back."

Lady Arabella had reached Fanny's side. She was out of breath and wheezing a little. She tucked a crumpled package into Fanny's hand.

"Sugar plums, my dear. Eat them on the journey. Keep one or two for the children. They will find them comforting. You always did, do you remember?"

"Yes, Great-aunt Arabella. Thank you very much."

Fanny's eyes pricked with tears. It was a good thing the old lady was too short-sighted to see them. Anyway, she had turned to remount the stairs. She had two woolly shawls round her shoulders. Her head, with its slightly awry lace cap, sank among them cosily. With her short broad stature and her skirts tending towards the crinoline, it was virtually impossible to pass her on the stairs. She was more comical than sinister. Surely she wasn't really sinister, at all. That had been only childish imagination in a dusk-filled room.

Now she had been kind, and Fanny wished passionately that she hadn't been. First it had been Amelia with her request for French ribbons, then George urging her to hurry back, and now Lady Arabella giving her comfits for her journey.

But she mustn't let these things shake her resolution. She wouldn't be back at Darkwater. Never again . . .

Hannah had appeared with the baggage, and Uncle Edgar came in briskly to say that the carriage was at the door.

"That's better," he said, looking at Fanny's smart appearance. Her fur-trimmed cloak, the smart shiny boots peeping beneath her silk skirts, her bonnet tied with velvet ribbon, all marked her as a young lady of taste and fashion. "You must look your best, my dear, otherwise you may find people trying to take advantage of you. Hannah!"

The elderly servant in her modest dark attire came forward. "Yes, sir?"

"I expect you to take good care of Miss Fanny. Don't let her do anything foolish."

Hannah's lips went together. It wasn't for her to say that the master must know Miss Fanny could be unpredictable at times. Didn't he remember the storms and tantrums at intervals in the past? But one had to admit she looked a well-bred well-behaved young lady at this minute, so perhaps all would be well. Personally she couldn't wait until the nerve-wracking journey in one of those fast smoky trains was over, the perils of London safely avoided, and all of them home again in the peace and quiet of Darkwater.

"Fanny! Fanny!" Amelia was flying down the stairs, her skirts billowing. "Here's the money for the ribbon. Papa gave it to me. Don't forget, it's to be striped. And if you can't get the exact shade, get the nearest you can." Amelia's cheeks were as pink as the ribbon she hoped Fanny would bring back from London. She was a silly little affectionate thing, and one didn't want to disappoint her . . . Reluctantly Fanny put out her hand for the money. Hannah could bring back the ribbon. Uncle Edgar was smiling indulgently. Aunt Louisa said, "Really, Amelia! You and your fallals. I hope you're not neglecting the serious reading Miss Ferguson recommended every day. Then come, Fanny. Trumble can't wait forever."

Darkwater . . . All the way down the curving drive, Fanny's head was thrust out of the carriage to look back. The sun was out from behind the clouds, and the house looked the way she loved it most, warmly red, the windows shining, smoke curling from the twisted chimneys. It was like a jewel lying against its backdrop of gentle green hillside. The flaring red of rhododendrons marked the path to the lake. The lawns were velvet. The peacock and the peahen strutted near the rose garden. Rooks cawed in the swaying elms.

"Put your head in, Miss Fanny, do."

Fanny fumbled for her handkerchief. She couldn't let Hannah see the tears on her cheeks. It was Hannah, long ago, who had told the children, and the avidly interested Lady Arabella the legend of the bird in the chimney. She had heard it from the previous housekeeper who had been in employment at Darkwater for forty years. And before that it had come from another superstitious and nervous servant.

It was only a legend. No one really believed it, not even Lady Arabella, although it pleased her to make startling announcements.

Indeed, there must often have been a bird caught in one of those many chimneys, a swift, perhaps, or a starling. But not that white forlorn sinister one that was a portent.

Yet Fanny had sometimes likened herself to the unfortunate creature. She too, had been caught in her poverty, in her orphanhood, in her inability to live a free untrammelled life because an unprotected young woman had little place in the world.

That was why she had determined to escape before she, like the bird, suffocated in the claustrophobic atmosphere.

But today she loved Darkwater. If only the morning had been dark and gloomy, the clouds pressing down, the wind whining. But the sun shone and she had a sense of identification with the great faded rose-red house lying against the hillside. It was as if she had known it, not only for the seventeen years of her residence there, but for centuries. She was going to long for it bitterly, as if she had left part of her heart behind.

A branch whipped her face. She drew back, a reason now for her tears.

"There, I told you," said Hannah. "Hanging out there like a great overgrown child. You're a fine one to be bringing little children safe home."

Fanny dabbed at her reddened cheek.

"I'm sorry, Hannah. I do foolish things."

"You don't need to tell me that, Miss Fanny." Hannah had been at Darkwater for fifty years. She came from the village where she, and her seven brothers and sisters had slept like peas in a pod in the bedroom of the two roomed cottage. Her father had been a labourer on the estate and her mother, in between being brought to bed with a new baby, had helped in the kitchen of the great house. Later, there had only been two brothers and a sister left. The rest, one by one, had withered away with a fever. Only four in the big bed had seemed lonely. Hannah had been glad at the age of twelve to begin work in the great house. Now she was sixty-two and had earned the privilege to speak her mind. "I can see I'll have my hands full with the three of you."

"No, you won't, Hannah. I'm going to be perfectly sensible."

Hannah reached out a neatly gloved hand to pat Fanny's. Being the eldest of eight children had given her a maternal quality that she had never lost. Her face, apple-cheeked and prim, within the sedate circle of her bonnet, was full of kindness.

"Of course you will, love. You can be when you wish. But don't look as if it's going to be such pain to you. Or is it that you're homesick already? Silly child. You're not leaving Darkwater forever."

Chapter 4

EVERYTHING had gone according to plan. Fanny and Hannah had arrived safely in London to find that the children were due from the ship docked at Tilbury by midday the next day. Fanny had contained her excitement about her own private plans sufficiently even to go shopping for Amelia's ribbon. She meant to go with Hannah to meet the children, take them by cab to Paddington and put them on the train for Devon, then take Hannah aside and say good-bye.

Hannah would be dreadfully upset, she might even be angry, but she was a servant and must do as she was ordered. She was quite capable of taking the children safely to Darkwater and breaking the news of Fanny's escape.

Escape? It was odd that that was the word that came to her.

Of course she didn't mean to tell Hannah where she was going. That could result in Uncle Edgar fuming and fussing to London to insist on her returning home. She would merely say she had a situation and was going to take it up that day.

It had all seemed so simple. The only thing she had overlooked was her emotional reaction to the new arrivals.

She hadn't thought they would look so small and desperately self-contained and lost. It hadn't occurred to her that she might see herself in them, herself as she had been seventeen years ago, just as frightened and lost, just as eager for a welcoming voice.

But there they were, the strange little trio, rooted to the ground with apprehension. Miss Nightingale and her nurses, the pride of doing a worthwhile task, the possibility of meeting some young man who would marry her for love, all swept out of Fanny's head. She was kneeling on the dusty sooty ground to gather the children into her arms.

The amah was bowing low. Behind her the strange man said, "I take it you are Miss Davenport?"

Fanny straightened herself. The little girl whom she had embraced stood aloof, her black eyes still staring warily, but the boy's cold hand was curled within her own.

"I am. And you're the gentleman from the shipping company who so kindly met my little cousins."

He bowed. "My name is Adam Marsh."

She hadn't needed to know his name. She wondered how she could best give him his guinea with dignity and bid him farewell. She thought he was behaving in a slightly too familiar way for a mere employee of a shipping company. He was really staring at her quite openly. His eyes were very dark brown, almost black.

"Thank you, Mr Marsh, for your help. My uncle will no doubt be writing to you. In the meantime, he instructed me to give you this."

She held out the guinea in her gloved hand. She thought that for a moment Mr Marsh looked surprised, as perhaps was not to be wondered at. He would hardly expect to receive money from a young woman. But in a moment his fleeting expression of surprise had turned to what seemed to be amusement, and he took the coin with another bow. He was well-dressed, she noticed, his coat of excellent cut, his linen immaculate.

"My thanks to your uncle, Miss Davenport. But surely we're not parting immediately. I believe I was to see you safely on your train for Devon."

"That's quite unnecessary. I have my maid waiting at the other side of the barrier. We have ordered a cab." She looked up at the waiting young man. Something made her add, "Though I would be grateful if you would see us to the cab and find a porter for the luggage . . ."

"The porter is waiting. And in the cab we'll perform introductions. I believe you don't yet know the children's names."

He was very self-assured. It was scarcely his business, a stranger, to make her known to her own cousins.

But she couldn't help the relief of being capably looked after. The old Chinese woman looked so remote and unapproachable, and the children seemed likely to burst into tears at any moment. It was nice to see Adam Marsh swing the little boy into his arms, and tell the girl to take Miss Davenport's hand. It made them a little family, filing through the gates, the amah discreetly a few paces behind.

The cab was waiting. The luggage was hoisted on top, and the children, then Fanny, followed by the amah who was plainly terrified of this new method of transport, got inside. Hannah, who was relieved to have everyone safely arrived, climbed in next, and Mr Marsh told the driver to take them to Paddington station.

As Fanny was leaning out to repeat her thanks to him, he lifted a long leg on to the step.

"Is there room inside for me? I think so. Nolly and Marcus and Ching Mei take up the space of only one small person. Marcus can come on my lap."

He settled down comfortably, his knees all but touching Fanny's.

"But, Mr Marsh—"

"Not a word, Miss Davenport. It's no trouble to me at all. Besides," he patted his pocket, and surely the gravity of his face didn't conceal the irreverent amusement, "I have been well paid. Now let me have the pleasure of presenting your cousins to you. This," he took the little girl's hand, "is Olivia, but I understand she has always been called Nolly. And this young fellow is Marcus. Shake hands with your cousin—" he hesitated questioningly.

"Fanny," said Fanny reluctantly, and only for the benefit of the children. This stranger was taking too much on himself. Hannah was looking at him with disapproval. It was the way she should be looking at him, too. Yet she couldn't help liking the easy way he held the little boy in his lap. He surely couldn't be just a lowly shipping clerk. Perhaps he was the son of the owner, learning the business from the ground up, as some young men did.

"Your cousin Fanny," he said, prompting the children, who reluctantly held out limp cold hands to be shaken.

The little girl spoke for the first time.

"Are we going to live with you?"

The unmistakably hostile and perfectly contained voice abruptly brought Fanny to a realisation of what she had let happen to herself. In a moment of emotion and pity and sympathy she had sacrificed her chances of happiness, happiness which for her lay only in living an independent and worthwhile life. She had gone down on her knees on a dusty smutty railway station and promised two strange children that they would be safe with her.

She never broke promises. She would particularly never break one made to a trusting child. But in the close confines of the cab the strange atmosphere of lostness and danger that had seemed to hang over the children had vanished, and they were just two children like any others, the girl with her cool hostile gaze, the boy not much more than a baby, his nose needing attention, his eyelids beginning to droop.

They would have been all right at Darkwater, with Hannah and Dora, and the little alien-faced amah who as yet had not said a word.

But now she had promised, and already they, or the girl at least, odd little precocious creature, was looking to her for reassurance. And anyway this interfering Adam Marsh obviously meant to stay until the moment the train left, with them all safely aboard. It wasn't any business of his. He was exceeding his duties. But one had to suppose he meant well.

Fanny's resentment against the children encompassed him, too. Did he think she looked the kind of person who would be content with living in the background all her life?

But how could he know she did that? She was the niece of a wealthy man. He probably saw her living a leisured and pampered life. Uncle Edgar had always meant outsiders to see just that.

Fanny impatiently loosened the fastenings of her fur-trimmed cape. It was hot in the cab. She could feel her cheeks flushed. And she was acutely aware that Adam Marsh was still subjecting her to his thoughtful scrutiny, as Nolly said again, patiently, "Are we to live with you, Cousin Fanny?"

"With your uncle and aunt, and your cousins Amelia and George—yes, and me, too," she answered meticulously.

"And her?" She pointed to Hannah.

"Yes, Hannah, and the other servants."

"It sounds a great many people," said Nolly, with her lack of expression. "I don't think Marcus will care for that. He's shy." And suddenly she flung round on the Chinese woman and began a flood of words in a strange language.

The woman replied sharply. The staccato exchange was over in a moment. Fanny noticed, with some bewilderment, that the amah's bright slit-eyes had gone over Nolly's head to Adam

Marsh's almost as if in supplication. She murmured something more, and he nodded, as if he understood.

"What are you saying? What is everyone saying?"

Adam replied quietly, "I think Nolly was begging to be taken back to Shanghai, and of course Ching Mei explained that was quite impossible."

"Do you speak Chinese?"

"A little. I had a trip to the Far East when I was a boy."

"Oh," said Fanny, satisfied. "So that's why you were chosen to meet the ship today. That was very sensible of the shipping company. It must have made everyone feel much more at home. It's very kind of you to take this personal interest, Mr Marsh."

"I think I haven't mentioned Ching Mei to you, Miss Davenport. She has made a great sacrifice in leaving her country to bring the children safely here. It appears she promised their mother to do this. But you can understand it was a tremendous enterprise for someone who hasn't travelled before and who speaks little English."

Fanny was too warm-hearted to let her own disappointments obsess her. She turned sympathetically to the amah in her high-necked black smock and impulsively touched one of the wrinkled yellow hands folded so quietly.

"You will be taken care of, too, Ching Mei. My uncle is very kindhearted and generous."

The slit eyes in the little alien face stared back uncomprehendingly.

"She won't understand you," said Adam Marsh. "But may I say to you, Miss Davenport, that if your uncle could find the opportunity to send her home when the children are settled, it would be a great kindness."

That was nothing to do with Adam Marsh, either. Uncle Edgar might decide that the cost of an old Chinese woman's return to her country was too high. But Fanny found herself nodding, and in her high unfamiliar voice, Ching Mei suddenly said, "Velly kind."

The cab was trundling through the dusty narrow streets that led to Paddington Railway station. In a few more minutes they would be there. If they could find an empty compartment the children could be bedded down on the seats and persuaded to sleep. Because she hadn't expected to make the long journey home, Fanny was now dreading it.

For no reason at all she was thinking of the sapphire pendant locked in her jewel box. She had purposely left it behind, disclaiming possession of it. Now she would have to wear it to Amelia's ball. It would mark her again as one of the family, and this seemed to her to be co-operating in a lie. She was no more one of the family than these children would ever be.

She realised she had never given a thought to the fact that their skin was as white as her own. She didn't think it would have worried her if it hadn't been, but at least Amelia would be profoundly relieved.

Mr Marsh had found them an empty compartment only one carriage from the dining car. He was efficient to the end. He helped them all aboard. Ching Mei, her bland wrinkled face showing no expression, though this must be one more tremendous ordeal for her, came last. Fanny helped Hannah settle the children then emerged into the corridor to see her lifting an intent face to Adam Marsh. He had just finished saying something to her. She gave the briefest nod, then with her neat silent movements, she left him, and he looked up to see Fanny.

"What were you saying to Ching Mei?"

He smiled very faintly.

"You're observant, Miss Davenport."

"Perhaps. These people are in my charge now. Your duties are ended. There was no need for final instructions."

He smiled more broadly.

"The final instructions you assume were merely reassurance. Don't you realise that poor little creature is scared out of her wits."

"I don't see what is so terrifying about Hannah and me," Fanny said coldly. "Why wasn't she afraid of you, too? Was that because you spoke in her language?"

"She isn't afraid of you, Miss Davenport, but of this great monster." He indicated the noisily steaming engine. "Of the travelling, the strange language, the future."

"You are very concerned about an old Chinese woman. Why not the children? Everything is strange to them, too."

She felt his eyes dwelling with their serious intent regard on her face.

"The children will have a future. They will have you."

"You have certainly summed up the situation in a very short time, Mr Marsh."

He was too observant. He had caught the asperity, or perhaps the undercurrent of grievance in her voice.

"You speak as if the situation isn't entirely to your liking."

Fanny lifted her chin. The momentary impulse to confide in him had been so strong and so surprising that she had to speak sharply.

"As far as it is in my power to make them so, the children will be happy. You have no need to feel so concerned for people who have crossed your path so briefly, and only as a matter of business."

He completely ignored her rebuke. He said softly, "I think you could make anyone happy, Miss Fanny."

To her confusion the colour flew into Fanny's cheeks. She had been right in her first opinion. This young man exceeded his duties in the most extraordinary way. He assumed a too proprietory attitude towards a strange family and now calmly called her by her first name. This apart from the intimacy of his remark. And yet . . .

"I think the porter is about to blow his whistle, Mr Marsh. Isn't it time you stepped off the train?"

"In a moment. Perhaps we will meet again one day."

"I should think it quite unlikely."

"Our meeting today was unlikely. Who knows? I have a great liking for the Devonshire moors."

With this remark he did step off the train. Fanny backed away to return to the compartment and the children, one of whom she could hear crying. But for a moment she was held, not quite understanding her upsurge of hope.

Perhaps there was to be something in her life, after all.

Because a shipping clerk, someone Aunt Louisa would call a mere nobody, had expressed a liking for the moors?

But then, if she were ever to marry, she couldn't expect a husband who was anything but a mere nobody. Unless, of course, he was someone swept off his feet by her beauty and tenderness, to the exclusion of all other considerations . . .

Mr Adam Marsh, standing on the railway platform looking up at her so intently, did give a vague impression that this might have happened to him.

Fanny's heart was beating uncontrollably faster. Then suddenly, folding the expensive material of her cloak around her, she realised that she looked what she was not, a rich young woman. Certainly rich by a shipping clerk's standards.

He was calling something to her.

"Remember—"

The steam was hissing noisily from the engine. She leaned forward.

"What did you say?"

"Remember me when we meet again."

The words made their own beautiful shape in the confusion of sounds. Then a cloud of smoke enveloped the platform and when it cleared the whistle had sounded and the train was moving out. It was no longer possible to see the expression in Adam Marsh's face. He stood, a tall figure, raising his hand in farewell. He grew smaller and smaller as the distance lengthened, and Hannah was at Fanny's side saying crossly, "Miss Fanny, come in, do. All that dirty smoke over your good clothes. And if you ask me, that young man had a great deal too much to say for someone in his position."

This was all true. But for once Fanny was going to be illogical.

"Oh, I don't think so. He talked the greatest sense. Where would we have been without him?"

"Where we are now, of course," Hannah retorted acidly. "And with the boy crying his head off, and that Chinese sitting like a foreign image, I declare I don't know how this journey is to be got over."

("I almost think, Hannah—I almost think I have fallen in love.") Fanny pressed her lips together, keeping back the impulsive confession. But she couldn't repress the flush in her cheeks, or her surge of gaiety. Now she was glad to be going back to Darkwater. Because if Adam Marsh liked moors he would make a point of spending time on them when he had the opportunity. He was certainly a young man who made his own opportunities. His company would have a ship sailing from Plymouth, perhaps, and he would break his journey down there to make a call at Darkwater to see how the passengers in whom he had taken such an interest were settling down.

Or he would invent some other reason. She had no doubt as to his versatility. And now his interest in the children and the Chinese amah no longer puzzled her. It had developed, of course, immediately after he had set eyes on her.

"Miss Fanny—"

"I'm coming, Hannah. Why are you worrying?" Fanny's voice was gay. "We are going to have a completely pleasant journey."

The children were sitting bolt upright. Nolly had refused to lie down, it seemed, so Marcus had done the same, a habit of imitation that Fanny suspected was frequent. There were tears still on his cheeks, and his large smoky blue eyes were woebegone.

Nolly, however, showed no distress. She sat primly, her feet in their shiny buttoned boots crossed, her hands clasped in her lap. She had something of the composure of the elderly amah, a discipline learned far too young, and hiding, Fanny guessed, a smouldering volcano. The black eyes stared with an unchildlike challenge. Small wonder that Marcus was dominated by a sister like this.

"They're not like children at all," Hannah said in an undertone to Fanny.

"Oh, I think they are," said Fanny. "I expect they won't go to sleep because they're hungry. Unpack that hamper, Hannah, and let us have some lunch. Then everybody's temper will be better."

This, however, was not a complete success. Marcus would have nothing more than a mug of milk, and his sister began a chicken sandwich which presently she laid down with the polite remark that she didn't care for the taste of it. Hannah's lips tightened, but Fanny merely said pleasantly, "Then try one of these biscuits. I assure you they're very good."

Nolly stared.

"Doesn't Marcus need to eat his sandwich either?"

"Train journeys," said Fanny, "are occasions when one isn't forced to eat anything one doesn't like. Naturally it is different at home. But we're not at home yet, are we."

"Home?" echoed Marcus hopefully.

"Don't be silly," said his sister. "We're never going home again. You know that. Mamma and Papa have gone to heaven and we have no home."

"And that," said Fanny, "is something I never want to hear said again. Hannah and I have travelled hundreds of miles to get you and take you home. What a stupid little girl you are. Now will you please ask Ching Mei to have another sandwich."

Nolly stared with her disconcerting unflickering gaze. She had a small slightly turned-up nose. Her mouth was soft and childlike. Dark ringlets hung beneath her bonnet. She was only a baby, one realised, if one could ignore her alarming composure.

"I don't think we care for you, Cousin Fanny."

"I'm sorry about that."

"Do you care for us?"

"Not immoderately at this moment."

"Then we have no friends."

"Don't be silly," said Fanny exasperatedly. "I'm your friend. So is Hannah. So is your Cousin Amelia and Aunt Louisa and Uncle Edgar." She spoke firmly, making her words persuasive. But Nolly was staring at her, disbelieving. Perhaps afraid to believe.

"It's true," said Fanny. "And now will you please do as I ask. Pass Ching Mei a sandwich."

The Chinese woman spoke suddenly in her high voice. Nolly pouted, then grudgingly did as Fanny had bidden her.

"There's going to be trouble with that one," Hannah whispered to Fanny. "You can't have her only taking orders from the Chinese woman."

"From Ching Mei, Hannah. She has a name. And Nolly's accustomed to obeying her. She'll learn to obey us, too."

"There'll be tantrums," said Hannah darkly. "Perhaps worse than yours used to be, Miss Fanny."

"One only needs to have understanding," Fanny said.

For she knew—Nolly was herself. Uprooted, unhappy, resentful, bewildered, impelled to fight dragons she couldn't see . . . The little girl pulled at her heart already.

Her own rebellion was dead. Or perhaps it was merely taking a different form. From now on she was to be the champion of these two orphans, and do her best to make them happy in an unwelcoming household. That was to be her purpose in life. That, and perhaps the visit of Adam Marsh to the moors . . .

"I don't know what's happened to you, Miss Fanny," Hannah muttered. "You're talking like an old woman. And you're flushed, as if you have a fever. Do you feel quite well?"

"I've never felt so well," said Fanny, with truth.

Chapter 5

LETTERS arrived for Edgar Davenport late that afternoon. One bore a foreign postmark, one came from London.

Edgar recognised the handwriting on each. He opened the one with the Chinese postmark first. He believed in facing bad news quickly.

It was, as he had suspected, from Hamish Barlow, the attorney who had first written to him about Oliver's death and the trust imposed in him regarding the two children. He fully expected it to contain a list of his brother's debts. This was not the case. Although the debts undoubtedly existed, Mr Hamish Barlow was, surprisingly enough, going to acquaint Edgar personally with them.

"By the time you receive this letter I shall be on my way to England. I have a passage on the tea clipper, the *Verity*, which, all being well, expects to make the journey in something like twelve weeks. So you may think of expecting me about the end of August or early in September. I have various business affairs to attend to, but I will not deceive you that the journey is being made chiefly in regard to settling your brother's estate. It has aspects which I would prefer to acquaint you with by word of mouth.

Also, I made a promise to your brother and his charming wife, now so tragically gone from us, that I would satisfy myself as to the safe arrival of the children who should be with you on receipt of this.

I sincerely trust they completed their journey without mishap. The Chinese woman, Ching Mei, is of the highest integrity, and intelligence.

I am looking forward, my dear Mr Davenport, to making your acquaintance, and this I propose to do as speedily as possible after my arrival in London. I shall inform you when this event takes place."

"H'mm," Edgar muttered, throwing the letter down.

He opened the other one. It was from his stockbroker. It informed him that much to the writer's regret it looked as if the Maxim Banking Company, an enterprise in which Edgar had invested a substantial sum of money, was, contrary to paying a dividend, likely to show a loss on the year's trading. The writer recommended salvaging as much money as possible at once, as he foresaw panic among the shareholders.

"I am sorry to say I predict your loss will be as much as seventy five per cent, or even more," the letter concluded.

Upstairs, Louisa Davenport was dressing for dinner. Since Hannah was not yet back from London, Dora, the new maid, was called in to help. She was slow and clumsy and terribly nervous. Louisa had little patience with inexperience. She increased the girl's confusion by ordering her to do too many things.

"Lay out my grey silk. No, not that. That's blue. Where are your eyes? The crinoline. Put it on the bed. Now come and lace me. How strong are you?"

Dora looked at her skinny arms. She was undergrown, plain, with crooked teeth, and only fourteen years old. She had just been promoted to the upstairs after two years of washing dishes and scurrying hither and thither for cook in the kitchen. The mistress had asked her if she were fond of children and she had said yes, because how could you say anything else? Anyway, it was true. There were ten brothers and sisters in the cottage on the moors and she found she had missed them painfully when she had come to the big house. She had been pleased and excited to be told that if she wished she could move upstairs and help to care for the new arrivals from far-off China.

But she hadn't known that would bring her to doing anything so terrifying as lacing the mistress.

"I'm very wiry, ma'am," she said nervously.

Louisa had found the new fashion of the crinoline much to her liking. The only drawback was that it necessitated a neat waist, and that she had not got.

"H'mm," she said to Dora sceptically, "We'll see. Take these two ends and pull. Oh, good gracious, girl, you haven't the strength of a fly. Amelia, is that you?" There had been a tap at the door. "Come and help this incompetent creature."

Amelia came bursting in, and promptly began to giggle.

"There's no need for impertinence, miss."

"I'm sorry, Mamma, but you do look funny. Do you really want these awfully tight? You know it makes your face flush."

"I shall have only six courses at dinner," said her mother. "Then I shall be perfectly comfortable. You know we have Sir Giles and Lady Mowatt coming."

"They're so dreary," Amelia complained. "The governor of a prison. Ugh!"

"Sir Giles is a man of importance. Your father likes him."

"Papa! But when is there going to be someone for *me* to like? Someone young. Doesn't Papa realise I'm grown-up."

"Of course he realises it. Don't be so stupid."

"He never seemed to notice Fanny was. He never did anything about her. And now she's getting old."

"Dora," said Louisa, "give me the hairbrush. I shall do my own hair. Miss Amelia will help me. You may go."

Dora bobbed thankfully and withdrew. Louisa turned crossly to her daughter.

"Haven't I told you before not to discuss family affairs in front of the servants?"

"Oh, Dora," said Amelia. "She won't gossip because no one listens to her. And Mamma, it's true what I said. Fanny has hardly ever met a young man, and now I'm seventeen I don't intend that to happen to me."

Louisa surveyed her daughter with mingled indulgence and criticism. It was a pity she wasn't ravishingly pretty. But her skin was good and she had animation. She would never be left sitting silent in a corner. Her fair hair tied in ringlets on either side of her face was quite charming. Being a little over-plump suited her style. She was a presentable daughter. There was only one trouble and that was one her father refused to admit or understand. Her looks faded to insignificance beside Fanny's. Fanny, when her emotions were aroused, had a way of looking incandescent. She reduced Amelia's chatter and smiles and fluttering lashes to the gauche tricks of a schoolgirl.

It was all very well for Edgar, with his exaggerated sense of fairness and responsibility, to insist on the girls being treated like sisters. But Edgar was a man, and men were blind to the subtler points of feminine behaviour. He had to be made to realise that this was Amelia's year, and Fanny must be kept in the background.

For instance, that extravagant unnecessary gift to Fanny of the sapphire pendant had been an error of major importance. It would only serve to make the girl flaunt her looks even more. Edgar refused to see that. But then Edgar always had been stupid. Stupid, stupid, stupid, thought Louisa, the comb snapping in two in her clenched hands.

Amelia sprang towards her.

"Mamma, have you hurt yourself?"

"Of course I haven't." Louisa laid down the broken comb calmly. "I was only wondering why you compare yourself with Fanny. The circumstances are entirely different. Your father and I will certainly make it our business to see that you meet plenty of young men, if not here, then in London."

"London, Mamma!"

"It occurred to me we might open our house there for your ball. But that will depend on your father."

Amelia clapped her plump small very white hands. (Some day someone would say to her, "You have very little hands like water lilies, see, just curving open." And then he would bend his head and kiss her palm.)

"Papa will do anything for me!"

"Will he, indeed. You know I won't permit him to spoil you. And don't be too confident. We have so much worry with George now, and these wretched children arriving are another problem."

"Fanny will look after them," Amelia said blithely. "George will help her. He'll love it. His adored Fanny!"

Louisa frowned. "Don't speak like that. I won't have this stupid infatuation of George's encouraged. It's nothing but an aspect of his illness. I'd ask you to remember, Amelia, that you are not the only person in the world whose happiness has to be considered."

"Oh, Mamma! It will take so little to make me happy. Just a ball in London, and a husband I truly love. And a little money, of course, and jewels, and—and—"

Amelia had her face pressed to the window. The moors, dark fold on fold, stretched away to the edge of the earth. The sky was colourless, like river water. There was the far-off cry of a bird. A heron from the lake, perhaps, or an owl. Or the trapped bird in the chimney that Grandmamma was always talking about.

Suddenly Amelia shivered. At dusk she hated the moors, she hated the thought of the grim grey prison ten miles away in its bleak setting. She hadn't minded so much when the prisoners had been French. That had seemed romantic. She had imagined them singing *La Marseillaise* and wanting to die for their country. But now the cold dank cells were occupied by the riff-raff from the streets of London and Liverpool, thieves, forgers, would-be murderers . . . Sometimes one escaped and the countryside was in terror, with the hounds baying in the mist—for an escaper always chose a time of thick mist when his capture would be doubly difficult. Amelia would imagine she saw the bearded desperate face at her window, and would be torn between terror and a terrible fascination. If it ever happened that a prisoner did appear at her window, would she scream, or hide him beneath her bed and temporarily have the violent creature at her mercy? She didn't know why such thoughts came into her head. She only knew that they made her long to get away from here. She would marry and have six children and live in London where one could go to the theatre or a dinner party every night. And there would always be lights, and no lonely night wind.

"Mamma!" she turned slowly, her voice intense, "I would do anything to get those things."

Her mother was clasping her topaz necklace—good enough for the governor of Dartmoor prison—round her plump neck.

"What woman wouldn't? It's always been her aim in life, a good husband and security."

"You got them, Mamma. You must be very happy."

Louisa's mouth went down at the corners. Happiness didn't consist of a house full of servants, a wardrobe overflowing with expensive clothes, a warm bed and a husband beside her who sometimes, but not now so frequently, woke to fumble beneath her nightgown. No, that wasn't happiness, she realised. But just as her mother hadn't pointed out that fact to her, she had no intention of pointing it out to her daughter.

"Of course I'm happy. Don't look so worried, child. You'll acquire all these things. But the effort will be as much mine as yours. I still have connections, even though I've been buried in the moors for so long. I'll do what I can with your father. Now run along and see if Grandmamma is coming down to dinner. If she is, see that she's wearing her cashmere shawl, and that her hair is tidy. Sometimes I believe she deliberately makes herself look like a scarecrow."

Amelia, her spirits recovered, giggled. "She does. She's naughty. George is the only one who can make her do things."

Louisa frowned again, remembering the many ways in which her mother spoiled her handsome grandson. But she merely said sharply, "Amelia, don't gallop out of a room like that. Learn to glide along quietly and gracefully."

Amelia paused. "Like Fanny, Mamma?"

"Nothing of the kind! I have never advised you to model yourself on Fanny."

"I never have," said Amelia blithely. "Anyway, Fanny can dash about when she's in a temper. You ought to see her then. Oh, Papa —I'm just going."

Edgar came into the room, scarcely noticing Amelia's departure. He was deep in thought.

"My dear, you haven't begun to dress. You must hurry. You know what a stickler for punctuality Sir Giles is. I suppose it comes from running a prison—"

"Louisa, don't chatter! Can't I have a little peace."

Louisa looked at him in surprise. He was normally a good-tempered and placid man.

"What's the matter? Has something happened?"

"Only a trivial but worrying thing. My brother's attorney from Shanghai is seeing fit to pay us a visit. I must say I regard that as a little nosey-parkering. Probably he imagines me as improvident as Oliver. But even if I were, there's nothing he can do about that. My brother's last instructions must be carried out."

"How old is he?"

Edgar stared at his wife perplexedly. He had never been able to understand the way a woman's mind worked, and had come to dismiss the whole process as unworthy of serious attention.

"Whatever has his age got to do with it?"

"Is he married? Or perhaps unaccompanied by his wife?"

"What are you thinking of?"

"What you should be thinking of, my love. Had you forgotten Amelia comes out this year? We shall require every eligible man possible if we are to have successful parties. Don't men ever think of these things?"

"Don't women ever think of anything else!"

"Now, Edgar, please don't get irritable. Amelia is your daughter and you must do your best by her."

"Confound it, I've promised her a very generous marriage settlement."

"So you have, love." Louisa gave his hand a perfunctory caress. "But a marriage settlement is of little use without a husband. I really think we must open the London house—"

"No! That's out of the question."

"But, Edgar—"

"Don't argue with me. I say it's out of the question."

"Oh dear. Amelia will be so disappointed."

"Have you being discussing it with Amelia? Without consulting me?"

His wife's full eyelids drooped slyly.

"I'm afraid we shall need to be persuaded that there are advantages in having a ball here."

"The London house hasn't been lived in for years. You'd find that everything needed re-decorating and re-furnishing. As it is, Murchison lives there and keeps a couple of rooms available for me, and that's all that's necessary. Advantages! My dear Louisa, it would only be a matter of several thousand pounds more to have the ball in London."

"Then," said Louisa, smoothly, "Amelia and I will expect a much more generous allowance for our wardrobe. Amelia needs several new gowns, and as for me,—"

"Stop it," said her husband harshly.

"Stop it! Please don't speak like that to me! I am merely asking for one small fur tippett." Louisa's full mouth pouted, reproachfully. "Only it must be of white ermine. Lady Mowatt has something similar, but of muskrat. Ermine is a much more rewarding fur. And really it is to be such a summer, with these strange children foisted on our household—why I meekly put up with them, I can't imagine—and then the utter fatigue of Amelia's coming-out. But it's the children who are worrying me so much. Your brother's, after all, and it's scarcely my fault that he turned out to be such a waster. I don't see why I, or Amelia, poor child, or any of us should be so put about—"

Again Edgar held up his hand to interrupt. He recognised the familiar grievance in his wife's voice. He knew that the ermine tippett would naturally extend to being a cloak costing a great deal more than he cared to think about. He also knew that life wouldn't be worth living until the cloak hung in Louisa's well-filled wardrobe.

"My dear Louisa, will you listen to me a minute? When I said that it would be out of the question to re-furbish the London house, I meant it. Money's short at present. I've made one or two bad investments lately and it's left me short of cash."

Louisa was alarmed.

"Edgar, it's nothing serious?"

He laughed easily. "Good gracious, no. It will right itself in time. Something else will come up. But in the meantime I'd be glad if you'd exercise a little economy in the house."

This was not amusing. Louisa pouted again.

"That won't be easy with two extra mouths to feed, and extra servants. Though it would be the least Fanny could do to offer some help. I hope you will speak to her, Edgar. And this, I might say, was certainly not the time to give her an expensive present. Why, that sapphire would have kept the children for a year, or—"

"Bought your ermine tippett?" Edgar observed. "This was exactly the time to give it to Fanny, if we expect her co-operation. Besides, the child deserved it. Remember, she didn't get a ball, as Amelia is going to."

"She'll share Amelia's. She can't expect more than that."

"A very different kettle of fish, my dear. As Fanny would be the first to realise. Well, I suppose I must dress."

Nevertheless, he sat heavily on the edge of the bed, making no move to go to his dressing room. He was sunk in thought.

"Edgar, what is it about this man coming from China that upsets you?" asked his wife shrewdly.

"Eh? What are you getting at?"

"Something's worrying you, and I know all that talk about money is merely a disguise."

"Oh, you do, do you?"

Edgar surveyed his wife. She was laced into her stays and hooked firmly into her crinoline. The neck of the bodice was low and displayed a too generous amount of white flesh. Her hair style, with its tight sausage curls liberally flecked with grey, was more fitting to Fanny or Amelia than to a middle-aged matron. Her cheeks were flushed, and the tip of her nose swollen and bulbous. She had already arranged her face into the animated expression that would last until her guests left. After that, the pouting lips and the look of grievance would return.

When he was in his early twenties, Edgar had fallen deeply in love with a delicate and nymph-like girl called Marianne. He had laid his heart at her feet and she had laughed at him. She had said in her clear laughing icy voice, "But, Mr Davenport, you look so exactly like a frog!"

Seven years later he had met Louisa who had not laughed at him. She hadn't been pale and nymph-like, but she was the granddaughter of an earl. Edgar had decided that ambition was a much more satisfying object to seek than love. Although he was not beyond expecting that Louisa's ample flesh might be pleasant. And so it was, if grudgingly given. Also she ran his house well, and for all her propensity to be a rattle, was shrewd. She had earned her diamond ear-rings and perhaps her ermine tippett. It was not her fault if he always saw Marianne's pale shadow behind her, and heard that cruel laughter.

"If you must know," he said, "I expect Hamish Barlow to arrive with a list of my brother's debts. It must be something serious to bring him so far. In honour bound, I shall have to try to settle them."

"How vexing!" Louisa cried. "Couldn't your brother have made a little money. I understand business people in China have."

"Not Oliver, you may be sure."

"Well, don't worry about it now," Louisa said briskly. "It's late and we must go down. Why don't we have a little music tonight? That always cheers you up. Amelia will play the piano. And next month Amelia and I must have a few days in London shopping. I shall have to find some reliable woman to make her ball gown. She will need a great many things—" Louisa swept up to kiss the top of her husband's head, "—and we may look at furs, too."

"You haven't listened to a word I said."

"Oh, indeed, to too many."

Edgar made haste in dressing, hoping for ten minutes alone in the drawing room with a glass of sherry before his guests arrived.

In this, too, he was disappointed, for he found Lady Arabella ensconsed in his favourite chair. Wrapped in her fleecy white shawl with her stiff black skirts spreading about her, she looked cosy and gentle and half asleep.

"Well, Edgar," she said in her husky voice.

"Good evening, Mamma." His voice was hearty, easy. He had quickly overcome the irritation of finding her in his chair, and the room not empty.

"It was so chilly, I had the fire lit. The summer's late, as usual."

"Good idea. Nice and cheery. Are you dining with us tonight?"

"I thought I would. I miss Fanny. She reads to me."

"Doesn't Amelia?"

"Oh, Amelia. That harum scarum." The old lady's voice was indulgent. "I'm looking forward to the new children. They'll help me to pass the time. Fancy, Edgar! Such skeletons in your family."

"Hardly skeletons, Mamma. My brother had a past, I admit. But that's no business of the children's. We won't have any of this sins of the father rubbish. I'm a broad-minded man."

"*And* wise and tolerant," Lady Arabella approved. "You know, I once thought my daughter was making a mistake in marrying you. But you've astonished me."

"Thank you, Mamma. I hope I have been a good husband."

The old lady smiled gently. Her eyes stared myopically into the fire.

"Giving her this splendid home, too. Do you know, I've discovered a new pastime since the children have got too old for stories. I've been delving into the history of Darkwater. If I had been a man I should have been an historian. These old tales fascinate me. Darkwater has quite a history, you know."

Edgar had lifted the sherry decanter. He put it down again, listening politely.

"All old houses have," he said. "I suppose you're referring to the legendary bird. The bringer of disaster, eh?"

"Not just disaster," said Lady Arabella enjoyably. "Death."

"Come, Mamma! How you love gloom."

"Ah, yes, gloom. And successions, too. Family trees. All those pictures of fruitful trees with babies in the branches. So pretty."

Edgar smiled indulgently.

"Where do you find all this stuff?"

"Oh, it's all here in the house. Some of the Davenports were admirable recorders."

Edgar's smile had faded.

"The library is my preserve. I really can't have you ferreting about in there, Mamma."

"All those books and no one bothering to open them," Lady Arabella said regretfully. "George and Amelia haven't inherited my literary tastes, which is a pity. One's mind should be cultivated. You mustn't deny me my little hobby, Edgar. Besides,

I hadn't realised the Davenports were such an interesting family. This house has seen some times."

Edgar stared at her. Her face was bland, innocent, lost in thought. She might have been telling this story to anyone. It wasn't directed especially at him. Or was it?

No one had rung for lamps to be brought in and the room was full of twilight. Sunk into the wing chair, with the uneven wash of the firelight on her wide black skirts and white lace cap, Lady Arabella looked like a monstrous mole. That's what she was, busily tunnelling her way into old books and diaries, all the musty paraphernalia of a very old house, swallowing the secrets and then letting them ferment inside her. She had a dangerous habit of embroidering and exaggerating. Not that it mattered much what scandals emerged regarding dead and gone Davenports. All the same, he should long ago have examined those old books himself.

"All old houses have seen interesting times," he said, then realised that he had made that platitudinous remark before, and added, "It won't see any more while I live here."

"But how can you be sure?" Lady Arabella said vigorously. She was embarking on her favourite theme. "Events are forced on us. These strange children arriving, for instance. They will change the atmosphere and a changed atmosphere provokes things. Then there is George's war injury. You can't deny that has made him almost a stranger. We have to learn to know him all over again. And had you forgotten that this is the year Amelia puts her hair up, and Fanny comes of age. These are the seeds of drama."

Lady Arabella's voice had become deep and vibrant as it did when she got to the terrifying part of a fairy story, the moment when she was going to deliberately shock and startle her audience.

"You will see, Edgar," she said portentously.

"Come, Mamma," said Edgar playfully. "You're just like a child wanting to stir muddy water to see what lies underneath."

The old lady pounced.

"Why is the water muddy?"

Edgar put down his glass of sherry, then picked it up and took a large mouthful.

"I don't know what you're talking about. I hope you will keep off such cryptic conversation at dinner."

"And why should I? It might liven things up. People enjoy hearing scandal about others."

"Scandal!" Edgar's eyebrows shot up in surprise. "What exactly are you referring to?"

Lady Arabella closed her eyes dreamily.

"How I adore other people's letters. So revealing. Your great-uncle was a talented correspondent. I fear it's a dying art in this family. Can you imagine George or Amelia writing really artistic letters. Fanny may, of course. She may have inherited the Irish gift for poetry."

"I still don't know what you're talking about," Edgar said good-humouredly. "My uncle's letters would be with the recipients, not here."

"Exactly my point. The replies, you understand, are still in existence. I find I have a knack with hidden drawers in desks. I'd have made an accomplished burglar. Then perhaps," the old lady chuckled, "I wouldn't have been coming down to dinner when you entertained your friend, Sir Giles Mowatt."

Edgar was bending over her.

"What did you find?"

"The next thing I shall investigate is secret panels. I can't think why I never thought of this fascinating pastime before."

"What did you find?"

"Edgar, don't breathe on me like that. I've told you what I found. Merely family letters. No secret hoard of sovereigns, unfortunately."

"Show them to me."

"Yes, indeed I will when I find them."

"You said you had found them."

"And since then I've mislaid them. Isn't it aggravating I've grown so forgetful. But they'll turn up, and then certainly you shall see them."

"Who were they from? You remember that, at least?"

"Someone called Philip. A connection of your great-uncle's. You've never explained the ramifications of your family to me. But he seemed to be a person of distinct literary talent. It's really a pity your children haven't inherited it. Still, they do other things. Amelia is clever with her needle, and in spite of his illness, George still rides superlatively. And by the way, Edgar, the boy badly wants a new hunter."

Their eyes met, Edgar's still and watchful, Lady Arabella's milkily dim. At last Edgar said, "George has a tongue in his head. If he wants something, he must ask for it himself."

Lady Arabella shook her head slowly. Her frizzy grey hair ringed from her lace cap in a frosty halo. She looked vague and gentle and only half-concerned with the conversation.

"He won't, Edgar. Since his illness he almost seems a little afraid of you. Isn't that odd?" Lady Arabella picked up her stick and poked playfully at Edgar's gently rounded stomach. "Such a fine figure of a man are you. I used to say to Louisa before she married you that you were an unprepossessing creature, but perhaps you would improve in middle age. And indeed you have, dear boy. That watch chain now. It must have cost a pretty penny."

"Mamma, keep to the subject. You were saying that George needs a new horse, but that he hasn't the courage to ask me for it himself."

"Poor boy. He used not to be like that. It's a great tragedy. We must make his life pleasant for him until he recovers his health."

"That doesn't involve pampering him. Do you know what a well-bred hunter costs? At least a hundred guineas." Edgar began to walk up and down, thoroughly put out. What was he, an inexhaustible purse into which all his family dipped? A pool to be fished? A muddy pool, Lady Arabella had insinuated. The devil take her. What was the devious old creature up to? He didn't underestimate his mother-in-law. But he had never remotely considered her a match for himself. The very idea was ridiculous.

All the same, it would be as well to get possession of those letters. If they existed . . . She was quite able to make the imaginary more dangerous than the reality. What did emerge from all this was that her great love for her grandson was going to ruin the boy.

Edgar's irritation burst out.

"Amelia requires ball dresses, my wife seems to think she will freeze to death without new furs, I have two penniless children arriving to be supported, children I neither begot nor approve of, and now you—you on behalf of my voiceless son, see fit to demand another horse which will probably break his neck! What am I, Mamma? Simply a bank account?"

"How comical!" Lady Arabella clapped her hands appreciatively. "What an apt description. Only you would have thought of it, dear boy. But that's what a lot of people are, isn't it? Mostly men, of course, but sometimes women, if they have the cleverness to keep their husbands' hands off their money. Such predatory creatures, men. You must admit, Edgar, a new ball dress or a piece of jewellery is negligible compared with what a man will desire."

"And what's that, Mamma?" came Louisa's voice from the door.

Lady Arabella blinked myopically at her daughter.

"Good gracious, Louisa, you look very grand. I must say Edgar dresses you grandly."

"What do you mean, Mamma," Louisa said irritably. "I've worn this gown a dozen times. I've just been telling Edgar that Amelia and I have a great deal of shopping to do. But why are you sitting here in the dark?" Louisa tugged at the bell rope. "Why is this house always so dark and cold? Even on a summer evening."

Edgar recognised the familiar tactics. They would go on until the new furs were bought. His family were leeches, he thought, with cold clarity. Only Fanny demanded nothing. Sometimes he wished she would so that he could be angry with her, too.

"Shall we tell George about his new horse tonight?" said Lady Arabella dreamily. "The dear boy. He deserves it. He nearly died for his country."

Chapter 6

TRUMBLE was waiting on the tiny station platform. Hannah carried Marcus who was asleep. Fanny had attempted to take Nolly's hand, but the child had firmly withdrawn it. She walked at Ching Mei's side, small and upright and independent. It was half past eight and she should have been dropping with weariness. Indeed, her face was colourless, but her eyes stared out as brilliantly as ever.

Fanny could see Trumble staring as they approached. Ching Mei's pigtail and her trousered legs obviously fascinated him. He had expected a Chinese woman, but dressed respectably in skirts and petticoats.

There was mist in the air. The wind was cool and fresh, like cold water. Fanny breathed deeply, smelling the familiar loved smell of damp earth and heather. Perhaps she would have withered away with longing for this and the moorland wind if she had gone abroad or stayed in London.

Trumble had doffed his cap and sprung forward to help with the baggage. As they were about to climb into the carriage Fanny's attention was taken by another small group who had left the train. She stared in pity and horror. There was a man, handcuffed, between two warders. He was on his way to the prison. Fanny caught only a glimpse of his thin bearded face beneath the flaring station lamps before he was hustled off.

She shivered. Imprisonment. It was terrible. There were so many forms of it. The prisoner's face had been expressionless, like Ching Mei's. Like her own must be, at times.

Fortunately no one else seemed to have noticed the episode. And in the carriage, when Marcus woke, and began to sob, Fanny suddenly remembered the sweetmeats Lady Arabella had given her. They had been left untouched in her reticule. She produced the small brown paper bag and distributed the sticky sweets.

"There," she said. "We'll be home in less than an hour."

She thought again, involuntarily, of the prisoner when the carriage had come to a standstill outside the front door, and Trumble was helping them all to alight.

For either by accident or deliberately, the curtains had not been drawn across the drawing room windows and in the glowing lamplight the scene within was visible in every detail.

Lady Arabella was dozing in the high winged chair by the fire. Opposite her on the sofa Aunt Louisa, her topaz necklace catching the light, was deep in animated conversation with Lady Mowatt. Uncle Edgar stood smoking a cigar and talking to Sir Giles. Uncle Edgar was wearing his most benevolent expression. He looked well-fed and content, a man without a care. Sir Giles must have just said something that pleased him for he made a deprecatory gesture with his cigar. Sir Giles, unlike the hapless creatures in his custody, had a ruddy jovial face as if he habitually dined well and had a cellar as well-stocked as Uncle Edgar's. His wife was a quiet creature, soberly dressed. Aunt Louisa, with her honey-coloured necklace and her massive crinoline looked almost flamboyant in contrast.

Beyond them Amelia and George were sitting at the card table engaged in a game of cards. George looked remarkably handsome. From this distance one couldn't see the lines of difficult concentration on his forehead or his intermittently blank gaze. Amelia wore her sprigged muslin with the blue velvet sash. She had her curls pinned high in an adult manner, and looked very grown-up and sure of herself, the cherished daughter of wealthy parents.

It was a pretty picture. It required no one else in it.

Again Fanny had the overwhelming sense of being excluded from any genuine place in the family. The wind blew in a sharp gust, making her shiver again. The horses moved restlessly on the cobblestones. Hannah was saying, "You can walk now, a big boy like you," and had set Marcus down. And suddenly Fanny knew that the strange children, Nolly and Marcus, were looking in at the warm room, too. She felt a small very cold hand slipped into hers. She looked down. It was Nolly at her side. The child hadn't looked up, hadn't made a sound. Her bonnet hid her face. Only her chilly fingers spoke. Fanny reached out her other hand for Marcus, and for a moment the three of them stood there, irrevocably bound.

There was no other way, she realised. She was now passionately identified with them. She was not sorry she had come back.

Then the heavy oak door swung open, the light streamed out on to the cobblestones, and Barker was there, urging them to come in out of the cold. The family in the drawing room had heard the commotion, and Uncle Edgar's deep genial voice was to be heard saying with what seemed like pleasure and excitement, "I believe the children have arrived. Do come and meet them. Lady Mowatt, would you be interested to see my poor brother's children? Louisa my love—"

It really seemed as if they were welcome.

They came inside. Hannah was discreetly whisking Ching Mei up the stairs. Fanny stood with the children still clinging to her.

"Well," said Uncle Edgar, putting his finger under Nolly's chin and gently lifting it. "This must be Olivia. I'm your uncle, child. I hope you'll grow fond of me. And this is the boy. Tch, tch, tears won't do. Now I have something that will interest you. Would you care to see my watch? I warrant your papa didn't have one like it. It plays a tune."

"Edgar, not now. Tomorrow," said Aunt Louisa.

"Mamma!" That was Amelia, her voice louder than she had intended from relief. "They're quite white."

"From exhaustion, I should think," said Aunt Louisa, and only Fanny saw her angry glance at her indiscreet daughter. "And a little grubby from the long train journey."

"By jove," Sir Giles, putting down his glass of port. "They're of a rather tender age, Davenport. I must say I admire your generosity."

"On the contrary," said Uncle Edgar, "the pleasure will be all mine. After all, who knows how imminently I'm going to lose my own children. Amelia makes no secret of being on the look out for a husband—"

"Papa!" Amelia shrieked.

"And Fanny is pretty enough to join her at any moment. So there you are, I have two to take their place. Come, my poppet," he chucked Nolly's chin again, "aren't you going to speak to your uncle?"

"They're very tired, Uncle Edgar," Fanny said.

"She's pretty," said Uncle Edgar, with great pleasure. "I believe she looks a little like her father. He had all the looks in our family."

"And see where they led him," came Lady Arabella's wheezing voice.

"To an early grave," said Uncle Edgar sadly, with admirable presence of mind.

"Fanny," Aunt Louisa spoke authoritatively. "Take the children upstairs. They look quite worn-out. Now, Edgar, don't interfere. They can see your watch tomorrow. Poor little creatures. They don't know what anything is about at this moment."

Fanny curtseyed to the company and led the children to the stairs. She had to pick up Marcus and carry him, he was stumbling so badly from fatigue. Nolly followed silently.

At the turn of the stairs she heard Sir Giles Mowatt saying again, "By jove, Davenport, I admire you. You take a thing like this in your stride."

"Well, they're not exactly here under duress, like your guests," Uncle Edgar said, and there was a great roar of laughter.

"They're really quite sweet," Amelia said in her high voice. "They look so innocent."

"Ah, yes. Innocence. A precious quality. One I don't see much of. We must be off, I'm afraid. I, too, was expecting an arrival on this evening's train."

"Oh, poor man!" cried Amelia. "What has he done?"

"I'm afraid he escaped from Wandsworth prison where he was doing a sentence for theft. They say he's a desperate fellow, but I warrant he won't escape from Dartmoor."

Ching Mei was standing in the centre of the room in which the children were to sleep. It was probably the first English bedroom she had ever seen. Her bewilderment simply took the form of rendering her motionless, her hands clasped in front of her, her slitted eyes dulled.

Dora was at the door, goggling. Hannah came bustling out muttering, "That heathen woman, what's to be done with her? She's useless. Not a bit of unpacking done, and as for getting the children to bed—"

Fanny pushed the children into the room. She said sharply, "Dora, how would you like to be stared at like that? Go down to the kitchen at once and get cook to make a bowl of bread and milk. Hannah, will you get the bed in the next room made up?"

Hannah looked at her in surprise. "For you, Miss Fanny? But it isn't aired! The room hasn't been used since the house party last November. Everything will be damp."

"Do as I ask you, Hannah. You can put a bed warmer in."

Hannah nodded slowly. She lowered her voice.

"I understand, Miss Fanny. You don't trust the Chinese woman." Hannah was refusing to call her by her outlandish name.

"Only to the point that she, too, may be nervous in such a strange house."

"But we're all upstairs, Miss Fanny! Just overhead."

"And which of you would wake if a child cried?" Fanny asked sceptically. "Besides, you know that Dora jumps at her own shadow, and so does Lizzie, and cook would say it wasn't her place, and none of you would wait on a Chinese woman. Would you?"

"Miss Fanny, you do say some things."

"Besides, I want to be near the children. Tomorrow, I shall have all my things moved up."

"Permanently, Miss Fanny?"

"Permanently."

Hannah, with her tired elderly eyes, stared at Fanny. Fanny said, "I know what you're going to say, Hannah. Start a bad habit and you'll have it always."

"No, I wasn't, Miss Fanny. I was going to say, bless your kind heart."

In the other room the children were chattering busily, but the moment Fanny went in, like startled birds, they were silent. All the same, their faces and hands were washed, they were dressed in their nightgowns and ready for bed. Ching Mei, when no strange eyes were on her, obviously worked swiftly and efficiently. She had even opened one of the trunks to get out the children's night things. Now she stood again in her familiar deferential attitude, with clasped hands and downcast eyes.

"That's wonderful, Ching Mei," said Fanny. "You are very quick. Dora is bringing up some bread and milk. Try to persuade the children to have some."

The Chinese bowed. Fanny said perplexedly, "How much English do you understand? You must have spoken it in my cousin Oliver's home in Shanghai."

Ching Mei stared.

"Didn't she?" Fanny appealed to Nolly.

"Not much," Nolly answered. "She was just beginning to learn when—when—" She pressed her lips together, to stop their trembling. "When we came away," she finished flatly. "After that we just talked Chinese."

"There'll be no more Chinese spoken," Fanny said firmly. "Do you all understand?"

Ching Mei bowed again. "Tly velly much, missee."

Fanny felt a lump in her throat. If one wanted a lesson in self-sacrifice and loyalty it was all there in this alien woman, with her sad wrinkled face, her expressionless eyes. Tomorrow she must tell Uncle Edgar what Adam Marsh had said. When the children were settled some way must be found to send Ching Mei back to her own country. She must not be allowed to die from homesickness.

The thought of Adam Marsh brought back a surge of warmth into Fanny's heart. Suddenly she wanted to be alone to think and dream. She kissed the children quickly, "This is your bed, Ching Mei," she said, indicating the narrow one placed at the foot of the children's, and was rewarded by Ching Mei's sudden giggle which meant understanding. But Ching Mei pointed to the floor, indicating she would prefer to sleep there.

Fanny nodded. "Do as you like. I'll be next door if you want me in the night."

"We're not babies to want people in the night," Nolly said.

Fanny faced her reproving gaze.

"I wasn't suggesting you were. Such a travelled young lady as you couldn't have remained a baby. Indeed, I'm surprised you haven't already found a husband."

Nolly pressed her lips together again, this time to prevent a surprisingly human giggle. Her hair stuck out in pigtails. She had, Fanny noticed, been hiding a doll under the blankets, for now its highly-coloured Chinese face and flat black hair emerged. She was only a baby, after all. Thank goodness, for her precocity had been a little alarming.

Only a baby . . . For in the night cold fingers touched Fanny's face.

"Cousin Fanny! Cousin Fanny! Marcus is afraid."

Fanny sat up, fumbling for the candle at her bedside. She struck a match quickly, and the frail light showed her Nolly's night-gowned figure. She was clutching the Chinese doll in its gaudy red kimono. Her eyes were dilated.

"What is it, Nolly? Why are you afraid?"

"Marcus is afraid," Nolly whispered. "He thinks he heard something."

Fanny wondered if George had been walking about, as he sometimes did long after midnight. The house, as she listened, was as still as it ever could be. She was so used to the infinitesimal creakings and rustlings that she scarcely heard them.

"Then come and let us see Marcus," she said, picking up the candle and taking Nolly's hand.

If Marcus were frightened he was being remarkably silent about it. It required only one look to see that the little boy was fast asleep. Ching Mei, in her lowly position, wrapped in a blanket, didn't appear to have stirred.

Fanny was beginning to realise Nolly's tactics. Marcus was at once her scapegoat and her possession.

"Come, Nolly, what was it you heard?"

The child looked round fearfully. The wavering candlelight cast moving shadows over the high ceiling and the panelled walls. In the long mirror of the wardrobe they were caught, two night-gowned figures, Fanny with her dark hair on her shoulders, Nolly with her pigtails and her intensely disciplined face looking medieval, the forlorn child in an old story. The breathing of the sleepers made a faint whisper. There was still no other sound.

"Something in the chimney," Nolly whispered. She pointed to the dark mouth of the fireplace. "Up there."

A cool prickle ran down Fanny's spine.

"What sort of noise?"

"A sort of fluttering, and something falling down." Her fingers tightened on Fanny's. "Has something fallen down?"

Fanny resolutely shone the candlelight on the hearth, and into the cavernous chimney. There was a smattering of soot on the tiles, nothing more.

"Look, that's all it is," she said. "Soot from old fires. It gets loose and suddenly falls. That's what you heard."

Nolly stared. At last she said, "It's dirty."

"Yes. Dora will tidy it in the morning. Now get back into bed."

Nolly went quite willingly back to her bed.

"It's a good thing Marcus didn't hear that," she said. "He'd have been frightened." And the amah sat up abruptly, mumbling in Chinese. She blinked. The candlelight seemed to dazzle her.

"Tlouble, Miss Fanny?" For the first time she used Fanny's name, with a pretty deliberation.

"Nothing, Ching Mei. Go back to sleep, both of you."

In the morning, which was grey and chilly, with a rising wind and the high tors black against the sky, Dora couldn't get the fire to burn. The sticks must be damp, she said, and a lot of soot seemed to have fallen down. Perhaps the chimney needed cleaning. With the fascinated children watching, she stuck the long poker up the chimney, and something fell to the hearth with a rush.

Nolly screamed. Fanny hurried in to see the small light-as-paper skeleton of the bird, wings still outspread in its vain attempt for freedom.

"It's a starling," she said matter-of-factly. "Poor thing, it must have been caught there last summer and no one heard it."

"I did," said Nolly. "I heard it in the night. You didn't, Marcus."

"I did," said Marcus. "I did so."

"Neither of you did," Fanny said. "That bird's been dead for a long time, poor thing. Take it away, Dora. And later today in the garden I'll show you some live starlings. They're coal black, but the sun shines like diamonds on their feathers. Dora, what are you waiting for?"

"I'd better not let Lady Arabella see, Miss Fanny. She'll declare it was white, and that would mean—"

"Dora!"

"Yes, Miss Fanny," Dora mumbled, balancing the light draggled burden on a shovel and hurrying away.

Omens, thought Fanny impatiently. They didn't exist. Intuition did, and perhaps a certain presentiment. But not omens. They were for the ignorant and the foolishly superstitious.

"Cousin Fanny, why was the bird in the chimney?" Nolly's clear precise voice demanded an answer.

"Perhaps it was building a nest. Perhaps it just fell down."

"Why didn't it fly out again?"

"I suppose it couldn't. The chimney's dark and narrow, like a tunnel. It wouldn't be able to spread its wings."

That was it exactly. Not being able to spread its wings . . . She had always thought so, from the moment she had identified herself with Lady Arabella's fanciful white bird.

"Then it should have flapped and screamed until someone came and rescued it," Nolly said with nervous distaste.

"Yes, darling."

"But suppose nobody rescued it?"

"That's enough about the poor bird. See, the fire's burning beautifully now."

She stooped to hold out her hands to the blaze. It was absurdly chilly for mid-May. She felt very cold.

She had to go down to her own room to put away her finery from yesterday and get out the poplin day dress, faded from many washings. Amelia heard her and came bursting in in her usual unceremonious way.

"Fanny, what do you think? Papa is buying George a new horse!"

"Is he?"

"You don't sound at all surprised or indignant."

"Why should I be?"

"Because George already has a perfectly good horse, and he knows he is free to ride any other of Papa's horses. Even my Jinny, if he pleases. But now he is to get a pedigreed hunter, and all I get is money for a paltry bit of French ribbon. You didn't forget to buy my ribbon, did you?"

"No, I didn't forget. I'll unpack it presently."

Amelia subsided on to a chair, her skirts flouncing out. She was still pouting and looking like a schoolgirl.

"Mamma says Papa is talking economy all the time, and yet when George asks for something—or when Grandmamma asks for him, as Mamma says she did, not a no can be said. Fanny, do you think Papa is afraid to say no to Grandmamma?"

Fanny laughed. "Don't be silly, Amelia. Your father isn't afraid of anybody?"

"No, I didn't think he was. But it's awfully unfair. This is supposed to be my year."

"I expect you will get what you want eventually," said Fanny, twisting her glossy hair into place. "And after all, George—"

"Don't you say it, too! I know he nearly died for his country. But that was just the fortunes of war. After all, he had lots of splendid times with his regiment before that, and he wanted to go into the army. Oh, I suppose I'm mean and selfish to talk like this. Am I, Fanny?"

"And vain," said Fanny.

"Oh, I declare! Fanny, you're the most unsympathetic person I ever met. And why did you sleep upstairs last night?"

"It's where I intend to sleep from now on," Fanny said calmly. "Dora is moving my things today."

Amelia's indignation grew again.

"But what if I want you?"

"One flight of stairs doesn't mean I am living on the moon."

Amelia giggled reluctantly.

"Fanny, you're in a mood this morning. I know Mamma thinks it will be nice if you take an interest in the children, but that isn't to mean you won't have time to do things for me. I must admit the children did look rather sweet last night. Papa was quite taken with the girl. And at least—wasn't it terrible the way I blurted it out—they're the right colour, so that worry is over. I may come up and see them in the nursery today."

"May you, indeed? Your own cousins, and it may please you to have the whim to visit them."

"Oh, I didn't mean it like that. Fanny, you are aggravating. You've changed somehow since you've had this journey to London. Turn round and look at me."

Fanny finished pinning up her hair. She turned with deliberation.

"Well, there you are. What do you see? The great metropolis written in my face?"

"No-o. But your eyes are so bright. If it wasn't impossible, I'd believe you'd fallen in love."

"Impossible?" Fanny queried coolly.

"Well, how could you, with Hannah at your shoulder, and then the wretched orphans. And besides who would you meet on a train?" Amelia suddenly jumped up. Her voice dropped to a whisper. "Fanny, you didn't see *him*!"

Fanny couldn't help her colour rising. How could Amelia know? Was her secret written so plainly on her face?

"If you mean the clerk from the shipping company—"

"Oh no, not him, I meant the new prisoner. The one Sir Giles said was arriving. Fanny, did you really see him?"

Fanny's voice was casual with relief. Amelia could be a destructive person with secrets, whispering them, distorting them . . .

"Just for a moment, yes."

Amelia wrung her hands together.

"Did he look awfully starved and desperate?"

"I don't think so. Really, Amelia, I believe you think Dartmoor prison is full of caged tigers or panthers, with claws and blazing eyes."

Amelia had gone to look out of the window. She was a little round figure with a cosy domestic look. A man would put his arm round that softly fleshed waist and think of warmed hearths and well-laden tables and filled cradles. He wouldn't think there was anything further to know about a young woman like that.

"I don't know why I have this longing to see one of them," she whispered. "I should be terrified, and yet—They are just human beings, aren't they, with a mother who once loved them. I suppose they have long forgotten about love . . ."

Fanny contrived to keep her colour when Uncle Edgar asked her, at breakfast, about the young man from the shipping company.

"We didn't have the opportunity to talk last night. But I take it all the arrangements went well. The company sent a reliable sort of fellow?"

"Very reliable, Uncle Edgar."

"Splendid. I shall drop them a line of thanks. I take it—"

"I gave him the guinea, Uncle Edgar." Fanny lowered her head for this time she could feel the warm colour in her cheeks. She was more and more sure that the guinea had been pocketed by Adam Marsh simply to save her embarrassment, that he was quite unaccustomed to taking money from a lady. She was almost certain that they would laugh about it in the future.

"Fanny looks well, doesn't she, Louisa?" Uncle Edgar boomed. "The little change has done her good."

"I said she had fallen in love," Amelia said boldly, then fell into her irrepressible giggle.

"Who with? Who, damn him!"

"George!"

His mother spoke so sharply that George fell back into his seat. He began to frown bewilderedly, the hard flush of anger leaving him.

"It isn't true, is it, Fanny? Amelia's teasing, as usual?"

"Yes, she is," Fanny said, because at this moment there was nothing else to say.

She looked round, seeing Aunt Louisa behind the shining silver teapot and coffee pot, at one end of the table, Uncle Edgar with his napkin tucked into his waistcoat, his attention apparently solely on his food, Amelia in her fresh blue morning gown keeping her eyelids lowered to hide the wicked sparkle that the result of her sally had aroused, and George momentarily forgetting the food on his plate, staring at Fanny in a way that the old George would have thought unmannerly and gauche.

Who would have thought the scene was anything but a pleasant friendly family breakfast? There was a bowl of freshly picked roses, still holding the night's dew, on the centre of the table. The furniture gleamed from the daily polish it had had before breakfast had been laid. There was a rich warm odour of well-cooked food and beeswax and roses, an odour as old as the house. Lizzie had come in with more hot water, and Aunt Louisa, lifting the teapot in her beringed hand, was saying, "More tea, Amelia? Fanny? What about you, my love? Lizzie, bring Mr Davenport's cup."

And no one would guess that a moment ago she had been hating Fanny intensely. She had never done more than tolerate her, but as a child she had been harmless enough, even useful as a companion for Amelia in the schoolroom, and later in many other little ways. She could still be tolerated if she hadn't developed those disturbing ravishing looks that only a blind or preoccupied person would not realise outshone Amelia's, and if George hadn't got into that irrational infatuated state about her.

Fanny knew all this. But though she knew Aunt Louisa's tolerance had turned to hatred, she didn't know about Uncle Edgar. He was a man. He would have a natural tenderness for a woman, even if she did represent a threat to his own children.

Amelia was young and silly, and affectionate. But she was easily influenced, and her mother could alienate her, too.

George—when his love was not returned? That was a dark question she could not answer.

But all those things lay beneath the calm privileged comfort of the breakfast table. And she was still not sorry she had returned to Darkwater . . .

"Well," said Uncle Edgar, heavily playful, "if Fanny didn't lose her heart on this journey, perhaps she will be able to put her thoughts to more practical things. My dear," he turned to Fanny, "as soon as my small nephew and niece are presentable, will you be kind enough to bring them to me in the library. I must set about making their acquaintance. They looked quite a promising pair, I thought. Oh, and the amah, too. There will be things she can tell me about my poor brother and the children's mother."

"She speaks very little English, Uncle Edgar."

Uncle Edgar looked up, puffing out his moustache.

"Nonsense! She must have spoken it in the household in Shang-hai."

"She says not."

"Then she's not telling the truth. These Chinese are a devious race, all bows and smiles, and not an atom of their true feelings showing. I've no time for 'em. Frenchmen, either, or Greeks. Even Americans. They had the impudence to turn us out of their country."

"Or anyone who isn't English, Papa?" Amelia said archly.

"Quite right, my dear, quite right. Oh, I grant you the other races serve some sort of a purpose, although I'm never sure what it is. Italians make good servants. And I remember getting some deuced good gloves in Vienna. But this Chinese woman must talk. I'll make her. Bring her down, Fanny."

Chapter 7

THE nursery was the old schoolroom where Fanny and Amelia and George, also, until he had gone away to boarding school, had endured so many years of Miss Ferguson's rule. The blackboard was still in the corner, and the dais where Miss Ferguson used to sit so that she could look down on her rapidly growing "young ladies".

Aunt Louisa had not made any extensive alterations for the new children. The old nursery fireguard had been returned to the fireplace, and several low chairs brought in. Fanny had been through the cupboards and brought out such toys and games as had survived George's rough treatment. There was a battered dolls' house for Nolly, and some toy soldiers for Marcus.

But the children had not yet developed an interest in a European child's toys, for when Fanny, obeying Uncle Edgar's instructions, came up to get them she found two small outlandish figures in a state of wild excitement.

Their trunks were standing open and the contents scattered about. Nolly was dressed in a scarlet kimono decorated with black and gold dragons, Marcus in silk trousers and jacket. Nolly not only had on a pair of high-heeled shoes much too large for her, but she had earrings hanging precariously from her ears, and rings which she clutched on her fingers. Ching Mei stood scowling fiercely, the situation obviously out of her control.

"Miss Nolly velly bad," she said to Fanny.

"Marcus is, too," Nolly declared. "He wanted his Chinese clothes on. It was his idea."

Marcus stopped his capering to look at Nolly with open mouth. His slavish following of his sister brought its own bewilderment.

But in a moment he was grinning happily and saying that they were being Chinese children.

"That's very amusing," said Fanny. "But at this moment your Uncle wants to see you downstairs. So quickly put on your proper clothes."

Nolly backed into a corner.

"No," she said. "We don't want to. We want to be Chinese children."

Her eyes had their hard black stare, there was a high spot of colour in each of her cheeks. But with her drunken jewellery and her shoes askew, she looked too comical to be taken seriously.

"Then I shall have to turn you into an English child again," Fanny said light-heartedly. "Take off those ridiculous shoes to begin with."

"They're not ridiculous," Nolly said in a low voice. "They're my Mamma's."

Fanny looked at the silver brocade shoes, slightly tarnished, too big for Nolly, but small for a grown woman. She felt a sharp pang of pity, thinking of the dead woman with her little feet and her love of flamboyant jewellery. For the stones Nolly was wearing were large dull green ones, not at all like the discreet pearls and garnets which English women wore.

"Miss Nolly velly bad," Ching Mei said again, helplessly.

Fanny nodded, but a little absently. Her feeling of pity had reminded her of almost forgotten scenes she herself had once created. She remembered shaking Amelia violently in her cradle a few moments after her mother had lovingly kissed her good night. There had been a great to-do and Miss Fanny hadn't been allowed near Baby for some weeks after. There had been tantrums in the schoolroom when Miss Ferguson, newly arrived, had had it explained to her that Miss Amelia was the daughter of the house, Miss Fanny only a sort of cousin. She had hated birthday parties, always, and even Christmas.

The little girl backed balefully into the corner now was not so strange.

Fanny was not concerned with winning a battle, but in making her happy.

She made an abrupt decision.

"Nolly, little sweet, you can't walk downstairs in those shoes. You'll lose them at once. So put on your own, and you may visit Uncle Edgar in your kimono."

Nolly stared.

"Won't he be angry?"

"He's very kind. Don't you remember last night he promised to show you his watch that plays a tune?"

Uncle Edgar was kind. She counted on that. But if he took exception to the way the children were behaving, Fanny intended to fight on their side. Didn't he know what it was to be so young and alone in a strange place . . . But of course he didn't. He never had been. She must rely on his kindness only.

She hadn't counted on his amusement. When he saw the two strangely-garbed children he burst into a roar of laughter.

"What's this, eh? A charade? Fancy dress party? Are these all the clothes you could bring with you from China? Is that all that was in those trunks?"

The last question was addressed to Ching Mei who stood in her familiar attitude, with bowed head and clasped hands.

"Uncle Edgar, she doesn't understand," Fanny said anxiously.

But Uncle Edgar suddenly wasn't listening. He was staring at Nolly. He went towards her, and again put his fingers under her chin, lifting her face.

"What are these gee-gaws you're wearing, child? A bit mature for you, aren't they?" He was chuckling softly. "By jove, rings, too. Trust a woman to like jewellery. Let me look at the rings. Give them to me."

Nolly backed away sharply, her hands clutched together.

"No," she said.

"Come, child. I only want to look. I have no designs on your circus jewellery."

Nolly's eyes blazed.

"Don't you dare touch them! They're my Mamma's!"

Uncle Edgar's colour had heightened, although he was still smiling.

"Fanny, here's a little girl who must be taught manners. We're not going to indulge in anything so vulgar as a fight. Take her upstairs and send her to her room. The boy—" But Marcus, sensing disaster, had dropped his lower lip, and was beginning to sob.

"Oh dear, dear!" said Uncle Edgar. "Our acquaintance is scarcely improving. Take the boy, too, Fanny." He pointed imperiously at the amah. "You stay."

"Uncle Edgar, Ching Mei—"

"My dear Fanny, I haven't been deaf. You've already explained several times that the woman doesn't understand English. Leave me to judge that for myself. For heaven's sake," he finished impatiently, "what is the boy crying about? He's not going to be a cry baby, I hope?"

"He was expecting to see your watch, Uncle Edgar."

"And he and his sister thought their behaviour deserved it? Oh, no, that must wait until another day."

At lunch Uncle Edgar had completely regained his good-temper. He spent some time describing a particularly memorable hunt in detail, and that reminded him of the horse he had promised George. When Amelia, with her modestly downcast eyes, said, "Papa, if George is to get a horse—" he interrupted good-humouredly, "So you think you should get something, too."

"It's only that I *need* so many things, Papa," Amelia said earnestly.

"We all do, my dear. Or we all think we do. By the way, Fanny —" it was as if he had just noticed her "—have you got your charges into a better frame of mind?"

"My charges, Uncle Edgar?" Fanny's chin was up, her voice cool. She was still upset by the disastrous and disturbing morning.

Uncle Edgar gave his vast chuckle, and went on pursuing his own amusing thoughts.

"Little foreign devils, eh? The girl's got spirit, though. Pity it isn't the boy. He seems a bit of a namby pamby. By the way, Fanny, your aunt will be going through the trunks they brought. It seems there are private papers. I don't want the servants touching anything."

"Did Ching Mei tell you?" Fanny asked in astonishment. "But I didn't think she could—"

"Speak English? She certainly doesn't have much of a vocabulary. But I contrived to understand her. Personally, I still think the woman is concealing her talents."

"She's so strange and homesick," Fanny said impulsively. "Adam Marsh thought it would be very generous of you if you could send her back to China."

"And who is Adam Marsh?" Uncle Edgar asked, with interest.

"Why, the gentleman from the shipping company. He was very kind and understanding."

"And couldn't mind his own business?"

"Oh, he didn't mean it like that. He was just concerned about her."

"And does he think an English household offers deadly peril? Are we going to return the woman to her loving family, finger by finger?"

Amelia shrieked in horror. Uncle Edgar explained expansively, "A charming little custom Chinese bandits have, I believe. Now, don't you worry, Fanny. Ching Mei is perfectly safe in our hands. When she leaves is for me to decide," there was the smallest hardening in his voice, "no one else."

She had been put in her place once more. That was obvious by Aunt Louisa's attitude when she came up to investigate the trunks.

"Take the children out in the garden, Fanny. I don't want a lot of noise and interruption. By the way, I see you have decided to change your room."

"Yes, Aunt Louisa. If that's convenient."

"Isn't it a little late to ask now that Dora has moved your things? I might say that room was one of the larger guest rooms."

"But surely you wouldn't want to put guests next to the nursery, Aunt Louisa."

"That wasn't the point I was making," Aunt Louisa said crossly. Her nose had taken on the grape bloom tinge that it did when she was excited or upset. She was already crouched over the battered trunks, like a great over-blown dahlia in her dark red full-skirted dress. Aunt Louisa had a tendency towards flamboyance in her dressing. The next thing, she would be wearing the green earrings in their ornate gold setting, provided, of course, it could be proved that the stones were semi-precious, at least.

"I merely meant," she went on, "that you might have had the courtesy to consult me about your new arrangements."

"But I thought it was taken for granted the children should be my responsibility."

Aunt Louisa recognised the familiar glint of rebellion in Fanny's eyes. One never knew what the wretched girl was thinking. And the exasperating thing was that she looked prettier than ever when she was indulging in one of her difficult moods.

"Naturally, Mr Davenport and I think it very suitable that you should take an interest in the children. And I agree that sleeping near them is an advantage. But you should have asked. I really think the trust Mr Davenport placed in you by sending you to London has gone to your head. You must try to quell those domineering tendencies in your nature. They're not becoming to a young woman."

"What are you going to do with those things?" Fanny asked, her voice no less aggressive.

Aunt Louisa was about to make a sharp rejoinder, but her attention was diverted to the heaps of clothing, tossed about untidily after the children's wild scramble through the trunks that morning. She frowned in distaste and perplexity.

"Burn most of it, I should think. It's probably full of germs."

"What if any of the things should be valuable?"

"If you're thinking of that barbaric jewellery Nolly was wearing, if any of it is of any value, which is most unlikely, considering the impecunious habits of my wretched brother-in-law, it will be put away safely in the bank until the children are of age. Does that satisfy you, miss? Why do you imagine I choose to do this tedious task rather than allow the servants to?"

Fanny resolutely dismissed her vague and unfair suspicions.

"I'm sorry, Aunt Louisa, I shouldn't have spoken like that."

"Speaking hastily is another of your faults. How many times have I told you that? But we'll say no more, except that even though your uncle and I are trusting you with further responsibilities, we will expect you to still have time for your usual duties. I'm sure I wouldn't care to face either my mother or Amelia if you neglected them. Now what, I wonder, is this meant to be?"

She was holding up a garment of Oriental silk made in no identifiable shape.

"Isn't it a cheongsam, Aunt Louisa? The dress that Chinese ladies wear."

"So tight," murmured Aunt Louisa. "And a split in the skirt. Surely that woman didn't wear anything so indecent. But I suppose one could expect anything—Well, what are you standing there for, Fanny? I asked you to take the children in the garden. And remember that you're a very fortunate young woman. Boredom, you know can be worse than unhappiness. That's why we must get that idle daughter of mine married as soon as possible."

Out in the garden Fanny had no envy of Amelia's idleness. It was a cool windy afternoon, with racing cloud shadows and flashes of brilliance from the distant lake when the sun shone out. The peacock was spreading his tail on the lawn against the copper beach, as if he had deliberately planned the rich gleaming backdrop. His mate was picking in the grass near him, ignoring his splendour. But he had an enraptured audience in Nolly and Marcus and the little amah.

Old William, the head gardener, came up and touched his cap, giving a sideways look at the Chinese woman. He said that there were some ripe strawberries in the kitchen garden if the little ones would care for one or two.

After that they went down to the pagoda by the lake. Nolly, her mouth smeared with strawberry juice, was suddenly a natural little girl, excited and happy. She ran happily round the pagoda, wanting to know what the table and chairs were for, and the bamboo screens.

Fanny explained that if they brought tea down to the lakeside and it began to rain, as it often did, they moved into the shelter of the pagoda.

"Can we have a picnic?" Nolly cried. "Ching Mei, wouldn't it be nice if we hung the windbells up here. See, the wind comes in everywhere. They'd ring all the time."

"Windbells?" said Fanny. "But how charming. We'll do that tomorrow."

Marcus wanted to put his feet in the lake. Where the water-lilies grew thickly he thought it safe to walk.

"No, no!" Fanny cried. "Only birds can walk on the leaves. You must never try to do that. You'd fall in and drown."

"Drown?" said Marcus, lifting his dreamy harebell eyes to Fanny.

"The water would go down your throat and choke you," said Nolly brutally. "Did you ever drown, Cousin Fanny?"

Ever since that long ago afternoon the lake had given Fanny a cool feeling of distaste. It was so smooth, so glassy. When the sun shone on it it looked inviting enough. But she had never gone in the boat since without a shamed feeling of apprehension. She would never forget Uncle Edgar's hands round her throat, dragging her out. And somewhere someone screaming. It had been one of the servants on the bank. The silly woman had had an attack of the vapours, and Uncle Edgar had been angry, because she should have whisked Fanny up to the house for a hot bath and dry clothes. Instead, Aunt Louisa had had to take her. And besides having been frightened to death, Fanny was made to realise that she had spoiled everyone's afternoon. How clumsy to fall out of a boat! Other people could reach for a water-lily without falling overboard.

Even the creamy water-lilies had been distasteful since that day.

The peacock screamed harshly, and Nolly flew to Fanny.

"What was that?"

"Only the peacock. You must get used to strange noises. There are other birds that come to the lake, and they all have different voices."

"Fanny! Fanny!" That was George standing on the slope of the lawn calling imperiously. "Come here. I want to see you."

A child holding each hand, Fanny walked slowly and reluctantly towards him. At the same time a window opened upstairs and Lady Arabella's white-capped head was thrust out.

"Fanny, is that you!" Her husky voice was quite audible across the garden. "No one has had the courtesy to bring the children to see me. Send them up at once."

"Who's that?" Nolly said, shrinking against Fanny.

"Your great-aunt Arabella. You must visit her for a few minutes. Dora will take you."

"She looks like a witch."

Marcus's eyes had grown enormous. Fanny said sharply, "Are you frightened, Nolly?"

"Frightened?" said Nolly, with contempt. "Me?"

"Then don't frighten your brother. Witches, indeed! Ching Mei, ask Dora to take the children to Lady Arabella. Lady Arabella. Do you understand?"

Ching Mei bowed. Marcus's hand dragged at Fanny's.

"Great-aunt Arabella has sugar plums," Fanny murmured. "Run along and see."

She watched them go. Already she had this absurd feeling that she shouldn't let them out of her sight. Why ever should she feel like that? The lake, and the vivid memory of her near-drowning had upset her.

George strolled towards her, scowling.

"Am I never to see you now without those brats?"

"George! Don't speak of your cousins like that."

"Isn't it true? They've been at your heels ever since you brought them home. And Mamma's quite content to make a servant of you. You know that, don't you?"

"I love the children already," Fanny murmured, uneasy beneath his intense regard. The little frown was on his forehead. His brown eyes were too bright, almost as if with a fever.

"Come for a walk. Let's go through the woodland on the other side of the lake."

"Not now, George."

"But you never will. I scarcely see you. You're so pretty, Fanny. I'd like to—" His fingers were at the neck of her dress.

"George!" She started back. "Please don't touch me!"

He was immediately contrite. Now his eyes were dull. He suddenly looked years younger, an overgrown schoolboy.

"I'm sorry. I wouldn't do anything to hurt you. But Amelia said you were behaving as if you had fallen in love on your trip to London."

"Amelia is teasing you," Fanny said indignantly.

"Yes. Yes, I thought she was." George passed his hand across his brow. "You must only love me, Fanny. I won't let—won't let—"

"George, dear, isn't it time for your rest? You know the doctor said you must rest every afternoon."

"Yes, I suppose it is. I get this headache. Let me walk in beside you, Fanny. I promise not to touch you. But don't let those brats take all your time. If they do—"

"What will happen?" Fanny asked, smiling.

"You know how I got this wound? That Cossack was swinging his sabre, like a devil. But I could use a sword. I still can. My sword arm isn't hurt. I used to be the best swordsman in the regiment, did you know? You're so pretty, Fanny. None of the girls at the regimental balls could hold a candle to you."

"Come inside," said Fanny uneasily. "The hot sun—"

"Yes, yes, I'm coming. When I stop getting these nightmares I'll be all right. You'll have patience, won't you, Fanny."

"Of course," Fanny promised. What else was there to say?

In Lady Arabella's room, with the curtains drawn against the sun because Lady Arabella loved this warm underwater gloom, Nolly stood staring with fascination at the empty birdcage.

Marcus was contentedly stuffing sweetmeats into his mouth, but Nolly held hers untouched in her hand.

"Where is the bird?" she demanded passionately.

"It died, my little darling. I told you. It was ninety five years old, I believe. And so bad tempered. Although I was dreadfully upset, I was also a little relieved to find it lying in the bottom of the cage one morning. Fanny, these children are charming. The boy's a poppet, but this one, the questions—" Lady Arabella shook her head pleasurably. "Oh, I shall have some times with her. Look at those bright eyes. They're going to miss nothing."

"You've been telling me a lie," Nolly said, turning on her. "The bird didn't die in its cage. It was in the chimney."

Lady Arabella blinked and stared.

"Oh, no, little love. You're talking about the white bird that struggles and struggles and can't get out. Not my scruffy old Boney. He was here, sure enough. He wouldn't have been up and down chimneys. Had too much sense. No, that was the white—"

"Great-aunt Arabella!" Fanny interrupted sharply. "Don't!"

"Don't!" The heavy-lidded eyes looked at Fanny in amazement. "You suggest I can't tell the child a story?"

"Not that one."

"Because the bird fell down the chimney this morning," Nolly said flatly. "Dora carried it away on a shovel."

Lady Arabella leaned forward, her cheeks pink.

"*No!* The white one? In your room? But what does that *mean?*"

"It was a starling," Fanny said. "It was black. Dora poked it down when she was trying to light the fire. It must have been caught there during the winter. It doesn't mean a thing. And I do wish you wouldn't tell the children these things."

"So why shouldn't I tell them stories. I told you plenty when you were this size, didn't I? And you enjoyed them. You wanted more. Besides, what is this? Are you making the rules in this house now?"

"Of course I'm not, Great-aunt. But already Nolly—"

Fanny looked at Lady Arabella's flushed hurt face and wondered what was the use. The old lady was so vain about her storytelling, she would never be stopped. And now the seeds of fear were planted in Nolly. She was brooding over an empty birdcage and imagining she heard things in the night.

But the sounds she had heard in the night had come before she had heard that tiresome eerie legend . . .

"Couldn't they play with Ludwig?" Fanny suggested.

"Ludwig! At his age! What does he care for romping with children? He creaks with rheumatism, the same as I do. But I have it!" Lady Arabella suddenly clapped her little plump hands. "We'll have a game of hide the thimble. Now that's something we can all play. Who shall go first? Marcus, of course. He's the smallest. And we girls go into the bedroom while he finds a hiding place. You understand, dear?" The old lady had put a silver thimble into Marcus's sticky hand. "Dear, dear, covered in sugar already. We shall be very clever and follow your trail. Now I will tell you a secret. Everyone looks under the clock, but nobody in my workbasket. Call when you're ready. Be quick."

Beginning to smile, Marcus looked round the room slyly. It was clever of Lady Arabella to think of something he could do in which Nolly didn't take the lead. There was no doubt, she could be like an enormous child herself, and throw herself with gusto into any game. This one, at least, seemed to have no pitfalls or sudden shocks.

Nolly was a little put out at not being the one chosen first to hide the thimble, but when Marcus called, she forgot to sulk and rushed eagerly into the room.

It was such a cluttered room, it was almost impossible to find anything that was well hidden. Cushions were tossed about, tablecloths lifted, vases tipped upside down. Nolly had emptied Lady Arabella's hairpin box, disclosing a fascinating collection of buttons, pieces of false hair, pins and unstrung beads. Lady Arabella was convinced that Ludwig, much discomposed in his demeanour, was sitting on the thimble, and had Marcus in shrieks of laughter at her antics. Nolly was lifting rugs and shaking the curtains.

"He's too clever, your little brother," Lady Arabella wheezed. "He's a magician, I believe. Now where is this thimble spirited to? How am I to do my sewing this evening?" She bustled about, looking in the same place twice, getting on her hands and knees to peer under the sofa and chairs.

"It's higher," Marcus choked. "It's not on the floor, Great-aunt Arabella."

"Then it is on a table. Or on the bureau. Or the mantelpiece. Fanny, what are you doing? *Put that down!*"

Fanny stood still in surprise, the pincushion in her hands. She had thought the padded top lifted off to disclose perhaps a small workbox. But the change from glee to sharp command in Lady Arabella's voice immobilised her.

"It's full of pins, you'll only prick yourself." Lady Arabella watched until Fanny, somewhat bewilderedly, put the pincushion back on the little table in the corner. Then she said in a changed, tired voice, "Well, Marcus, you've been too clever for us. We give in. Where is the hiding place?"

"Here it is, Great-aunt Arabella!" the little boy cried triumphantly, taking it out of the pocket of his jacket.

"You cheated, you cheated!" Nolly shouted. "You're not allowed to hide it on yourself. Is he, Great-aunt Arabella?"

"He's very little," said the old lady. "And suddenly I am very tired. Come and see me again tomorrow. Now be off with you!"

In the morning, when the mail had been brought up from the village post office, as it was each day, Uncle Edgar sent for Fanny to come and see him in the library.

He had a letter in his hands. He looked puzzled and, Fanny thought, perturbed.

"Fanny, this young man who escorted the children from Tilbury—what did you say his name was?"

Fanny's heart gave a paralysing leap. Had Adam written to say he was coming to the moors? Written to Uncle Edgar himself? Or perhaps to enquire after the children and Ching Mei?

"It was Adam Marsh, Uncle Edgar."

"And he was a perfectly respectable type of person?"

"Yes, indeed he was. I could swear to that, and so could Hannah. Why, what has happened?"

Uncle Edgar tapped the letter.

"Because the shipping company writes to apologize deeply for their man failing to contact the children. He reported that there was no sign of them, and that he had made a fruitless journey."

"But that couldn't be so! Why, Mr Marsh seemed to know about them—he even—" Good heavens, Fanny thought in horror, he had even accepted her guinea!

"Then he's an impostor."

"An impostor? How could that be?"

"*Why* could it be? That's what I'd like answered. What was that young man up to?"

Chapter 8

THE mystery about Adam Marsh remained unsolved. Of course he had not given her any address, Fanny said indignantly in answer to Uncle Edgar's questions. Ching Mei could give no information in her limited English except that the man had been there and offered his help. "Him velly kind," she said simply, her flat yellow face expressionless. It was impossible to tell whether she was puzzled by a complete stranger's action, or whether she just didn't understand what was being explained to her. Yet Fanny found herself remembering Adam Marsh pausing to have that last word with Ching Mei. Had it been as innocent as it had seemed?

"He spoke Chinese," she said involuntarily, and Uncle Edgar looked at her sharply.

"You didn't tell me that before."

"I just remembered."

Nolly and Marcus were also questioned.

Nolly said in her dispassionate voice, "We liked him. Marcus liked him."

Marcus, prodded into speaking, merely repeated in his parrot-fashion what his sister had said, "We liked him," clearly without having the faintest idea who was being discussed.

"Is he coming to see us?" Nolly asked presently.

"Not that I am aware of," said Uncle Edgar. "Although now I begin to wonder. Perhaps this mysterious gentleman will turn up."

Fanny tried to keep her face as expressionless as Ching Mei's. She knew the attempt was useless. Her mouth, her eyes, always treacherously showed her feelings.

310

Adam Marsh had said he loved the moors—not that the moors might be his excuse for coming to see the family from China again.

It was the children he had been interested in, not her at all. How could she keep the devastation of that discovery out of her eyes?

The Chinese windbells had been hung in the pavilion by the lake, and their delicate tinkling seemed the voice of the summer days. For one whole week the sun shone.

Then the wind changed, and the mist rolled up again. But not until the evening. In the afternoon they had their first picnic of the summer by the lake. Uncle Edgar had suggested it at breakfast. The Hadlows from Grange Park were coming to tea, and since it was such a fine day surely they would prefer a picnic to stuffing indoors.

His eyes twinkling with heavy roguishness, he added that Amelia would surely like the opportunity to take Robert for a walk through the woods.

Amelia coloured indignantly.

"Papa, he's only a schoolboy!"

"Three months younger than you, to be exact. I grant you a young man hasn't the advantage of springing his grown-up personality on the world, simply by the trick of putting his hair up. But he'll age, my dear, he'll age."

Amelia pouted, but kept her next thoughts silent. At least Robert was too young to interest Fanny. In the past, young men had shown an infuriating tendency to desert her side for Fanny's, and Fanny had blatantly encouraged them, her eyes shining wickedly. She didn't care two figs for them, yet she thoroughly enjoyed wielding her power over them.

Now that she was grown-up, Amelia thought, tossing her curls, she would prove that she was a match for Fanny. There was this mysterious Adam Marsh, for instance, and the way Fanny had been looking so distrait ever since her trip to London. If that gentleman turned up, as Papa seemed to think he might, she intended to flirt outrageously with him, perhaps even fall in love with him, since he must be quite attractive. She intended to have her own back on Miss Fanny.

Then there was to be Mr Hamish Barlow, the attorney, arriving from Shanghai. He would be here at the time of her ball. One

311

hoped he also would be attractive and interesting, with the glamour of foreign places on him. And he must be a bachelor. It wouldn't do at all if he had a wife. Altogether, Amelia reflected pleasurably, it was to be an exciting summer. She might even be coquettish with Robert Hadlow this afternoon, simply to get some practice.

She lingered in her room, prinking in front of the mirror, until after the Hadlows had arrived, and their carriage been taken to the stables. She intended to saunter down to the lake in a leisurely manner, being the last to arrive so that all eyes would be on her. She would carry her parasol instead of wearing a hat. Everyone would think what a charming picture she made, Miss Amelia Davenport in her lilac muslin, strolling by the lake on a summer afternoon.

As it happened, she wasn't the last to go down to the pavilion, for as she left her room and romped along the passage—her graceful approach could be saved until there was someone to see her—she almost bumped into her father coming out of Lady Arabella's room.

"Oh, Papa! Isn't Grandmamma coming to the picnic?"

It was a warm afternoon. Papa's face glistened faintly with perspiration. He shut the door behind him with a bang.

"She's gone down some time ago," he said shortly. "And why aren't you also looking after your guests?"

"Why aren't you, Papa?" Amelia retorted.

She had always been able to joke with her father, but she had chosen the wrong moment now.

"Because I'm a busy man and can't be at everybody's beck and call. Where are the servants? No one answered the bell when I wanted someone to go up and see to that atrocious cat. Your grandmother had somehow shut him in the wardrobe."

"Was he crying, Papa? I didn't hear him."

"You were too busy listening to your own thoughts, I expect." Papa was recovering his good humour. He pinched her cheek. "You're looking very pretty. Who is this toilette for? Robert?"

"I intend only to practice on him," Amelia confessed, and at last Papa laughed.

"You're a minx. Then let us go down. Don't say anything to your grandmother about the cat. She'll only want to come up and assure herself that he's all right. We don't want the picnic spoilt."

All the same, he was still strangely absent-minded, and she had to make the same remark twice before he heard her. Also, he had spoiled her plans for an impressive solitary approach. But for all that it was a successful picnic.

Three maids, with flying cap strings, brought a succession of trays with hot scones and muffins, strawberry jam, bowls of the rich yellow Devon cream, and, for the centre of the table, an enormous fruit cake. Mamma poured tea from the Queen Anne silver tea service, into the green and gold Dresden cups. The Hadlows, Mrs Hadlow, Anne and Robert, sat on the light bamboo chairs, but Lady Arabella, distrusting their resilience, had had her own sturdy rocking chair brought down. The Chinese windbells tinkled with a tiny glassy foreign sound. Fanny sat on a cushion on the grass, a little aloof from the rest, not bothering for once to fascinate Robert Hadlow who was looking more grown-up and almost handsome. The children sat quietly beside her. Nolly had her quite hideous Chinese doll in her arms. Ching Mei stood a little distance away. George lounged against a tree, watching. Watching Fanny mostly, but occasionally his quick glance darted over everybody. He made no attempt to talk. He behaved exactly as he pleased now. If polite conversation bored him, he remained silent. Sometimes Amelia wondered how much he was shrewdly exploiting his illness.

The sun shone brilliantly. Dragonflies darted over the gleaming water. The trees rustled gently and the windbells tinkled. It was an idyllic English summer afternoon scene. After Papa's arrival the slightly stilted quality left the party and there was a lot of laughter. Papa adored picnics, and was so good at them. It really was exactly like all the other ones they had had. Even the tiny slender figure of the Chinese woman stopped seeming so foreign and heathenish, and anyway was so unobtrusive among the tree shadows that one could almost forget she was there. Robert Hadlow pretended to think she had been imported to go with the pagoda.

"Is she real? Shall we stick a pin in her and see?"

Really, Robert was growing quite amusing. But all the same . . . an older man, more worldly . . . someone who would kiss her hand . . . Amelia dreamed, and the shadows grew longer, and the first hint of the rising mist obscured the sunlight.

Presently it was chilly, and the ladies were reaching for their shawls, and preparing to go indoors.

"Well, children." Amelia watched her father take out his fat golden watch. "You've been as quiet as two harvest mice. So shall we now see if this can make a better sound than those tinkling bells."

He wound the watch and held it out, smiling at their absorbed faces. The little chiming tune played itself through.

"Oh!" whispered Nolly. "It's pretty." Marcus put a shy stubby finger on the watch's plump face. Ching Mei was laughing, a tinkling sound not unlike the windbells, a sound of pure delight.

The mist had rolled up so quickly that it was drifting in opened windows when they returned to the house. The sun had completely vanished, and it was as if it was another day altogether, grey and chilly and filled with the sound of the rising wind. There was a great scurrying to and fro as windows were closed, billowing curtains stilled, and lamps lit. Fogs over the moor were a part of winter, but no one liked the summer ones that rolled up, stealing the light and warmth with a sinister rapidity.

Fanny left the children to Ching Mei and Dora, and went to dress for dinner. She had been happier today, because the children had been noisy and completely child-like and even Ching Mei, who had seemed strangely nervous of both Uncle Edgar and Aunt Louisa, but chiefly of Uncle Edgar, had relaxed enough to laugh. All the other days she had been shut in silence. Once she had wanted to write letters to her family and Nolly, who already showed a precocious grasp of her alphabet, had showed her how to laboriously address the envelope, writing the name of her brother in spidery Chinese characters, and the address Shanghai China, in English. Fanny had permitted her to walk into the village to post the letters because it was a pleasant walk for her and the children. It was the only occasion on which she had left the house.

As she went downstairs Fanny heard the hounds barking. It was a far-off sound, fragmentary and melancholy. It made her think of wet heather and scudding clouds, and the smell of fear. Once she and Amelia and George had followed the hunt on their ponies, and seen a fox torn to pieces by the hounds. She had never gone to a hunt again.

Now it was long past the hunting season, and she wondered whose hounds were loose. The baying was so far away that it seemed she might have imagined it. But the prickly sense of apprehension was not imaginary. It stayed with her after the sound of the hounds was lost.

Lady Arabella came wheezing behind her on the stairs.

"Fanny, that was very naughty of you, letting the children in my rooms to play when I wasn't there."

Fanny turned in surprise.

"They haven't been in your rooms, surely!"

"Playing hide the thimble," Lady Arabella grumbled. "Things upside down. Poor Ludwig taking refuge in my bedroom."

"When did this happen?"

"When I was down at the lake, I imagine. It was the only time I went out."

"But the children were there, too," Fanny said. "They were with me. Anyway, I'm sure they wouldn't go into your rooms un-invited. They're too—" She stopped. She didn't want to say they were too frightened. Nolly was unduly imaginative about the empty bird cage and Marcus more than half-scared of the old lady herself.

Surprisingly enough, Lady Arabella had begun to chuckle wheezily.

"So that's it, is it?" she said to herself. "Of course, I should have guessed. We'll say no more about the children."

"What are you talking about, Great-aunt Arabella?"

The old lady wagged a thick forefinger.

"Fee, fi, fo, fum, I smell the blood of an Englishman," she quoted enjoyably. "I've been watching the mist rolling up. Isn't it exciting the way it blots things out, wipes them away? I thought I heard dogs barking a little while ago."

"So did I," said Fanny uneasily. "I don't like the mist as much as you do. It hides things."

But it wasn't until they were all going in to dinner that George came bursting in, his eyes blazing with excitement.

"There's an escaped prisoner! They've got the bloodhounds out. Did you hear them?"

Amelia screamed.

"Oh, I knew something would happen. I knew it all afternoon!"

"It's because of the mist," said George. "They always make a break in the mist. If the search comes this way I'll volunteer to help."

"You'll do nothing of the kind," said his mother sharply. "You're an invalid."

"I can still fire a rifle and use a sword," George said indignantly. "Dash it, I'm not going to miss all the sport."

"Hunting a fugitive is scarcely sport," Uncle Edgar said calmly. "And one doesn't usually shoot the poor wretch down. Anyway, if this fellow has been clever enough to escape, he'll be miles from here by now. I suggest we don't let him spoil our dinner. Come, Amelia, my dear." Uncle Edgar gave his deep amused chuckle. "You look as if you imagine he's hiding under your bed already."

"Oh, Papa!" Amelia said faintly. "How can you joke about it?"

"I'm not joking. I'm admiring the poor devil's adventurous spirit. Who wouldn't make a bid for freedom in similar circumstances?"

"He may be dangerous," Aunt Louisa protested. "Really, Edgar, you can carry your philanthropy too far."

Uncle Edgar chuckled again. His colour was rather high. He looked as if he had been at the whisky decanter more than once before dinner. He was often mellowed by liquor, while never being overcome by it.

"Don't be alarmed, my love. I should, of course, hand him over to the authorities if, for instance, I tripped over him in the dark. But let's admit we all have a lurking sympathy for him. Fanny? Isn't that true?"

Fanny was remembering the hollowed face and the thin silent figure of the prisoner she had seen on the railway station the other night. She could imagine him now, crouching in the wet bracken, scarcely breathing, praying the hounds would go another way. He was a stranger, yet he had momentarily touched her life. Touched all their lives . . .

"Hunt him like a fox," said George, the excitement burning in his face.

There was a clatter at the sideboard as one of the maids let a dish slip. The curtains were drawn across the windows, a dozen candles burning on the long table. It was warm and safe in this room. No one was hiding, or hunted, or desperately hungry, or afraid . . .

After dinner Sir Giles Mowatt arrived on horseback. He stopped for a hasty glass of port, and to warn them that he believed the prisoner was hiding somewhere in that vicinity.

"But if we don't get him, he'll make for the high ground, and try to cross the moors to Okehampton. So you ladies don't need to be nervous."

316

"Was it the man who came down from London the other day?" Fanny asked.

"Yes, that's the rogue. He made a break in the fog, and got over the wall. He's as slippery as an eel. But we'll get him never fear."

"Does luck never go the way of the criminal?" Uncle Edgar asked reflectively.

"Only the ones who never have their crimes brought home to them. And we hope there aren't many of those. But this is hardly a subject for the ladies. And I must be off. I'll send word when we've made a capture. Good night, all."

Aunt Louisa rang for Barker to go round the house checking that all the windows and doors were locked. She drew her shawl round her ample shoulders, shivering.

"I've always hated the moors. Who else has to live in danger like this?"

"Good gracious, my love, the man's a thief, not a cut-throat."

"How do you know what he may become if he's desperate? Yes, Dora, what is it?"

Dora had tapped timidly at the open door, and now stood anxiously twisting her fingers.

"Please, ma'am, the children are upset. Master Marcus is crying and Miss Nolly's in a state about her doll. Could Miss Fanny—"

"Can't the Chinese woman control them? Really, Edgar, why are we keeping her here if she can't keep two small children in order?"

"But she's gone to look for Miss Nolly's doll," Dora broke in. "It was left down by the lake, and she really won't go to bed without it. It's the only thing she makes a fuss about." Dora looked round, listening. "But Ching Mei's been gone an awful long time," she said uneasily.

Fanny sprang up.

"She's lost her way in the fog, I expect. I'll go and find her."

Uncle Edgar stepped forward, detaining her.

"No, you won't. Not with a fog, and a prisoner at large."

"I should certainly think not," said George vigorously. "I'll go. I'll take my rifle."

"Oh, don't shoot anybody!" begged Amelia.

"Barker and I will go," said Uncle Edgar. "We'll probably

317

meet this foolish woman on the doorstep. How did she expect to find a doll in pitch darkness?"

"It would have been in the pagoda," Dora faltered. "She had a candle to light. Miss Fanny—"

"Yes, I'm coming upstairs," said Fanny. She wanted to hurry to the distressed children, but more urgently she wanted to go out and find Ching Mei. She didn't know how to explain this feeling of urgency, except that she could have sworn Nolly had had her doll when they had returned from the picnic. Uncle Edgar, in high good humour after his success with his chiming watch, had carried Marcus up to the house on his shoulder, Nolly clinging to his hand. There had been shrieks of excited laughter. One might have known they would later turn to tears. But Uncle Edgar had scored a very big success indeed if he had succeeded in making Nolly forget her beloved doll.

She was thinking of the eerie tinkling of the windbells in the mist, and of the ineffectiveness of one feeble candle in a whole world of darkness. The mist always wreathed closely over the lake, disguising the water as effectively as the water-lilies did. Supposing Ching Mei, unfamiliar with the paths, missed her footing . . .

"How long has she been gone?" Fanny asked, following Dora's little scurrying figure up the stairs.

"Oh, I couldn't say, miss. Before the children began their bread and milk, and I've bathed them since."

"But, Dora, that must make it nearly an hour!"

"I wouldn't know, miss. I hadn't thought about it until Miss Nolly wouldn't go to bed without her doll. Then I forgot myself and said the silly woman must have tumbled in the lake, and Master Marcus began to howl."

Marcus was still crying, though less uproariously, when they reached the nursery. Sheer exhaustion had left him with only breathless hiccuping sobs. There were no tears on Nolly's cheeks. She was standing at the window, the curtain drawn back, to peer out. When Fanny came in she turned, and Fanny saw her face as white as her nightgown, her eyes angrily accusing.

"What's everyone done with Ching Mei, Cousin Fanny?"

"Everyone, as you say, hasn't done anything with her. She must have lost her way in the fog. Uncle Edgar has gone out to find her. She'll be here presently. Now I want you two children in bed."

318

"Then will you kiss us good night, Cousin Fanny?" Marcus asked exhaustedly.

"Of course I will. Don't I always? Come, Nolly. Into bed with you. You shall have your doll when Ching Mei comes."

"Will you watch for her, Cousin Fanny?"

"No one can see anything in that fog." Fanny briskly twitched the curtain into place. "Dora, put some more coal on the fire. I'll sit beside it until the children fall asleep."

"Will you blow out our candles, Cousin Fanny?" Nolly was coming reluctantly to the bedside.

"When you're asleep. Not before. I promise."

"Will Ching Mei be afraid in the dark?"

Fanny was tucking Marcus in. She said, "Ching Mei did a very brave thing coming to England with you. I don't think she'll be afraid of a little dark." She added offhandedly, "Nolly, do you remember leaving your doll in the pagoda?"

"No, I didn't leave her there. I had her under my arm all the time. Then we were running up to the house. At least—I think I had her."

"Then you're not sure, so she is down there. Well, she'll soon be rescued. Dora, you may go now. I'll be here until Ching Mei gets back."

Marcus was asleep almost instantly. Fifteen minutes later, just as Fanny was about to blow out the candles, Nolly said sleepily, "I hope those dogs didn't get my doll."

"Dogs?"

"The ones we heard barking. Marcus said they were wolves. Isn't he silly! Wolves!"

Nolly, too, was asleep, her lashes long and dark on her white cheeks. Neither child stirred when Aunt Louisa came to the door to whisper stridently, "Fanny! Your uncle says it's no use trying to search any more in the dark. He says either the woman will come back, or she's run away."

"Run away!" Fanny exclaimed in astonishment. "She wouldn't dream of doing such a thing!"

Aunt Louisa was a shadow in the doorway, an enormous domineering bossy shadow.

"I don't see how you can claim to know, Fanny, any more than the rest of us how the oriental mind works. I myself have never trusted the woman. I'm perfectly sure she has understood every

319

word we have said. So is your uncle. Now, pray don't spoil the children by sitting there all night."

Fanny started up.

"But is that all that's to be done about Ching Mei? With a prisoner at large, too."

"My dear girl, what do you suggest? That we start dragging the lake in pitch darkness? You may sit up and listen for her if you choose. I, for one, am going to bed."

Aunt Louisa probably didn't mean to be callous. She just didn't attach much importance to the safety of one small silent suspicious foreigner, and a servant, at that. Uncle Edgar, whose kindness always had a practical element, would be the same. George would think only of discharging his rifle at shadows. So it was left for Fanny to put on her cloak and her outdoor shoes and grope her way across the terrace, past the rose garden, and down the path to the lake.

The wind had dropped. There wasn't a sound until suddenly the tall outlandish shape of the pagoda loomed up out of the fog and the thin intermittent tinkle of the scarcely-swayed windbells sounded.

She had brought matches. She struck them, one after another, as she went into the pagoda and saw the bamboo chairs and the table where, so long ago, they had had the light-hearted tea party.

She called softly, "Ching Mei! It's me, Fanny. Answer me, if you can."

The mist formed a halo round the tiny flare of the match. On the lake something made a muted splash. The bells tinkled again, very faintly. There was no other sound, no movement.

Uncle Edgar had been right. There was no use in trying to search in the dark. Ching Mei had obviously strayed out of her way and would shelter beneath a bush until daylight. It was cold, but not dangerously so. She shouldn't come to any harm.

Reassuring herself with those thoughts, Fanny made her way towards the house. Just beyond the rhododendron bank someone sprang on her, holding her fiercely.

"There you are at last, you foreign devil!"

"George! George, let me go at once!"

George's alarmingly strong hands pressed her head back. He was trying to see her face.

"George, it's me! Fanny!" It was as well she had recognised his voice or she would have been scared out of her wits.

"Fanny!" He loosened his hold. The hard substance pressing into her side was his sword, sheathed, thank goodness. Had he had that naked in his hand he could have run her through.

"I thought you were one of the foreign devils."

"Foreign devils?"

"Russkys, Chinese, what's the difference? Don't you know the dark isn't safe?"

"I came out to look for Ching Mei. I haven't been able to find her. Take me back to the house."

"Not for a minute, Fanny." His arm had tightened round her again. He was pushing the hood of her cape back from her face. "I never have the chance to get you alone like this."

He had kissed her before she could turn her face away, a hard bruising greedy kiss that filled her first with revulsion, then with furious anger. It was the first time she had been kissed. Her first kiss, and it had to be like this! Her eyes stung with angry tears. She wrenched herself free and resisting an impulse to beat and claw at George, she made herself stand still and face him in the darkness.

"George Davenport, if ever you dare to do that again, if ever you dare—"

"I told you the dark wasn't safe," George muttered, but the fire had gone out of his voice. Inevitably, the anger in Fanny died, too. She knew how he would look if she could see him, shame-faced, bewildered, sulky, his slowed brain trying to understand the violence that leapt in him.

He wasn't safe, Fanny was thinking uneasily. And yet the inevitable pity was filling her. It wasn't his fault that he had become like this. Somehow one had to have patience until he got better.

"I'm sorry if I hurt you, Fanny. Truly, Fanny, I wouldn't hurt you."

"I'm telling you, George, if ever you do that again I believe I could almost kill you."

"But you wouldn't, would you, Fanny. You only kill enemies, not friends. So stay my friend, Fanny, and you'll be safe."

Back in her room, Fanny found Nolly's Chinese doll lying face downwards on her bed. She stared at it in stupefaction. Had she absent-mindedly put it there herself? Or had Nolly forgetfully dropped it? Anyway, there it was, the culprit.

It was a very small and innocent toy to have caused the death of one old Chinese woman.

Chapter 9

FOR the gardener's boy found her in the morning lying among the water-lilies in scarcely eighteen inches of water. She had been battered about the head. Whether she had been drowned, or had died of those brutal blows, it wasn't possible to say.

But it was clear her death was no accident. There seemed little doubt what had happened. In her search for Nolly's doll she had encountered the escaped prisoner. He, as Sir Giles Mowatt confirmed, was a desperate and dangerous man. He couldn't risk the alarm being given, and had attacked his innocent discoverer violently. A stronger person might have survived his blows, but Ching Mei was a small old woman with fragile bones. She had had no chance.

It was all very tragic, and the search for the prisoner was redoubled. All the comings and goings, men on horseback and on foot, kept Nolly and Marcus at the windows, full of interest, and they even seemed to believe Fanny's story that Ching Mei had suddenly grown too homesick to stay with them. She had crept away quietly last night to catch the train to London, and a clipper ship to China.

"Will she write to us?" Nolly asked. "She can. I've taught her how to write letters."

"Then perhaps she will, later."

"That means in years and years," Nolly said dispassionately, her nose pressed against the window pane. "Oh, Marcus, do look at that dog with the white tail. That will be mine. You can have the black one."

"No, I want the one with the white tail."

"You're a silly baby, wanting it just because it's mine. You can have the black one."

"I want the white one!"

"Then very well, you can have the white one, and it's got great big teeth and it will bite you in half!"

"Nolly!" Fanny exclaimed, as Marcus burst into the inevitable loud sobs. "That wasn't very kind. Tell Marcus you're sorry."

"Why should I? He always wants my things. He will have to be careful, Papa says, or he will have no mind of his own."

It was easy enough to see that Nolly's quarrelsome mood came from taut nerves, but that didn't make the task of restoring peace any easier. The child was uncannily intuitive. How much did she guess, or know? Her next question froze Fanny's blood.

"Cousin Fanny, why didn't Ching Mei take her sandals?"

"I expect she did."

"She didn't. Not her best ones. They're in the wardrobe wrapped in tissue paper. She kept them for feast days and long journeys. That's why I know she hasn't gone on a long journey."

Fanny thought of Ching Mei's lonely journey, and it was all she could do to answer quietly, "Then perhaps one day she'll come back. In the meantime neither of you must worry because I will take care of you."

She thought the hideous day would never end. The mist had turned to rain, and this had obliterated any tracks the fugitive might have left.

If he had been this way . . . Fanny was doing her best to shut out of her mind the episode with George in the dark garden last night. Had she been the first unprotected woman he had sprung on, in his obsession about a foreign enemy?

But surely, surely, what Uncle Edgar, the police, and Sir Giles Mowatt said was true. The prisoner was desperate. In his previous escape from Wandsworth he had bound and gagged a housewife in her kitchen, and stolen bread and half a leg of lamb. There would very likely be more acts of violence in lonely dwellings on the moor before he was recaptured.

One had to believe it was the prisoner who had caused Ching Mei's death.

Fanny realised this even more after she had sought out George in the billiard room, and found him in one of his quiet and contented moods.

"Hullo, Fanny. Come to have a game with me?"

"No, I haven't time. I must stay with the children."

"Can't the servants do that? What about the Chinese—oh, but

she met with an accident, didn't she? I forgot for the moment."

Were servants really of such little importance to him as human beings, or hadn't it penetrated his mind that Ching Mei was dead? Watching him place the balls with skill, his handsome face completely absorbed, Fanny was genuinely bewildered.

"George, you do remember being in the garden last night?"

"When I bumped into you? Sorry if I scared you. I was only fooling."

"*Fooling!*"

"Lord, Fanny, you don't think I'd kill a woman, do you? I thought you were the escaped prisoner, until I got my hands on you. Knew then you were a woman—skirts and things."

"George!" Fanny breathed. "Ching Mei wore trousers."

"What's that got to do with it? Dash it, Fanny, you don't think I go about fumbling an oriental!"

The horror in his voice was convincing. He looked so affronted that Fanny almost found the situation comical. She compressed her lips. She found herself longing to laugh, light-heartedly, carelessly, at anything. Laughter seemed a very long way away.

"No, you save those favours for an English woman," she said with asperity. "And I won't have it, George. I told you last night."

George looked abashed. "Sorry," he mumbled. "Lost my head. Guess the opportunity won't come again. If it does—can't promise—"

At this moment it was impossible to imagine George a murderer, he was merely lovesick and embarrassing. But his moods changed, and he was, perhaps conveniently, unable to remember. Sometimes he was still pursuing Russians. Asking him questions got one nowhere at all.

To Amelia, the day had been intolerable. She had had to spend most of it alone, for Mamma was with Papa, talking first to Doctor Bates, and then to the hastily summoned police. Grandmamma, on an occasion like this, was someone to be avoided. She would have been talking about omens and portents, and probably that ghastly bird in the chimney. And Fanny wouldn't let Amelia come into the nursery, because she had foolishly wept (not for the strange little Chinese woman, but from shock and depression, and a curious strung-up state of expectation), and her eyes were still reddened.

"I won't have the children upset," Fanny had said. "They

think their amah has gone back to China, but they're quick enough to guess anything. Anyway, why are you crying?"

Amelia sniffed and mopped at her eyes.

"Fanny, you're getting altogether too bossy. Mamma says so, too. And why must you spend all day with the children? I need some companionship as well."

"But, Amelia, they're so little!"

Amelia pouted.

"Then they don't understand this terrible thing. I do. I can't bear to be alone. I keep thinking—"

"Thinking what?" Fanny asked curiously, seeing Amelia's furtive and frightened eyes.

"That that dreadful man might break into the house. You know —that a curtain might draw back and there he would be."

"Oh, Amelia, darling! Hunted people like him don't come into houses. They hide on the moors, in caves, under hedges. He'll be miles away by now. Sir Giles says so."

"I wonder where," said Amelia fearfully.

The day, of course, did end. Even dinner was over. Only Amelia and Lady Arabella had stayed downstairs afterwards. Lady Arabella had fallen asleep by the fire, and Amelia, unable to face the thought of her bedroom all alone, stayed at the piano, picking out tunes, singing a little, but only halfheartedly. To cheer herself up, she had put on her best blue silk, and tied blue ribbons in her hair. She had expected Mamma to scold, but no one, not even Papa, had made any comment, or seemed to notice her. It had been a horrible day, and thank heaven it was almost over.

A log fell with a muffled crash in the big fireplace. Lady Arabella didn't stir. Amelia gave an exclamation of exasperation and bad temper. She brought her fingers down on the keys with a resounding chord, but still Grandmamma, sunk deep in her slumber, didn't wake. Something made a pecking sound at the window behind her. A bird? A branch of the wistaria climbing the wall? Amelia turned and stared fascinatedly at the drawn curtains.

Actually, they were not quite drawn. There was a space of two inches that showed dark window pane—and was that something moving?

Amelia's hands flew to her throat. The tapping came again, peremptorily.

She didn't know where the courage which impelled her to the window came from. She really wanted to scream until Papa or George or Barker, or anyone, came. Instead, she was drawing aside the curtain, and looking into the wild shining eyes of the man outside.

He made urgent motions for her to open the window.

Again she didn't know what kind of hypnotism compelled her to obey. But in a moment the window was open, the cold wind in her face, and the man, pressed against the wall, under cover of the wistaria, was whispering harshly, "Get me some food! I'm starving. You look like an angel."

"You're the p-prisoner!" Amelia gasped.

"Never mind what I am. Shut the window and get me the food. Quick! Don't wake her."

He nodded towards Lady Arabella, still fast asleep, her cap tilted sideways, her chin sunk into her plump breast.

Amelia suppressed an hysterical giggle.

"Nothing wakes Grandmamma."

"Then hurry! You wouldn't let a man starve."

Just for one horrifying thrilling moment his fingers, cold and hard, touched hers. Amelia snatched her hand away and held it pressed in her other palm as if it had been wounded.

"Will you promise not to get into the house?"

"Yes, yes, I promise. Shut the window. Draw the curtains again. I'll be here. But hurry."

Suddenly Amelia realised that her fright was really intense excitement. She did as he told her to, closing the windows softly, and pulling the curtain across. Then she flew out of the room and down the stairs to the kitchen where the lamps were lit and a fire burning cosily in the big stove. Lizzie was washing dishes, and Cook sitting at the long scrubbed table finishing her supper.

The kitchen was familiar and comforting territory to Amelia. Her plumpness was largely due to her fondness for coming here to be petted by the maids, and consume freshly made biscuits and hot scones.

"Cook, make me a sandwich, please. A big one."

Cook, who also found food the chief pleasure in life, threw back her head and shouted with laughter.

"Miss Amelia, you'll never get an eighteen inch waist this way, bless your heart."

"Please, Cook. Cold meat, if you have it, and a piece of plum cake. Honestly, I couldn't eat a thing at dinner. Everyone was so quiet and glum, as if it was one of us who had died."

(And was that the murderer crouched beneath the wistaria, trustfully waiting for her?)

Cook was shaking her massive head. "We couldn't make anything of that heathen idol. She gave us the creeps, to tell the truth. All right, Miss Amelia, don't fidget so. I'll make your sandwich. Lizzie, get me that cold joint out of the safe. And the bread. Lizzie will bring it up to you, Miss Amelia."

"No, I'll wait and take it. But hurry. I'm so tired, I could die."

She yawned convincingly. She hoped the high colour in her cheeks was put down to over-tiredness by Cook and the inquisitive Lizzie. They seemed to dawdle so over cutting the bread and buttering it that she could have screamed with impatience. But at last it was ready, with the large slice of plum cake, and Cook was chuckling with admiration at the thought of Amelia's unashamed greediness.

Clutching the plate to her, praying she wouldn't encounter anybody, and that Grandmamma hadn't woken, she hastened back to the drawing room.

Everything was as she had left it, the songbook open on the piano, the fire crackling, Lady Arabella snoring gently. It was such an innocent scene. She scarcely believed that when she drew back the curtain and opened the window the hungry hand would enter and snatch at the food.

Indeed, for a moment, when she had undone the catch, there was no movement without. She had a crazy feeling it had all been a dream. She was wildly disappointed.

Then the leaves rustled, and the shock of dark hair, the thin face, appeared.

He didn't snatch at the food. Instead, he looked steadily into Amelia's face.

"I think I have never seen anyone so beautiful," he said.

Amelia felt the hot flush of startled pleasure flood her whole body.

"Here's your food. Take it and go."

He emptied the plate quickly, putting the sandwiches and the cake carefully in his pocket. Then, much as she wanted him to go, taking the fearful excitement with him, Amelia detained him.

"Have you been hiding about here all day? How was it the dogs didn't find you?"

"Because I haven't been here. I went the other way last night, then at midday I doubled back, to fool them. I'm making for Plymouth. I'll get aboard a ship."

"You—weren't in this vicinity last night?"

He grinned, showing remarkably good white teeth.

"Sure, I was not. I slept under a boulder stinking of sheep."

"Why do you trust me?" Amelia whispered.

"Because when I saw you sitting at the piano there, with the light in your hair, I knew you could be nothing but an angel. I'll never forget you. Now I'm off. God bless you."

There was an infinitesimal rustling in the leaves, and he was gone. He was as quick and silent as a fox. Amelia had no doubt he would get to Plymouth, and get safely aboard a ship sailing for France or Holland, or perhaps one of the Americas. She was glad she had helped him, glad! She would never breathe a word about him having been there. If necessary, she would lie until the day she died. For he had done something for her that so far no other man had done. He had made her feel beautiful, and a woman. She didn't think she could ever talk to a schoolboy like Robert Hadlow again.

As she softly closed the window, Lady Arabella woke.

"Ugh!" she exclaimed, shaking herself. "It's cold. The room's full of draughts. What are you doing at the window?"

"Just looking to see if it's a clear night," Amelia said.

"And is it?"

"Yes, the moon's shining."

"Then they'll most likely catch that criminal. He won't have the fog to hide in. Ugh!" She shuddered again. "It's cold. I feel as if I have that dead woman's blood in my veins. Now what is it, child? Why are you looking so frightened?"

Amelia pressed her hands to her pounding heart. She had just realised a terrible thing. Only she knew that the prisoner had not killed Ching Mei, but by keeping her secret, no more effort would be made to find the real culprit. And who was it? *Who?*

Chapter 10

THE hunt moved the other way, towards Okehampton and Ashburton, and the Somerset border. Trains going to London were searched, and shopkeepers in small villages warned to be watchful. It seemed as if the prisoner's break for freedom might have been a success.

The episode had passed like a disastrous storm over Darkwater. The villagers, from having been hostile and unfriendly towards the little foreign woman, were now belatedly sympathetic and shocked. It was arranged that she should be buried in the village churchyard, her grave lying between honest Joseph Briggs, blacksmith, and old Martha Turl, centenarian, dead a few weeks previously. She was in respectable company now, people said with satisfaction, but Fanny kept thinking of how Ching Mei, Chinese to her core, must be fretting for the paper house, the food and the cooking utensils, which she would require for her long journey. Even her feast day sandals, which Hannah had briskly bundled up, together with her other modest belongings, and taken away to be destroyed.

There couldn't be letters written to her family in Shanghai because no one knew who they were. Hamish Barlow's arrival would have to be awaited, to see if he could produce any information. Fanny had the strange suspicion that Adam Marsh, too, might have been able to throw some light on the subject.

But Adam Marsh remained as great a mystery as Ching Mei's Chinese relatives, and the gloom hanging over life at present was hard to dispel.

Strangely enough, Amelia seemed to be touched by it, too. She was restless and distrait. Amelia without her boisterous talkativeness was another person. Lady Arabella noticed the change in both girls and although she approved their extreme sensibility —delicately-reared young women must naturally be deeply shocked by violent death—she finally grew impatient of it.

"Louisa, those girls either need a good dose of rhubarb or a change. Why don't you take them to London for a week or two? I'll speak to Edgar if you like."

"Thank you, Mamma, but I'm quite able to speak to my husband myself. Why should he listen to you more than to me?"

Lady Arabella rocked back and forth in her rocking chair, smiling gently.

"Because he has a respect for old age, probably."

Louisa looked at her mother suspiciously. The reply was too innocent. She hadn't noticed her husband's respect for age lead to any great generosity. Though there was the matter of George's new hunter which Mamma had wheedled out of him.

"Anyway, there's no need to speak to him. He has agreed that we may go to Plymouth and shop, particularly for Amelia. This is her year, after all. Edgar has been very generous."

Indeed, he had. He had thrown a pile of sovereigns on to the bed last night and said offhandedly, "See how far you can make that go. I don't expect wild extravagance, but make Amelia—and Fanny, of course—look as they should. Eh, my love?"

Then he had kissed her on the cheek.

"You see, I'm not such a bad husband after all."

Louisa, for once, was at a loss for words. At that moment she found his portly figure impressive and admirable, his eyes not merely tolerant and a little facetious, but loving.

"Have you overcome your financial difficulties?" she asked.

"Things are looking more optimistic, yes. There are still problems, but I hope and expect to overcome these."

"You will, I am sure. You always have."

"And then you will begin to think about your ermines?" His eyes twinkled with the kindness he could show so many people, orphans, impoverished villagers, people struck by misfortune, but not always, Louisa had to admit, herself. Nevertheless, at this moment, he was showing it to her. She was sceptical but pleased.

"Edgar, sometimes I believe you really are a good man."

For some reason he found this remark diverting. His heavy jowls and his stomach shook as he chuckled rumblingly.

"Then let us settle for that. Sometimes I am good, and sometimes you are tolerable. But I must admit—" he laid his hand on her shoulder, "—you pay for dressing. I expect you and my daughter to do me credit at this ball."

"Is Fanny to go to Plymouth also?" Lady Arabella asked.

"If she wishes to," Louisa replied shortly.

But Fanny didn't wish to go on the shopping expedition. She couldn't bring herself to leave the children. She didn't know why she had this obscure dread that the tragedy of Ching Mei might spread to them . . .

So Aunt Louisa and Amelia, with Trumble on the coachman's seat, went, and arrived home after dark, laden with silks and brocades, lawn and striped taffeta, also trimmings for bonnets, ribbons and braids, and feathers, and an enchanting white fur muff and bonnet to match for Amelia. The children had not been forgotten. Uncle Edgar had particularly asked that they be fitted out as became their new position in life, so there was a plaid coat and bonnet for Nolly, frilled pantaloons and petticoats, and shiny black-buttoned boots, and for Marcus a sailor hat and suit, and a cord with a whistle on it.

There was even a length of the new foulard silk for Fanny. It was for her ball gown, Amelia explained. Amelia had quite recovered her spirits, and chattered endlessly.

"We do hope you like the silk, Fanny. Mamma and I took ages to choose it. And the next time we go to Plymouth you're to come, too, so that you can go to Miss Egham for your measurements to be taken. She's to make all our gowns. Lady Mowatt says she's terribly clever, and even makes things for the Duchess of Devonshire. Isn't it jolly, because it means several visits to Plymouth, and although it isn't London, at least it's better than being cooped up here. Miss Egham has let us bring home some of her fashion books. Do you want to see them?"

"Later," said Fanny, absently.

She had to admit that Aunt Louisa and Amelia had chosen well for her ball gown. The silk was a deep rose instead of the pastel colours worn so much, and it would set off very well her black hair and vivid colouring.

But they had had to choose carefully, because Amelia's ball was going to be a large important one, and everyone belonging to the family must do her credit.

Fanny hated herself for her thoughts. She hated dressing the children in their new clothes and telling them that they were for Sundays only, when they would be going to church. Afterwards, they must be taken off and hung away carefully until the next Sunday.

"I don't think Marcus likes his," said Nolly.

Marcus stood uncomplainingly in the sailor suit. Indeed, there was an innocent look of pleasure on his face.

"I think he likes them very well," Fanny said.

"Then Ching Mei won't when she comes back. She doesn't like us in any clothes but the ones she gets ready for us."

This was all too true. Ching Mei had been extremely vain and particular about her washing and ironing of the children's clothes. But how did one explain to a highly suspicious little girl that time didn't stand still, that clothes wore out and unfamiliar hands had to prepare new ones. That Ching Mei was never coming back . . .

It seemed impossible that Nolly, aged six and a half years, could have divined what had happened and kept the knowledge to herself. Yet there was that look of austere acceptance in her face and she had never cried.

She made scenes instead. There was the scene when she couldn't find the marbles.

"What marbles?" Fanny asked patiently. "Dora, do you know anything about Miss Nolly's marbles."

"I've never seen them, miss."

"But you must know about them. Everyone knows about them!" Nolly stamped her foot, her black eyes sparking. "They were in a little bag that Ching Mei sewed for us, and Marcus and I are always playing with them. Aren't we, Marcus?"

"What?" said Marcus.

"Playing with our marbles, stupid!"

"We haven't for a long time," said Marcus. "Where are our marbles?"

"Don't you understand, that's what I'm asking Cousin Fanny!" The loss of the marbles, whatever they were, was not serious enough to provoke such anguish in Nolly's face.

Fanny averted the real tantrum by suggesting a walk.

"We'll go to the village, and I'll show you the church where you'll be wearing your new clothes on Sunday."

It was late afternoon and the sun had left the long windows over the altar. The church was dim. Fanny walked slowly up the aisle, the children tiptoeing after her.

"What's that?" whispered Marcus. "What's that, Cousin Fanny."

Fanny looked round. He was pointing to the tomb of a long-ago Davenport, the one who was reputed to have built the house at Darkwater. Hugo Davenport, born 1521, died 1599. He lay, tall and thin, carved in cream-coloured stone, his shoes narrow and pointed, his beard trim, his long nose rubbed flat with the centuries. His wife, Elizabeth, lay beside him, her Elizabethan ruff holding erect her small firm chin. Their feet rested against a greyhound, which lay humbly loyally curled, not deserting them in death.

It was the dog which fascinated Marcus.

"I'd like it," he said.

"You can't have it, it's stuck there," said Nolly.

"It's a memorial," Fanny explained. "It's so people will always know that once there lived a man called Hugo Davenport and a woman called Elizabeth, and they had a faithful greyhound. What would you like to be at your feet?"

"When we're dead!" said Nolly in astonishment.

It couldn't happen to a little girl of six years. It could scarcely happen to someone who was almost twenty-one. But it had happened to the homesick, alien Chinese woman, as loyal as the Davenport greyhound. It could happen to anyone . . .

"I'd have a dove, I think," said Fanny.

"I'd have a peacock!" said Marcus.

"And what about you, Nolly?"

Nolly lifted her small chin. It looked remarkably like that of her ancestor Elizabeth. It didn't need supporting by a stiff ruff.

"But I'm not going to die!"

Someone had opened the church door. It creaked, and sunlight fell across the flagstones. Then the door closed softly, and the man stood within.

His face was in shadow. There was something about his bearing that was familiar. Why did he just stand there as if he hoped to remain unseen? Marcus gave a small whimper as Fanny's fingers tightened on his. Nolly said in her clear low voice, "Cousin Fanny, there's a man watching us."

Fanny stepped briskly into the aisle, a child at each side. She

333

hoped to reach the door without her palpitating heart rendering her speechless. She was almost sure . . . She *was* sure . . .

She held out her hand with easy grace.

"Why, Mr Marsh! So you have come on your visit to the moors."

She had thought she had remembered every detail of his face, but she found she had forgotten the squareness and strength of his chin, the faint disturbing grimness of his eyes before they left her face and turned to the children with a look of assumed surprise and delight.

And the unwanted thought flashed through her head—how long had he been in this part of the country without making his presence known?

"Miss Davenport!" Her hand was all but crushed in his grip. "And Miss Olivia and Master Marcus! I had hoped to see you hereabouts. I fancied it was you I saw going into the church."

"We were looking at the dead lady," Marcus said.

"Dead lady?" repeated Mr Marsh, and Fanny tried to signal to him that if he had heard about Ching Mei, not to say her name.

"The one on the box over there," Marcus said. "She's squashing a dog with her feet."

"She's not squashing it, Marcus," Nolly said severely. "She's just resting her feet on it. It likes it, anyway. It's a faithful and true dog. Would you like to see it, Mr Marsh?"

"Very much."

So the little procession filed back to the tomb, and while the children, brought to life by his sudden appearance, rushed forward to caress the dog's cold ears, and trace its stony outline, Fanny said softly, and hurriedly, "Ching Mei—the Chinese woman—I don't know if you remember her, has d-died—" To her horror she heard her voice trembling. Belatedly, and at this highly inconvenient time, she felt herself about to weep for the patient silent loyal woman who also would have curled up at the feet of her master and mistress in eternal devotion.

"I know. They told me in the village. I'm staying at the Darkwater Arms."

His fingers had barely touched hers before the children were looking round, demanding attention. But the gesture had warmed her to her heart, and more than ever her tears were difficult to control.

"Mr Marsh, will you be coming to call on us?" That was Nolly, remembering her manners and her dignity. "Ching Mei, we're

334

sorry to say, has left us, but we have new clothes, and a great many toys to play with."

Mr Marsh bowed.

"I hope to, Miss Olivia. I have been meaning to renew my acquaintance with you ever since the day I said good-bye to you in London. Wasn't it good fortune, Miss Davenport, that I was able to give assistance to these small travellers when they arrived in a strange country in such bewilderment."

He realised that she must know by this time that he had not been the shipping company official, and that an explanation was due. But it was a little belated. Why couldn't he have told her at the time and saved her the embarrassment of the guinea tip? At the thought of that, Fanny's colour rose angrily.

"It was very kind of you, Mr Marsh," she said in a clipped voice. "But it has since caused my uncle, and myself, also, some mystification. Perhaps you might have explained your identity a little earlier."

"My identity?" He was smiling. Had she imagined that earlier grimness in his eyes? Now they seemed to hold nothing but gentle amusement. "What am I? Let us say, a traveller in search of a home. The same as Olivia and Marcus. Perhaps that's why I had sympathy for their plight. I apologise deeply for any misapprehension I caused. Later I will apologise to Mr Davenport personally."

"Later?" She was furious for letting the anticipation be heard in her voice.

"I told you I love the moors. I intend to spend some few weeks here. Perhaps longer if I find a suitable house."

"You would—live here?"

"I explained, Miss Fanny, that I am a traveller in search of a home. I have moved about too much in my youth, but now I intend to settle down. Indeed, your uncle may be able to give me advice. Do you think it would be convenient if I present myself tomorrow afternoon?"

"I think—yes, I am sure it would be." Fanny felt herself behaving more like a schoolgirl than Amelia did. "He'll look forward to having the mystery of the traveller on the train cleared up. It has puzzled us all."

(And you particularly? his intent gaze was asking.)

"And now, perhaps I may see you part of your way home?"

335

"Oh, no. Please don't. I think it would be better—I mean, if you were to call formally—"

"As you wish, Miss Fanny. We shall meet, of course. And talk of what has happened."

He was referring then to Ching Mei's death. Naturally he would want to talk of it, since he had been interested in her welfare, and spoken to her in her own language.

But was it coincidence that his arrival had taken place so soon after her death?

"I wonder what brought him just now."

She realised she had spoken aloud, as she and the children made their way down the narrow lane, deep-set between hawthorn hedges.

"I wrote him a letter," said Nolly, tossing her curls.

Fanny stopped short. "Nolly, what are you saying?"

Nolly's bright black gaze faltered.

"I know how to spell and write."

"But you didn't write and post a letter. Where would you have sent it? You're not telling the truth, Nolly."

"Marcus posted it. He pushed it into the box."

"Marcus, did you?"

Marcus's wide innocent eyes were full of indignation.

"That was Ching Mei's letter to China. Nolly, you're not telling the truf."

Nolly burst into loud sobs.

"I hate you! I hate you both! You say I tell lies."

"Nolly, darling!" It was the first time the child had cried like this. Fanny recognised it as a release of her pent-up grief for Ching Mei's disappearance. She welcomed the tears, noisy and untidy as they were. "Nolly, my pet, come here. Let me dry your eyes. No one's cross with you. We love you. Don't we, Marcus? And you see, even without a letter, Mr Marsh has come. So all is well, isn't it?"

It was only when they got home, and Fanny had left the children with Dora, and was in her room thinking she had only ten minutes to dress for dinner, that she realised her appearance. Her poplin gown was darned in two places, the cloak she had thrown over her shoulders, was threadbare, and quite the oldest she possessed. She had had a scarf tied over her head. There was certainly no grand lady about her this time. She must have looked like a servant.

Looking into the mirror at her flushed cheeks, Fanny began to dimple with mirth. She had been saved the trouble of an explanation to Mr Marsh of her own position. He must by now be as puzzled about her as she had been about him!

Chapter 11

BUT this situation didn't seem so amusing the next day.

Marcus had developed a slight fever during the night, and had to be kept in bed. He was fretful and restless, and wept every time Fanny left his bedside.

"Cousin Fanny, are you going on a journey, too?"

Ching Mei's disappearance had shaken him as much as it had Nolly. He remembered his mother and his father disappearing. He distrusted everybody.

Fanny scarcely had the opportunity to dress, or tidy her hair. When, half way through the morning, Lizzie came up with a message that the master wanted her in the library, she had an impulse to send back a message that she was unable to come. Then the thought sprang into her mind that Uncle Edgar might have come to hear of Adam Marsh's presence in the village, and wanted to speak of it.

She hurried downstairs straight from Marcus's bedside. Her long black hair was escaping from its hasty pinning up, and, because of her nursing chores, she had put on her oldest gown.

Voices in the library should have warned her. She was so intent on getting the interview over, and hurrying back to Marcus that she failed to realise that the voices were not only Uncle Edgar's and Amelia's.

She saw him standing near the window immediately she entered the room. He had been talking to Amelia, bending a little towards her attentively. Amelia, her fair hair brushed and shining, and tied with black velvet bows, and a spotless muslin fichu draped over the shoulders of her pretty blue morning gown, looked charming and animated and deliciously young. The contrast between her and Fanny, at that moment, could not have been more marked.

It showed on Adam Marsh's face as he turned and saw her. She was aware of his moment of keen assessing regard before he bowed and smiled.

"Miss Fanny! We meet again."

Uncle Edgar, wearing his most benevolent expression, came forward.

"Fanny, my dear, why didn't you tell us you spoke to Mr Marsh yesterday, and that we could expect a visit from him?"

"Why, I—" Why had she wanted to keep their meeting secret? Because she had anticipated that scene of him bending so attentively over Amelia?

No, no, Amelia was only a gauche schoolgirl. Or had been until very recently. One couldn't quite decide when, in the last week or two, she had suddenly acquired moments of dignity and a certain mystery. Had it been since the tea party in the pagoda, when she had conversed so animatedly with Robert Hadlow? She didn't giggle so much, and she dreamed, and now, with the stimulation of a personable man's attention, she was really pretty.

They were all waiting for Fanny to finish what she had begun to say. Aunt Louisa was there, too, and George. They had been having glasses of Madeira and biscuits, showing hospitality towards the stranger even though they must want to know a great deal about him.

"Marcus has developed a fever," she said. "I've thought of nothing but him. Anyway, I was under the impression that Mr Marsh said he would probably call in the afternoon."

"Marcus ill!" Mr Marsh exclaimed. "I'm sorry to hear that."

"It's only a little fever—"

"We must call Doctor Bates," Uncle Edgar interrupted. "Why hasn't it been done already?"

Aunt Louisa's nose, whether from the Madeira, or the pleasure of entertaining a good-looking and presumably unattached young man, or her husband's implied rebuke, had taken on its familiar grape colour.

"Fanny said the fever was slight. As you can see, Mr Marsh, Fanny is a practical young woman, and already so devoted to the children. My own daughter, I am afraid, has still to learn the practical things of life."

At her mother's indulgent tone, Amelia's lashes drooped on her

339

pink cheeks. She looked unbearably smug. And suddenly Fanny hated them all for what they had just done to her, letting her come unaware into the room looking as she did so that the comparison between her and Amelia was inevitable.

They had meant to do it. She wished passionately that she had run away that day in London. Then she remembered the children upstairs, utterly dependent on her, and was ashamed of her selfishness. But the anger stayed in her eyes, and in her jutting lip. Let Amelia smile coquettishly. She would be herself, refusing to be meek and humiliated.

"Fanny, Mr Marsh has been telling us how he came to be of such inestimable help to the children on the train that day. The shipping clerk was dilatory. Mr Marsh found Ching Mei in a state of distress. Being able to speak Chinese, he soon ascertained the facts. Isn't that so, Mr Marsh?"

"Miss Fanny expressed surprise that I spoke Ching Mei's language." Mr Marsh's eyes as they rested again on Fanny were ironic. "I didn't explain to her, as I have to you, that my father was a well-known collector of Chinese porcelain and jade. He made several trips to the East, and on two occasions I accompanied him. I should add that I was at Tilbury that day because the *China Star* was bringing some new pieces for the collection which I now own."

"And he is looking for a house in which to keep it," Amelia exclaimed, unable to keep silent any longer. "And in which to live himself, of course. Mr Marsh, if it were to be somewhere in this vicinity I should be delighted—I mean, we should all be delighted."

She blushed at her transparency and Adam Marsh smiled.

"That is charming of you, Miss Amelia."

It was funny, thought Fanny, that when he looked at Amelia that almost grim expression left him, and he looked light-hearted and gay. He wasn't summing her up as he was Fanny. But then Amelia needed no summing up. She didn't look like the daughter of the family one day and a servant the next.

"Yes, I'm tired of wandering," he went on. "I intend to settle down. As I told Miss Fanny, I have a great fondness for this part of England. Our meeting has been quite a coincidence, hasn't it?"

"A fortunate coincidence, Mr Marsh," said Aunt Louisa warmly. "I hope we can persuade you to come to some of our gaieties this year. We are giving Amelia a ball later."

"And by jove, my brother's attorney from Shanghai will be here, too," said Uncle Edgar. "A Mr Hamish Barlow. I don't suppose you have heard of him?"

Did something flicker in those dark brown eyes? They were unreadable eyes, Fanny had decided from the first. Amelia could get out of her depth in them. So, for that matter, could she.

"I'm afraid my acquaintance of China is confined mostly to Peking. But I shall be interested in meeting Mr Barlow."

"I have suddenly remembered!" Amelia cried. "The other day Robert Hadlow said that Heronshall was going to be put up for sale. Old Mr Farquarson is going to live entirely in London. That's scarcely ten miles from here. It's a Georgian house, Mr Marsh, with lovely light rooms. Not nearly so dark and dreary as these."

"But this is a beautiful house," said Mr Marsh.

Fanny found she couldn't bear to stay there while Amelia excitedly arranged this stranger's future. Surely he wouldn't allow her to do it! Though if he were speaking the truth and wanted to buy a house, Heronshall was eminently suitable. The long windows would display to perfection his collection of Chinese porcelain—if it existed . . .

She interrupted the conversation, speaking quite calmly.

"If I may be excused, I would like to return to Marcus."

"Certainly, my dear," said Uncle Edgar. "But don't make yourself a prisoner in the sickroom. You know there's no need for that."

"Fanny used to think she had a vocation for nursing," said Aunt Louisa indulgently. "Then later she began to talk of convents. I think she used to imagine she had something of the martyr in her. It's her Celtic ancestry, I expect."

"She's much too pretty for convents or hospitals," Uncle Edgar boomed. "And to add to our festive year, Mr Marsh, Fanny has a twenty-first birthday which of course will be suitably celebrated."

How clever they were, Aunt Louisa suggesting that her tendency to martyrdom made her stay in Marcus's sickroom and wear her oldest clothes, Uncle Edgar hinting that twenty-one was so much more than the delicious freshness of seventeen.

Or did she imagine these things because she had fallen in love and all her senses were unbearably heightened? She knew she would have to walk a tightrope to achieve happiness. She was more likely to fall and hurt herself irremediably.

341

She had got out of the room and longed only to escape to the children, now her allies and her uncritical unquestioning friends. With dismay she heard Adam's voice at the door.

"I was greatly taken with the children. I promised them to come. Would I be out of place for two minutes in the sickroom?"

"But how thoughtful of you, Mr Marsh." Aunt Louisa's voice was acquiescent as courtesy demanded, but a little bewildered, a little put out.

"It may be the measles, Mr Marsh. Pray don't catch them." Amelia laughed, but she was a little put out, too.

Fanny hurried up the stairs, not thinking at all. She didn't want him in the nursery. He had already been too officious, too overpowering. He made glib explanations and got his own way. He probably broke hearts right and left. She wouldn't have Nolly and Marcus fretting for him.

"Miss Fanny!"

They were at the turn of the second flight of stairs. There was no one about. From the nursery Fanny could hear Marcus whimpering.

"I've heard how Ching Mei's death happened. Is it true?"

She had to turn and look at him.

"How could it not be?" she asked slowly.

"There was no other reason?"

"Not that I know of. My cousin George—you must have noticed how he is. He hasn't yet recovered from his war wound. But he has been trained to kill with a sword, not—not his hands."

"Then it was the escaped prisoner?"

"It must have been. The coroner decided so at the inquest." She looked into his intent eyes. "Why do you care?"

"Because I find a mystery provoking. Very provoking."

"You are staring at me," said Fanny. She put her hands to her hair, an inevitable feminine movement, trying to smooth it. "Is there anything wrong?"

"Everything."

"Then you had better go back and talk to my cousin Amelia. She has had time to make her toilette this morning."

He began to laugh as if her tartness amused him, then stopped, and said thoughtfully, "Yes, your cousin Amelia is a delightful creature. I fancy we shall be seeing quite a lot of one another. If I had known I would have come much sooner."

"Known what?"

"Why, that the moors can be so fascinating. Exciting, dark, unpredictable, stormy, tragic, and then warm and glowing like a summer's day, full of light, innocent, irresistible."

He was talking of the moors. But he made them sound like a woman.

Chapter 12

LADY Arabella had awoken with a start to the knowledge that something was going on about which she knew nothing. This had happened also the other evening when she had opened her eyes to find Amelia at the window and the room full of cold air. She never had discovered what Amelia had been doing, which was aggravating. She didn't intend to be left out of what was happening upstairs now, with Nolly laughing hysterically and the sound of a man's deep voice.

Had Doctor Bates been sent for to examine Marcus? But Doctor Bates was elderly, prim and serious, and most unlikely to make a child laugh.

Sighing and struggling, Lady Arabella heaved herself out of her low chair, put her cap straight, and waddled off to her vantage point at the head of the stairs. The windowseat was shadowed by the heavy velvet curtains. It was surprising how often she had sat there quietly in her black dress and never been seen, though occasionally a startled maid had dropped what she was carrying and exclaimed in confusion. She had heard many intriguing fragments of conversation from there, and if they hadn't always been interpreted correctly, that made it all the more interesting. Lady Arabella was all for a little embellishment of the truth.

Her harmless ploy was well-rewarded today, for she had scarcely sat down before the door of the nursery on the second floor opened, and footsteps began to come down the stairs.

Fanny led the way, followed by a stranger, who seemed to be on terms of some intimacy, for he was saying in a low almost conspiratorial voice, "I will come again, I hope frequently. I've taken a fancy to those children. I shall be interested in their future."

Fanny, bless the girl, never minced matters.

"If you have such paternal feelings, Mr Marsh, I wonder that you don't do better than borrow other people's children."

"Perhaps I intend to."

Amelia must have been lurking at the bottom of the stairs, for she called in her high assured young voice—now there was someone who was rapidly learning the artifices, the gushings and the vapourings, that Fanny despised—"What is it you intend to do, Mr Marsh?"

"He intends to find a wife," Fanny answered.

"How interesting." Amelia's voice bubbled with interest. "We wish you luck, Mr Marsh. Don't we, Fanny?"

As Lady Arabella had expected, no one noticed her sitting quietly in the shadow, but she was able to take a swift look at Fanny with her geranium-flushed cheeks and ruffled hair—that girl would look beautiful in sackcloth, in childbirth, in extreme old age—and then a much longer one at her companion. She noted the hard chin and the broad clever brow. She also noticed or divined a look of intense speculation in the almost black eyes. This, however, disappeared as the man caught sight of Amelia in the hall below. He paused a moment, looking down with a smile and an unruffled face. He could change his expression like an actor. He was someone to be watched, this young man. Lady Arabella made a sharp guess at his thoughts. Of the two girls, Fanny was the prettier, but Amelia was the richer. The children upstairs? They merely provided an original and convenient excuse for establishing himself in the house. Lady Arabella itched with curiosity. Who was he?

She had to wait until her pre-lunch glass of Madeira before her son-in-law satisfied her curiosity. Edgar, also sipping Madeira, was as anxious to discuss his uninvited guest as Lady Arabella was to hear about him.

"Well, that's cleared up the mystery of the man on the train. Fellow's story seems plausible. With his connections with China, the Chinese amah attracted his attention, naturally enough. Any gentleman would have done what he did."

"Even to coming all the way to Devon?" Lady Arabella murmured.

Edgar paced up and down, reflectively.

345

"He seems to want to live in these parts. Call that coincidence, if you like. If he buys a property, we can't doubt his integrity."

"And do you now?"

"Eh? Doubt a gentleman's word? I should hope not."

"What are you worrying about, Edgar? That he will run off with Fanny?"

"With Fanny!"

"Didn't it occur to you that it might be Fanny who has brought him to these parts?"

It was obvious that such a thought had not occurred to Edgar. His brow cleared. He gave his rumbling chuckle.

"Well, now, I must have been blind not to see that. Of course, Fanny is an attractive young woman. But I'm afraid this won't suit my wife and daughter. They plan to lay claim to Mr Marsh. I've said they must wait until we know more about the gentleman, but you know what women are. Louisa sees him as an asset to our entertainments this summer, and Amelia—" Edgar shrugged his shoulders with tolerant amusement—"you may have noticed that what that young lady wants she intends to get."

"I've noticed," said Lady Arabella. "I've also noticed that Fanny isn't completely without a will of her own. She hasn't Amelia's material assets, of course. That should provide a test to Mr Marsh's character. The contest should be remarkably interesting, don't you think?"

"Remarkably," said Edgar shortly.

Lady Arabella watched him beneath her eyelids.

"I notice you worry less about the young man now you realise his interest is of the heart only."

Edgar shot her a quick glance.

"What other object did you imagine he had in coming here?" Lady Arabella murmured. She waved her small white hands. "No, don't bother to invent an answer, because I know that is all you will do. But I wouldn't underestimate even this romantically-inclined gentleman."

"Wouldn't you?" said Edgar sharply.

"He is strong. Very strong. I feel it. I feel—no, never mind. I can see you despising my old woman fancies. And anyway, as you say, Louisa intends to fête the young man, Amelia intends to pursue him, so even if we think him a menace we're helpless."

"Really, Mamma, you would make a country bumpkin, a clod,

346

into a menace." Edgar stared at her angrily, accusingly, "You do it to amuse yourself."

"Oh, yes, my dear, I make up stories. I turn the frog into the prince, and vice versa. It's a harmless occupation. Like my little forays into local history. By the way, isn't it strange how that letter that I was telling you about has disappeared, so that neither of us can find it?"

She lifted her eyelids, letting him have her full round innocent gaze. He returned it, puffing his cheeks out in angry frustration.

"Whatever that letter is, if it exists, it's nothing to do with me. It's only against my better judgment I'm making arrangements to buy George a new hunter. Does that satisfy you?"

"In the meantime," said Lady Arabella meekly.

Edgar made his voice genial.

"What else is it you want, you old witch?"

"What else? Only George's happiness. Even to his marrying Fanny, if he insists."

"Marry Fanny!" Edgar exploded. "What poppycock! I'll never hear of it. Neither will his mother."

"Edgar, you're getting red in the face. Is your health what it should be? I only make this comment now because I don't think it will do for Fanny and Mr Marsh to form an attachment. George wouldn't care for it."

"George, George, George! Is he to run this house?"

"One day, we hope." The old lady gave Edgar her heavy-lidded glance, a sly secret look she invited him to share. "If things go as I suspect they must."

"I am the master here!"

Lady Arabella seemed to be falling into one of her sudden naps. She didn't appear to notice his changed and furious face.

Outside the window, on the sloping lawn, the peacock suddenly set up its harsh penetrating squawking.

Lady Arabella opened her eyes.

"I have never disputed that, Edgar. But even you won't live for ever. Though longer than some, perhaps. And if you are the master, could you demonstrate it by finding out why the luncheon gong is two minutes late. I, for one, am famished."

It was true that Amelia had already set her heart on having as much of Adam Marsh's company as she could get. Her mother was cautious, pointing out that although Adam seemed a perfect gentleman they didn't yet know anything about him.

347

"Your Papa will make enquiries," she reiterated.

"Oh, Mamma, it's perfectly plain what he is by his face and his manners. I think it rather impertinent to even suggest investigating him. Anyway, no matter what you might find out, I intend to have him here a great deal."

"None of that talk, miss."

"He likes me," said Amelia. "He will help me to forget."

Her mother turned in astonishment.

"To forget what, for goodness sake?"

"All faces are not as easy to read as Mr Marsh's."

"Amelia, *what* are you talking about?"

Amelia flung her arms round her mother passionately.

"Oh, Mamma, I want a kind safe husband. I don't want to be—tortured."

"Good gracious, child! Whatever books have you been reading to get such ideas? Tortured, indeed! As if your Papa or I would allow you to meet that kind of man."

Amelia gave a small hollow laugh. "No, I know you wouldn't if you could help it."

"I still don't know what you're talking about," said her mother, losing patience. "You're a very fortunate girl. You live a sheltered life."

"Yes, Mamma," Amelia whispered, her eyes dark. "I know."

Amelia's prediction about Marcus's illness came true—he did have the measles, and by the end of the week Nolly had come down with them, too. So the children were not able to wear their new clothes to church on Sunday. The Davenport pew was occupied only by Uncle Edgar, Aunt Louisa, Amelia and George. It was taken for granted that Fanny should stay in the sickroom since, by her own behaviour, she had made the children so dependent on her that they were unmanageable when she was absent. No one else seemed to understand that two such little ones, deprived cruelly first of their parents, and then of their faithful nurse, must have some security in their lives.

Though perhaps Lady Arabella understood a little. She had taken it on herself to come and sit for long intervals in the sickroom, sometimes bringing Ludwig to sit in her capacious lap, sometimes her many-coloured wools and embroidery. She urged Fanny to take walks in the garden so as not to lose her pretty colour. At first Fanny was reluctant to do this, knowing Lady Arabella's propensity for making children nervous. But she had become so quiet and gentle that Nolly and Marcus seemed to like her sitting in the big armchair, as dozy as the cat in her lap. It was only when, after a day or two, they grew better, and restless, that she began to tell them stories.

The outcome of this was that when Amelia came rushing up to the nursery after church Nolly burst into loud hysterical screams.

No one could tell what was the matter. The day was bleak and rainy, and Amelia had taken the opportunity to wear her new white fur hat and muff.

It emerged, at last, that on her first glimpse of it Nolly thought it was a white bird.

Fanny turned on Lady Arabella.

"You've been talking about that bird again!"

"No, I haven't, dear." Lady Arabella's eyes were milky and innocent. "Except to point out to the child that it was white, and not that wretched black skeleton she found the other day. A white bird. A beautiful pure creature. And on that day the mistress of the house shall die."

Amelia said scornfully, "Grandmamma, you can't scare us now with that old myth. It isn't true, anyway. Do you think a silly old bird is going to warn Mamma when she is going to die!"

"Need it be your mother?" said Lady Arabella softly.

"Well, who else, if it is to be the mistress of the house? Pay no attention, Nolly. See, I'll take my hat off and you can touch it. It's only white fur, so soft."

But Nolly wouldn't be lured into touching the fur. She shrank away, hiding herself beneath the blankets, and although later she protested loudly that she hadn't been frightened, Fanny knew that that particular fear had been tucked deeply into her mind and that it would be a long time before it ceased to haunt her.

That was when it came to her that Lady Arabella might be more than a foolish, imaginative and mischievous old woman. In her desire to shock and in her desire to wield power she might be dangerous.

But why she should feel that, Fanny couldn't have said. She was becoming as overwrought as Nolly. Perhaps poor old women were happier than rich ones. They might be tired to the bone with washing and ironing great baskets of laundry, or scrubbing and cleaning, or hoeing the potato patch or caring for a clutch of grandchildren, but they were not so hopelessly bored with their idleness and uselessness that they weaved strange schemes in their heads.

It appeared that Amelia had rushed up to the nursery on her return from church for the express purpose of telling Fanny that she had talked with Adam Marsh. She had to wait until Fanny came down for her brief walk outdoors to seize her, and say, "Don't you want to hear about Mr Marsh? He looked so elegant and everybody talked to him. And what do you think, Sir Giles Mowatt had heard of his father and of his famous collection of Chinese ceramics. So Papa has to admit now that all his actions have been perfectly innocent."

"Innocent?" said Fanny.

"Mamma and I believed him on sight, but I suppose fathers of marriageable daughters have to be careful, and even suspicious."

"How can you *be* so smug?" Fanny breathed passionately.

Amelia opened her eyes wide.

"Smug? But why? Mr Marsh is unattached and we expect to be seeing a great deal of him this summer—by the way, he intends looking at Heronshall—and after all I am considered something of a catch. That isn't being smug, Fanny. It's simply looking at things the way they are."

Fanny pulled her shawl more tightly round her shoulders. The wind was chilly. It was because of her that Adam had come here! Not because of this bright-eyed baby of a cousin, this plump naïve creature scarcely out of the schoolroom.

But then he hadn't known about Amelia in London. He had imagined her, Fanny, the pampered daughter of the house . . . As Amelia had said, one had to look at things the way they were.

"Do be a little more sympathetic, Fanny. Otherwise I won't be able to tell you my affairs of the heart."

Fanny laughed out loud.

"Affairs of the heart, indeed! You're only a child."

Amelia flushed indignantly. "Mr Marsh doesn't think so. He complimented me on the way I looked. You had only to see the expression in his eyes." Already she had forgotten her anger with Fanny, and was carried away with the happiness of her recollections. "He is so masculine. He makes me feel truly like a grown woman. Only one other—person has ever made me feel like that." Amelia's eyes were suddenly inward-looking, strange. "Do you know," she said in a rush, "all the time I was in church I kept thinking of that wretched Chinese woman buried outside. Sometimes I am frightened . . ."

Fanny stared at her.

"Why? Because the prisoner may come back?"

Amelia shook her head.

"Sir Giles says he is afraid he has got away completely. To France or Belgium, or the Hook of Holland." Her next words were almost inaudible. "I think that is why I am frightened . . ."

George, tapping his riding crop against his leg, said to Fanny, "You're not having your head turned by this fellow Marsh, too, are you?"

"I think my head is fairly securely attached."

"Mamma and Amelia are behaving as if they had never seen a man from the city before. He must be laughing at them." George's eyes, with their look of feverish excitement, were on Fanny with the intensity she was beginning to dread. "You won't let him laugh at you, will you?"

"I don't suppose he's laughing at anybody."

"I saw you looking at him yesterday. Don't do it again, Fanny." His voice was very soft. "I don't care for you to look at another man."

"Oh, George, leave me alone! I can't bear this possessive attitude of yours. It's suffocating me. You used to tease me and despise me. Be like that again. Please!"

"Never!" said George. "Never!"

"You will be when you are well."

"I love you, Fanny. Being well won't change that."

Fanny was near to tears with exasperation and tiredness and strain.

"Then if you must love me, you must. But please don't persecute me, or I'll have to tell your father."

An indescribably sly look came into George's eyes.

"That wouldn't be much use, you know. Not poor old Papa."

Then he turned and left her, the once handsome young lieutenant of the 27th Lancers, who had flirted shamelessly with every pretty girl, a shambling young man whose once immaculate clothing was now always a little untidy, and whose breath frequently carried the fumes of brandy.

George was a tragedy. But how long could one have patience and forbearance with that kind of tragedy! How long was it safe to do so? Fanny couldn't help thinking constantly of Ching Mei's

351

death and the convenient way in which it had been blamed on the escaped prisoner. Had anyone else seen George in the garden that night? Uncle Edgar? For why had George begun to speak of his father with pitying contempt? Poor old Papa . . .

It didn't seem, after all, as if Adam Marsh were laughing at Amelia with her transparent admiration for him. For he invited her to accompany him to look over the property, Heronshall. They went on horseback across the moors. Amelia rode almost as well as George did. On her mare, Jinny, she lost her dumpiness and her coquettish flutterings, and was a figure worth watching. They made a fine pair as they rode away. Fanny could scarcely bear to watch them go.

There was a shuffling sound behind her.

"A well-matched pair," said Lady Arabella's throaty voice. "Don't you agree?"

"Amelia scarcely comes to his shoulder."

"She is on a level with his heart. That used to be the thing in my young days. Don't girls have these romantic notions nowadays?"

"You know that Amelia has her head stuffed with romantic dreams," Fanny said irritably.

"And you? You're too practical for such things?"

Fanny turned away.

"You know I am not," she said in a low voice, as if the words were forced from her.

Lady Arabella patted her hand.

"Your turn will come, my dear. Don't despair."

Fanny snatched her hand away. She found the old lady's kindness more intolerable than her sarcasm. How could she not despair when Amelia and Adam rode through the honeyed sweetness of the moorland air, talking perhaps intimately, perhaps touching hands. It was no use to wonder what Adam Marsh saw in an emptyheaded rattle like Amelia. He would discover that she had beautiful small white hands, that her yellow curls blew across her throat when disordered by the wind. A man didn't then seek for a high intelligence.

They arrived back late in the afternoon. Amelia came flying upstairs calling, "Fanny! Mr Marsh has things for the children. Are they well enough to see him? Oh, and you should have seen that divine house. Mr Farquarson's things are gone and the rooms are empty, but one can imagine exactly what is needed. Mr Marsh has a fine Arabian carpet which he says will perfectly fit the drawing room. The staircase must have portraits on either side. It is so light and airy compared with all the dark stairways in this house. And the master bedroom has the most beautiful view across the moors."

"Did you furnish that, too?"

"Fanny! What a thing to say. We merely discussed what could be done. And it was all perfectly respectable as Mr Farquarson's housekeeper was still there. Mamma naturally wouldn't have let me go otherwise. Then is Mr Marsh to come up?"

Fanny wanted to refuse to have Adam in the nursery, but it would give the children pleasure. She said he might come for five minutes, no more.

The wind had raised a glow in his sallow skin. Although he was smiling he looked strangely serious. He had brought gingerbread cookies, bought from old Mrs Potter in the village that morning.

"For the invalids," he said. "I hope they are recovering fast. You see, Mrs Potter gave the gingerbread men spots, too."

The children studied the figures liberally sprinkled with coloured sugar, and laughed with delight.

"Marcus got the measles first, Mr Marsh, but I had the most spots," Nolly declared.

"I had the most spots," Marcus said.

"You did not, Cousin Fanny said I had more. And anyway my gingerbread man has more spots than yours."

"No, it hasn't. Mine has."

"Then count them. Come over here and I'll teach you to count." While they were wrangling, Adam turned to Fanny.

"Miss Amelia has been telling me a great deal about you."

"About me!" Fanny exclaimed in astonishment. She could scarcely believe that they could find nothing to talk of but her on that long ride across the moors. She couldn't prevent a dimple appearing momentarily in her cheek.

"Amelia usually finds herself the most absorbing subject."

"Perhaps it was because I asked her questions."

"What kind of questions?" Fanny's face had gone still.

"Why, how you came to be in this position."

"Yes, I suppose you must find it rather different than what you imagined it to be when we met in London."

"Amelia tells me your parents died when you were very young.

353

Your mother—your father—tell me what you know about them."

"I know so little. My father died of a consumption. He had artistic leanings, I believe. I can't remember him at all." Fanny frowned, feeling the old familiar bafflement. "My mother was Irish, of landed but poor gentry, Uncle Edgar has told me. Her name was Francesca, like mine. I try to imagine what she was like, but I know so little. I feel as if I had dropped from the sky. What I do know," she finished briskly, "is that poor Papa's illness took all his money. That's why he left me in my uncle's care. To be quite accurate, Uncle Edgar isn't my uncle, but a second cousin."

She realised, all at once, his interest and was startled and a little disturbed.

"Why do you ask me these things?"

"I have an inquisitive bent," he said pleasantly.

Fanny frowned again. "I think I find your inquisitive bent, as you call it, a little presumptuous. So now you know without any doubts that I am a poor relation. Have you some better position to offer me?"

"Cousin Fanny, Cousin Fanny! Marcus has eaten all his gingerbread."

Nolly's imperative voice broke in on their small duel. For duel it was, and Adam seemed to welcome the interruption. He went over to sit on Nolly's bed.

"When you are quite recovered how would you like a picnic on the moors? We could take a hamper. Have you seen the moorland ponies? They will come for crusts of bread."

"Sandwiches like we eat?" Nolly asked.

"Yes, indeed. They have cultivated tastes. But they all need a brush and comb taken to their manes and coats."

Nolly laughed delightedly. Marcus clamoured, "Me, too. Can I come, too."

"Naturally. And Cousin Fanny, of course. One day when the sun shines."

He had a way of making people adore him, Fanny was thinking coldly. Not only children, but adults, like Amelia. Even Aunt Louisa. But the strange conversation they had just had had confirmed her suspicions about him. She knew now what he was about.

He was looking at her to see if she shared the children's enthusiasm about the proposed picnic.

"If you are disappointed I am not an heiress, I am sorry," she said. "I am afraid no amount of conjecture can achieve that." She wanted to go on and say that he would have to be satisfied with Amelia, a compromise that didn't seem too displeasing to him.

She wasn't prepared for his frowning anger.

"I must have been very clumsy to deserve a remark like that. I assure you—"

But at that moment Amelia came bursting in.

"Mr Marsh, Mamma insists that you stay to dinner. We're not going to dress. Say that you will."

He inclined his head. "Your mother is very kind."

"Then come downstairs." She had taken his arm proprietorially. Miss Ferguson's patient lessons about etiquette and modesty seemed to have escaped from her flighty little head. "I think it's sweet that you should be so interested in my little cousins," Fanny heard her saying as they went. "But you mustn't let them monopolise you."

That was the moment when Fanny decided he was never to have the satisfaction of knowing what he had done to her.

In spite of Amelia's lofty decree that because Adam was in riding clothes, no one should dress, Fanny took great pains with her appearance that night. She wore her grey taffeta, old to be sure, but she let the neckline fall as low as possible over her shoulders, and she decided, with deliberation, to wear the sapphire pendant Uncle Edgar had given her. Above all, pity was not the emotion she wanted Adam Marsh to feel for her. She brushed her hair into a state of velvet softness and instead of wearing it in ringlets, as was all the rage, she twisted it low on her neck so that her ears and all of her round white forehead were visible.

She went downstairs late, so late that the gong had gone and everyone was just about to go to the dining room. Everyone looked at her. Aunt Louisa was about to scold when Uncle Edgar saw the sapphire and beamed with pleasure.

"And very well it looks on that pretty neck," he whispered conspiratorially, making sure, nevertheless, that his words were quite audible.

"I had a fancy to wear it," Fanny murmured. "Somehow I was feeling happy. The children are recovered, and it's summer, and everything is so beautiful."

She looked vaguely out of the window, suggesting that her remark about beauty meant the garden, and the trees heavy with mid-summer leaf. But her lingering gaze went round the room.

"May I sing to you later, Uncle Edgar. It seems a night for singing, I hardly know why."

"You may indeed, my dear."

"Fanny has a very pleasant voice, Mr Marsh," Aunt Louisa said repressively.

"It's more likely we may hear a nightingale if we go outdoors," said Amelia. "Are you an admirer of the nightingale, Mr Marsh?"

So now he was caught between the two of them. Fanny found herself waiting for his answer with more amusement than pain. The pain would come later, when he strolled in the warm dark scented garden with Amelia, as inevitably he would, while she sang to Uncle Edgar, or Lady Arabella, dozing in her chair, or George with his worshipping eyes—or the uncaring moon.

"Perhaps if the windows were to be opened, we would hear both nightingales."

"Bravo, Mr Marsh! Worthy of a diplomat," applauded Lady Arabella.

"Coward, Mr Marsh!" Fanny murmured.

Adam's eyes met hers over Amelia's ringletted golden head. They had a strange intense glitter that shook all her resolutions and left her silent for the rest of the meal.

But later, half way through a song, when the wind from the open window was causing the candle flames to gutter in their own grease, she realised that he and Amelia had disappeared.

"Don't stop, my dear," said Uncle Edgar. He was a bulky shadowy figure in the winged chair. "But perhaps something a little more gay."

Fanny's hands came down on the keys in a jagged discord. She saw that the room was empty except for Lady Arabella sunk, as usual, in her gentle after dinner slumber, and Uncle Edgar. Even George had not stayed. But George didn't care for music. He could be forgiven. No one else could.

"Most songs are sad," she said.

"But not all of them are about death. Although, indeed," Uncle Edgar was sipping his second glass of port, "we must be practical and realise our ultimate destiny. And that reminds me that now you're almost twenty-one, Fanny, my dear, you must make a will."

"A will! But I have nothing to leave to anybody."

"It's more tidy to do so. After all, where would you have been,

356

as indeed where would Olivia and Marcus have been, if your separate fathers hadn't left instructions about you. True, you haven't children. Nor have you a fortune. But you do have a little jewellery, my dear, some of it of a certain value. And your aunt and I intend you shall have more. So one day we'll draw something up. I'm sorry if I sound morbid. Some people think that by signing a will they hear the nails going into their coffin. George made his before he went to the Crimea, and naturally Amelia will also do so later. My own has been made this thirty years, and look at me! No nails in my coffin."

Fanny was taken aback, more surprised than repelled.

"What made you think of such a thing just now?"

"Your song about death. And seeing you wear that sapphire tonight. You will naturally want to choose your own recipient for that."

It was ironic, macabre, hilarious, even vaguely flattering, since it indicated she wasn't completely without possessions. She had come down meaning to be so gay and to steal the evening into her hands, and this was what happened. She and Uncle Edgar had an absorbing conversation about death!

Amelia and Adam came in just as she was laughing with uninhibited mirth.

"Whatever is the matter now?" Amelia demanded. She had been flushed and a little sulky all evening, knowing Fanny's ability to steal a scene. "I only took Adam out to insist that he smell the new red rose William is so proud of, and immediately we go you and Papa start having private jokes."

"About mortality," said Fanny. "A very amusing subject. Although I don't imagine Ching Mei found it so. I hardly—" She stopped what she was going to say—what had it been going to be? The wind from the open window was making her shiver violently, to the exclusion of all thought. One of the candles on the piano had blown out. The room seemed too dark, the faces all looked at her too intently.

George and Aunt Louisa had also come back, and, about to ask what was going on, the words had died on their lips. It was a strange petrified moment, without rhyme or reason. Did anyone else but herself perceive that all at once Darkwater had turned treacherously into its haunted state?

Someone walked about here who thought too much about death. Was it the name, Ching Mei, that had brought the silence?

Chapter 13

AMELIA's ball was only six weeks away, and Hamish Barlow, the attorney from Shanghai, was due to arrive within a month or so. Everyone seemed to be on edge. Uncle Edgar was probably wondering how he was going to explain Ching Mei's death to Mr Barlow, and Aunt Louisa was constantly fussing about the arrangements for the ball.

Finally, instead of making frequent journeys to Plymouth, Miss Egham, the dressmaker, had been installed in the house, and Amelia divided her time between fittings, riding on the moors with George, or alone (did she have a rendezvous when she went alone?) and wandering about with a moony look on her face.

Adam Marsh kept his word about the children's picnic, and Amelia, who hitherto had found Marcus and Nolly little but a nuisance, suddenly discovered that she couldn't resist so delightful an outing, and was sure that there would be room for her in the pony trap, too.

Fanny thought that Adam looked put out when he met them at the crossroads. But if he had, his ill-humour was gone in a flash, and he was welcoming them all with the news that if they followed the uphill road a little farther he had found a perfect spot, out of the wind. Sheltered by an outcrop of rocks they spread their rugs on the turf and prepared to bask in the sunshine. Amelia had brought her parasol, a frivolous affair of purple lace. She said how fortunate Fanny was to have a complexion that was not harmed by the sun, and could even toss aside her wide-brimmed hat. Her own skin was so delicate it would be burned to a cinder without protection, and with her ball so near Mamma was constantly chiding her about her appearance.

"It's a terrible thing to be a woman," she said, sighing deeply.

"It certainly seems a pity to have to sit upright under a parasol on a picnic," Adam agreed gravely, and then said that he was taking the children to find some of the friendly moorland ponies. Perhaps Fanny would care to come, since Amelia had her complexion to protect?

Fanny resisted both the invitation and her desire to laugh. She said that she would busy herself unpacking the luncheon basket. She meant to keep Mr Adam Marsh at arm's length, and anyway Amelia would look so forlorn if she were left, sitting primly under her parasol, playing at being a lady when all the time she wanted to throw dignity to the winds and romp after the children.

"I think he was laughing at me," Amelia declared indignantly.

"I sometimes think he is laughing at us all," Fanny said.

"Why? What is ridiculous about us?"

"Perhaps I used the wrong word. Perhaps, 'examining' would be a better one."

"He does ask a great many questions," Amelia admitted. "He says he is interested in human nature. I wonder, Fanny, if he is a dilettante." Amelia's eyes shone. "I confess I would find that irresistible."

"Getting your heart broken?" Fanny asked dryly.

"Oh, I shouldn't allow that to happen. But he does make all the other men we know seem dreadfully dull. Do you know," she finished in a burst of confidence, "it is my ambition this summer to make him fall in love with me. If he isn't already," she added dreamily.

"I think you are a silly little girl," Fanny said.

And so she was, sitting there in her too elaborate clothes, the ridiculous parasol outlined against the wild beautiful landscape.

But her silliness could not be entirely dismissed. She was the one with the dowry which was undoubtedly a feature of great attraction. It could compensate for her affectations and her constant chatter and her childish enthusiasms. And she would develop poise. Indeed, she had disturbing moments of it already, when one saw the woman too prematurely. She was irritating and endearing, and Fanny would love her if only she would fall in love with Robert Hadlow, or some other harmless young man.

But now she had to be an enemy, because, innocently, she was exposing Adam's weakness. Or what one imagined was his weakness . . .

The children came back, with flushed cheeks and happy laughter.

"Cousin Fanny, Marcus thought the pony was going to bite him. It took his sleeve, like this!" Nolly nuzzled at Marcus's jacket, and he shrieked with laughter.

"It had big teeth, Cousin Fanny. Mr Marsh said it used them to gnash at its enemies."

"There were hundreds of ponies, Cousin Fanny. And Marcus is hungry. Can he have something to eat?"

Whatever this man was, he knew how to make children happy.

"Let us all sit down and eat," said Fanny calmly. "Adam—have you a large appetite, too?"

He didn't fail to notice her use of his first name. He gave her his quiet unsmiling look.

"I don't know which looks the more edible, the food or the young ladies."

Nolly giggled wildly. "Pray don't eat them, Mr Marsh! At least, not Cousin Fanny. She puts us to bed and listens to our prayers."

"I would leave her eyes to the last," Adam said. "Because they are the colour of heaven."

"That's where Mamma and Papa are," said Marcus in surprise.

Nolly plucked nervously at Adam's sleeve.

"You wouldn't actually? Would you, Mr Marsh."

"I am a maker of bad jokes. I deserve to go without anything to eat at all."

"That child would be afraid of a mouse," Amelia put in, with some peevishness. She hadn't cared for the conversation.

"And so would you, I don't doubt," Adam retorted. "Come, Nolly. You be a mouse, and scare Cousin Amelia from under her pretty parasol."

Amelia shrieked wildly, forgetting to be a lady, as her ruffled and starched petticoats were threatened. And Fanny found herself storing in her memory what Adam had said in his flippant voice.

At the end of the day, as if he were tossing them a trivial piece of information, Adam said that he had arranged with Mr Farquarson to take a year's lease of Heronshall, and that his Aunt Martha would be arriving to organise the household.

"If at the end of the year I want to buy, I will do so," he said. "But in the meantime it's a place to call home. I have travelled so much I can scarcely remember what it is to have a home."

360

Amelia was excited and too unsophisticated not to show her jubilation.

"But how wonderful! I believe you have done it this year, for me, because it is my coming-out year. Anyway, it pleases me to think so."

Adam bowed. "If it pleases you, Miss Amelia, then it is true, of course."

"Your Aunt Martha?" said Fanny involuntarily. This latest information surely made him a completely honest person.

"Yes, you must meet her. She's delighted that I seem to be settling down at last. She has a particular fondness for children, so one day I will send for these two to come to tea."

"Surely you will give more than children's tea parties," Amelia said, pouting.

"To be sure, if Miss Amelia Davenport has time to spare from her numerous social activities."

Amelia giggled. "The most I do at present is stand and be poked and prodded and pinned by Miss Egham. Really, you have no idea what it is like to be a woman."

Amelia's light chattering voice went on, but Fanny no longer heard what she was saying. For her own first overwhelming feeling of pleasure at Adam's news had died. Why was he merely taking a lease on Heronshall? His reason, to be sure, sounded plausible enough. But was the true reason the fact that he hadn't the capital to put down, that first he must marry to advantage? And was his Aunt Martha, so respectably sounding, a willing conspirator to this end?

Amelia, with her feather brain, would be the last person to recognise this. But would it matter, if she married someone she ardently loved? Miserably, Fanny knew that it wouldn't. She would do the same herself. Only she would never never have the chance.

As Trumble took the pony trap away and they went into the house, George appeared and took Fanny's arm. He didn't say anything, but just welcomed her in this possessive manner, as if she were already his wife.

Fanny shook herself free, trying not to be irritated.

"I must take the children up."

"I wouldn't go up there just yet. The doctor's there."

"Doctor?"

"Doctor!" echoed Amelia. "Who's ill?"

"Grandmamma had a fall. It's nothing serious, I believe."

"But how did she fall?" Fanny asked.

"She tripped over Ludwig. Poor Ludwig." George gave a high-pitched giggle. "It's a wonder he survived."

Amelia and Fanny hurried upstairs. They met Aunt Louisa coming out of Lady Arabella's room. She looked harassed and worried.

"Oh, there you are at last. Grandmamma's had a fall. Doctor Bates is going to bleed her."

"Then it is serious!" Fanny exclaimed.

"He doesn't think so, but at present she's dazed and he can't be sure—" Aunt Louisa lowered her voice, "—that it isn't a slight apoplexy. She says she fell over a cushion on the floor, but it must have been the cat, of course. Poor Mamma sees so badly.

"She broke her spectacles," Aunt Louisa went on, "so now she can't see at all. Oh dear, this is very vexing, just at this time. We can only hope she won't be an invalid for long. And Amelia, Miss Egham has been wanting you. She can't get on with the tarlatan until she has had another fitting. I did think you might be back a little earlier. Let me see your face, child!" Aunt Louisa's voice reached a new pitch of anxiety. "Oh, I do declare you've got your nose sunburnt! Really, how could you be so careless?"

Fanny felt a rubbing against her skirts, and looked down to see Ludwig, the fat tabby, ingratiating himself. He had missed his tea, no doubt, with Lady Arabella in bed. He usually had a small dish of cream, and a sardine. He showed no sign of having been stumbled over by a very heavy person.

"Why is Great-aunt Arabella so unkind?" Nolly asked.

"Unkind?"

"To step on poor Ludwig like that. Like on a beetle." She stamped noisily on the floor to establish her point.

"It was an accident. She didn't do it on purpose."

"Ludwig doesn't let me step on him. He runs away too quickly."

It was uncanny that the child had had the same thoughts as herself. Fanny said sharply, "Stop making so much noise. You can be heard all through the house."

Nolly ignored her defiantly.

"Come on, Marcus. Stamp on beetles. Like this."

Marcus needed little encouragement to join in such an original game. Fanny had to seize them both and hold them firmly.

"Such behaviour!"

"Ching Mei would let us play that game."

"Ching Mei would," Marcus echoed.

It was the first time Ching Mei's name had been mentioned for days.

Nolly's eyes were flat and hard and bright.

"Is Great-aunt Arabella going to die?"

"No, she isn't, foolish little one. Kiss me, and be good."

Hannah was sitting with Lady Arabella when Fanny tapped and asked if she might come in.

"Go and get some rest, Hannah," she whispered. "I'll stay here."

"But what about your dinner, Miss Fanny?"

"Lizzie can bring me something on a tray later."

"Bless your kind heart," said Hannah. "Miss Amelia, I suppose, is too concerned about her fripperies to have time to come and see her old grandmother."

Hannah, for all her long service, was getting too outspoken. Ever since the journey to London and the arrival of the children who had touched a chord in her soft heart, she had been an ally of Fanny's.

"Never mind Miss Amelia, Hannah. How is Lady Arabella?"

"Very hazy, Miss Fanny, but it's from the doctor's medicine to quieten her more than the fall."

"Who found her?"

"Lizzie, when she brought up her tea tray. She let out such a squawk, you'd have thought the peacocks had got indoors. And then the master and Barker had to get her on to the bed. It was quite a task."

Fanny looked down at the inert form in the big fourposter. Sunk into the feather bed Lady Arabella looked unexpectedly small. Her frizzed grey hair stuck out from under her nightcap, her cheeks were pink and white like a child's. Her eyes, too, when she opened them, had a surprising childlike innocence. It was because they were without the customary spectacles, of course, and so short-sighted as to be almost blind.

She stared up at what must be a very hazy form at her bedside, and said testily, "Who is it? Come nearer, can't you?"

"It's me, Great-aunt Arabella. Fanny."

363

"Bend closer. Let me see."

As Fanny obeyed, the old lady grasped her shoulders with unexpected strength and pulled her so close that the pale round myopic eyes a few inches from Fanny's. Her breath was on Fanny's cheek.

"Have to be sure," she muttered. "Can't trust everyone. They said I tripped over Ludwig. Stuff and nonsense. Who tells such lies? It was a cushion, put there purposely to trip me. They picked it up, of course."

"Who is they?"

"Now how would I know?" the old lady said in her husky irritable voice. "Someone with a tidy mind, I expect. There are tidy minds in this house. But my poor Ludwig. He never got in the way of my clumsy feet. Bring him in to me, Fanny. My prince."

Fanny did as she was bid, because Lady Arabella didn't seem in a mood to be crossed. She was definitely wandering a little in her mind, and very petulant.

The elderly cat settled down comfortably on the bed, and the fat ringed hand caressed his head.

"My prince. He wore a sky-blue uniform. He had such elegant moustaches. And his manners. He would click his heels and bow and kiss my hand and say I was adorable. I was, too," Lady Arabella added sharply. "You may look disbelieving, as I know you are. My skin, my eyes—ah well—and I had such a figure. Louisa has all my husband's worst features. That was why she had to marry a plain man like Edgar Davenport. Still—" a sly smile lay on the curved pussy-cat mouth, "—he has proved quite a man. Fanny, bring me my needlework."

"Now, Great-aunt Arabella? But you're ill."

"Stuff and nonsense. I'm only in this condition because that ridiculous doctor had leeches clamped to my neck while I was still unconscious. Said there was probably neither cushion nor cat, but that I had had a seizure. Oh, yes, I heard him. I heard a great deal while they thought I was still beyond listening. But bring my work basket, as I told you. My scissors, my tapestry, everything."

Fanny obeyed, knowing that without her spectacles Lady Arabella wouldn't be able to see a stitch.

"And my pincushion," the autocratic voice followed her. "Bring all those things and put them at my bedside."

When Fanny had done so, the old lady groped to feel the shape of the objects, satisfying herself that the wicker work basket, overflowing with coloured wools, the fat round pincushion, and the half-finished tapestry were there.

Then she subsided with an odd sigh of relief.

"There's nothing wrong with me that a new pair of spectacles won't cure," she said in her hoarse husky voice. "But I may find being an invalid quite amusing." Her eyelids were closing. Doctor Bates' soothing dose was beginning to take effect. "Send George to me," she murmured. But she was already asleep.

When Hannah came back some hours later Fanny had been almost asleep herself. She felt in a dream that was half nightmare. She knew that both Aunt Louisa and Uncle Edgar had tiptoed to the bedside, satisfying themselves that the invalid would do until the morning, but that now seemed so long ago. The wind was blowing softly, and the slightly moving curtains, the shadow of the fourposter wavering across the ceiling in the moving candlelight, and the gentle snoring of Lady Arabella were all somnolent. She had had to struggle to keep awake, welcoming the familiar and sometimes unfamiliar creakings and murmurings of the old house. Even a sudden flurry in the chimney, and then a fall of soot, stirred by a wayward breeze, had been not so much startling as another means of keeping her heavy eyes open.

"What time is it, Hannah?"

"Midnight, Miss Fanny, and you must get some sleep."

Hannah was bundled up in a crimson flannel dressing gown. She, too, looked another person, a friendly succourer in the alien world of the night and the sick.

"She hasn't moved since eight o'clock. I don't think there's anything to be alarmed about."

Fanny took the candle Hannah held out to her. She stumbled a little from weariness as she went into Lady Arabella's sitting room. She noticed that Ludwig was back in his favourite place on the rocking chair. The couch was littered with cushions and it seemed very possible that Lady Arabella, stirring from her afternoon nap, had dislodged one without noticing, and then had stumbled over it. In the flurry of finding her prostrate, someone must have picked it up without remembering doing so.

Did it matter what she had fallen over, if anything at all, since her fall had been an accident? So why was Ludwig being blamed so strenuously?

Chapter 14

LADY Arabella recovered to a certain extent. She maintained, however, that her legs gave way, and that she couldn't walk without assistance. She refused to be a prisoner indoors, and said that she must have a wheelchair. When this contraption arrived, Dora was ordered to push it. Lady Arabella chose Dora for the reason that the girl was timid and wouldn't be tempted to go too fast down slopes, or push her chair, occupant and all, into the lake.

Within the family, it was decided that poor Grandmamma had grown a little weak in her mind. Uncle Edgar said the persecution complex was a common one. All this talk about dangerous cushions, for instance (Lady Arabella refused to have any in her room now), and not allowing anyone she didn't trust near her. Also, there was her insistence that she must have her embroidery, her wools, her work box and paraphernalia with her all the time, although her plump idle fingers never touched it. The whim to work might come on her, she said. So she sat cosily in the chair, cashmere shawls round her shoulders, a jet-trimmed bonnet nodding on her head, a fringed parasol erected above her, for all the world, Amelia giggled, like some eastern potentate taking the air.

Presently she became expert with the mechanism of the chair, and indoors was able to operate it herself, taking pleasure in coming up silently behind people and waiting for them to discover her. Fanny had the suspicion that the wheelchair was nothing but a pretence, that Lady Arabella could walk very well if she tried, but she kept this thought to herself because the old lady was kind to the children, and occasionally let them ride with her, the three of them whooping with delight as they negotiated slopes or startled the gardeners at their work.

Sometimes George took time from his riding or his billiards to wheel his grandmother. He was the only other person permitted to push the chair.

Summer moved on, the roses were over and the dahlias and michaelmas daisies out. A haze of heat lay over the moors. The dabchicks' family on the lake had grown to full size, the strawberries were finished and the blackbirds had had their fill of sun-reddened cherries. The carriage, coming round the curve of the long drive, raised a trail of reddish dust. It was a hot summer, and Amelia prayed that the weather would last until the night of her ball. It would be so much more romantic if couples could take the air on the terrace, or even wander daringly across the lawns beyond the illumination from the ballroom.

"Have you ever been kissed?" she asked Fanny. She didn't expect an answer. She was quite sure it would be in the negative. For only a serious suitor would kiss a girl, and only a flighty girl would allow herself to be kissed under any other conditions. Amelia pursed her red lips and determined that she would be kissed on the night of her ball. She also knew who would kiss her. She spent a great deal of time in front of her mirror nowadays, studying her reflection from different angles. She was growing vain. She could never forget the words of that wild and hunted man, "I have never seen anyone so beautiful," and sometimes, by candlelight, when her face looked older, more fragile and shadowy, she saw exactly what he meant.

She intended Adam to see her that way, in the half-light near the fountain, on the night of her ball.

But when he bent over her, would she see that other face beyond him, ruthless, half-starved, desperate . . . Amelia pressed her hands to her own face, afraid to look any more, afraid of the unknown within herself . . .

A stranger, a Mr Solomon, short, heavily-built, with small sparkling black eyes, came to spend a night. He had business to do with Uncle Edgar. It was obvious Aunt Louisa didn't think much of him. She was cool and distant with him at dinner, and afterwards, when Uncle Edgar took him to the library she sighed with relief and said to Amelia and Fanny, "There will be no need for you girls to wait up to entertain Mr Solomon. Papa has affairs to discuss with him."

Mr Solomon departed immediately after breakfast in the morning. The business must have been concluded satisfactorily, for he and Uncle Edgar exchanged a cordial handshake.

"Remember, Mr Davenport, I will be happy to be at your service at any time."

He had scarcely noticed the women of the household. Fanny, who had often preferred to be overlooked, and Amelia, who had discovered the pleasures of male admiration, found it strange to meet a man who was much more deeply interested in something other than them.

"Who is he, Papa?" Amelia demanded. "What does he do?"

"Busybody!" said Uncle Edgar, ruffling her hair affectionately. "If you must know, he is a diamond merchant from Hatton Gardens in London."

Amelia's eyes became round.

"And now you may ask questions until your voice wears out, but you will get no answers at present." He went off, smiling to himself, in high good humour.

And it was no good Amelia persecuting her mother with questions, either, for Aunt Louisa declared she knew nothing whatever about the matter. Although Fanny thought there was something distrait about her manner, and a look almost of uneasiness in her eyes.

The next visitor was Hamish Barlow.

Trumble met him at the station and he arrived before lunch. Amelia, always eager to meet someone new, went down early. Fanny was late. She hadn't meant to be, because she didn't want to make any kind of entrance, but Marcus had been difficult over his lunch and she had stayed to help Dora get him into a better mood. So that eventually she came flying undecorously down the stairs just as everyone was going into the dining room.

She was aware of the stranger's face looking up at her with sudden intent interest. It was a narrow pale face, with reddish eyes, neat ginger-coloured eyebrows and a small ginger moustache. Hamish Barlow was meticulously dressed in a black frockcoat and dark grey trousers with braided sideseams. He looked a gentleman. But there was a quick alertness about him that immediately made Fanny think of a fox.

"And this late arrival," Uncle Edgar was saying, "is my niece Fanny. She has taken the children completely under her wing. You must talk to her about them. Fanny, this is Mr Barlow."

He bowed exaggeratedly like a pigeon to its mate, Fanny

368

thought, his head well down, coat-tails in the air. Involuntarily she smiled at her foolish imaginings. Foxes, pigeons . . . was Mr Barlow an animal, a bird, or simply a human being, very anxious, for some reason, to make a good impression.

It was pleasant enough to have a visitor from the other side of the world, who talked well about China and his travels in the east. Fanny planned to have him gratify her curiosity about the children's parents, especially their mother, at a later time when they might have a few moments alone. Though she wasn't sure that she particularly desired a tête-à-tête, for he was proving to be one of those men who couldn't keep his eyes off her. He ignored Amelia, and only good manners made him turn occasionally to Aunt Louisa.

"The wonders of the ancient Chinese civilisation," he said directly to Fanny, "are uncountable, but against them you must put their primitive and barbarous habits. Binding women's feet, cold-bloodedly murdering female infants, or selling their unwanted daughters into slavery. When it comes to a woman's country, Miss Fanny—Miss Amelia," he added belatedly, "you must be very content with your own."

Fanny was reflecting that there were different subtle forms of slavery when George suddenly leaned forward.

"Why do you look at Fanny all the time, Mr Barlow?"

No one could have warned Mr Barlow about George's strangeness. It must have come as a shock to him that this handsome adult young man was asking the question of an ill-mannered and jealous child.

Aunt Louisa said quickly, "George, don't be foolish. Mr Barlow is talking to all of us, and most interestingly."

"Perhaps," said Mr Barlow easily, turning to George, "because I find an English woman such a pleasant sight after years of lemon-coloured faces."

He was quick-tongued and clever. But George was clever, too, in his fumbling intuitive way. He saw what was already happening. Fanny noticed that Uncle Edgar's eyes were narrowed in thought. His expression was bland. Only her own heart was beating more quickly in nervousness and frustration. Hamish Barlow. She had instinctively disliked him on sight.

But she had to be polite to him because he was a guest in the house and because she wanted to talk to him a great deal about the children's parents.

Nolly and Marcus did not remember him.

"But Miss Olivia is such a young lady now," Mr Barlow said admiringly. "She was only so high when I last saw her." His hands, spread out, were pale-skinned with a dusting of large coffee-coloured freckles. "And Marcus in his cradle. That was when I visited your Mamma and Papa in Shanghai, but you won't remember."

Nolly would have nothing to do with him. She forgot her manners and hung back against Fanny, giving her malignant stare. But she was not good with strangers. That was all that was wrong. Adam was the only stranger who had known the way past her prickly defences. Marcus was pleased enough to be noticed, and answered Mr Barlow's questions as best he could.

"Ching Mei went away," he said quite happily. "She left her sandals. Cousin Fanny looks after us now."

"And very lucky children you are."

"Yes we are. I have a new suit. It's red velvet. It's to wear to the ball. Nolly has pink ribbons on her dress. Would you like to see my toy soldiers, Mr Barlow?"

Nolly tugged at him sharply.

"You're showing off, Marcus."

"And I wonder what Cousin Fanny is to wear to the ball," Mr Barlow said softly.

Nolly's hand tightened in Fanny's. She seemed to recognise the unwarranted intimacy as much as Fanny did.

But there were questions to be asked. She had to be pleasant. She didn't intend Nolly to spend her whole life wondering what kind of a woman her mother had been, grasping at half-memories.

"I haven't heard your plans, Mr Barlow. Are you to stay for my cousin's ball?"

"Your aunt has been kind enough to invite me. I am looking forward to it with the greatest anticipation. You can't know what this means to me after so many years in exile, a gracious house, this truly English garden, with its ancient oaks and cedars, the wonderful hospitality your aunt and uncle are giving me, and now beautiful women at a ball. I was only nineteen when I left England and I have been away for seventeen years. I feel almost like that nineteen-year-old young man again, full of hopes and dreams. Does that sound foolish to you, Miss Fanny?"

He spoke sentimentally and quite movingly. One wouldn't have thought those emotions dwelt behind his narrow and calculating face. Was he inventing them to gain her sympathy?

"Then you have been an unwilling exile, Mr Barlow. I wonder why."

"No, you mustn't misunderstand me. The East has me in its spell, just as it had these children's Papa. I intend going back as soon as my business here is completed. But apart from winding up the late Mr Davenport's affairs and assuring myself that his children are happy, as I promised him I would—it was my last assurance to him, poor fellow—this interlude makes me absurdly sentimental."

Fanny made no reply to that. She wished he wouldn't look at her so boldly.

"But I must talk alone with you sometime, Miss Fanny."

"Why?" she asked bluntly.

"For this reason and that. I hope you will give me the opportunity."

Amelia teased her mercilessly.

"I believe you have made a conquest, Fanny. The way he looks at you. It's almost ill-bred, but I suppose the poor man can't help it if he's so overcome by passion."

"Amelia, be quiet!"

Amelia giggled. "But he really is. I've even remarked on it to Mr Marsh."

Fanny's face became still. "And what did Mr Marsh say?"

"Why, that you deserve a good husband."

Such rage swept over Fanny that she could scarcely speak coherently.

"He dares to say that! He dares to patronise me! I won't have it. And I won't have you, Amelia, running to him with every bit of foolish tittle-tattle. What must he think of you? That you're empty-headed and a gossip and a silly little rattle."

Amelia refused to be drawn.

"I know exactly what Mr Marsh thinks of me," she declared complacently. "And really, Fanny, if you get so upset over a simple remark like that you must be entertaining some feelings towards Mr Barlow."

Everyone else seemed to like the man, and there was no doubt that he set himself out to be entertaining. Aunt Louisa took even more care than usual over her toilette, coming down in the evening looking like the rich and well-bred matron she was, and Uncle Edgar was frequently in Mr Barlow's company, showing him over the estate, or sitting closeted in the library with him when no doubt every aspect of poor Oliver's affairs was discussed.

Once the door was left slightly ajar, and in passing Fanny heard Uncle Edgar speak the word "Gee-gaws" in an amused and slightly rueful voice.

"Are you absolutely certain, Mr Davenport?"

"But of course. I had them examined. If there had been anything else, the Chinese woman must have disposed of it. Tell me, can you trust these Chinese? You've lived among them long enough to know. It seems to me that they say one thing and think another. They're like icebergs, their words are a fragment on the surface, their thoughts—oh, very deep." He laughed delightedly at his metaphor.

Mr Barlow laughed, too, and agreed, and added, "I'm sorry that after the debts were paid there was no cash left at all. But you expected that."

A faint whispering sound behind her made Fanny turn to see Lady Arabella wheeling her chair expertly away across the polished floor.

"No change there, my girl," she said over her shoulder, and then laughed hoarsely at her unwitting pun. "Come and help me upstairs."

As Fanny heaved the large soft body, like nothing so much as a bag overstuffed with wool, out of the chair, she was sure again that Lady Arabella was much more active on her legs than she let anyone know.

"I've listened at doors all my life and I've never learnt anything pleasant yet. It's not a habit to be commended."

Fanny flushed but made no excuses.

"I was thinking of Ching Mei. I hoped Mr Barlow might have been her friend."

Lady Arabella gave Fanny her opaque unreadable stare.

At last she said, "Ching Mei doesn't need friends now," and leaning heavily on Fanny's arm struggled slowly up the stairs.

It appeared, however, that Ching Mei was in Hamish Barlow's thoughts also, for a day or two later he joined Fanny and the children in the pavilion by the lake.

He had cleverly learned that the best way to cope with Nolly's hostility was to ignore her. Seeing that the children were absorbed in their own game of building a house with toy bricks and twigs, he asked quietly if he might sit by Fanny and talk to her. He admired the tinkling windbells, saying they almost made him homesick, then, with a suddenness that made Fanny draw in her breath sharply, asked what her version of Ching Mei's death was.

Adam Marsh, she remembered, had asked a similar question. Adam's interest had been in Ching Mei as a person, this man's was for some other reason.

"Why, it was an accident, of course."

"You're a very intelligent young woman, Miss Fanny. You really believe that?"

"What else would I believe? Didn't my uncle tell you the story? It was a thick mist that night and there was this escaped prisoner, desperately anxious not to be seen. If he had been caught—"

"I understand all that. The laws for prisoners are harsh enough. Then if this is what you believe, I accept it."

Fanny frowned. "You mean, you accept what I say when you doubt—other people's views?" She had no intention of discussing her Cousin George with a stranger.

"I repeat, I admire your intelligence."

Fanny's eyes fell beneath his regard.

"You think it your duty to make these enquiries, of course."

"Naturally. I take the trust imposed in me quite seriously. Does that surprise you?"

She could have talked to him if only he would leave the personal note out of the conversation.

"Mr. Barlow, I have heard so little about Oliver Davenport's wife. One day Nolly is going to ask what her mother was like and no one will know. I understand this, because I too was orphaned very young. Won't you tell me about her?"

"I knew very little of her background. Her family had returned to England after she had married. I believe they had only been travelling in the East when she met and fell in love with Oliver. She was young and beautiful—"

"Who was young and beautiful?" came Nolly's voice, her ears alert at precisely the wrong moment.

Mr Barlow sprang up.

"I see a boat tied up at the jetty. Won't you come on the lake,

Miss Fanny? The children are fully occupied with their own affairs."

Extraordinary as it seemed to her afterwards, Fanny forgot her dislike of water and assented eagerly. On the lake they would be safely out of earshot of the children and she could hear more about the woman who had worn the flamboyant green ear-rings and the high-heeled dancing slippers.

She allowed Mr Barlow to assist her into the boat, and push it smoothly out from the jetty. Away from the shadow of the willows the sun was deliciously warm, the summer wind on her face. The reflections of the yellow flag irises hung like lamps in the water. Dragonflies skimmed in darts of light. There was no sound but the far-off chirping and chattering of the children, mingled with bird cries.

Mr Barlow sent the boat forward with a long pull on the oars.

"At last," he said, "I have you to myself. The only way to escape me is to jump overboard, and personally I don't care for the look of those water weeds. They could drag a person down."

The sun was not so warm after all. But it was silly to feel this chill. He was only joking.

"Once, when I was a child," Fanny said, "I did fall in. Uncle Edgar rescued me. And why do you think I want to escape you, Mr Barlow?"

"Am I wrong? I had the impression that Miss Fanny was fully occupied with the children, or reading to her great-aunt, or perhaps doing some highly important needlework. She always seemed to be just a flick of a skirt round a corner when I came near. Except at mealtimes, of course, and then she had to be polite."

"I lead a busy life," said Fanny coolly, "as you have noticed. And now I think we came out here to talk about Nolly and Marcus's mother. You said she was beautiful?"

"But not one half as beautiful as you."

Fanny made an impatient exclamation.

"Mr Barlow, please be serious, or I shall have to ask you to take me ashore."

"But I am serious. Never more. You are the most beautiful woman I have ever seen. I recognised it the first moment I saw you."

"Mr Barlow—"

"No, please listen." His face was quite pale. Perspiration glistened on his brow. There was no doubting his intensity. "I know

374

your circumstances. All that makes not the least difference to me. I want to marry you. I want to take you back to China with me. I've spoken to your uncle. Now it only requires your consent. Fanny! Fanny, are you listening! I want you to be my wife."

She had been gazing into the distance, trying not to hear his words. Trying not to hear Adam Marsh's words, if ever they had been spoken, "*She deserves a good husband . . .*"

She had known this was going to happen at some time during Hamish Barlow's stay. A woman couldn't fail to sense that kind of thing. But she would have given anything for it not to have happened. Now she had to be grateful, grateful and flattered. Her first kiss had been George's violent searing one, and now her first proposal—perhaps her only one—came from a man with a foxy face whose hands were covered with blemishing freckles.

She wasn't grateful or flattered. She was furious with the fate that had done this to her.

"Mr Barlow, you've tricked me, and I don't enjoy that. Will you please take me back to the shore immediately."

"But, Fanny! How extraordinary you are! How different! You came out here to hear about a dead woman and you're angry because I offer you life. Yes, life, my dearest. Don't think I haven't seen how you live here only through your uncle and aunt's courtesy and sense of duty. You're a woman who needs her own household, her own family. And I would give it to you. I'm not a poor man. I'd show you the wonders of the East, and later you could choose your own house, in Peking, Shanghai, Hong Kong, wherever you pleased. I'd show you the world, Fanny. Doesn't that interest you? Answer me!"

"Mr Barlow—later I will thank you for the compliment you have paid me—just now I am not interested. I never will be interested. So please row back to the shore."

He stared at her in growing resentment and incredulity.

"You can't mean this! To choose to be a poor relation, little more than a governess—"

"Cousin Fanny! Cousin Fanny!"

The children were on the bank staring across the lake. Nolly had sensed something. She was agitated.

"Cousin Fanny, come back. Our house fell down."

"Come back!" Marcus echoed.

"What is wrong with me? Why do you dislike me!" He was leaning nearer. His eyes had a reddish glow. "Don't you want a husband who would adore you?"

His hand was on her skirt. It came nearer, intent on clasping hers. Fanny drew back sharply, forgetting the precariousness of her position, and her movement made the boat rock violently. For one heart-stopping moment she felt the water coming up close to her face, and that other long-ago memory swept over her, the cold, the choking, the darkness . . .

Then the boat steadied, and she was aware of Mr Barlow, temporarily forgetting his ardent courtship, looking at her anxiously.

"I am afraid of water," she murmured. And then, unaccountably, "Ching Mei drowned."

He picked up the oars.

"I'll take you back," he said curtly.

She would have given a great deal not to go down to dinner that night. She was still shivering intermittently. Nolly had been wiser than she. Nolly had known Hamish Barlow for an enemy immediately. An enemy? When he wanted nothing but to love and cherish her? The thing was, what he might do if he didn't get his desire. She recognised the driving force in him, the refusal to be thwarted.

What *could* he do?

She was overwrought and hysterical, or she would not be imagining that disasters could follow a simple refusal to marry a man she did not love. She would go down to dinner simply to disprove any accusation of cowardice.

And as it happened, the conversation at the candlelit table couldn't have been more innocuous.

Hamish Barlow, impeccably dressed, was calm and seemingly contented. He had turned the conversation to his youth, comparing it with that of the children today.

"Our toy soldiers wore a different uniform," he said. "The Duke of Wellington was the great hero. Poor old Boney was in prison, and harmless, but we still played at battles defeating him. Then we had hoops, and skipping ropes, and of course marbles. By the way, Marcus seems to be grieving about the loss of his marbles. Do you know anything about them, Miss Fanny?"

It could not have been a more innocent question. She could only wonder why the table seemed so silent.

"I never saw them here. I think they must have been left behind on the ship. Yes, he has complained about their loss."

"If that's all he wants," Uncle Edgar said, "we must get the little fellow some more. Nothing could be easier."

Chapter 15

UNCLE Edgar sent a message to Fanny that he must talk with her. She found him in the library, strolling up and down, his thumbs tucked in his waistcoat pocket—he was wearing a silk waistcoat of maroon stripes on silver grey that gave him a peacockish air. He had a habit of showing small vanities in his dress that was pleasing because he carred it off with such an air of boyish pleasure. He was, Fanny saw at once, in an affable and relaxed mood.

She hoped the traces of her own disturbed night didn't show too clearly on her face. Last night she had never felt so alone. There was no one to whom she could talk or turn to for sympathy. Hamish Barlow's taunt had kept returning to her, "To choose to be a poor relation, a governess!" and at last she had wept into her pillow. Courage belonged to daylight. In the morning, she would face her chosen future more calmly.

"Well, Fanny," said Uncle Edgar pleasantly, "Mr Barlow has been surprising me."

"Surprising you, Uncle Edgar?"

"Indeed, yes. I didn't think you would be foolish enough to refuse an offer such as, speaking candidly, you are never likely to receive again. You have decided hastily, of course."

So Uncle Edgar wanted this to happen. Probably Aunt Louisa did, too. Only by marriage would they be rid of her. Otherwise she was likely to remain an encumbrance to them, and later to George or Amelia, until the end of her life.

Fanny bit her lip, and answered, "Hastily, perhaps, Uncle Edgar. But quite finally."

Uncle Edgar smiled and patted her shoulder. "Finally is a long word, my dear. Mr Barlow will be here another three or four

377

weeks. He understands young women can be over-emotional and too precipitate. He will give you an opportunity to change your mind."

"Would you have me marry a man I not only don't love, but actually dislike?"

"There you are, you see. You are over-emotional. Now sit down and let us talk about this. What is it about Mr Barlow that you don't like?"

"How can I explain that? It isn't a list of criticisms, it's a matter of one's senses."

"Illogical, too!" Uncle Edgar chuckled gently. "I told Barlow you wouldn't be able to put a finger on your reasons for refusing him."

"But I can!" Fanny cried hotly. "It would be terrible to travel to a foreign country with a man one didn't love. To spend the rest of one's life . . ." She paused a moment, contemplating the appalling prospect. Then she added more quietly, "Besides I can't leave the children. I have promised them."

"The children don't come into this question." For the first time Uncle Edgar's voice had a hint of harshness. "You can't sacrifice your life for them. They will be cared for very well whether you are here or not. After all, you didn't have a kind Cousin Fanny when you came here as a child. And you survived, didn't you? So put them out of your mind, and think of the brilliant future you can have. Mr Barlow has told me his financial position, and his prospects, and all I can say is that for a young woman without a dowry you are extraordinarily fortunate. Now, Fanny, your aunt and I won't let you throw away this chance."

"But, Uncle Edgar, marrying Mr Barlow is the last thing I wish to do."

"The young man has been a little impetuous, I grant you. I told him so. But you must be tolerant, Fanny. He is quite infatuated with you. By George!" Uncle Edgar chuckled again, "I've never seen a man so smitten. I want you to reflect again. For instance, would you regard my brother's children as an obstacle if you were really in love?"

If it were Adam Marsh who had sat in the gently rocking boat telling her of his undying love? Fanny's eyes fell. What could she answer?

"You want to be rid of me," she murmured.

Uncle Edgar leaped up, his face flushed with distress.

"Fanny! Don't you ever dare suggest such a thing again! Haven't you always been one of the family! Haven't George and Amelia been a brother and sister to you? This makes me ashamed. How have I failed you?"

Remembering a thousand things she remained mutinously silent. If she showed gratitude at this moment she would be lured into making a promise she could never keep.

She watched Uncle Edgar stare at her with such earnest appeal that at last she had to say defensively, "It's just that I won't marry a man I don't love."

"And you think your unfeeling and heartless uncle is forcing you to? I won't force you, child. But I will do my best to make you change your mind. Have you contemplated the life of an unmarried woman in this country?"

"Do you imagine for a moment I haven't!"

"And yet you still say no to such an eligible suitor? Illogical, emotional, romantic . . . I think you have more than a little of your Irish mother in you, my dear. Amelia, three years your junior, has far more good sense."

(*But Amelia has a dowry and is free to choose. The wonderful forbidden wealth of that word, choose!*)

"All the same," Uncle Edgar had regained his comfortable placidity, "I think you will come to look at this matter in a different light. Mr Barlow is remaining with us until after Amelia's ball. Between now and then I expect you to have a complete change of heart."

It was an order. Uncle Edgar's most serious orders were always given in that over-soft kindly voice.

Fanny lifted her chin.

"Am I the kind of person to have a change of heart, Uncle Edgar?"

His eyes narrowed.

"It is a possibility for everyone. Everyone, my dearest Fanny. What is more, your aunt and I will give you as fine a wedding as we intend for Amelia. And you will make a very beautiful bride." He patted her hand again. "Now run along and make Amelia jealous. She always expected to be the first to marry, the little rogue."

Amelia, it was true, was full of curiosity, but it was Aunt Louisa who behaved in the most disturbing way. While Fanny was being fitted for her ball gown Aunt Louisa said to the dressmaker, "You

379

had better make arrangements to stay on for a little while, Miss Egham. Miss Fanny will be requiring a bridal gown."

"But I won't, Aunt Louisa! Didn't Uncle Edgar tell you—"

Aunt Louisa behaved as if she were nothing but a dressmaker's dummy.

"She has a pretty waist, hasn't she, Miss Egham? I am always telling my own daughter to control her appetite for sugar plums."

"Fancy, ma'am! And where will you be going to live, miss?"

Miss Egham's eyes were popping with curiosity. The round-about question was intended to give her a clue as to whom the bridegroom was to be. If there were to be one, since this seemed to be a remarkably reluctant bride . . .

But the question presented a much bigger problem to Fanny. Where would she be going to live when this dismal affair was over? Supposing they wouldn't let her stay with the children . . .

"You have made the waist pinch a little, Miss Egham. Aunt Louisa, can't we discuss this—other matter another time?"

"Certainly, my dear. But I wasn't aware there was anything to discuss."

So Aunt Louisa had adopted her husband's bland attitude that Fanny would allow herself to have a change of heart. A reluctant bride was no uncommon thing. She was none the worse for that in the end.

Amelia, knowing Fanny's stubbornness, was not so certain. She was only cross that Fanny refused to talk to her about either Hamish Barlow or her own feelings.

"A proposal and you won't tell me how it happened," she sighed. "Fanny, you are mean. Did he kneel at your feet? Did he kiss your hand? Or your lips, Fanny? Is that why you won't tell me?"

George said nothing at all. He only seemed to be around more than usual, seldom now going out to ride although he was in-ordinately proud of his new hunter. He watched Fanny, but he watched Hamish Barlow even more. For once Fanny was not afraid of what he might do. She even had a dark dream of Hamish Barlow at the bottom of the lake, tangled in the waterweeds . . .

It was inevitable that Nolly should sense what was happening. She said very little, but it was difficult to persuade her to eat, and Dora reported that she pined all the time Fanny was not in the room. Fanny worried, and wondered what to say to the child, and then was saved an explanation by Nolly herself suddenly clinging to her and saying fiercely, "You promised! You promised!"

"I promised what?"

"That you would never leave us. Marcus thinks you're going to leave us."

"Then you must tell Marcus that he's wrong."

Nolly's face was taut and unchildish. She wouldn't let it relax. "I don't think he will believe you."

"Then he's a silly little boy. I'm sure you have much more sense, and know that people don't leave other people they love. Nor go away with people they don't love . . ."

The child's black eyes bored into her. What she saw must at last have satisfied her for she gave the smallest nod.

"That's what I told Marcus," she said.

What Adam Marsh thought—and he must surely have heard such a brilliant piece of news through Amelia—she hadn't the faintest idea. She only suspected that he, too, didn't care for Hamish Barlow. Or had she imagined that faint antagonism when the two men had met?

There was no reason for antagonism, she thought bitterly. Mr Barlow must have noticed how Mr Marsh was Amelia's lapdog, a role that couldn't have suited him less. But perhaps it would get him what he wanted, where Mr Barlow's own tempestuous tactics in love had failed.

It was as well that the night of the ball was almost on them, and there was little time during the daylight hours to think of anything else.

Chapter 16

HANNAH had been sent away to see that Amelia was safely dressed and not prostrate with too much excitement. Louisa and Edgar were alone in their bedroom. Louisa's face already echoed the wine colour of her low-cut wide-skirted velvet gown. She wore the diamond ear-rings which Edgar had given her just a few minutes previously.

He had kissed her brow, and murmured, "A mere trifle, my love. Just a memento of the coming-out of our daughter."

It seemed a very short time ago that Edgar had been preaching economy. Louisa didn't understand business, but she imagined the stock market must have greatly improved, or some other windfall which naturally was her husband's affair, had come Edgar's way. Nevertheless, her delight over the unexpected gift was vaguely tinged with uneasiness, she didn't know why.

"So that explains Mr Solomon's visit."

"As usual you are right, my dear. Well now," Edgar adjusted his waistcoat, and took a glance at his sideview in the mirror, "isn't it time we went down? Let me say you are looking extremely well. If Amelia looks as well, she'll be safely launched."

Louisa preened herself, knowing very well that for all her weight, she was still a fine figure. But she was too hot already. What ever had made her choose velvet? She had thought it a regal material, forgetting its suffocating warmth. She waved her feather fan jerkily. Although the windows were wide open no coolness, only a dark tide of warm air, came in.

"Edgar! I'm worried about Fanny."

A little of the satisfaction left Edgar's face.

"So am I. Does she show signs at all of changing her mind? Tonight is her last chance."

"She doesn't confide in me," said Louisa shortly. "I know there's that problem, too, but what I'm worried about is tonight. She's in a strange mood. She can spoil Amelia's ball."

"Spoil Amelia's ball! Come, my dear!"

"You know how she can be if she sets out to gain attention. Nobody looks at anyone else. Certainly not men. She has only to lift her eyes and give them that bold look."

"Bold? Fanny bold?"

"Oh, you know what I mean," Louisa said snappishly. "She has never learnt it in this house, but she knows how to use her eyes, in a way our innocent daughter never will. I believe men feel they are drowning, or something equally stupid. Mr Barlow tried to explain it to me, but of course he's in a state of ridiculous infatuation."

"I am quite aware that Fanny has magnificent eyes," Edgar said slowly. "And also great vivacity when she pleases. Sometimes, I am reminded—No, never mind. What makes you think she won't behave well tonight?"

"Because she is desperate. She will finally have to marry Mr Barlow, of course, but first she may throw discretion to the winds. And you have insisted in dressing her in a gown that will make every other woman in the room look insipid," she added bitterly.

"I haven't even seen her gown," Edgar said mildly.

"Oh, well, perhaps that was Amelia's fault. She insisted the rose-coloured silk was Fanny's colour, that pastels didn't suit her."

"Then haven't you taken care that Amelia looks just as well."

"Amelia is suitably dressed in white. She looks like a rose. But Fanny will look like—I don't know—a poppy perhaps. Something too vivid."

Edgar smiled reassuringly.

"You're understandably suffering from nerves, my dear. At least Adam Marsh seems to prefer a rose to a poppy, and that, I can make a guess, is all Amelia wants of this night."

"That's another thing, Edgar. Who is Adam Marsh? We have never satisfactorily discovered. Oh, I know Sir Giles has heard of Matthew Marsh the famous collector. But it has never been proved he really is Adam's father. We've never met any of his family. I grant you he's a pleasant young man, but how do we know he tells the truth?"

"That's a thing we can go into another time," said Edgar, with faint exasperation. "I believe Adam's aunt is arriving to live at Heronshall in a week or so. So that will be someone of his family whom you can meet. Our immediate worry, and I've emphasised this to you before, is to see that Fanny accepts Hamish Barlow."

"Yes," said Louisa, following her own thoughts. "I think it will be a relief to have her out of the house."

"We will miss her, naturally. But we must think of her future. It is vitally important that she should do this. Vitally important."

"Edgar!" Louisa's vague unexplainable uneasiness had come back. "You speak as if she has no alternative."

"Neither she has. Now I believe I hear the first carriage. It's time we went down."

Amelia was by no means prostrate. She was revolving round her room in a waltz, making the candles dip madly, and catching glimpses of herself, a fairytale figure, she thought, in the mirror. Hannah and Lizzie were watching admiringly.

"Do you think my dress will be admired, Lizzie?"

"Only them as is blind wouldn't, Miss Amelia," Lizzie said, unable to take her eyes off what she thought was the most beautiful dress in the world. Its low round neck and puffed sleeves showed Amelia's pretty, plump neck and arms, the crinoline skirt, looped up in front and trimmed with white roses, revealed a crisply flounced underskirt. Amelia's bead-trimmed reticule hung on her wrist, her fan was made of silk and ivory, her white satin slippers peeped beneath her wide skirts. She looked like a dressed-up ringletted very shining and clean doll.

Then there was a tap on the door and Fanny came in. Lizzie went on thinking loyally that Miss Amelia was the prettiest thing ever, but Hannah was aware at once of the superior elegance of Miss Fanny.

The rose colour was not fashionable, her shoulders were too thin, there were faint hollows at the base of her throat (she seemed to have grown thinner in the last week), but when the heavy dark lashes of those blue eyes, the exact blue of the jewel she wore round her neck, lifted, then who could not be shattered by their brilliance? Certainly not that little ginger man from the East, or any other man, unless his thoughts were entirely on a fortune in the bank, and not on what he might hold tenderly in the curve of his arms. Hannah was an old woman and had not missed any of the aspect of life which came within her province of bedroom and upstairs sitting room. She saw her ladies before and after gaieties, she saw them unrobed or in their finest feathers. She saw their smiles fall off like their gowns, their undisguised weariness, their boredom, their secret hopes, and their unsuccessfully hidden fears. She heard the chatter of women alone, or the whispers of the husbands, the scufflings, the sometimes raised voices, or the muffled sobs. She had learned human nature in the most revealing room of all, the bedroom.

And she knew in that moment that no one could meekly make Miss Fanny take second place, or marry a man whom she detested. She would rather proudly remain alone all her life.

"Fanny," said Amelia, "you look very nice, but I do think that dress needed a little decoration. Miss Egham thought so, too. Some beading, or at least some ribbon bows. It's quite severe, isn't it? Now me, don't you admire my roses? And the necklace Papa gave me?" She fingered the pearls round her neck, "He got it from that Mr Solomon. He says I am too young for diamonds, but they'll come all in good time. He is such an indulgent Papa."

She was wholly wrapped up in herself, and certainly wasn't sharing her mother's fears that Fanny might spoil her evening.

"You ought to go down," said Fanny. "It's time."

"Yes, I know. Oh, dear, I'm so excited I could die. What about you, aren't you coming down?"

"In a little while. I'm bringing the children. We'll wait until the dancing begins."

"Fanny! Aren't you going to tell me I'm beautiful."

"Really, Amelia! You're growing impossibly vain. You look very well, certainly."

Amelia pouted and tossed her head.

"I don't look just 'very well'. Already one man has told me I'm beautiful, so I don't imagine it."

Fanny watched her go down the stairs, her ringlets bobbing, her feet hardly able to resist breaking into a run. Certainly she did look pretty enough tonight, to turn any man's head—whose head, like Adam Marsh's, was not already turned. Fanny should have been more generous in her praise. She should have tried, for a moment, to forget her breaking heart.

The first dance was almost over when Fanny, with Nolly in her starched petticoats and Marcus looking pale and fragile in the rich scarlet velvet, came downstairs. The servants were in a huddle at the foot of the stairs, trying to see into the ballroom. They made way for Fanny, and cook said boldly, "The foreign gentleman was looking for you, Miss Fanny. Dora will keep the children if you want to dance."

"Cousin Fanny!" whispered Nolly penetratingly. "You promised you would stay with us."

"And so I will. But do come and look at the lights and the fine dresses."

Nolly stared into the brilliant room. All the windows were thrown wide open, but the hundreds of candles, swaying like yellow broom flowers, made the room already unbearably warm. The musicians on a raised dais played with verve and energy, and the dancers, the ladies with their great skirts ballooning, passed in small gales of wind. Uncle Edgar was dancing with Aunt Louisa, both of them looking flushed and triumphant, Amelia with, of course, Adam Marsh. Fanny made her eyes slip over those two, and sought for George and Hamish Barlow. Neither appeared to be on the floor. She sighed with resignation and led the children to chairs along the wall. She would have liked to stay in the anonymous darkness of the hall with the servants, but that wouldn't have been fair to Nolly and Marcus. So let everyone see her sitting here, looking like a governess.

"Cousin Fanny! Cousin Amelia's dress is only white. It isn't nearly as beautiful as yours." Nolly leaned smugly against her.

"There's Mr Marsh," cried Marcus, pointing.

"He's looking at us," said Nolly. "Mr Marsh! Stop dancing and come and talk to us."

"Nolly! What behaviour! People don't stop in the middle of a dance to talk to children."

"Mr Marsh would to us."

"Yes, Mr Marsh likes us."

"Be quiet, both of you, and listen to the music."

But their unobtrusive entrance had not gone unnoticed. They were not to be left in peace. Fanny had just noticed Lady Arabella sitting in her chair at the other end of the ballroom, and was pondering joining her, when Hamish Barlow stood over her, giving his exaggerated bow.

"Miss Fanny! I have been looking for you. May I have the pleasure of the next dance?"

"Cousin Fanny—"

Fanny shushed Nolly silent.

"Thank you, Mr Barlow, but I have promised the children to sit with them for a little. This is a great event for them."

"I appreciate your kind heart, Miss Fanny, but surely their nursemaid—"

At that moment the music stopped, and the dancers began returning to their seats. Fanny was aware of Uncle Edgar, pompous and benign.

"By George, it's a warm night. This tells on an old fogey like me. Well, Barlow, are you persuading Fanny to dance. I promise myself one with her a little later if she will bear with me."

"Uncle Edgar, the children have never seen an English ball. I've promised to stay with them."

"And not dance! God bless my soul, what nonsense! Where's that girl, Dora." He snapped his fingers. A servant came hurrying. "Tell Dora to come and take charge of these children. Your zeal, my dear Fanny, does you credit, but it's quite unnecessary."

Nolly aimed her little pointed boot at Uncle Edgar's shin and administered a sharp kick.

"I hate you!" she said under her breath.

Uncle Edgar burst into a roar of laughter. It was loud enough to make many heads turn. The little group was the centre of attention.

"So! You would bite the hand that feeds you, little girl? And you looking like an angel in that pretty white dress. Just like a woman, eh, Mr Barlow? You pamper and cosset them, and what happens? Something displeases them and they let you know it. By George, I love the dear creatures. Whims, pouts, tempers and all."

Marcus's lip was trembling. Nolly prepared to outstare her uncle, her eyes glittering, but Dora had come and Uncle Edgar gave a sign of satisfaction, and moved away to his guests. The little incident was brushed-off as completely trivial, yet for all she had meant it otherwise, Nolly had played into Uncle Edgar's hands. Once more he was able, in his jovial benevolent way, to show the assembled company his generous heart.

"Do you dislike dancing with me so much?"

She was so thankful that he wore gloves. At least those freckles which gave her such a feeling of revulsion would not touch her. But his curved pale mouth beneath the sandy moustache, his narrowed eyes, his sharp alert face, were too close to her. She couldn't escape his gaze while she danced with him.

"I love to dance," she murmured non-committally.

"And you do it beautifully. Those little feet are like birds flying. What's wrong now? Don't you like my choice of words?"

"I would prefer you not to compliment me."

He gave a short unamused laugh.

"Really, Miss Fanny! For a woman not to care for compliments! I've scarcely seen you lately. I think you've been avoiding me."

Fanny seemed to be intent on the dance. She looked beyond him to see who Amelia was dancing with. The Talbot boy. Then who was Adam with? She failed to see him.

"Miss Fanny! I asked if you had been avoiding me?"

"I have been busy."

"Oh, yes, I know about that. But I hoped also you were taking time to reflect on my proposition. Your uncle promised me that you were."

"Really!" Fanny's eyes flashed angrily. "It is wrong for one person to guarantee another's thoughts. At least that is something one has in private."

"And these so private thoughts—have they been a little kind towards me?"

It was too late for mere politeness, too late to cover a rebuff in carefully chosen words. This man would understand only finality.

"Mr Barlow, I gave you my answer on the lake. I am not the kind of person to change her mind."

He returned her gaze. His eyes hardened, seemed to gleam with some curious kind of triumph, as if he were turning disappointment to something he almost enjoyed. But Mr Hamish Barlow had looked a self-centred man who would pamper rather than inflict hurt on himself.

"Then I seem to have been wasting my time," he said stiffly. He added, almost under his breath. "I wonder if you realise what you have been doing. You are a fool. Your uncle will never forgive you."

Fanny had a moment of remorse. Hamish Barlow had paid her the biggest compliment it was possible for a man to pay a woman. She should have been more appreciative. But at this moment she wanted only to escape from his gaze, and his touch on her arms. She wanted never to see him again. She scarcely paid any atten-

388

tion to his impertinent remark about Uncle Edgar's feelings. She merely said, "That is scarcely your business. Besides, you exaggerate."

"Miss Fanny, what do you think I came to England for?"

"To wind up Oliver Davenport's affairs."

"Precisely."

"Perhaps it was to find a wife as well?"

"Perhaps." He seemed to be reflecting with himself. "You will see. You will see." He added, almost with humility, "I wish you could have liked me a little. It would have been so much simpler for everybody."

Fanny forced herself to say, "I am sorry. And now I can see that Marcus is crying. Will you excuse me?"

"Certainly."

They found they had stopped dancing immediately in front of Lady Arabella, ensconsed in her chair, her only concession to the grandeur of the occasion a jewelled comb in her hair.

She insisted that Fanny stay and talk to her, and Hamish Barlow bowed politely and left.

Lady Arabella smiled conspiratorially.

"So I see you have got rid of the fox from China."

"How do you know?"

"My dear child, too much gets written on your face. Learn to conceal your feelings. That is the beginning of power. Well, I thoroughly agree with you. The man is a poor little runt." She waved her fan impatiently at Uncle Edgar who was approaching. "Go away, go away! I am talking to Fanny."

"I'm sorry, Mamma, you can't monopolise Fanny at a ball. Come, Fanny. Dance with me."

"I was about to go to Marcus, Uncle Edgar. He is in tears."

"Then let the servants dry them. You're spoiling those children. I'll have to put my foot down. Come!"

He had taken her hands and drawn her towards him. She knew precisely why he was doing this. He had seen Mr Barlow leave her and had to know the outcome of their conversation. But she was saved the awkwardness of telling him, for Lady Arabella was waving her fan, and saying in her hoarse carrying voice, "You've been foiled, Edgar. Ha, ha, ha! But if Fanny hadn't had the courage, I should have come to her rescue, you know."

"What does she mean, Uncle Edgar?" Fanny asked.

Uncle Edgar didn't answer for a moment. He seemed to be

finding dancing too agile an occupation for a man of his years and weight. His face was almost the colour of Aunt Louisa's dress.

"Your Great-aunt Arabella," he said at last, "I am sorry to say, is a mischief-maker. I suppose it is a danger that threatens all old ladies with too little to do. So am I to understand that you've dismissed Mr Barlow, Fanny."

"Yes."

"That was very foolish. Very foolish indeed." Uncle Edgar's voice had gone soft with what seemed like sincere regret and even sympathy.

"Uncle Edgar, my future at present is with the children."

She hated having to plead. But supposing he took Nolly and Marcus away from her.

"Yes, yes." He dismissed that subject as if it were of little importance. His eyes were rather persistently on her throat. "Do you know, you look extremely well tonight. You remind me of—"

"Of whom, Uncle Edgar?"

"Eh? Oh, of someone I knew a long time ago. The long white throat . . ." The inward look in his eyes was strange, it seemed to hold more loathing than admiration. Who was the woman he was thinking of? Someone who had hurt him as she had just hurt Hamish Barlow?

"Well," he said, and he seemed to be speaking to someone else, "let us be friends in spite of all. Now I will release you to go to those pampered children."

But Dora had taken the children out, and Fanny, still affected by Uncle Edgar's oddness which she would not admit had frightened her, suddenly had to escape from the hot ballroom. She slipped into the conservatory hoping no one would be there. It was such a mild still night that most people seeking air would go on to the terrace.

She was unlucky, of course. There was someone there already. She knew him instantly from the set of his shoulders. And in the same moment he must have sensed her approach for he turned.

"Well, Miss Fanny!" said Adam Marsh. "You look distressed. I realise some of us are not expert dancers."

"I have more than sore feet," Fanny burst out, and then was angry that the temptation to confide in him was so great. What did he care for her and her problems?

He came towards her, his eyes twinkling maddeningly.

"You are looking very charming. Has someone been telling you so too pointedly? Mr Barlow, perhaps?"

"They can't make me marry him?"

"They?"

Uncle Edgar's strange look, a mixture of love and hate it had seemed, was still with her. She couldn't understand why the shiver of fear had gone over her.

"I would marry you," said Adam Marsh, in an undertone, as if speaking to himself.

She flung round on him furiously. "Don't joke with me. Go back to Amelia. She will be missing you."

He didn't move. His eyes, too, were on her throat. But not in the way Uncle Edgar's had been.

"That's a very valuable jewel you are wearing for someone who says she is penniless."

"If you imagine I have a jewel box overflowing with these things, Mr Marsh, you are mistaken."

Their eyes met in a hard unflinching stare.

It was Adam who spoke first.

"I wasn't imagining anything of the kind. I expect your uncle gave it to you."

Fanny's hand was over the sapphire pendant. Why did he have to make his harmless words suggest that the gift had been some kind of bribe? The unreasonable fear caught at her again.

"What is the matter?" she heard him asking in concern.

"I have tried," she said intensely, "I have tried to get away from here. But the children came to stop me, and now—"

"I beg you not to go."

"You? Why?"

He came closer, not answering. His eyes had that deep strange glitter she had noticed once before.

"Because I would hate you to go."

Her voice had lost all its assurance.

"Go back to Amelia."

"You said that before. I have no intention of doing so—" his arms were actually about her waist and she was weakly letting herself be drawn towards him, "—until I have kissed you."

She felt the hardness of his body against hers. She knew she should struggle, but her lips were parting, her eyes closing. Very well, he would kiss her. What was a kiss? Surely not this strange bewildering ecstasy that made her so dizzy. She had to lean against him, waiting for the touch of his lips which never came.

For a moment later she was snatched back so roughly that she almost fell.

"Don't do that, Marsh," came George's voice.

His grip on Fanny's shoulder was so firm that she would have had to struggle ignominiously to get away. She said furiously, "George, you are a devil!"

George laughed with pleasure and triumph. His eyes were too bright with what seemed to be an uncontainable excitement.

"Fanny is mine, Mr Marsh, as you must have observed. I've had to make that clear to Mr Barlow, too."

Adam was very pale, his mouth angry.

"Don't you think you are taking too much on yourself, Davenport? I fancy your cousin isn't a person who can be dictated to. I suggest you take your hands off her?"

"So you can kiss her in a dark corner! Not a chance!"

No one had heard Aunt Louisa come. Suddenly she was standing there, like a great crimson peony, visibly palpitating with annoyance.

"Fanny! What's going on here? Are you letting these foolish men quarrel over you? George! Mr Marsh! I'm surprised. Is Mr Barlow here, too?"

"Mr Barlow isn't here, Mamma," George said smugly. "Fanny and I have sent him packing. And I've just had to explain to Mr Marsh here the lie of the land. Now Fanny is coming to dance with me. You don't need to worry, Mamma. I have the situation under control."

Fanny wrenched her arm away from George. She was blazing with anger.

"I'm not going to dance with you, George. Now or ever! I'm not going to dance with anybody. I have a headache. I ask to be excused."

"But, Fanny—"

"No, George! The situation isn't under control after all."

"But, Fanny—"

"Fanny!" Aunt Louisa exclaimed. "You can't leave the ball!"

"Would you have me faint at your feet, Aunt Louisa?"

"What nonsense! You have never fainted in your life."

Fanny was already at the door. George, flushed and perplexed, made an impulsive movement towards her. Adam stood perfectly

392

still, his face composed and expressionless. He might have opposed George, but he was too gentlemanly (or too cowardly?) to oppose Aunt Louisa. Once again she faced her disillusionment. As George had said, he had wanted only a snatched kiss in the dark.

So her beautiful dress, her pleasure in the dancing, her eternal optimism that perhaps tonight something wonderful would happen to her, were all wasted. She had not had the opportunity to dance with Adam once. She had only quarrelled with him, and then weakly surrendered to him. Now she despised him only slightly less than herself.

It was true that she felt dizzy and faint, and for the first time without hope.

She turned and ran up the stairs before anything more could be said.

Hannah came to her room to see if she would have a soothing drink, or needed help to undress. Fanny sent her away. She only wanted to be alone.

She had let her ball dress slip to the floor, and lay on the bed in her petticoats. She could hear the violins and the sound of voices and laughter. They were distant, because her room was at the opposite end of the house, facing the yew garden and beyond it the copse. She supposed it would be almost daylight before the carriages rolled away and the guests who were staying overnight came upstairs.

Her head ached badly, and it was a long time before she could fall asleep. When she did she was woken with shattering suddenness by a hoarse scream.

She started up in terror, the nightmare darkness pressing on her.

Oh, but it was the peacock, she realised, almost but not quite able to laugh at her foolish imagination. Although it still seemed so dark it must be nearly dawn.

Chapter 17

AMELIA already dressed in her morning gown of lavender muslin stood at the door.

"How are you feeling now, Fanny? Wasn't it sad that you had to leave the ball? Mamma said you were feeling faint."

Fanny had overslept. She struggled up on the pillows, feeling heavy and dull.

"I'm better, thank you. What's the time?"

"It's after ten. Mamma said we were both to sleep all morning, but I couldn't. I scarcely slept at all. I can still hear the violins." Amelia began to waltz round the room. "Wasn't it all heavenly. Except—" She began to frown a little, and Fanny asked, as she was expected to, "Except what?"

"Oh, well!" Amelia decided to be philosophic. "It isn't something that can't be remedied. It's only that I had expected to be kissed, I was determined to be. But somehow I was never able to get the opportunity. There were so many people round me, wanting to dance, or talk to me. Mamma says I was a great success."

"And it wouldn't have mattered who kissed you, so long as you achieved this great event?"

"Fanny! How can you be so stupid? Oh, I see, you're teasing me as usual. But, Fanny!" Amelia was able to stop thinking of herself for long enough to tell the news which had brought her up to Fanny's room. "Whatever happened between you and Mr Barlow last night?"

Fanny's heart missed a beat. She was suddenly sharply apprehensive. "Why do you ask?"

"Because he's left! Either he walked, or got a lift with some of the guests leaving last night, and caught the early train to London this morning."

Relief swept over Fanny. She could have heard nothing that pleased her more.

Then suddenly she was remembering George's peculiarly smug look last night, his words, "Fanny and I have sent him packing."

Fanny and I . . . What had George had to do with it?

"But didn't he say good-bye?" she asked breathlessly. "Didn't anyone know he was going?"

"Oh, yes, Papa did. He said Mr Barlow asked for his bags to be sent on. Now that he had suffered such a great disappointment—that was the way Papa said he expressed it—he only wanted to be away as quickly as possible. I suppose no one can blame the poor man. Fanny, you were cruel to him."

If he had told Uncle Edgar he was leaving, it must be all right. She had no reasons for these superstitious fears. She tried to concentrate on what Amelia was saying.

"Would you marry a man you didn't love?"

"No, of course I wouldn't," Amelia admitted honestly. "I don't blame you. Neither does Papa."

"Doesn't he?"

"Well, he thinks you have thrown away a wonderful opportunity, but he has decided to forgive you."

Hamish Barlow, in that strange almost deadly voice, had said, "Your uncle will never forgive you . . ."

"Papa is the kindest man," Amelia said. "You needn't be afraid he will be angry with you."

But would he have been very angry indeed if Lady Arabella hadn't taken her side? Why the old lady had done that was now perfectly plain. George must not be made unhappy. And for some reason Uncle Edgar always listened to Lady Arabella, even though he thought her a mischief-maker.

So on the one side there had been Hamish Barlow, and on the other George. There was always George who, even without his grandmother's help, would get his own way by any means. She didn't think she wanted to live.

Dora brought her hot chocolate and fresh brown bread and butter.

"There you are, miss," she said, her rosy face full of affection. "The mistress said I was to bring it because you were poorly."

Instead of chiding her they were cosseting her. Fanny couldn't understand it.

"I hope you're feeling better, miss, though what we all need after last night is a good sleep. Just fancy, even the peacock was upset. Screeching at three o'clock!"

Fanny had forgotten that moment of frozen horror. Now it came back to her vividly.

"Did you hear it, too, Dora?"

"I swear I did, miss. Hannah and cook say I'm crazy, what would the peacock be doing awake at that hour. But I heard it as plain as daylight. Or else it was—"

Had it been only three o'clock? What a strange time for the peacock to cry out. Some of the dancers must have sought it out on its perch and disturbed it.

She was only half listening to Dora.

"Or else it was what, Dora?"

"Why, that—that other bird, miss!"

"In the chimney! Making all that noise! Dora, don't be daft!"

"No, miss," said Dora, relieved. "It was only the peacock. He's cranky in his old age, William says."

The strange thing was that Hamish Barlow's name was scarcely mentioned again. Uncle Edgar made only one reference to the matter. His voice was uncharacteristically humble.

"Your aunt and I were thinking of your own good, Fanny. But if you're content to stay with us, we're content to have you."

Something impelled her to say, "Did you see Mr Barlow leave, Uncle Edgar? Was he very upset?"

Uncle Edgar pinched her cheek.

"Little rogue! It's too late now to worry whether he was upset or not. But he was, I assure you. He looked like a man in a daze, poor fellow."

Aunt Louisa's silence was perhaps more eloquent. She had obviously been instructed by her husband that Fanny was not to be scolded. So she contented herself with looking cold and reproachful every time Fanny appeared. But even this attitude was hard to maintain, for she was so busy with the aftermath of the ball which everyone had pronounced a great success. Invitations were rolling in, and it seemed that Amelia was to lead at last the social life for which she craved.

When Fanny's name appeared on invitations, Fanny begged that apologies be made for her. She wished to devote herself to the children, she said. They were about to begin lessons in the schoolroom.

Aunt Louisa interpreted this as a desire on Fanny's part to retire into the kind of life that would now be her future, since she had refused what was probably her only chance of marriage. She willingly agreed, since who knew when the wretched girl would behave unpredictably and disastrously. But Fanny sincerely wanted to be with the children and avoid all those empty social festivities where she was always "Amelia's cousin", some nameless person who was there by courtesy only. Even her slightly malicious pleasure in stealing the limelight had ceased to be an amusing game. She preferred the company of Nolly and Marcus.

She was nearly twenty-one and she must grow sober, quiet and restrained. In another ten years she would have lost her love of attractive clothes and be content with her governess's grey gown. She didn't suppose she would ever wear the rose-coloured ball dress again.

Those were her resolutions and she thought she made them with calm resignation.

They all vanished to the four winds when the invitation came from Heronshall for Miss Fanny, Miss Amelia, and the children, to come to tea to meet Miss Martha Marsh, Adam's aunt.

There was no hint as to whether Adam would be there. Fanny hadn't seen him since that brief scene in the conservatory when she had as near as possible accused him of being a fortune hunter. Also, Amelia was to go, and Amelia was now as possessive of Adam as George was of Fanny.

Yet Fanny's lethargy had vanished, and she was filled with life and vigour. She hadn't known she could despise a man and still love him. Nor had she realised that just to set eyes on the person one loved, even if no words were spoken, was the most acute and bittersweet pleasure. Perhaps even if he married Amelia she would still feel this. But he was not yet married and she was not a half-dead elderly young woman after all. She could no more keep the light out of her eyes than she could stop the sun shining.

Heronshall, in contrast to Darkwater, was full of light. It was already most tastefully furnished with turquoise velvet curtains and rose-coloured carpets, a startling combination of colours that set off perfectly the plain white walls, and the few well-chosen paintings and ornaments. There were several pieces of Chinese jade and porcelain.

The effect was so simple as to be extremely luxurious. Could Adam need to marry a fortune when he could live in a house like this? But she had heard of men expending their last shilling on the gamble of making the correct showing.

She despised herself for her thoughts as they were welcomed by Adam's aunt. Miss Marsh was a tall bony commanding-looking old lady with unexpectedly gentle eyes. From the beginning, although she greeted Fanny and Amelia with the greatest courtesy, it was evident she was almost entirely taken up with the children.

"I love children," she explained, and then made no effort not to devote her attention to them.

Amelia began to fidget. This was not her idea of a visit at all. She was accustomed to being the centre of attention.

"Is your nephew home, Miss Marsh?" she at last asked boldly.

"Adam? Oh, yes, he'll be in shortly. Then we'll have tea."

Amelia settled more happily then, patting her curls, and retying her bonnet strings. The children fortunately had taken to this rather unexpected elderly woman, and were shyly but politely answering her questions. She must have a good deal of Adam's gift for dealing with children, for even Nolly's hostility had not been aroused.

But when Adam came in he, too, devoted himself to the children and what remarks he addressed to the young ladies were made chiefly to Fanny regarding Nolly and Marcus. Had they enjoyed watching the ball? How were they progressing with their lessons? What were their favourite games?

Nolly answered that question herself. She clamoured for a game of Hide the Thimble when they had finished tea.

This was not Lady Arabella's cosy dishevelled room with a thousand hiding places. Nevertheless, Miss Marsh agreed good-naturedly to the game and suggested the morning room should be used, also. This necessitated a great deal of running to and fro, and so it was that Fanny, at one stage, found herself alone in the drawing room. She was fascinated by the Chinese ceramics, and was standing studying a small camel in some kind of earth-coloured pottery that looked older than the tors on Dartmoor when she was aware of Adam at her side.

"Do you like that? It's a Bactrian camel. It was one of my father's favourite pieces."

"It has such a look of age."

"Yes. The craftsman who made that has been dust for many centuries."

398

Adam had picked up the piece and was studying it. Fanny no longer saw it, but only his strong square hands holding the fascinatingly ugly creature so surely. She was conscious of the most overwhelming desire that it should be one of her hands he held like this, turning it over, examining it lovingly. She felt hot and on the verge of trembling. If he were to take her in his arms now she would make very sure that his lips reached hers. The very thought made her draw in her breath sharply, and to cover her odd behaviour she said in a rapid voice, "Mr Marsh, I am sorry for the things I said to you on the night of the ball."

"What did you say?"

Had he forgotten? Had her words had so little effect on him?

"Why, that you might be interested in whether I had other valuable jewellery besides the sapphire pendant."

"And so I was interested. But entirely for your sake. Fanny, if ever you are in doubt—" His hand was on her, gripping her wrist. He had a look of wanting to say something of the greatest importance. But it was never to be said, for the children, followed by Amelia, came running in.

"Cousin Fanny, Marcus found the thimble! Wasn't he clever. It was in—Cousin Fanny, why are you looking at that funny camel. A thimble couldn't be hidden in it."

"Have you ever heard about camels, Olivia?" Adam asked. "They are beasts of the greatest courage. They can keep going in the desert when it seems certain they will die of hunger and thirst. But they never stop expecting to find the oasis with green palms and cool water and date trees."

"And do they find it?"

Adam balanced the Bactrian camel on his hand.

"This one did. And you see it became too happy to die. It has lived for hundreds of years. But it is important always to remain optimistic, to be sure the oasis is there."

Nolly laughed delightedly.

"Tell us more stories, Mr Marsh. Marcus likes stories."

"Fanny!" Amelia's voice cut sharply across the conversation. "Isn't it time we left? We have a long drive."

"Yes. Yes, indeed." Fanny's voice was distrait. She was only vaguely aware of Amelia's petulance, and had scarcely heard Adam's fanciful tale of the happy camel. Her fingers were clasped lightly round her wrist, as if they would preserve the unbearably

399

exciting feel of Adam's grip. She had the most foolish desire to burst into tears.

At the last minute, as they were saying their farewells, Nolly remembered the most important thing.

"Cousin Fanny, can we ask Miss Marsh and Mr Marsh to Marcus's birthday party? Marcus will be five next week, Mr Marsh. Cousin Fanny says we can have tea in the pavilion if it's a nice day."

"But it isn't really a party, Nolly dear."

Amelia leaned forward in the carriage, her face suddenly much more cheerful.

"Why don't we make it a party? I'm sure Mamma will agree. We could play Hunt the Thimble outdoors, or have a real treasure hunt. Let's, Fanny. You're clever at thinking up things. Do you remember when we used to play paper chases? Miss Marsh, do say you will come. Mamma will write to you. And we can ask the Hadlows, and the Grey children for Nolly and Marcus."

"A party seems to be being born," said Adam. "What about it, Aunt Martha?"

His aunt gave the remarkably sweet smile that transformed her stern face.

"I should like nothing better than to go to Marcus's party."

"I'm five," said Marcus, realising his importance.

"Not until next week, you silly!" said Nolly. Her face relapsed into resignation. "I shan't have a birthday until next April. It's an awfully long time to wait. Cousin Fanny has one before then. Shall we have tea in the pavilion for you, too, Cousin Fanny?"

"Hardly, in October. There are fogs then, and the leaves are falling."

"Oh, do come, Fanny! We must go." Amelia was petulant again. For some reason Fanny had had far too much attention today. Who was interested in a woman's twenty-first birthday? So old!

"I do think, Fanny," she said aggrievedly, as Trumble whipped up the horses, and they began their long drive across the moor, "that you didn't behave very well while we played that game. Just making it an excuse to talk to Mr Marsh alone. No wonder Mamma says you're a born flirt. What with poor George, and poor Mr Barlow, and now Mr Marsh."

Fanny was in too dreamy a state to be annoyed by Amelia's maliciousness.

"Why don't you say poor Mr Marsh, too?"

"Because he is much too intelligent to be taken in."

"Have you discovered that yourself?" Fanny asked innocently. Amelia coloured angrily.

"Don't be ridiculous! I don't flirt. I'm entirely sincere."

When they had alighted from the carriage, at Darkwater, Amelia hurried inside, still sulking. Dora came out to get the children, but Fanny, following them, was called back by Trumble.

"Miss Fanny! I have a package for you."

"A package?"

Trumble took a neat brown paper parcel from beneath his driver's seat.

"Mr Marsh asked me to give it to you when we reached home. Quiet-like." The old man almost winked. His faded blue eyes were twinkling kindly.

"Oh!" Fanny had that absurd feeling of being about to tremble again. She took the package, and automatically slipped it inside her cloak. She would wish passionately to keep it private even if Adam hadn't already hinted that she should do so. She could scarcely get up to her room quickly enough to open it.

It was the Bactrian camel.

"Oh, no!" she whispered. "It's too valuable. Oh, Adam!"

If he had been there she would have flung herself into his arms.

So it was as well he was not, she told herself soberly. But why did he give her a present like this? Was it to disprove her sordid doubts that he might be a fortune hunter? Did he care so much for her good opinion?

She could only stand there, lost in delight.

It was some minutes later that she noticed the thin sheet of white paper that had fallen to the floor with the wrappings. It was a hastily scrawled note.

"My dear Fanny—what I was interrupted in saying to you—if ever you have doubts as to what is happening, if ever, I repeat, you are uneasy, will you tell me, or send a message to me or my aunt? If this injunction seems like nonsense to you now, it may not always be nonsense. I will be very happy if you will accept this small gift as a—let us say—happy omen."

And then, at the bottom, was written, "I would not have let you marry Barlow."

Chapter 18

"Well, how do I look, Master Marcus?" Uncle Edgar demanded in his rollicking voice. He stuck out his stomach, and patted his elegant striped satin waistcoat. "Made especially for your birthday party, my boy."

The children adored Uncle Edgar in this expansive mood. Marcus judged it a good moment to ask to hear the fascinating chiming watch, and Nolly, delicately touching the fine new waistcoat, remarked judiciously that she thought it beautiful.

"So you've forgiven me, have you, young lady?"

Nolly lifted her unafraid eyes.

"Marcus thinks you're being kind on his birthday. But I shall kick you, if I please."

Uncle Edgar roared with laughter.

"By George, we'll never find a husband for you, you little spitfire. Don't say you're going to be as stupid as your Cousin Fanny."

"Cousin Fanny isn't stupid!"

"All right, all right, we won't malign your paragon." Uncle Edgar sounded suddenly irritable, his good humour a veneer that could easily crack. "But remember, your Cousin Fanny isn't indispensable, and you children can't monopolise her life."

"What does indispensable mean, Uncle Edgar?" Nolly demanded, following him out of the room.

"God bless my soul, child, keep off my heels. It means that I could find you and your brother quite dispensable, except that it's my duty to keep you, and except that it's Marcus's birthday and I believe we're having a picnic in the garden. Or aren't we?"

"Yes, yes, yes!" shouted Marcus.

"Does dispensable mean not being here?"

"In a way it does." Uncle Edgar's voice was growing more testy. "Where's your nursemaid? Where are the servants?"

Nolly stood quite still.

"Then isn't it your duty to keep Cousin Fanny?"

"It is my duty to keep your Cousin Fanny until she is twenty-one years old, which means she is of age, and free to do as she pleases. If she chooses to go away I will have no legal right to stop her. Now, miss, will you leave me in peace?"

"Who is going away?" came George's voice from the stairs.

Nolly and Marcus had treated George warily, not understanding his alternating hearty friendliness, and moodiness. But now Nolly darted to him.

"Cousin Fanny!"

"Never!" said George.

He suddenly seemed very tall, and Nolly shrank back, although he wasn't looking at her but at his father with that look of frowning frightening anger. His blue eyes burned.

"Well, God bless my soul," Uncle Edgar muttered in assumed helplessness. "I am good-humoured enough to indulge this child in her interminable questions and like all women she immediately jumps to the wrong conclusion. No one is going away, as far as I know, anyway. I was merely explaining the legal situation, which I am sure, my boy, you understand already. If you don't, I've no doubt your grandmother will explain it to you. So would you mind having the good manners to look at me with some respect. I am your father, I would remind you, not your enemy."

The tense little situation was broken up by the ladies, Aunt Louisa, Amelia and Fanny, coming down the stairs in their light summer dresses and wide straw garden hats with fluttering ribbons.

The scene had been like the day, gloomy with thunder threatening. But now the sun had come out again, and it was very hot and bright.

"George," said Aunt Louisa, "your grandmother is waiting for you to help her downstairs. See that she brings an extra shawl. I don't trust the weather. It's too warm. Well, children, what are you waiting for? Why don't we go down to the lake? Our guests will find us there. Fanny, see that Olivia and Marcus look after little Charles and Amanda Grey. They're old enough to begin understanding their social responsibilities. We don't want any tears or tantrums."

"I can't keep it, of course," Fanny said in a low voice, later.

"Why not?" demanded Adam Marsh. His voice was hard. "Why not?"

"It's much too valuable. And besides, why—"

She had known the opportunity to speak privately to Adam would only last a moment. Already Amelia was at their side at the lake's edge saying vivaciously, "Has Fanny explained the list of things to be found on the treasure hunt? Some of them are awfully difficult. Twelve varieties of wild flowers, a lady's handkerchief—you should have no difficulty with that one, I am sure, Mr Marsh—a windfall apple, a toadstool, a bird's feather. And what else, Fanny?"

Fanny laughed. "It is mainly for the children, Mr Marsh."

"But everyone must join in," Amelia insisted. "And I shall need help because I confess I scarcely know two varieties of wild flowers. I shall prick my fingers or get caught up in a hedge." She contrived to make the picture of herself caught in a hedge a beguiling one. Adam laughed.

"I shall be glad to assist you, Miss Amelia. And to whom do we bring our offerings?"

"To Fanny, of course." Amelia looked from one to the other of them. She sensed something and said impatiently, "It's only a game, of course. You're not actually making her a gift."

No, it couldn't have been a gift, any more than Uncle Edgar's giving her the sapphire pendant had been a gift. Yet she persisted in believing that the little camel was a wholly impulsive offering, with no underlying intention. Even in the dark water of the lake her face looked up at her rosily. She was happy. She knew that happiness was the most fragile of all emotions yet while it was there she never imagined it departing.

When the game began she watched without a pang Adam accompany Amelia. She was beginning to know her strength, yes, and her power. Lady Arabella had been right. Power lay behind a calm and secret face.

In spite of having been told they must look after the Grey children Nolly and Marcus stubbornly ran off hand in hand, Nolly's white dress and wide-brimmed straw hat blown on to the back of her neck, and Marcus's fair head flickering behind the rushes on the far side of the lake. Robert Hadlow now that Amelia had gone, was left to rather sulkily escort his sister, and Uncle Edgar, declaring sportingly that he could at least pluck a feather from the peacock's tail, sauntered off in a leisurely manner. George refused to play the childish game, unless Fanny joined him. Lady Arabella could surely be trusted with gathering the trophies and announcing the winner.

But George's method of playing would be to attempt to put his arm round her waist the moment they were out of sight. Fanny refused pleasantly.

"No, George dear. If you want to please me, help Charles and Amanda. They don't understand where to look for things."

George looked at the shy and gaping children with the greatest distaste.

"There's a prize," said Fanny softly.

"By jove, is there!" George's voice had the anticipation of a small boy. But his eyes were on Fanny's lips. He looked as if he meant to demand another sort of prize.

Fanny sighed, and then forgot the perpetual worry of George as she observed the way Aunt Louisa and Miss Martha Marsh were getting on so amicably. For some reason this seemed to amuse Lady Arabella, or something amused her, for she sat a little distance away in her wheelchair, smiling to herself, her idle fingers resting on her work basket and her hopelessly tangled wools.

The close airless heat had increased. There wasn't a breath of wind. Black clouds loomed, then parted and exposed the sun's blazing heat, only to gather again after a few minutes, threatening imminent thunder. Bird cries were sudden and sharp, the lake was a black mirror, the dipping dragonflies making stitches across its gleaming surface.

"You were taking a risk, Fanny," Lady Arabella observed. "Sending everybody out with a heavy shower about to descend. Amelia, I've no doubt, will enjoy it. She can huddle under a tree with Mr Marsh." Her eyes were sly. "Had you that in mind, Fanny? But what about the children? If it thunders they'll be frightened."

"Charles and Amanda have George," said Fanny calmly. "And Nolly and Marcus aren't in the least afraid of thunder. Indeed, Nolly enjoys it."

This was true, for the last storm there had been had filled Nolly with a delighted excitement that kept her at the windows on tip-toe, wanting to dance every time the thunder rolled.

"But I hope they'll take cover if it begins to rain," she added, and as she spoke the first drop fell.

It was isolated, but the clouds had converged overhead, and the first broken roll of thunder sounded.

Aunt Louisa sprang up, exclaiming in vexation.

"Now isn't this just like our English weather! Having lived in London, Miss Marsh, I expect you haven't had the experience we have of ruined picnics. That's no doubt why my husband's ancestor had this pavilion built."

"And which Davenport was that?" Miss Marsh asked politely.

"Well, now—I'm not exactly sure. My husband acquired the property from a cousin. He knows its history better than I do."

"Perhaps Fanny knows," Miss Marsh suggested, her long gentle face turned towards Fanny.

Fanny, who had never been encouraged to feel that Darkwater was any part of her lineage, was startled that she should be addressed.

"I believe it was the father of the previous owner, John Davenport," she answered. "He would have been my great-great-uncle and I expect Uncle Edgar's great-uncle. That would be right, Aunt Louisa?"

"My family," said Aunt Louisa in her most lofty tones, "were more inclined to follow the Greek and Italian style of architecture. We had a lot of statuary, and a folly, of course. Ah dear, there's the thunder again. And which children are those?"

She was peering across the strangely darkening landscape. Fanny followed her look, and saw the children running on the edge of the copse, Nolly's white dress glimmering, and Marcus following some yards behind.

"They must have all their trophies," declared Miss Marsh. "They're hurrying."

This was true, for Nolly, her long starched skirts billowing out behind her, was literally flying out of the copse, with Marcus stumbling valiantly behind her.

It was Marcus's sobs that reached their ears. Nolly wouldn't wait for him. She wasn't usually unkind like that. Taller and light on her feet, she had outstripped him and he was bawling.

Fanny went towards them, calling, "Wait for Marcus, Nolly. There's no need to hurry like that. No one else has come back yet."

She realised at once that her words hadn't reached Nolly, that even if the child had paused to hear, she was in no condition to take anything in. As she came within reach, Fanny saw that she was half-crazed with fear.

At last she flung herself into Fanny's arms, panting and trembling. In spite of the violence of her exertions her face was colourless, her eyes absolutely black.

"Nolly! Nolly, what is it?"

She had lost her hat somewhere. Her hair was tumbled and damp with sweat. Some wild flowers, hopelessly crushed, were held forgotten in her clenched hands.

"Nolly darling, what frightened you?"

The other ladies were gathering round. It was Miss Marsh who went to Marcus's rescue, picking up the hot noisily sobbing little boy.

"N-nolly wouldn't wait!" he accused. "She ran away from m-me."

"The thunder's frightened them both," said Aunt Louisa practically. "They shouldn't have gone into the wood. It probably got very dark in there. Get them calm, for goodness sake, Fanny, before the others came back."

Nolly's grip round Fanny was unbreakable. The child obviously couldn't stop trembling.

Perhaps it had been the thunder. Safely indoors watching a majestic sky was one thing, but in a gloomy wood it was another. Perhaps a startled bird had flown in their faces.

"You're safe now, darling. Tell me what it was."

Nolly's face, pressed into Fanny's breast, didn't move.

"Marcus, what happened in the wood? Can you tell us?"

Marcus's sobs had died to hiccups. His drowned blue eyes held nothing but reproach.

"Nolly ran away. And I fell over a stick, and she said 'Quick!' and she wouldn't wait for me."

"Perhaps there was a wild pig," said Lady Arabella. Her eyes gleamed pleasurably. "Was there a great old boar snorting and snarling, Marcus? Or did your sister think the thunder was one? I expect that's the explanation, you know. She thought the thunder was an animal. And perhaps it is, or perhaps a herd of huge animals, bigger than elephants, growling and stamping about in the clouds."

"Please, Great-aunt Arabella!" Fanny begged.

"Oh, Nolly isn't afraid of that. She likes my stories. Come on my lap, child, and I'll find you a sugar plum."

The others were drifting back with their spoils. Uncle Edgar stood over Fanny demanding to know what had happened, and listening intently. He was perspiring, Fanny noticed. He was too heavily built for exertion in the heat. Adam listened intently, too. Amelia said that the thunder had scared the wits out of her.

"Didn't it, Mr Marsh? You saw how terrified I was."

George came back, his two small companions, the Grey children, trailing a long way behind him as if he had deliberately lost them. Everyone declared that he or she had not been in the copse and seen Nolly and Marcus.

"They shouldn't have been allowed to go in there alone," said Uncle Edgar. "They could have got lost, apart from being torn on brambles. It's too wild. I intend to get it cleared up one day. They probably did meet a wild pig."

The rain was about to descend in volumes. Aunt Louisa sensibly decreed that they should all hurry indoors, and the servants would gather up the chairs and the picnic things.

There was a great scurry to get to the house before the rain began. The thunder reverberated again, and a flash of lightning sent Marcus scurrying for Fanny's other hand.

The lake was as black as ebony when they left it. The willows were just beginning to sigh in the rising wind. With a sound of eerie gaiety, the windbells began to chime. For no reason at all, Fanny was vividly remembering Ching Mei's death.

Nolly had to be put to bed. She would neither talk nor eat. Her white face was a little alarming. Fanny stayed with her, so didn't know how the party ended, although Dora reported that Master Marcus had behaved nicely, and blown out the candles on his cake quite cleverly.

The thunderstorm was over in a very short time. Afterwards everything dripped in a brilliant yellow light. The lifting of the gloom seemed to lessen Nolly's fear, or else she was naturally recovering from some shock she had had. She sat up and was persuaded to drink a little warm milk. At last it looked as if she would be persuaded to speak. Only by talking about what had happened, Fanny realised, would the nightmare leave the child.

"What was it, little pet? Did it grow too dark? Did you see a wild pig?"

"No," said Nolly. "I saw a black bird."

Birds—the child's phobia. The dead starling tumbling down the chimney. The empty cage in Lady Arabella's room. Amelia's white fur hat that had made Nolly scream.

One might have realised it had been a bird, perhaps a blackbird or starling fluttering out of a bush. But that wouldn't have sent Nolly into such an ecstasy of terror. Fanny sensed more to the mystery. She probed gently.

"Nolly darling—was it the white bird you saw? You know, it would have been a pigeon, or even a white owl who thought it was night time with the dark clouds."

"No, it was black," Nolly's voice was shrill. "It was black, black, black!"

"But you wouldn't be frightened by a harmless little blackbird. You often see them in the garden."

Nolly's fists beat at her.

"You are stupid, Cousin Fanny! Uncle Edgar says you are stupid! It wasn't a little blackbird. It was big, big like this!—" She stretched out her arms dramatically.

"And where was this bird? In a tree?"

"No, it was on the ground. Marcus didn't see it. I told him to run. We both ran. I tore my dress."

Suddenly she had flung herself into Fanny's arms, trembling and saying in her high shrill voice, "You are so stupid! You have to keep saying it was white when it was black."

Once, in the dark, she had gone out to look for Ching Mei. Now it was only twilight, the half-light. Dawn and dusk, Lady Arabella used to say, were the times when frightening things happened, when nothing was quite real.

Fanny wasn't afraid now, only tense and just vaguely apprehensive. She was sure she would discover the thing that had frightened Nolly, a dead hawk perhaps, or even something that wasn't a bird at all. What was echoing in her mind was Nolly's insistence that she was stupid because Uncle Edgar had said so. Nolly's hysteria had given the remark a significance out of all proportion, and now, in the gloom of the copse with its tangle of bracken and brambles, it came back to haunt Fanny. Why was she so stupid? What was it she hadn't seen? That black was white, or white was black?

Now she was allowing her fancies to take possession of her just as Nolly's had. She must concentrate on what she had come to do, pick her way, her skirts held up, down the vague track which Nolly and Marcus had followed.

The bracken shook with raindrops. The heat had been swept away with the storm, and the air was full of a damp chill, as if autumn were truly here. The young birches shivered audibly in the dying wind. A blackbird, a real vociferous blackbird, plummetted out of a bush and flew scolding into the dusk. Fanny stopped at a glimmer of white on the ground. It was an uprooted toadstool, obviously dropped by Nolly in her flight. So she was on the right track.

The strange thing was that as she stopped there was the faintest crackling of bracken which ceased almost at once, as if someone else had stopped, too.

She must have imagined it. She stood very still, listening. There was no sound but the shiver of the beeches. The half-light gave very little perspective. Surely nothing moved behind that broad tree trunk!

She gave herself a little shake, telling herself that if she were going to be afraid she should have sent someone else to find out what had startled Nolly, George or Uncle Edgar, or Adam, or one of the gardeners. It was foolish to think that they might not have eyes to recognise what would frighten a sensitive child, or that perhaps they would not tell the truth about what they found.

Was there anything to find? The children could not have gone very far through this tangle of bracken and moss-grown logs. There was a strong smell of damp rotting leaves and earth. Had she noticed that before? But of course she had. The bracken seemed to have been trampled down a great deal as if indeed a wild pig, or some animal had crashed through here.

A twig snapped behind her. She was instantly motionless, petrified. Her own footstep hadn't snapped that twig. She turned her head, listening. Her thumping heart deafened her. It seemed to have grown very dark.

Who was following her?

"Who's there?" she called softly. "Is it you, George?"

There wasn't the faintest sound.

"George, I'm not an enemy to be stalked."

But supposing she were to stumble on to something she shouldn't see, just as Nolly had . . . Just as, perhaps, Ching Mei

had . . . *Fanny is so stupid* . . . *The white bird is a black one*
. . . *There is no escaped prisoner tonight* . . .

Was that someone breathing? Or just the whisper of the beech
leaves? It was so dark, she couldn't *see*. The tree trunks were
men. She had to go back, but somebody, something, barred her
way.

To George, with his blurred brain, everything that moved in
the dark was an enemy. She found she didn't dare to go back.
She had to go to the left, in the direction of the lake, leaving the
half-formed track behind and plunging through the nettles and
fallen logs and drifts of dead leaves. It couldn't be very far. She
would come out on the far side of the lake directly opposite the
pavilion. She had been crazy to come here so late in the day. She
shouldn't have waited for Nolly to talk, she should have come
immediately the rain had stopped.

Had that other person come then, and waited ever since?

She didn't stop to listen now for pursuing footsteps. She was
intent only in bursting out of the copse, as out of prison. Her
skirts would be ruined. She would have to ask Uncle Edgar for
another dress. She would have to explain she had ruined this one
in running away from his son, and Lady Arabella would tell him
not to be so foolish as to encourage her to run away from George,
let George have his way . . .

The light hadn't gone from the sky after all. When Fanny at last
emerged only a few yards from the lake she saw that the water
held the last glow of sunset, and was the colour of candlelight.
It looked beautiful and reassuring, and even warm. And a few
yards away a figure stood motionless, watching her.

Fanny froze. She could feel her feet sinking into the damp rushy
ground. She couldn't have turned and run. Her breath had left
her.

"Fanny! Whatever are you doing bursting out of the woods
like a witch." Adam Marsh was standing over her. "Your hair is
tumbling down."

"What are you doing here?"

"Reflecting, in the quiet of the evening. But my aunt will be
getting impatient. It's time we were leaving."

"Weren't you in the copse?"

"A short time ago, yes?"

She searched his face, his figure. She saw that he was perfectly

411

calm, that his clothing was unruffled, no dead leaves clung to his trousers as they did to her skirts.

"I thought someone was there," she said uneasily.

He looked over her head to the dark line of the trees.

"Perhaps there was. I believe we've all been down at one time or another searching for Nolly's scarecrow. Or perhaps it was that wild pig your uncle said was there."

"Uncle Edgar said there was a wild pig?"

"Both he and George and one of the gardeners found indisputable evidence, I believe. So there is Nolly's ghost." His eyes searched her. "And what did you find?"

"Nothing at all. It was too dark."

"What did the child finally tell you?"

"Oh, only some exaggerated story about a black bird. Nolly has this unnatural fear of birds. I'm afraid it's Great-aunt Arabella's fault. I expect it was a crow or a starling. Nolly has a weakness for exaggerating. But I wanted to reassure myself, all the same."

"And you didn't reassure yourself?"

"I thought someone followed me."

Adam took her arm.

"It wasn't me. It should have been. Pin up your hair, my dear. Or we will look guilty when we are innocent."

She was still too disturbed and distressed to notice the regret in his voice.

Chapter 19

"WELL, aunt, what did you think of her?"

"She's a nice enough child. Empty-headed, of course."

"Empty-headed! Fanny!"

"How was I to know which one you meant, you give so much attention to the other."

They stared at each other across the jolting carriage. Adam saw the humorous gleam in his aunt's eyes and knew that she hadn't been missing anything. He laughed softly, in appreciation.

"And sometimes at that I fancy Miss Amelia isn't so empty-headed."

"She must be if she is taken in by you."

Adam stopped laughing, and frowned.

"Yes. That's what I hope and count on. Then she won't be hurt too deeply. But don't you agree that I must go on. There is something. That child wasn't in a state of absolute terror today over nothing at all."

Miss Marsh leaned forward.

"What do you imagine it was?"

"Not that wild boar everyone is talking about. Although I grant you there were traces of a boar. I saw them myself. No, I haven't the slightest idea, aunt. Or if I have, it's too fantastic to put into words. No, no, aunt, I don't know. I thought I was in the copse before anybody else, but there was nothing to find, nothing that hadn't flown away."

"If you ask me, Adam, it's time you stopped being so secretive."

"No, I disagree entirely. As I explained to you, it isn't only the children, it's Fanny."

"Tut, boy! You have no grounds whatever for your suspicions.

Besides, Fanny is a grown woman, and by the look of her, very capable of taking care of herself. The children—" Miss Marsh sighed, it seemed with longing. "You shouldn't have let Mr Barlow get away like that without having it out with him."

"How was I to know he would behave like that? Like a sulky child, not like a man at all. Good lord!"

Miss Marsh tapped his knee with her fan.

"And how would you behave in similar circumstances?"

Adam looked out of the window at the darkening moor.

"You must have noticed her beauty, aunt," he said in a low voice.

"I have noticed that, and all her other qualities. You have my sympathy, but not my patience. I'm nervous, Adam. I confess it. Find out whatever it is you have to, and be done with it."

"Another two months," Adam murmured. "I don't think it can be any longer than that."

"Winter," said Miss Marsh. "The leaves fallen, that old house full of draughts. Rain, wind, snow. Why must we wait until the winter?"

"Because that is when Fanny becomes of age."

Chapter 20

It was later that Fanny thought how strange it was that Adam Marsh seemed always to be there at the unexpected moment. On the railway station on that first day of all, in the church in the village, at the lake in the dusk when she had been so frightened, and when the other men had been indoors—or were when they themselves returned. All those meetings could not have been accidental. Perhaps none of them had been . . .

Once she had had the thought that he was watching over the children, because, having come to their rescue on their arrival in England, he fancied he had some responsibility for them. But lately he had seemed always to look first at her. If he were trying to warn her about something, why didn't he tell her what it was? Or didn't he know? Was he, too, haunted by this feeling of premonition?

Nothing was different, and yet somehow everything was. Nolly had never quite recovered her spirits since her mysterious fright, for some time she refused to be left alone and cried at a shadow moving. It was never established exactly what she had seen, but it seemed certain it had been a wild pig, for Uncle Edgar organised a shoot a few days later and two boars and a sow were slaughtered.

Lady Arabella told her rumbustious stories, as usual, and was in high good spirits when the children visited her, letting them handle all her treasures, and even coax Ludwig to play with a ball of wool. But she ended every session with the words, "I'm so glad, Fanny, you had the good sense to send that little red fox of a man back where he came from. We'll keep her safely here, children, won't we?" Later, she had secret sessions with the children from which Fanny was excluded. It was something to do with making her a birthday present, an occupation that made Nolly's eyes shine with happy importance.

Amelia was quite openly talking of an Easter wedding, although no one had yet proposed to her. Her thoughts were easy enough to read. And George, with just a shade more confidence and possessiveness, kept trying to persuade Fanny to bring the children down to the stables where they could grow accustomed to the horses before beginning riding lessons. He was shrewd enough to know that that was the only way he might persuade her to go with him, since she refused to be in his company alone.

Aunt Louisa had dismissed Miss Egham, and told Fanny that if she needed a good workaday gown to wear in the schoolroom she was at liberty to choose the material and make it herself. That was the way the wind blew in that quarter. Poor Aunt Louisa, Fanny thought, stuck with her unwelcome niece after all, but perhaps making the best of it, since when Amelia married the house would be very quiet.

Uncle Edgar was exactly as he had been before the Hamish Barlow episode, affable, good-tempered, laughing just as heartily at his own jokes, becoming a little more conceited, perhaps, in his dress, and showing a great propensity for social occasions. There were always visitors at Darkwater, or the carriage was ordered for some dinner party or another. Uncle Edgar vowed every morning that he was exhausted, worn out, too old for all these gaieties, but that it was his duty to arrange them for the sake of the girls.

That was the subtle difference. Whereas previously Fanny had been allowed to make excuses for her absence, now Uncle Edgar insisted that she accompany them everywhere.

"You know why Papa is behaving like this," Amelia said. "He's giving you another chance to find a husband. He's quite forgiven you, you see. He's so kind-hearted, dear Papa."

But Fanny didn't think that was the reason at all. She thought that Uncle Edgar was merely making it publicly known once more how generous and worthy a man he was, and how sincerely he loved the waifs thrust on him. It would have broken his heart if his dearest Fanny had gone to live in far-off China . . .

It was the only way she could reconcile his present fond demeanour with his previous emphatic insistence that if she did not marry Hamish Barlow she would never be forgiven.

The letter with the London postmark arrived for her one late October morning when she had just returned from a walk with the children. Usually all mail was taken to Uncle Edgar who enjoyed distributing it, though the bulk of it was for himself. But today Amelia happened to be there when the postman arrived, and caught sight of Fanny's name on the top envelope.

"Fanny!" she shrieked. "Have you an admirer you've never told me about? Do you think this is from Mr Barlow? Do open it quickly and tell me."

Her interest was forgiveable. Fanny never received letters. There had been no one from whom to receive them. And the London postmark was highly intriguing.

Fanny's own fingers trembled as she tore open the envelope. The thin delicate writing didn't look like a man's. Mr Barlow didn't come to her mind. She had no clue as to the writer, only again this unreasonable disquiet.

The thick sheet of notepaper was open in her hand. She read, "My dear Miss Davenport, You will not perhaps recognise my name since I have been retired for some years, and am now a very old man. But as your late father's attorney and friend, I would like to extend to you my very best wishes on your coming of age. Indeed, since I have not seen you since you were virtually a baby, I have an old man's whim that you might, when you next make the journey to London, call on me at my house in Hanover Square. I have no doubt that under your uncle's excellent guardianship you have bloomed. It would please me to see this with my own eyes. Would you be so kind as to bear the thought in mind? Your obedient servant, Timothy J. Craike."

It was like a hand reaching out from the past. Someone who had known her father, and perhaps her mother. Fanny had to read the letter twice to assimilate its contents, and then, forgetting all propriety, she went flying into the library.

"Uncle Edgar! Oh, I am so glad to find you here!"

"I scarcely had time to disappear, since you gave me no warning," said her uncle dryly.

"I'm sorry. I should have knocked. I was so excited. Look, Uncle Edgar! I have a letter. Read it!"

She thrust the sheet of notepaper at Uncle Edgar, wondering for the first time as she waited impatiently for him to read the thin careful writing, why he had never mentioned Mr Craike to her.

But in a moment he had unwittingly explained her doubt.

"God bless my soul, I thought the old man dead long ago."

"Then you know him, Uncle Edgar?"

"Certainly. He attended to your father's affairs after his death. But it's years now since I had occasion to see him, and as he was an old man then I'd no idea he was still alive. Let me see, he must be as near ninety as anything."

"Then how wonderful of him to remember me. Oh, I should like to meet him."

"For a young woman who seems to show a remarkable scorn for males of her own age, I find this deep interest in a gentleman approaching his century very strange."

"Uncle, please be serious!" Fanny begged. "It isn't Mr Craike I'm interested in. He remembers my father, and perhaps my mother. I should dearly like to talk about them to him."

Uncle Edgar clasped his hands on his stomach, leaning back in his chair. His eyes were inscrutable.

"So you want to make another journey to London."

"Oh, I do, please! I know it's a tremendous favour to ask, but if you would try to understand how I have felt with no memory of my parents, and now here is an opportunity of getting one."

"And supposing you hear something you wouldn't care to know?"

"What do you mean? There is nothing like that about my parents. What could there be that I shouldn't know?"

Uncle Edgar was chuckling gently.

"Be a little calmer, my dear. If I know anything at all, Mr Craike will tell you you are your mother over again, wilful, turbulent, a proper handful, eh? That's how he'll describe you." He was patting her hand in his familiar reassuring way. "Don't look so anxious. You shall go to London and see this gentleman. We shall both go."

"You mean you will come with me!"

"I will certainly come with you. Looking as you do at this moment you could certainly not be trusted to travel alone."

He submitted to Fanny's impulsive hug with amused tolerance.

"Perhaps you'll even have a good word to say for your uncle when we get to London."

"But of course, Uncle Edgar. When can we go? Tomorrow?"

"One day next week, perhaps."

"Oh, but, Uncle—"

Uncle Edgar made a sudden impatient movement, as if his good-will were only superficial. Fanny had a cold feeling that he already regretted his promise.

"Am I to cancel all my appointments, no matter how important, for a sentimental old man who has already waited almost twenty-one years to see you? Come, my dear, be reasonable."

"Yes, of course. It must be at your convenience. I didn't think."

"Never mind thinking." He reached in his pocket for his snuff-box. "Pretty women shouldn't think." As he opened the box some of the snuff was spilt. How strange. Uncle Edgar's plump fingers were never clumsy. But he was laughing softly again. "And a man should never allow himself to be upset by a pretty woman."

"Have I upset you, Uncle Edgar?" Fanny asked bewilderedly.

"Yes, you have. The hunting season begins in ten days. I shall have to miss the first meet. The devil take old Craike who should have been in his grave ten years ago."

Amelia had found the little Chinese camel. She was holding it in her hands when Fanny came into the room. She started guiltily at Fanny's entrance, and Fanny exclaimed, "Amelia, how dare you! Going through my things!"

"I was only looking for some cotton in your work box. Why did Adam give you this? Did you ask him for it?"

"*Ask* him for it!" Fanny snatched the camel from Amelia in high indignation. "No, I did not. He merely saw that I admired it."

"And so, as if you were the Queen, he had to give it to you!" Amelia's face was flushed, her voice sneering. "Why is it that you have to get everything these days, even another trip to London to see a silly old man in his dotage. I don't know what has come over Papa. But now, all the time, it's Fanny must do this, Fanny must have that, as if—I don't know. Why didn't you marry Mr Barlow and go away?"

"Amelia!"

"You needn't think Adam cares for you just because he's given you that ugly old camel. To tell the truth, he's just sorry for you. He told me so."

"And why is he sorry for me?" Fanny asked in a low voice.

"Good gracious, how could he not be? Everyone's sorry for poor relations."

"I think you're just being spiteful."

"No. I'm speaking the truth. Mamma says it should be me getting the trip to London. It's time I went to operas and theatres. But I don't really grudge it to you. You'll have little enough."

"Will I?" Fanny asked dreamily. The little camel cradled in her hands felt like the whole world.

"Don't look like that!" Amelia cried, stamping her foot. "You look lovesick and silly. Adam isn't going to marry you. He's going to marry me."

"Has he—told you so?"

"I'm not blind!" said Amelia and suddenly burst into tears and ran out of the room.

In his own way George made a worse scene than that. He had got it into his head that Fanny was going to meet Hamish Barlow in London. It was useless to tell him that she wasn't, that Hamish Barlow had long ago sailed for the East, "Then who is it you're going to meet? It must be a man. You wouldn't look excited like that for a woman."

"Yes, it is a man, but a very old man. Nearly ninety. Does that satisfy you?"

"It would if I believed you," said George. His eyes were sulky and smouldering. "Are you going to come back?"

"Of course I'm going to come back!" Fanny said exasperatedly. "Though sometimes, the way you behave, I'd like to stay away."

"If you do, I'll follow you. I'll follow you and kill you both."

One day George would do something like that—if he hadn't done so already. Fanny's thoughts inevitably went back to Ching Mei and the riddle of that tragic evening. Then he would have to be put away, either in a mental hospital, or behind the grim grey walls of Dartmoor prison. How terrible to ride past the prison and know that Cousin George was there. And yet what a relief it would be. Neither his parents nor his besotted grandmother recognised his potential danger. She had loyally tried not to recognise it herself, but the time was coming when she couldn't endure his persecution any longer, when something would have to happen.

Aunt Louisa was the other person who thought the trip to London a piece of extravagant folly.

"Why can't Fanny write to Mr Craike?" she asked her husband.

"Because she wants to see him and talk to him. It's very understandable."

"Then why don't you have the old man come here?"

"Because he is quite beyond travelling. I gather he has only a short time to live. One can't refuse a dying man's whim, my dear."

Aunt Louisa tossed her head impatiently.

"Oh, you and your sense of duty! Do you ever stop to consider the inconvenience caused to others by it? Fanny has already spoiled those children until the servants can scarcely manage them. There'll be trouble the moment she's gone, and the brunt of it will fall on me. Really, Edgar, I seem to have spent the whole of my married life coping with your obligations. What other woman would have done it—no less than three strange children —the house practically an orphanage—"

Uncle Edgar bent to press his lips against his wife's plump neck.

"You have been an angel, my love. Angels are sometimes rewarded." He gave his throaty gurgle at her face suddenly full of anticipation. "Not another word at the moment. But you haven't the worst husband in the world—" his fingers found her breast— "I assure you . . ."

Once again Fanny packed her neat carpet bag with the essentials for a journey. But this time she could leave out her most precious possessions, for she very definitely was coming back. She would have liked to have had the opportunity to tell Adam about her journey. She fancied he would have been pleased for her. But he had not called lately, and it hardly seemed sufficient reason to write to him since she would be back within three days. Two days for travelling, and one to visit Mr Craike. Yet it would have been a wonderfully satisfying thing to write a note to Mr Marsh. Even forming his name on paper would have made her lips curve with pleasure. So he was to marry Amelia, was he! She would see about that!

"Cousin Fanny, why are you always smiling? Is it because you are leaving us?"

Nolly's eyes were black with hatred.

Fanny began to laugh, and shook the child gently by the shoulders.

"If you continue to look like that I will be very glad to leave you."

"Marcus says you won't come back."

"Marcus says nothing of the kind. And you are to be good children while I'm away. If Dora tells me you haven't been, there will be no gifts in my bag."

Marcus immediately began to clamour for a toy trumpet.

"I need one to blow for my soldiers. Cousin George says there must be a trumpeter to sound the alarm. What does alarm mean, Cousin Fanny?"

"It means when the enemy is in sight."

"Then you mustn't blow it, Marcus! You mustn't!" Nolly cried, in agitation.

Marcus, five years old, was at last beginning to realise his superiority over a mere girl. He strutted about, saying derisively, "You're scared. Cousin Fanny, Nolly's always getting scared of something."

Nolly made a wild dash at him, to tug at his hair.

"I am not scared! I am not scared!"

"Lawks!" cried Dora, running to separate the screaming children. "Miss Nolly, you'll be going to bed without your supper."

Nolly stood glowering.

"I am not scared at all. I am only over-sensitive. Great-aunt Arabella says so. She says I must be treated gently and not frightened. She says this house is enough to frighten any child."

"And now that speech is over," said Fanny, "what is there about the house to frighten a child?"

There was a red spot in each of Nolly's cheeks. Otherwise her face was paper white and looked alarmingly delicate. She was a bunchy little figure in her starched petticoats and her wide-skirted gingham dress, but Fanny knew that when the clothes were stripped off her she was far too thin and light. And her flat little chest was the storing place for too many conflicting emotions.

"Nolly," Fanny said, "I will be back for my birthday. You know that, don't you?"

This was suddenly, to Nolly, an irrefutable argument. Her face lit up, showing its infrequent dazzling prettiness.

"You will have to be, Cousin Fanny. Because I am making you a present. You wouldn't be too stupid not to come back for your presents."

In spite of that victory, Fanny was still not entirely easy about leaving the children. It was only that she wanted so badly to go and see Mr Craike, and besides Hannah had assured her that she was wrong to let the children possess her too much.

"You're only making a rod for your back, Miss Fanny," she said. She looked round quickly to see that no one else was within hearing, and added, "You know what it's been, running errands for Miss Amelia all your life, and now being tied to the nursery when you should be living your own life. All this nonsense about not getting a husband. You had only to see how that gentleman from China was turned silly about you, so why shouldn't others be. You ought to be thinking of children of your own, Miss Fanny."

"Bless you, Hannah. I don't know why I worry about Nolly when you're here. It's only if she gets one of her frights—"

"And them all imagination!" Hannah said briskly. "It's a pity she ever heard that old story about the bird in the chimney. I know it can be scary for a child. You found it scary yourself when you were a little one. But if you ask me, half Miss Nolly's frights are invented." Hannah shook her grey head wisely. "She sees she gets plenty of attention from them."

"Perhaps you're right, Hannah. Anyway, she's convinced, for some reason, that I'm stupid. Perhaps that's the reason."

Fanny wanted so much to be convinced that she allowed herself to be. The children could come to no harm in three days. Dora would sleep in the nursery with them. Hannah would be within call.

But in the late afternoon of the day before her departure everything changed. Nolly and Marcus went to Lady Arabella's room as usual, Nolly to work on the mysterious birthday present, and Marcus to amuse himself with whatever new fascinating object Lady Arabella might produce.

A few minutes later there were piercing screams.

When Fanny rushed into the room it was difficult to get a coherent story from anybody. Lady Arabella was just shuffling on her sticks from her bedroom, the lamps had not been lit, and the living room, with its claustrophobic collection of furniture and knick-knacks was in gloom. Nolly was standing in the middle of the room screaming with terrifying regularity. Her figure was rigid. As that other day by the lake, she obviously was in no condition to say what had happened, and it was left for Marcus, beginning to sob with infectious fear, to stutter that Nolly had touched the bird.

"What bird?" Fanny demanded.

Marcus pointed towards the empty birdcage. "In there."

Lady Arabella shuffled forward. "There's no bird in there. The cage has been empty for months. Didn't I tell you about my parrot. He died—But my goodness, Fanny! Look! There is a bird."

The white shape, wings outspread, was clearly visible. It was hanging motionless against the bars of the cage. All unawares, Nolly must have brushed against it and it had pecked at her.

Marcus had caught Nolly's fear, and now, in an unreasoning overwhelming wave it swept over Fanny.

There was only a not very large white bird hanging motionless in a cage in a gloomy room yet the atmosphere was heavy with dread.

"Where are those lazy servants?" cried Lady Arabella. "Why aren't the lamps lit?" She fumbled for the bell rope, and suddenly, from the deep chair in the corner, George began to laugh.

"Ho, ho, ho! You've all been nicely taken in. It's only a dead bird."

Fanny spun round on him.

"George! Why are you hiding there? Is this a horrible joke you've played?"

"I didn't play the joke. I didn't put the bird there. But it was funny to see Nolly jump. You'd really think it had bitten her."

Lizzie had come hurrying to answer the bell. Lady Arabella turned on her angrily.

"Why haven't you lit the lamps half an hour ago? You know Miss Olivia comes here to sew. Do you expect her to do it in the dark?"

"But I did light them, ma'am!" Lizzie protested. "Really I did. They must have gone out. Look, this one's still warm."

Nolly's face was buried hard against Fanny's breast. Fanny only hoped her own rapidly beating heart was not further upsetting the child. But she couldn't help her feeling of unexplained dread. Someone had played a horrible trick on the children, put a dead bird in the birdcage, blown out the lamps . . . Why?

"Then didn't you fill them?" Lady Arabella snapped. "Can't you be a little more thorough in your work? Here I fall asleep on my bed, and am woken by banshee shrieks all because you've been too lazy to see that the lamps are burning properly. The child wouldn't have got a fright if she could have seen this bird properly. Let's have a look at it."

Lizzie, muttering something under her breath about the lamps being properly attended to, re-lit them, and in the soft glow the poor mute motionless creature was clearly visible. It wasn't even a real bird, but just a realistic concoction of feathers with a small sharp beak. Fanny remembered seeing it somewhere before, and suddenly recognised it as belonging to one of Aunt Louisa's bonnets. She had used to wear it to church last winter, nestling among veiling and ribbons.

It was only someone who knew Nolly's phobia about birds who realised how much of a fright this would have given her. But who, apart from George with his retarded sense of humour, would have wanted to frighten a child?

The disturbance had brought Aunt Louisa and Amelia hurrying upstairs.

Aunt Louisa was furious.

"Who has been destroying my bonnets? Mamma, surely—"

Lady Arabella's eyes went completely cold.

"I'm not senile yet, Louisa, much as you might like to think I am. No, I don't go about blowing out lamps and frightening children."

But she had always enjoyed frightening them with her stories, Fanny remembered, and then comforting them with sugar plums. She had enjoyed her power over them.

"George! Amelia—"

"Mamma, don't be idiotic," said Amelia. "A silly old artificial bird. I wouldn't even think of such a thing."

George was laughing again, the snigger of a schoolboy who has enjoyed a practical joke.

"I don't know who did it, but it was deuced funny. I say, make the child get over it, Fanny. She can't have been that scared."

But Nolly, Fanny realised, was not going to get over this last shock. Too many shocks had been accumulating inside her. She had gone suddenly limp in Fanny's arms, and seemed as if she were really ill.

"I'm taking her to bed," she said. "I'm sorry, Aunt Louisa, but I think this time the doctor ought to be sent for."

There was a great fuss about that. Aunt Louisa pooh-poohing pandering to what were probably only tantrums, but at that moment Uncle Edgar came upstairs to see what was going on and was instantly alarmed.

"The child's sickening for something. By all means, the doctor must come. I'll have him sent for immediately."

"She isn't sickening for something, Uncle Edgar," said Fanny.

"She's merely had a very bad fright. But can we talk about that later?"

She was carrying Nolly's limp too light body back to the nursery, Marcus clinging to her skirts whimpering. She heard Uncle Edgar's loud voice as she went, "God bless my soul, Mamma, what next! If you want a new parrot I'll buy you one, but to play games with dead birds!"

"If I play a game, Edgar," came Lady Arabella's voice, slow, distinct, and far from senile, "it will be a much cleverer one than that. And one that I will win."

By night-time Nolly had a high fever. The doctor had been, and given her a sedative which had sent her into a heavy sleep. He had heard the story of what had happened and said that contrary to sickening for some disease, the fright, to such a highly-strung child, might well bring on a brain fever. The utmost quiet and good nursing were essential. And there must be no more shocks. Her short life had held too many already.

Leaving Hannah (Dora was infected with the uneasiness in the house and jumped every time a door opened or a curtain billowed in a draught) beside the sleeping child, Fanny went downstairs. She didn't want dinner, she was too distressed for that, but there were things that must be said. She had reached a conclusion in the last hour that made her more angry than afraid.

The meal was over, and the family was in the drawing room.

George sprang up eagerly at her entrance, and Amelia asked, "How is poor little Nolly?"

"Sleeping," said Fanny briefly. "Uncle Edgar, I shall not, of course, be able to accompany you to London tomorrow."

Uncle Edgar pushed aside his glass of port, and said in distress, "My dear child, is that sacrifice really necessary? You had set your heart on this expedition."

"Yes, Uncle, I had. But someone is equally determined that I shouldn't go."

Now she had everybody's startled attention.

"Whatever is this, Fanny?" Aunt Louisa demanded. "I admit I never thought that extravagant journey to see an old man who has probably lost his memory was at all necessary. But this stupid childish joke with the bird in the cage was meant only to amuse the children, surely. It had nothing to do with you. I never heard anything so extraordinary."

"I think it had everything to do with me," Fanny said clearly.

"Someone must have been jealous of my going, or perhaps had an even more serious reason for stopping me. Anyway, you all knew Nolly's fear of birds. Whoever put the bird in Great-aunt Arabella's room was quite aware that the child would be scared out of her wits, and probably ill. And that consequently I wouldn't leave her. It's really very simple indeed."

As they all stared, she added, "If it was only meant to frighten the children, then that's even worse. I think whoever would do that is a devil."

She rubbed her hand across her forehead, wearily, and heard Aunt Louisa saying in a put-out voice, "Edgar, surely it isn't necessary to question the servants. Fanny is making a mountain out of this silly business. After all, I should be the one who is upset. It was my bonnet that was ruined."

"It isn't a trifling business, Aunt Louisa," said Fanny. "Nolly is seriously ill."

Uncle Edgar was on his feet, looking as perturbed as his comfortable after-dinner flush would allow.

"Now come, Fanny, if you're finding hidden meanings in a prank, I can surely find one in your implication that neither your aunt nor Amelia nor any of the servants, even Hannah who has seen you all through enough illness, is capable of looking after that extremely spoilt little girl. Stop talking nonsense, and prepare to leave for London in the morning, as we arranged."

"You know I can't. You know I won't. You must have heard the doctor say Nolly could develop brain fever. She has already been crying for Ching Mei. She hasn't mentioned her amah's name for weeks. Next she will cry for her mother. And if I disappear, too, then what do you imagine the consequences will be? No—" her eyes went round the room, "if someone played this horrible trick to keep me here they have succeeded very well. I will write to Mr Craike explaining the position."

Nobody had wanted her to go to London, she knew that. They had all had their separate reasons. Even Uncle Edgar hadn't wanted to miss the hunt. But now, because she made the accusation, they all had smooth astonished faces, as if incredulous that she could think herself so important.

The fact that no one could deny was that the bird had been put in the birdcage, and had succeeded far too well in providing the necessary upset.

George was the most likely culprit, and yet it seemed at once

427

too clever and too simple a plot for him. Perhaps he had had his grandmother whisper in his ear. Aunt Louisa had grudged the money spent on Fanny, and Amelia the attention. Uncle Edgar's seeming acts of generosity were not usually such unselfish ones . . .

"Oh, poor Fanny!" Amelia cried, suddenly springing up and throwing her arms round Fanny. "It is true, she gets all the worry. Let's make up to her for her disappointment, and give her a really wonderful birthday next week."

"A splendid idea," said Uncle Edgar in a relieved voice. "And you write a letter to Craike, Fanny. Ask him all the things you want to know. He'll answer them as well in writing, as in an interview. Get it done tonight, and give it to me. I'll see it gets away by the post in the morning."

"And Fanny, don't sit up with that child all night," Aunt Louisa ordered. "I'll look in before I go to bed, and the servants will take turns. You've really brought this indispensability on yourself, by your own behaviour."

"If Ching Mei hadn't died, it wouldn't have happened," said Fanny, and again the blank faces looked at her.

"Well, you'd better have that out with Sir Giles Mowatt," said Uncle Edgar. "He let the prisoner escape. He's tightened up regulations now, he tells me. Vows there'll be no more escapes. Fellow's away to Australia by now, I believe."

"Aus-Australia!" echoed Amelia unbelievingly.

"That's what they think. A ship bound for the Antipodes sailed from Plymouth a day or so later. And there goes a murderer scot-free. He'll probably make his fortune in the goldfields. Ah well, life's a funny thing. Most unfair at times. Most unfair."

Amelia made a movement as if to say something, then stopped. Her face was white, her eyes darkened.

"Papa—"

Her father waited indulgently for her comment. When none came, he said, "What is it, my dear?"

"Are you all right, Amelia? You look pale."

"I'm quite all right, Mamma. It's just that talk of escaped prisoners makes me nervous. Sometimes at night—the ivy taps on my window—and I almost scream."

"My poor darling, you mustn't be nervous. I tell you, Sir Giles declares not even a weasel could slip out of that jail now."

Amelia looked at her father with her dilated eyes. Then Lady

Arabella, who had been dozing the entire time, woke with a great start, and murmured in her hoarse voice, "Fanny is a good girl. She deserves more than a party."

And it seemed as if after all she might have been listening all the time.

Chapter 21

SHE was caught—she was the bird struggling and suffocating in the chimney. The bird had died . . .

Fanny, dozing in her chair at Nolly's bedside, started up, wide awake again, the questions without answers going round and round remorselessly in her brain.

The fire was dying, and the room almost dark. She got up to carefully shovel on more coal. In spite of her care, Nolly stirred, and muttered, as she had several times in her half-delirium, "Cousin Fanny! When will Ching Mei come back for her shoes?"

Soon the coal caught alight, and the room grew more cheerful. Nolly slept again. The Chinese doll that lately she had wanted much less was tucked in beside her. It had seemed to comfort her. That it had been the innocent cause of Ching Mei's death, fortunately the child didn't know. And, just as it was likely she would never discover who had put the bird in the birdcage, Fanny had never known who had tossed the doll on her bed that night.

But none of the queer episodes, not even Nolly's fright in the copse, had seemed quite as sinister as the imitation bird tonight.

Or perhaps Fanny felt that simply because she was so tired and overwrought and disappointed about her cancelled journey to London. So alone . . .

She had no one to whom to turn except Adam Marsh. Should she turn to him? Could she trust him? She kept remembering his injunction in his letter to her, "*If ever you have any doubts . . .*"

Now she had too many doubts. Whether they were the kind to which he referred, she didn't know, but on an overwhelming impulse she tiptoed to her room and got writing paper from her bureau.

". . . It isn't for myself, but for the children that I am worried. Someone is deliberately trying to frighten them. Nolly is ill to-night. I can't leave her to go to London. I am wondering if that pleases our tormentor, if it is what was intended. I confess now that I have never been entirely convinced that Ching Mei's death was due to the accident of her encountering the escaped prisoner. I think someone outside the family should know that my cousin George is more seriously ill than it was at first thought. Families can be too loyal . . ."

Putting her anxieties on paper gave her intense relief. She finished the letter, melted wax over the candle flame to seal the envelope, then slipped it into her pocket to ponder later how she would see that it reached Adam. She couldn't leave it in the hall to be taken with the rest of the post. Everyone would want to know why she was writing to Adam Marsh.

That letter finished, she began the one of apology to Mr Craike. She begged him to write to her telling her all he could of her parents. Perhaps at a later date she would be able to visit him.

There was no worry about the posting of this letter. Uncle Edgar had promised to see that it was dispatched first thing in the morning.

The wind had risen and it had begun to rain. The summer was over, and the leaves were falling. With this wind, the ground would be carpeted in the morning and the lake scattered with drowning leaves. The misty days and the long dark nights were coming. That was when the house really came to life, not with fires and parties and gaiety, but with its multitudinous creakings and sighings in the gales that swept over the moors, with the moonlight caught in uncurtained windows, and the snuffings of candles by immense disembodied breaths. Fanny shivered. She loved the drama of the winter, but this coming one she dreaded. She couldn't see its end.

Nolly was better in the morning. She drank a little warm milk, stared at Fanny with a shadow of her old truculence, said, "Stay here beside me! All the time!" and fell asleep again, this time deeply and quietly.

It was still raining in a fine drizzle by mid-morning when Amelia came flouncing in, wet and bad-tempered. She had been out riding and Adam hadn't met her.

Fanny looked at her in astonishment.

"Do you mean to say you have a rendezvous with Mr Marsh when you go riding?"

Amelia nodded. "Of course. I never did enjoy riding alone. Oh Fanny, don't look so shocked. This is the nineteenth century. Or is it that you're jealous?"

"Then your meetings were never by accident?"

"The moor's a bit big for accidental meetings, isn't it? No, he waits for me by High Tor. But he didn't come today, the coward. Surely he's not afraid of a little rain."

Fanny's fingers were closing over the letter in her pocket, crumpling it viciously. *If ever you are in doubt,* he had said. What was she in at this moment but the most miserable doubt?

"And does he encourage you—to confide in him?" she asked.

"Of course. I tell him everything. He's so wonderfully sympathetic. Fanny, I do really think I'm in love."

"Think!" said Fanny contemptuously.

Amelia frowned, "How can one ever be absolutely sure? Could you be sure?"

"No, I couldn't," Fanny admitted, her colour high. "Sometimes I don't know which is which, love or hate. Or whether they're both the same thing."

"You looked as if you hated us all last night," Amelia agreed. "So I understand what you mean. Because I'm sure you really do love us all. Even maddening George."

"I hate whoever frightened Nolly so badly," Fanny said in a low voice. "Who was it? I must know."

"Then don't ask me." Amelia was uncomfortable. "I expect it was Grandmamma, really. But she'd mean to amuse Nolly, not frighten her. You've made an awful scene out of such a trivial happening, Fanny. Mamma was very angry with you."

"Does she think Nolly being ill trivial?"

"No, of course not. How is she this morning, anyway?"

"Better," said Fanny briefly. "Dora is with her. She must be kept quiet."

"Will she be allowed downstairs for your birthday?"

"I don't know. How can I say."

"Oh, well!" Amelia sighed and yawned. "You're lucky to be so interested in children. What am I to do for the rest of this dreary day? I hate sewing, I hate reading, there's absolutely nothing to do. That silly Adam, why couldn't he have come out in the rain!"

When she had gone Fanny took the letter out of her pocket and tore it into small pieces. Then she burst into tears which she had to hastily dry when Dora came knocking at the door to say Miss Nolly was awake and fancied a little jelly. There was no peace for her, not even the peace of having a sympathetic ear into which to pour her troubles. Amelia had stolen that from her. It seemed that Mr Adam Marsh had a pair of very inquisitive ears, and enjoyed the secrets and heart-searchings of young women.

"Now, Fanny," said Uncle Edgar that evening, "we must be business-like. You come of age on Monday, so, as I mentioned once before, you must make your will."

"But I have nothing—"

"I don't want to remind you of the value of a gift I have made to you," Uncle Edgar interrupted, "but I would point out that that sapphire pendant has a cash value as well as a sentimental one. Surely you would like to choose who is to be its recipient?"

And there was the little Chinese camel, Fanny thought, with a pang. Adam's gift. Of course, Uncle Edgar was quite right, she must choose her own beneficiary.

"I would like to leave the pendant and—other personal things to Nolly," she said unhesitatingly.

"I thought you would say that, my dear. And a very nice gesture on your part. The day will come, a very far-off day, I trust, when the child will appreciate this. The other essential thing in a will, as you probably know, is that you must name a trustee. I make the suggestion from a purely practical point of view that that task should be left in my hands. If you agree, we'll draw up a very simple document that can be signed on your birthday."

"Do what you think best, Uncle Edgar."

She was too tired, after her long vigil at Nolly's bedside, to think clearly. Anyway, the subject was a minor one. It was only men who had this passionate desire for tidiness in their business affairs. She would give the pendant to Nolly long before she died, anyway. But the camel—that would remain her own until the end, no matter what memories it gave her.

"Craike will get your letter, and write again," said Uncle Edgar as an afterthought. "I hope you've forgotten all that nonsense you talked last night. Your aunt and I understand that you were overwrought. You spoke as if we were all your enemies. Oh, I know that someone played a prank, but not a malicious one. A fine

433

brainstorm you turned on, eh, my dear? But it's all forgiven and forgotten."

So she was the one to be forgiven! Fanny was too tired even to be indignant about that. Tired and hopeless. Unless Adam had had private reasons for meeting Amelia and listening to her garrulous tongue.

Perhaps that was it, Fanny thought, her mood turning to sudden high excitement. He was aware that somehow all was not well—as indeed he had hinted to her—and was pursuing his own methods of obtaining information. If that were so, she must see him. Yes, she positively must see him, and have the whole matter out with him. Why torture herself with doubts when ten minutes' conversation would solve the whole thing?

She would ride over to Heronshall. When? Tomorrow, when the family was at church. If Nolly continued to improve she could be safely left for three or four hours with Dora and Hannah. When the family returned from church and found her missing she could explain, on her return, that she had been impelled to get some fresh air.

The next day it was still raining and blowing a half gale. On Amelia's horse, Jinny, Fanny took the short cut across the moor. Even so the ride took her more than an hour, but the wind and rain in her face were wildly exhilarating. After being shut in a sickroom she felt one of her swift changes of mood to an almost intoxicated state of hope and freedom. It even occurred to her that she might find Adam waiting at his rendezvous beneath High Tor for Amelia. She would surprise him by her appearance, tease him, ask him if he were not bitterly disappointed.

But there was no horse and rider beneath High Tor, only a grey huddle of sheep sheltering from the rain.

Fanny rode on, and came at last to Heronshall. She was soaked through, but glowing with warmth. She didn't give a thought to her dishevelled appearance, knowing that Miss Martha Marsh would at once invite her in to dry herself by the fire, and drink hot tea. And Adam—she could already visualise the expression on his face, puzzled, pleased, welcoming.

Strangely, she had to lift the heavy knocker and pound on the door twice before it was opened.

Then a manservant, dressed rather casually in a leather apron, whom she hadn't seen before stood within, looking at her in some surprise.

"Is Miss Marsh or Mr Marsh at home?" she asked. "Would you

be so good as to tell them that Miss Fanny Davenport has called?"

"I'm sorry, miss. They be away."

Fanny stared at the man, scarcely taking in his words. Both Miss Marsh and Adam couldn't be away—not after her picture of a glowing fire, a warm welcome.

A gust of wind blew her wet hair across her face. She pushed it back impatiently.

"Oh, they've gone to church, of course."

"No, miss, they be gone to Lunnon. There be only Bella and me here. The house is shut."

"To London!" Fanny repeated. "But he never told us. He didn't even tell Amelia. He let her ride out—" She realised she was thinking her astonished thoughts aloud, and said quickly, "When did they go?"

"Day before yesterday, miss."

"For long?"

"That I can't say, miss. But the servants was to have yesterday and today off."

Fanny tried to collect herself after her profound disappointment, her unreasonable sense of having been abandoned.

"Is there someone who could rub my horse down? Could I rest her for half an hour?"

"I'll see to it myself, miss," said the man good-naturedly. "Will you step inside, into the dry, while you wait?"

The hall which she had thought so light and airy and attractive was as cold as doom. She sat on the edge of a carved oak chair and shivered. No one came near her. She tried to rationalise what had happened. Adam and his aunt had probably found the grey windy weather depressing and had decided on an impulse to go to London to see friends, an opera perhaps, or a new play. They had no obligation to inform anyone at Darkwater of their plans. They would be back before anyone knew they had gone.

But Fanny failed to comfort herself. Apart from Adam's thoughtless behaviour towards Amelia, he had given her the unmistakable impression that he would always be there if she needed him. And now he just wasn't there, the house was cold and empty, and she had the greatest difficulty in controlling her tears. Could nobody at all be trusted?

On the way back across the moor in the early dusk she saw a rider approaching, and her heart suddenly leaped. Adam, after all! He had returned. He had ridden out looking for her.

The rider on the superb black horse who galloped up, reining in his mount with easy authority, was George. His highly-flushed face was full of pleasure at having found her.

"They said you'd gone out riding. Amelia's furious that you took Jinny. How far have you been?"

"Only to High Tor."

"That's where Amelia waits for Mr Marsh. I've seen them." George's face was suddenly suspicious. "You haven't been looking for him, too?"

"Of course I haven't. I only had to get some fresh air. I'm going back now. Don't wait for me. Jinny can't keep up with your horse."

George laughed. "Don't be silly. I've been looking for you. Simon can suit his pace to Jinny's. Let's take as long as we like getting home."

"Not in this weather. I'm frozen."

"You don't look frozen. Your cheeks are scarlet." George suddenly leaned across and took Jinny's bridle. "Wait a minute, Fanny. I was jolly glad to hear you'd gone riding. I knew I'd get a chance to see you alone at last. I want to know when you're going to marry me."

"*Marry* you!"

"Well, don't sound so surprised! What do you think I've been trying to tell you for the last six months?" George's voice had turned sulky. Already Fanny's reaction had hurt him. "Look here, Fanny, I've waited long enough. You'll be twenty-one tomorrow. Even if Mamma and Papa oppose us, you'll be free to decide for yourself. So I want your answer then."

Jinny moved restlessly as the hold on her bridle tightened. George's face, flushed, too bright-eyed, oddly triumphant, was uncomfortably near to Fanny's. She felt caught and pinioned, unable to escape. And Adam had deserted her.

"George, let me go!"

"All right. I'll let you go now. But tomorrow I want your answer. And after that I'll never let you go. Never!"

He gave a sudden wild laugh, and abruptly releasing Jinny's bridle, spurred his horse and galloped off. But before he had gone far, he turned and came back, circling round Fanny on her slower mount, laughing and showing off his superb riding skill. He did that all the way back to Darkwater. It was, Fanny thought, like being hovered over by a bird of prey.

Chapter 22

She was twenty-one. Everyone had gifts for her. Amelia gave her a cameo brooch and Aunt Louisa a cashmere shawl. Uncle Edgar kissed her soundly on the cheek, and handed her a small packet containing ten sovereigns. "Buy yourself some gee-gaw," he said affectionately. Great-aunt Arabella's gift was a topaz ring set in heavy silver, but George was mysterious about his, saying that whether he gave it to her or not depended on her answer to his question yesterday.

Fanny knew that it must be an engagement ring, and her heart sank. She dreaded the scene she would have to face sometime today. She was physically afraid of George's reaction.

She tried to forget this in her pleasure at the children's gifts. Nolly, downstairs for the first time since her illness, importantly handed her a flat parcel, then went back to sit on Lady Arabella's lap while Fanny opened the parcel.

It was a sampler, "Remember Life's Sunny Hours" and "This sampler was worked by Olivia Davenport, aged six years, in the year of our Lord, eighteen hundred and . . ."

"It isn't quite finished," Nolly explained. "I had only that last bit to do when I got sick. But Great-aunt Arabella said I should give it to you on your birthday and finish it later."

Tears sprang to Fanny's eyes. She went to take Nolly in her arms.

"It's the very nicest gift of all."

"You haven't got mine!" shouted Marcus. "Here's mine."

This proved to be a box of sugar plums, and everyone laughed and agreed to sample one, and Fanny said tactfully that certainly Marcus's gift had been the sweetest.

"Well, Fanny, don't you feel awfully old?" said Amelia. "I intend to be married and have children by the time I'm twenty-one. Just think, if you had married Mr Barlow you would have been celebrating your birthday in China."

"She isn't in China, she's here, where she belongs," said Lady Arabella, with finality.

It was still misty and dark outdoors, the trees almost leafless after the gale. In contrast, the warm room with the fire blazing, and the comfortable circle of people, had an illusion of happiness and security. Was it really an illusion? Had she been unfairly suspicious and mean-spirited to imagine undercurrents? It almost seemed possible this morning to wipe away all her doubts and enjoy the pleasure of being the day's most important person in the bosom of her family.

Uncle Edgar said, "Since we are all here, and since it's a solemn occasion, I think we might read a chapter out of the Bible. Then, Fanny my dear, we'll get a couple of the servants to witness that brief document I drew up last night, and you'll really be your own mistress. Does that alarm you?"

She was thinking that the ten sovereigns, more money than she had ever had at once before, would pay for her journey to London if it became necessary to go. Or to Exeter or Bristol or Liverpool or any part of England. She need no longer feel completely a prisoner. The knowledge gave her a great sense of freedom and lightness of heart. She could even take the children . . .

"No, Uncle Edgar. I am not alarmed."

"She's a rich woman," said George unexpectedly. When everyone looked at him, he said, "How does a woman spend ten sovereigns? I'd know what to do with it, mind you."

"Then never mind your dissertations," said his father, with some sharpness. "Now be quiet. I am going to read the twenty-third psalm."

He had a good voice for reading aloud, rich and sonorous. Fanny had heard it every day of her life, when the servants gathered with the family for morning prayers. She had also heard it thrown out impressively from the pulpit in church when Uncle Edgar frequently read the lesson. But it had never sounded more moving than now on this, her twenty-first birthday, when she was in the grip of so many emotions. Excitement, pleasure, uneasiness about George, anxiety for the children, a most bittersweet feeling about Adam Marsh, and above all an unexplainable tense anticipation of some event about to happen.

Though I walk through the valley of the shadow of death I will fear no evil . . .

"There," said Uncle Edgar, closing the big Bible with a clap, and reaching for the bell rope.

When Lizzie answered the bell he said, "Can you write?"

Lizzie looked bewildered, bobbed a curtsey, and said proudly that she could.

"Good. Then I want you here, and someone else who can write a good hand."

"Cook can't, sir, but Rosie in the dairy can."

"Then ask Rosie to come."

"Yes, sir."

As Lizzie bobbed, and hurried away, Uncle Edgar produced the narrow sheet of parchment which he had inscribed in his own thick deliberate writing.

"If you want to peruse this, Fanny, you may. But I assure you it isn't necessary. I've done exactly as you asked. I am your Executor, Olivia your ben—, well, never mind. That child will want to know the meaning of the word, and I've already had experience of trying to answer her questions. She will at once imagine you—har-har-harumph." He chuckled good-temperedly, and handed Fanny the parchment.

Fanny glanced quickly at the script. She saw her own name in large letters, "Francesca Davenport" and further down "to my cousin Olivia Davenport all my personal effects including one sapphire and diamond pendant" (now there would be the cameo brooch and the topaz ring as well for Nolly to receive). Further down she read "to my said Executor Edgar Davenport all the rest and residue of my estate" and thought, with slightly grim humour, that if she died quickly enough, Uncle Edgar was ensuring that he got back his ten golden sovereigns!

The two maids had arrived, Rosie nervously hanging back in the doorway.

Uncle Edgar dipped his quill pen in the silver ink-well, and handed it to Fanny. She took it and signed her name where he indicated. She was in a curious state of unreality, the words *Though I walk through the valley of the shadow of death . . .* mingling in her head with the formal phrasing of the will.

"Where did you learn these legal phrases, Uncle Edgar?"

"Ah, that's easy. I've signed enough documents in my time. Now, if you'll just stand there, Fanny, while Lizzie and Rosie append their names as witnesses."

With much heavy breathing, the two women complied. Rosie gasped in dismay as a small blot formed beneath the nib, but Uncle Edgar swiftly blotted it away and said kindly, "Take your time, my girl. Don't be nervous. You're not signing your death sentence."

Fanny found Nolly at her skirts, whispering agonisedly, "What are you writing, Cousin Fanny. Does it mean that you'll go away, now you're twenty-one?"

Fanny said, "S-sh, Nolly! It's only something grown-ups do. Something you'll do one day. Ask Uncle Edgar."

"Yes, child," said Uncle Edgar absently. "Yes, if you have some jewellery and a little money. It's everyone's duty."

"You're wasting your time, Fanny," said George suddenly and harshly. "A married woman's property becomes her husband's."

Uncle Edgar lifted his heavy white eyebrows blandly.

"A married woman, George? But our dearest Fanny isn't married. So what can you be talking about?"

"George—" began his mother, uneasily.

"Be quiet, Mamma, Papa. I've waited long enough to speak. I knew you wouldn't allow Fanny to marry me before, but now she's her own mistress, as you just said. So she's free to do as she likes. And I'm asking her to marry me. I won't be put off any longer. Fanny, I want your answer now."

In that moment George sounded strong and dignified. But the speech had cost an effort of concentration that had made the moisture stand out on his forehead and heightened his colour alarmingly. His blue eyes had a fixed expression of determination and desire that made Fanny wince. She was only glad that this unwelcome proposal had been made in company where she was safe. Had they been alone George would have inevitably tried physical persuasion.

Aunt Louisa made a movement to speak again, but this time Uncle Edgar stopped her.

He said himself, in a perfectly quiet reasonable voice, "Well, Fanny? What is your answer?"

Fanny felt Nolly's small hand holding her own in a hot and panic-stricken grip. She felt almost as panic-stricken as the child, but she made herself speak calmly, "The answer is no, as George has always known it would be. I have never given him the slightest encouragement. I am sorry, George, but you can scarcely be surprised—"

George took a step forward. His brow was creased in concentration, his big hands held out. He seemed to be having trouble in understanding her words.

"Fanny, I told you yesterday on the moor that today I would be doing this. I want you to be my wife. We'd be happy together. You'd be mistress here—"

"Fanny! Mistress of Darkwater!" cried Amelia suddenly, deeply shocked. "But she's only—"

"Be quiet, Amelia!" That was Lady Arabella, her husky voice full of authority. "What is there about Fanny that makes her unsuitable to be the mistress here? She is beautiful, kind—oh, hot-tempered, I agree—but a lady. I commend George's taste."

"Mamma, you're talking as if I were dead!" exclaimed Aunt Louisa in high dudgeon. "I anticipate being mistress here for the next thirty years, at least, and this whole conversation is nonsensical. George is still ill and quite unfit to marry. I won't hear of such a thing. I thoroughly disapprove of cousins marrying, anyway. Fanny, be good enough to take the children upstairs. They shouldn't be listening to this conversation. And George, you are very flushed, I'm afraid your head is bad again. You had better rest."

Aunt Louisa's tactics had always been to reduce them to the status of children. To speak in a loud bossy voice, and wield her authority.

This time, however, George, at least, was not to be intimidated.

"My head is fine, Mamma, and I don't intend to ask the doctor's permission to marry. I shall do so when I please. So, Fanny! Listen to me! I warn you whether you do or not, I shall get my own way."

Fanny's refusal burst from her. "No!" she cried. "No, no, no! I won't be persecuted in this way. I can't stand it any more. What do you think I am? A servant to be bribed and bullied into giving in to your wishes? You're nothing but a bully, George. You always were. I'm glad to say it at last."

George's hands slowly opened and closed. His face had gone a curiously dark colour.

"I've told you I would kill anyone who came between us." His

441

hands closed again, convulsively. "I can kill. I've been trained to."
He gave a sudden high laugh. "That's one thing the Crimea
taught me. It's no trouble at all. A sword and a dark night . . ."

"George!" His father's voice was icy. "There are young ears
listening. Have a little self-control. Or if you can't, leave the
room."

George's face suddenly and distressingly collapsed into that of
a harshly scolded child.

He turned momentarily to Lady Arabella.

"I must have her, Grandmamma!" he exclaimed, and then
rushed headlong from the room.

In the shocked silence that followed, Aunt Louisa put her handkerchief to her face and began to cry. Amelia ran to her side.

"Mamma, it was only George in one of his moods. He'll forget
it. It's ridiculous that he should want to marry Fanny. Imagine—
Fanny!" But her eyes sought Fanny's in astonishment and resentment. "That's two proposals you've had in three months. At least,
you won't be able to say you've never been asked."

"How could I marry George who is practically my brother?"
Fanny demanded. "And I've said before I will only marry for
love."

"A nice sentiment," said Uncle Edgar, "though sometimes difficult to fulfil." His eyes rested very briefly on his wife. "Amelia,
get some smelling salts for your mother."

"Yes, Papa." Amelia hurried from the room.

"A nice sentiment, indeed," came Lady Arabella's deliberate
voice. "But quite impractical, Fanny. Quite impractical."

Her grey eyes, round as a cat's, met Fanny's with a look of
stony hostility. Fanny's heart missed a beat. She had never
thought Lady Arabella her enemy.

The tense atmosphere was broken by Marcus demanding
whether Cousin George would sound his trumpet before he used
his sword.

"I wanted a trumpet," he said wistfully.

"Did you, my boy? Then you shall have one." Uncle Edgar was
trying to restore the previous mood of happiness and normality.
"And Miss Olivia? What are her present desires?"

But Nolly wouldn't answer. She was very white and still clung
to Fanny. Fanny wished uselessly that that scene hadn't taken
place in front of the children. She murmured something about
taking Nolly upstairs, it was time she rested. She didn't want to

442

look at anyone any more, Aunt Louisa weeping angrily because always, always, this interloper, this girl with more looks and spirit than her own daughter, ruined things, Uncle Edgar earnestly trying to retrieve the happy birthday spirit while his eyes glinted with other thoughts, and Lady Arabella with her look of implacable hatred.

But a flicker of her never quite extinguished optimism came back as she saw the postboy coming up the gravelled drive.

"Uncle Edgar, here's the post. Do you think there might be a reply from Mr Craike?"

"Couldn't be yet, my dear. Don't be so impatient. He's an old man and sick. Give him at least ten days, if he replies at all. Cheer up, child, cheer up. Forget that affair with George. He's not himself, and you did quite right. Don't be afraid of his wild threats. We all know him, eh? But I'll have the doctors back, if necessary."

"Uncle Edgar, I've always wondered about that night Ching Mei—" She had to stop, because again the children were listening.

Uncle Edgar, surprisingly, didn't deride her unspoken suspicion. Instead he said, soberly, "I can't deny I've had my own thoughts, too. But that's over, past, can't be undone. So run along and begin to enjoy your birthday. Marcus, Olivia, if within an hour you have made your Cousin Fanny laugh you shall each be allowed to make my watch play a tune yourselves."

So, on the way upstairs, Marcus enquired earnestly the best way to make Fanny laugh, but Nolly, with a shadow of her former spirit, remarked dispassionately that when next she saw Cousin George she would cut his throat.

"Nolly!" Fanny exclaimed. "Such a thing to say."

"How?" Marcus asked with deep interest.

"With a knife, of course. Like William uses for wild pigs. He told me."

"I thought you'd use a sword," said Marcus.

"Children!" said Fanny, almost on the verge of laughter after all.

Life was so crazy. It swung from the fearful and the grotesque to the absurd and the touching without giving one time to change one's mood. Now she found that the alarming scene with George had jolted Nolly out of her apathy. There was colour in her cheeks, and her ingeniously macabre imagination was hard at work to find a way to protect her beloved Fanny. A little warmth and happiness had come back to the day, after all.

When Amelia came into the nursery to report that George had gone out riding, galloping his horse wildly across the parkland to the moors, she relaxed a little more. That meant he wouldn't be back for hours and when he came he would be tired and wanting only a hot bath and a brandy. So the house was safe until dark.

Safe? That was the word that had instantly sprung to her mind.

"Goodness, Fanny, you've upset everybody."

"I?" said Fanny indignantly.

"Mamma says it's your fault. She's talking of sending George to London for the winter. She says he needs a change of people and scene, and he'll come back cured. Grandmamma just says, 'Try, Louisa. See if he'll go.'" Amelia was amusing, the way she could imitate Lady Arabella's hoarse voice. "And Papa says nothing at all except that this will blow over. George is merely suffering from a foolish infatuation, like most young men. But you must admit, Fanny, that it wasn't a very *romantic* proposal of marriage. It was more like a threat, somehow. I'd hate my first one to be like that."

There was something wistful in Amelia's voice that made Fanny say, generously, "You don't need to worry. Your first one will probably be from the right man."

"Will it?" said Amelia, and strangely looked about to weep.

She didn't, however. She sprang up, crying, "Poor Fanny! What a birthday. First it was so nice, then so horrid. Let's make it nice again. Let's play games this afternoon. Everyone is to dress up as some well-known character, and the rest must guess who it is. Nolly and Marcus, too. Grandmamma will lend us things. It won't frighten Nolly, will it?"

"I don't think so. But it might be better if she sat and watched. She isn't strong yet."

"Yes, I suppose so. Then I wish we had some guests. I wish Adam were here. But who knows, he might ride over."

"He might be away," suggested Fanny.

"Oh, no. He'd have told me if he were going away. Anyway, let's do this, Fanny. We must do *something* this long dark afternoon. Why don't you dress up Dora and Lizzie, too? And I'll take Marcus."

It was a very long time since Fanny had been up to the long narrow room in the very eaves of the house where a miscellany of articles over the years had been stored. She and Amelia and

George had used to go there as children, opening the old chests to explore the musty and quaintly old-fashioned clothing stored in them, and playing carriages with the discarded furniture. But one day a rat had run across the floor and scared them out of their wits, and they hadn't been up there since.

Now, when Fanny took Dora up the final almost vertical flight of stairs, she found that the door to the attic room was stuck, or locked.

This was odd, since no one ever went there nowadays. Both girls pushed valiantly, but the door remained fast shut.

"Perhaps Hannah has a key, miss," Dora suggested.

"Yes, run and find her, Dora."

But Hannah, when she came, said she had never had a key to that particular door. She didn't know there was one.

"Anyway, I wouldn't have locked the room," she said. "There's nothing but old junk in there."

"Shall we get Barker or one of the gardeners?" Fanny asked.

"Wait a minute, Miss Fanny. Sometimes these keys I have fit two or three locks. All the linen cupboards can be opened with the same one, and I wouldn't be surprised if this one for the ironing room fits here."

After a little manipulation, to everyone's delight, the rusty lock gave and the door creaked open.

"Goodness, it's dark," said Fanny. "And musty. Dora, run down and get candles. How cold it is in here. Ugh!"

The long dim room with its peaked ceiling was full of strange shapes. Fanny knew that they were made only by upturned furniture and chests, but she waited with Hannah on the threshold until Dora returned with the branched candlestick.

Quickly the candles were lit, and the wavering light made the conglomeration of rocking chairs, tables, a child's high chair and wooden cradle, a paint-faded rocking horse, dark pictures in heavy frames, and old-fashioned travelling trunks quite unsinister.

"Put the candles there," Fanny instructed, indicating a dusty table. "Goodness, here's the old newspaper reporting the Battle of Waterloo. I remember reading that years ago, and George made me be Buonaparte and Amelia the King of Prussia, while he, of course, was the Duke of Wellington. We knocked over the furniture while we fought and made a terrific noise. Do you remember, Hannah?"

445

"That I do, Miss Fanny. Master George was never happy without a sword in his hand. He should have ended up a general, if—well, then, he's shed his blood for his country, and we must just remember that."

"Yes, Hannah. I do. Always." There was no need to explain that that was the only reason she had tolerated George's persecution. Hannah was not blind. She must know, too, by the servants' infallible grapevine, what had happened this morning.

In the candlelight, in the dark musty room, Fanny found Hannah's unspoken loyalty more comforting than anything that had happened today.

Dora had opened a chest and was exclaiming over the smell of the clothes.

"Faugh! They do need an airing, miss. If you knew what things you wanted I could take them out and give them a good shaking."

"Yes, there's a ball gown that I think was Lady Arabella's—it's the Empire style, in white lace. There should be a shawl and shoes and a fan that goes with it. I know, because I wore it once at Amelia's birthday party when we dressed up. I don't suppose it's been touched since. And I remember a velvet cloak—I think that was in one of these chests—"

She was engrossed now in the clothes and the old memories. She impatiently pushed the wrong trunk aside, and there was a little cascade as several boxes slid down. This disclosed two unexpectedly new-looking travelling bags, quite modern in design.

Fanny looked at them in surprise.

"These must have been put here by mistake. They're not in the least antique. I wonder what's in them."

She lay one on its side and undid the straps and fastenings. The lid opened and displayed the neatly folded Norfolk jacket, which lay on top of a miscellany of masculine clothing.

"Goodness!" said Hannah. "That's certainly got here by mistake. It's a good new garment. I wonder who it belongs to, miss."

Fanny was staring at the neat brown checks of the good expensive tweed in a fascination of horror. She could almost feel the boat rocking beneath her, see those hot eager red-brown eyes fixed on her, the freckled hands reaching towards her. She knew every detail of the jacket Hamish Barlow had worn that day because she had had to keep her eyes fixed on it rather than on his face.

446

"But he's gone. His things were sent on!" she whispered in desperation.

"Whose things, miss?"

"Mr Barlow's. The gentleman—from China." She couldn't bring herself to touch the jacket. She stared at it in horrified distaste.

Hannah had caught her feeling of unreasoning horror.

"But he did go. His things were packed. The master gave orders."

"He couldn't have travelled to London in his evening clothes!"

"Then who brought the bags up here? To a room locked for goodness knows how long."

"Why hasn't he sent for them? What's he been wearing in the meantime?"

Dora, who had said nothing, only stared with enormous eyes, suddenly exclaimed, "I heard rats, one night. Don't you remember, Hannah?"

"Yes," said Hannah derisively. "And you thought you heard the peacock, too! In the dark, long before morning."

"The peacock!" whispered Dora. "Screaming!" And clapped her hand to her mouth.

Chapter 23

"WHAT will you do, Miss Fanny?" asked Hannah at last.

"I don't know." (Ching Mei had left her shoes, Nolly kept saying. But compared to that, Mr Barlow was practically naked. He had gone out into the world in a set of evening clothes which, no matter how distraught or even drunk he may have been, would have to have been changed by morning when he took up his ordinary life.)

"I'll have to tell my uncle," she added. "I wish we hadn't come here. I wish that door had stayed locked." Again, her eyes met the fearful eyes of the two servants. Who had locked the door?

"I'll go down now," she said at last, standing up and brushing her skirts. "Lock the door again, Hannah, and Dora, go to the children. Suggest another game for them to play. Not dressing up. Tell Miss Amelia I said so."

Was she only twenty-one today? She felt older than Hannah, older than Lady Arabella. She walked down the three flights of stairs and along the twisting passages as slowly as if already her body were fragile and dried-up. She moved in a dream and for the first time in her life forgot to knock as she entered the library.

The two men looked up in surprise. Sir Giles Mowatt's expression immediately changed to a welcoming smile, Uncle Edgar's to an annoyed frown.

"Fanny, my dear—here is Sir Giles—we were having a private conversation."

"I'm sorry, Uncle Edgar! But I must speak to you at once. There's been a—a strange discovery. Uncle," she burst out, "where is Mr Barlow?"

There was the smallest silence—of surprise, of consternation?

448

"Gone back to where he came from, I believe. And entirely due to you, young lady." Uncle Edgar was fiddling with a paper knife. His voice was slightly jesting and affectionate because Sir Giles was there. Fanny knew that he would not have been so tolerant, otherwise. "I hope you haven't suffered a change of heart at this late day."

"No, uncle. We only wondered how he could have travelled without luggage."

"We?" said Uncle Edgar sharply.

"Hannah and Dora and me. We found his bags and all his clothes in the attic room. They look as if they had been hidden there. The door was locked. Hannah had a key that opened it. Uncle Edgar, he *couldn't* have travelled in his evening clothes!"

"Is this the gentleman from the East who was your brother's trustee?" asked Sir Giles with interest. "Why, Davenport, you didn't tell me this young lady had sent him packing with quite so much speed that he abandoned his luggage."

"But I didn't mean to," Fanny cried. "He had seemed to accept my decision with fortitude. I thought—"

"Never mind about your female intuition just now, Fanny," Uncle Edgar interrupted. "And Mr Barlow's bags will keep. They seem to have done so for some time already. Sir Giles and I—"

"Let us know what she thought," put in Sir Giles. "I'm interested in this. It sounds quite a mystery."

"Yes," said Fanny. "I think perhaps you should know. Everyone should know. Uncle Edgar, you heard George say this morning that he would kill anyone who came between him and me. Well, it isn't the first time he has said that. And he warned me about Mr Barlow. I'm so afraid—"

"Of what?" asked Uncle Edgar, smiling, amused by the nervous imagination of the feminine sex.

"The peacock screamed that night. Both Dora and I heard it. But it was still dark, and the sound came from the yew garden. I have never seen the peacock in the yew garden. And it never calls after dark. Then, in the morning, Mr Barlow—had gone."

Sir Giles sprang up with a decisive movement.

"Davenport, I don't know what this means but you'll have to have it investigated." Uncle Edgar made to interrupt him, but he motioned him to be silent. "Miss Fanny, you're an observant young woman. I wonder if you can throw any light on another affair. It has just come to my knowledge that that escaped

449

prisoner was seen in another area altogether on the night he got away. A farmer in the Okehampton district, an illiterate fellow, has chanced to mention it at this late day. That was the night, you will remember, that the unfortunate Chinese woman died."

"What does this mean?" Fanny breathed.

"It's up to the police, whether they decide to re-open the enquiry or not. But your suggestion that your cousin George is, let us say, not entirely responsible for his actions, throws another light on the affair."

"He was in the garden that night," Fanny said. "I know, because I ran into him." She caught her uncle's eye, and declared agitatedly, "I must say this, Uncle Edgar! I must. George isn't safe. He will kill sometime—if he hasn't done so already . . ." Her voice died away. She was shuddering at the thought that she had been kissed by a murderer, almost with the blood still on his hands . . .

"Now if I may at last be allowed to speak," Uncle Edgar said mildly. "First, George had nothing to do with Hamish Barlow's bags. He hadn't furtively disposed of a body—forgive me, Fanny, but that is what you intended to suggest—and then tried to dispose of the evidence. No, it was I who put the bags in the attic room."

"You, Uncle Edgar!"

Uncle Edgar smiled, as if he were enjoying the effect of his revelation.

"Yes, I. At the dead of night and like a criminal. But my intentions were innocent, I assure you. It was merely to stop gossip among the servants. The wretched fellow, in his hasty departure, promised to let me know where to have his bags sent, but he never did so. So I merely had them put out of sight, pending hearing from him."

"You mean he's never let you have a word!" Sir Giles said in disbelief.

"Well, he had a broken heart, so I suppose we must forgive him. And he did have an overcoat, Fanny. He would have arrived in London, or wherever he went, quite respectably. Also, he was a man of means, you know. A little lost luggage would scarcely worry him. These fellows seem to make their fortunes in the East, Sir Giles."

"But your brother failed to, I understand?"

"Ah, Oliver. My brother, I am sorry to say, was always the exception to the rule. But there's your little mystery explained, Fanny. You see, there was no need to exercise your very fertile imagination over it. You and that child Olivia are a pair. Now Amelia may be a little flighty, but she has a sensible head on her shoulders. None of these melodramas for Amelia, thank heaven."

"But where *is* Mr Barlow, Uncle Edgar?"

"Oh, forget the man. It was you who sent him packing. If you must know, I wrote to the shipping company enquiring for his whereabouts, and they replied that they thought he had decided to travel back to China overland. Adventurous fellow. I suppose it's as good a way as any of getting over a broken heart."

Uncle Edgar stood up. "Can I offer you a little brandy, Sir Giles?"

"No, thank you. I must be getting on my way. I thought it only fair to warn you about this other matter in case the police should call."

"Thanks, my dear fellow. Very good of you. But you can put that poppycock about my son out of your head. What on earth was the Chinese woman to him? I don't believe he'd ever spoken to her. She was only a servant, you know."

Fanny couldn't help lingering after Sir Giles had gone. At the risk of completely offending her uncle she had to say, "I don't believe a word of what you said, Uncle Edgar!"

His eyes narrowed, and became a foggy unfathomable grey.

"So?"

"No, I believe you made it all up to protect George. And that you're just as afraid as I am."

She clenched her hands. She could hardly put into words her final fear.

"Mr Barlow is still here, Uncle Edgar. I know."

Chapter 24

NOLLY and Marcus were in Lady Arabella's sitting room where Nolly was painstakingly finishing her sampler. They were pleased to see Fanny come in, but too occupied to pay much attention to her. Fanny sat quietly beside Lady Arabella on the other side of the room. The high back of the sofa separated them from the children. She didn't want to talk, or even to think, but neither of these things could be escaped.

She should have asked Uncle Edgar to show her the letter from the shipping company saying that Mr Barlow was on his way by overland route to China. But Uncle Edgar would merely have said he couldn't lay his hands on it. Fanny was quite certain that no such letter existed.

"The child has the wrong text on her sampler," Lady Arabella said suddenly. "It should have been one about charity."

Fanny kept her voice low so that the children sitting in the window getting the last light of the day wouldn't hear.

"Great-aunt Arabella, I couldn't agree to marry George."

"No. You are too selfish for sacrifices. Or charity. Not that marrying George would have constituted either. Humour him and you'd have found a kind considerate husband."

"I don't want a husband who has to be humoured all the time," Fanny said, with asperity.

Lady Arabella gave a derisive laugh.

"H'mm. You've a lot to learn, my girl. What do you think every wife has to do?"

"But not to be humoured like a child," Fanny persisted. "George is quite childish most of the time. And when he isn't he—"

"He what?" Lady Arabella's eyes were stony.

"He's frightening, Great-aunt Arabella. I think he's dangerous."

"Fiddlesticks! You only have to know how to manage him. I hadn't noticed you being particularly quailed by anyone before. I had thought you a young woman of remarkable spirit." Lady Arabella was stroking Ludwig on her lap. His fur crackled. He stretched sensuously and showed his claws. "I am very disappointed," said Lady Arabella. "But you will see reason eventually. You will marry George and have a child and become a contented woman."

"I won't marry a mur—" Fanny stopped abruptly, remembering the children.

Lady Arabella's eyes flickered. She gave no other sign of having understood what Fanny had been about to say.

"Why do you all want me to marry against my wishes?" Fanny went on. "But you will forgive me, Great-aunt Arabella, just as Uncle Edgar forgave me about Mr Barlow."

"I am a great deal stronger than your uncle," said the old lady. "Also, I am not a forgiver. I love George dearly, more than any other person in the world. I shall see that he gets what he wants. I have ways."

"You may have ways of intimidating other people, but not me!"

"You, a young dependent creature with no future," said Lady Arabella cruelly. "You must learn to know yourself, Fanny. And life. My daughter had to marry against her wishes. Almost all women do. You will see."

Fanny was at last goaded into saying, "But hasn't Uncle Edgar told you about Sir Giles Mowatt's visit? Don't you know the police may re-open the case about Ching Mei?" She was whispering now, her eyes warily on the children in the window. "And if they do—if they do, Great-aunt Arabella—I shall tell them how I met George in the garden that night, how—" She pressed her hands to her face, shuddering uncontrollably. "Mr Barlow has disappeared, too," she said. "I don't need to remind you of George's—insane jealousy."

Lady Arabella's face was old, older than Fanny had ever imagined it could look.

"There must be an investigation," Fanny insisted.

Lady Arabella straightened herself.

"Nonsense! Nonsense! George is as innocent as the day he was born."

"Only because he is mentally irresponsible—"

Marcus suddenly came running across the room.

"Cousin Fanny! Look what Great-aunt Arabella found for me. You turn it upside down and all the leaves fall."

It was a glass kaleidoscope filled with a shower of autumn leaves. When they had fallen, in their pretty amber pattern, to the bottom, they lay in a heap round a minature dead tree. They stirred some obscure memory in Fanny's mind.

"It's pretty," she said to Marcus. "It's like the story of the Babes in the Wood. Do you remember how they covered themselves with leaves?"

The smell of wet dead leaves recently stirred . . .

"Oh, it's too dark!" Nolly cried exasperatedly. "Why doesn't somebody bring the lamps? Cousin Fanny, I'm tired. I want to sit in your lap. What are you and Great-aunt Arabella talking about?"

There was a tap at the door and Amelia came bursting in.

"Is this where you all are? Fanny, why didn't you dress up after all? Dora came in looking as if she'd seen a ghost. But I hadn't time to find out what was wrong. I had to be with Mamma. She's terribly upset. Do you know that just now Papa has been saying George may have to be put—"

"Amelia!" said Lady Arabella in a voice of thunder.

Amelia, for once, was not intimidated by her grandmother's anger. Her words were tumbling over themselves as usual, but now Fanny noticed there was a look of intolerable excitement in her eyes.

"Hasn't Papa told you about Sir Giles' visit? Don't you know that poor escaped prisoner was miles from here that night?"

"Hearsay!" declared Lady Arabella contemptuously. "We won't discuss this in front of the children, if you please, Amelia. You ought to have more sense. And must we sit in the dark? Fanny, ring for lights. And take the children to the nursery. Wait! Before they go I have a gift for Nolly."

"Me, too," cried Marcus.

"No, greedy. You have the kaleidoscope which you may keep. Nolly is to have my pincushion. The one I cherish particularly."

Nolly's eyes opened wide.

"But, Great-aunt Arabella, you don't let anyone touch it."

454

"I will let you touch it."

Nolly's nose wrinkled in distaste.

"It's only an old thing. I don't care for it."

"Of course it's an old thing. It's an antique. It belonged to my grandmother, and perhaps to her grandmother before her. It has held the pins used to make gowns for the Court of Charles the Second. Now do you call it merely an old thing in that rude voice?"

"I still don't care for it," Nolly muttered, but she took the fat faded pincushion in her hand and went off with it to the nursery.

When Marcus boasted that he had the best present she hissed, "I will stick a hundred pins in you! Needles, too!"

Before Fanny could follow the children Lady Arabella called to her peremptorily, "Fanny! Help me downstairs. I must see your uncle."

Amelia, deprived of her audience, cried with strange desperation, "Don't leave me alone! I'm afraid." She gave a ghost of her old happy giggle, "Of I don't know what."

Her grandmother's eyes slowly went over her, from head to foot.

"That's a pity," she said at last. "That you should be afraid of your own brother. Fanny!"

The old lady was heavy on Fanny's arm. She had an odour of lavender water and wool, a familiar odour that in the past had represented some security. Lady Arabella's broad lap which welcomed children had been all the mothering Fanny had known. It was impossible to think of her as too implacable an enemy. She was merely indulging in her favourite game of intimidation.

"He'll be in the library," said Lady Arabella, panting slightly. "Don't come in. Leave us alone."

Her chair was at the bottom of the stairs in its usual place. Lady Arabella got into it and rapidly wheeled herself across the hall. She disappeared into the library and the door closed, but not completely, behind her.

"Fanny!" came Amelia's voice from the top of the stairs. "Why should I be afraid of George? What's Grandmamma got in her head?"

Fanny ignored her. There were no servants about. The hall was empty. She crossed it softly, and stood with her ear against the chink of light from the library, listening.

But only for a moment. She had to move away quickly into

455

the shadows beneath the stairs for hurried steps were approaching. Uncle Edgar's voice was raised in agitation.

"Thank God, Mamma! I was just coming for you. One of the servants has seen George down at the lake. He's behaving oddly. Walking up and down, in a distraught way."

"He's not going to drown himself!" Lady Arabella cried.

"I don't know. What with the disappointment about Fanny this morning and the state of his damaged mind—If anyone can stop him, you can."

"Fanny can. He loves her."

The door of the library had opened and Lady Arabella, wheeling her chair furiously, had appeared, followed by Uncle Edgar.

He was saying in a low hurried voice, "No. The sight of her may send him over the edge. Poor fellow! Let me push you, Mamma. Quietly. We don't want all the servants rushing down, and a scandal. You and I can handle this. I expect the truth is he's taken a little too much to drink."

They had almost reached the big oak door with its heavy fastenings. Fanny never knew what made her run forward.

"Great-aunt Arabella! Don't go!"

The two stopped, turning startled heads.

"Don't go!" Fanny cried again. She was, quite irrationally, remembering the kaleidoscope in Marcus's hands, with its little flurry of leaves settling, settling. And Hamish Barlow saying coldly and finally, "Your uncle will never forgive you . . ." It was Great-aunt Arabella who was the person who didn't forgive, not Uncle Edgar . . . And perhaps poor distraught George really was hesitating on the edge of the lake, trying to make up his mind to plunge into the blackness and the iciness.

Amelia was flying down the stairs.

"What's happening? Where is Papa taking Grandmamma at this hour?"

"Great-aunt Arabella, don't you remember? The cushion. The fall you had. It's dark outside. Your chair runs away down the slope . . ."

Fanny was aghast at what she had said. The words had come compulsively, without coherent thought. But Lady Arabella was turning her chair round, and slowly getting out of it. When Uncle Edgar put out his hand to assist her she pushed it away.

"No, Edgar, I can manage alone. Fanny! Come here at once. What is in your head?"

Nolly's little Chinese doll tossed negligently on her bed, Fanny was thinking, the dead bird in the cage, the cancelled trip to London, Uncle Edgar's insistence that she signed her will.

"You're not signing your death sentence," he had said to the two maids . . .

"Nothing that makes sense," she said. "But let us all go down to the lake and find George. *All* of us. Amelia! Barker, Hannah and Lizzie and cook! Barker will push your chair, Great-aunt Arabella."

Her hand was on the bell rope.

"Fanny! Leave that alone!" Uncle Edgar ordered. His voice went soft. "You interfering creature! You have defied me long enough. There's a limit—" But before he could finish what he was saying, and before Fanny could realise the fury in his face someone rapped on the door, lifting the heavy knocker and letting the sound thud through the house.

"George!" Lady Arabella gasped thankfully.

Barker appeared, looked surprised at the gathering in the hall, and retired discreetly, as Uncle Edgar himself opened the heavy door and saw the light shine on the tall figure without.

"Marsh!" he exclaimed. He recovered himself quickly, stepping back for Adam Marsh to come in. "I wasn't aware you were expected. Did my wife—Amelia, perhaps—"

Amelia had made a sound of pleasure, but it was Fanny who ran forward, whose feet, acting as compulsively as previously her tongue had, carried her straight to Adam Marsh's arms.

"Fanny!" ejaculated Lady Arabella.

"Fanny!" shrieked Amelia. "How could you?"

Fanny's face was pressed hard into Adam's bosom, her waist was likely to be crushed by the strength of his grip. The pain was ecstasy, she wanted to suffer it forever.

"You went away without telling me!" she said furiously. "I rode over. There was no one there."

"It was urgent," said Adam. "I couldn't help it. But I got back in time for your birthday."

"Back from where?"

He pushed her away.

"From London, of course. And I brought you a present."

"Ah!" said Lady Arabella icily. "So now Fanny, your behaviour becomes clear. How long has this intrigue been going on? And don't stand there, the two of you, as if you were on the moon. Mr

Marsh, we are suffering the most intense anxiety as to the whereabouts of George, and you burst in, uninvited, full of your private
affairs!"

Adam bowed with the greatest courtesy.

"Lady Arabella, forgive me! I was carried away. And if you're
worrying about George, he is at present drinking in the village
inn. Or was, not half an hour since. I imagine he'll be there for
some time yet."

"So!" The old lady had collapsed back into her chair. Her chin
was on her breast. Fanny knelt quickly beside her, but in a moment she was waved vigorously away. Lady Arabella's chin was
up, her eyes as cold as the lake water on a grey day. Nevertheless,
her voice was almost grotesquely gay.

"Edgar, we will have things to talk of later. But not in front of
these young people. I suggest you sit down, Amelia, and try not to
indulge in anything as futile as an attack of the vapours. Mr
Marsh, it seems, simply has a birthday gift for Fanny. A charming
sentiment. Perhaps we may all be permitted to look at it."

"Certainly," said Adam. He handed Fanny a small jeweller's
box of red morocco. "You might be interested to hear, Mr Davenport, that I patronised your friend, Mr Solomon. He has an interesting collection in that extraordinarily dark shop of his, hasn't
he?"

Before Uncle Edgar could reply Aunt Louisa came hurrying
downstairs, exclaiming in her petulant voice, "Is this where everyone is? Fanny, Dora finds it impossible to control those children.
You'd better go up—oh, Mr Marsh, we weren't expecting you.
Did I hear the name Solomon? Surely you haven't been buying
diamonds from him!"

"Louisa, be quiet!" Hastily Uncle Edgar tried to smooth over
his anger. "We are all bursting with curiosity to see Mr Marsh's
gift. Open it, Fanny."

Fanny knew it wasn't a real gift. She knew it was being made
like this, publicly, for a purpose. As Adam's eyes reassured her,
she pressed the catch and the little box sprang open.

She almost dropped it.

"But no! They're Nolly's. The green ear-rings!"

"Emeralds," said Adam casually, as if he might have been
mentioning green bottle glass. "And they're yours now, Fanny. I
bought them. You may, of course, like to give them to Nolly at
some future date."

"What right have you, Mr Marsh, to stick your nose into my affairs like this?" Uncle Edgar demanded stiffly. "It seems to me like damned inquisitive impertinence. And I don't apologise for my language. I am within my rights, as my brother's trustee, in disposing of his property as I think fit."

"And I within mine for buying property legally for sale," Adam replied. "Your brother must have done better than you expected him to do in China, Mr Davenport. Weren't you a little hasty in labelling him a failure? Could it be that you had always disliked him? Perhaps envied his popularity? I know how a prejudice will arise. But you shouldn't have assumed he died penniless."

Uncle Edgar's brows rose in angry astonishment at Adam's attack.

"I assumed nothing of the kind."

"I think you did at first. And you made no statement to correct that impression when you made that rather momentous discovery."

Aunt Louisa started forward.

"Edgar, do you mean that bag of green stones, the things the children called their marbles, were emeralds! Why, you told me they were some sort of inferior jade."

"A fortune," said Adam softly. "Your wastrel brother, Mr Davenport, was making sure of his children's future after all."

Aunt Louisa pointed a trembling finger.

"But you lied to me, Edgar! You must have stolen those jewels!"

Strangely, her words gave back to Uncle Edgar his poise. He thrust his fingers into the pockets of his elegant flowered waistcoat with an air of negligent ease.

"Not stole, my dear wife. Merely invested. Mr Marsh, who seems to have a passion for secret investigation, may care to inspect my investments. I would remind him again that I am legally the children's guardian, and perfectly within my rights to dispose of property. Mr Barlow would bear me out. We talked of this at length."

"But could it be," said Adam, in his deceptively soft voice, "that there was a conspiracy between you and Mr Barlow? Unlucky fellow that he was."

"Unlucky?"

"I understand the bargaining point was your niece Fanny. He

459

was to take her off to China, and nothing more would be said about the children's assets. Am I right?"

"Adam! Adam!" Fanny cried, unable to be silent any longer. "Mr Barlow's bags are still here. We found them today. I'm so afraid—"

Adam's grip on her fingers was remarkably soothing. Almost in a moment her terror quietened. She could even think of that pile of autumn leaves without such great distress.

"You think the poor fellow is still here? Perhaps he may be. Wild pigs can be destructive, can't they, Mr Davenport?"

Uncle Edgar stared at him, his pale eyes expressionless. Adam went on, "A man buried not very skilfully, and in evening dress, could easily seem like a large black bird to a child, if a wild pig had previously investigated the grave and some part of the body, perhaps an arm, protruded. You followed the children that day, didn't you, Mr Davenport? And made some quick repairs. I expect you made a much more thorough job later in the night. But I have taken the liberty of asking the police to investigate. They're in the copse now, with lanterns."

He looked at the horrified women, and said, "I apologise for the grisly nature of this conversation. But it isn't really as distressing as a hunt for a live prisoner. A man, a human being, hunted like an animal. And conveniently at hand when the little Chinese woman, who knew too much about the wealth of her charges, was lured down to the lake, looking for a doll that had already been safely secreted."

"And encountered a desperate man on the run," Uncle Edgar said, speaking at last his well-rehearsed statement. It had been said to the police and the coroner many times.

"Did she?"

"Of course. Oh, there's recently some hearsay evidence against it, but—"

"Papa!" That was, surprisingly, Amelia. White-faced, with brilliantly shining eyes, she faced her father. "It isn't true about the prisoner. You know it isn't. And so do I!"

There was all the usual indulgence in Uncle Edgar's voice as he answered his daughter.

"Your kind heart does you credit, my dear, but you know nothing whatever of this. Kindly stay silent."

Amelia's head was up, her face strangely mature.

"I do know something about it, Papa. I must speak. The prisoner was here the night after Ching Mei's death. The next night! He told me he had come from Okehampton, miles away. I gave him food. Cook will tell you. She wonders—" Amelia's voice trembled in a travesty of her light-hearted giggle, "—where my appetite has vanished to lately. I don't want sandwiches and slices of fruit cake after dinner any more. But the prisoner wasn't here the night Ching Mei died, Papa. I know."

Uncle Edgar's eyes went from one to another. He seemed to come, regretfully, to a long-expected decision.

"Then I am afraid the police will have to interview my son."

Aunt Louisa made a violent movement.

"Edgar! How dare you! Putting the blame on your innocent son!"

The eyes of husband and wife were locked. Twenty-five years of marriage culminated in that moment of Aunt Louisa's bitter disillusionment, no longer hidden, and Uncle Edgar's aggressive dislike.

Yet Uncle Edgar spoke quite quietly and gently.

"It's something we can no longer make a secret of, my dear. George isn't safe. The police should also be told about his hatred for Hamish Barlow." He threw out his hands. "I hate to disappoint you, Marsh, but I myself am entirely innocent. Your assumptions are fantastic. I merely sold some jewels and invested the proceeds on behalf of my nephew and niece. And may I add I find your whole manner and actions extremely offensive."

"But there is another thing," said Adam insistently. "I didn't travel alone from London. I persuaded a very old gentleman to travel with me. He's staying at the inn in the village at present. He needed to rest. But he will be calling on Fanny tomorrow. He has some extremely interesting and vital information for her. His name, I scarcely need to tell you, is Timothy Craike."

Chapter 25

THAT was when the distintegration of the man who, with his jokes, his whimsicalities, his naïve pleasure in himself, his vanity, his desire for public esteem, and his autocratic will, as befitted the master of the house, began.

He sat down very slowly in one of the carved hall chairs. His chubby hands were fiddling restlessly with his watch chain. His jowls had dropped, his face had grown thinner and lost its ruddy colour. His eyes were very tired.

"What an extraordinarily interfering young man you are," he said to Adam, almost mildly. "So now you know everything, and I observe you are quick to have an eye for an heiress into the bargain. All the summer, it was my poor little Amelia, with her promise of a substantial dowry. But your affections seem to be easily transferable."

"My affections," Adam said quietly, "have always been with Fanny, as I think she knows. To my great regret I have had to hurt her and puzzle her occasionally. I also can't apologise sufficiently to Amelia for misleading her so wilfully. But she was too useful to my purpose. She made me welcome here. She talked a great deal, and unwittingly gave me important information. It was she who told me about Fanny's disappointment over not getting to London to see this Mr Craike who had written to her. It was my first real clue about Fanny's affairs. I had waited all summer for it. But I am deeply sorry it had to be discovered at the risk of hurting Amelia." He turned to Amelia, holding out his hand. "Can you forgive me?"

Amelia promptly burst into tears, and ran to her mother. Aunt Louisa said in a strangled voice, "I don't understand one word that has been said. Fanny can't be an heiress! Why have I never been told? Is this another of my husband's machinations?"

"But it isn't true!" whispered Fanny incredulously.

Her eyes were caught by Lady Arabella's expression. It was unreadable. Her eyelids drooped until her eyes were mere slits. But it seemed as if she might be hiding triumph. Almost, as if she might have been waiting for this hour.

"Adam?" said Fanny urgently. "What has Mr Craike to tell me? Have I got a fortune, also in jewels? Was the sapphire pendant really my own all the time?"

It was at that moment that there was a flurry at the top of the stairs. Dora was crying helplessly, "Miss Nolly! Come back at once. Oh, I declare!" But her words were useless, for Nolly was flying down the stairs in her nightgown.

"Cousin Fanny! Cousin Fanny!"

Fanny started towards her. "What is it? Nothing's happened to frighten you—"

But it was not fright, she saw at once, that possessed Nolly. The little face was illuminated with excitement, and had its moment of blazing prettiness.

"Cousin Fanny, this dear little pincushion Great-aunt Arabella gave me opens! Look, the top comes off and makes the sweetest little box. I shall keep my jewels in it."

"Is that all?" said Fanny. "Does it please you so much?"

"Yes, it does. And I found this letter in it. I think it's about you. See, here is your name. F-a-n-n-y."

Suddenly and rather frighteningly Lady Arabella began to laugh.

"Ah, Edgar! You searched so hard. And such a simple hiding place. I used to keep my love letters there when I was very young. I baffled you, didn't I? And I wasn't bluffing about that letter. But it would never have been discovered if I hadn't realized you would kill for it." Her mirth had left her. Her eyes were fully open now and full of implacable revenge. "Fanny, send that child upstairs!"

"Yes, Nolly. Run up to Dora."

"But don't you think the little pincushion is delightful?"

"I do. And tomorrow we'll find some treasures to keep in it. Run along."

Nolly went reluctantly and Lady Arabella continued her conversation as if she hadn't interrupted it.

"I decided to dismiss that clumsy accident you arranged for me, Edgar. Just the threat of a schoolboy, I thought. Give her a fright and who knows, the old lady might have a stroke. But to-day, this evening, everything has changed. I would have had another accident down at the lake, wouldn't I? Just a feeble old woman tripping in the dark. Fanny knew. I underestimated you, Edgar. I even despised you. Now I must admire your—how shall I put it—diabolical simplicity. But I don't forgive it. You would have blamed your son. I share my daughter's feelings for you at this moment. I hope, Edgar," she finished, slowly and distinctly, "that you hang."

Uncle Edgar made no attempt to defend himself. He sat with his head slumped, his eyes far-off, almost as if he were in a dream.

Then he said, "I am very tired. It has all been a great strain for too long."

Looking at him, Fanny had the impression of reading him as if his life were written in his face—the over-sensitive pompous young man laughed at by the girl he loved, looked down on by his wife and mother-in-law, scorned by his gay reckless brother as dull, given only the qualities of steadiness and reliability by relatives who found him useful—no wonder he had had to puff himself up into a turkeycock of importance, seeking and finding the wherewithal for his family, his household, his village and the whole community to revolve round him.

"Uncle Edgar—" she began.

Uncle Edgar lifted his extinguished eyes.

"No, child. Don't come near me. I would have killed you, too. Don't you realise that? I could never have let you find out that I had spent your capital and taken possession of your property. Yes, you would have died. A fall off the train, I thought, on a jour-ney to London. Or perhaps a skating accident on the lake. There were so many possibilities."

"Edgar!" Aunt Louisa had difficulty in speaking. Her face was so alarmingly flushed that it seemed she would have a seizure. "Do you mean to say that Darkwater, everything, belongs to Fanny!"

"Completely, my dear. It is a pity you were such an avaricious woman. Always wanting, wanting, wanting."

"I had to have something!" Aunt Louisa cried thickly.

"You had me. And I had never told you about Marianne—always there behind your eyelids. You didn't know my private

464

ghost. Fanny sometimes reminds me of Marianne. That long white throat." He curved his strong thick fingers thoughtfully. "It's a matter of love and hate. You can kiss and kill—yes, almost simultaneously. But there it was. I comforted myself by marrying an earl's granddaughter and acquiring property. I bought diamonds for my wife. My son had a commission in a famous regiment and my daughter a dowry. But finally Fanny's fortune was not sufficient for the needs of my extravagant family. I hardly knew where to turn when the second plum fell in my lap. My brother's orphaned children, and a bag of uncut emeralds. How was that for luck? And the intricate plotting, the timing, the manipulating of people. The stimulation of it! But of course one's luck couldn't last forever. Time runs out."

"Edgar, you are mad!" cried Aunt Louisa, horrified.

The shrunken man, with his enormous calm, said, "Don't let those men you brought knock all the copse down, Marsh. I can take them to the exact spot. I agree that I did a careless job on that. I never realised the fellow would be so heavy. I had to risk leaving the body concealed by leaves and do the burying the next night when I could wear suitable clothes. Even so, it was quite a task getting garden debris cleaned off myself so as to present myself back in the ballroom. Luckily there was no blood. I have strong hands. And a man taken by surprise—I had asked him to step outside to discuss some business—has little defence. I must have a discussion with Sir Giles about these spontaneous crimes. They seem to be the most successful. Haphazard, but unsuspected." Uncle Edgar seemed almost to relish re-living the success of his macabre tactics. "Barlow was an unlikeable fellow, anyway. I can't think how my brother trusted him. Well, that's how it was. And now," he moved wearily, "I suppose I had better be getting along."

"Where are you going, Edgar?" Aunt Louisa cried.

"To the police, naturally. Marsh will perhaps accompany me, since he has already assumed so much responsibility. One knows when the game is over. One must behave with dignity. Time—oh, speaking of time, Fanny," he had taken the large gold watch, as yellow as a pumpkin, from his pocket, "give this to Marcus in the morning. The little fellow was always fascinated by it."

He wound it absently, and the tiny delicate tune hung in the air, as frail as a dream.

"Don't fret, Louisa." Uncle Edgar spoke with a shadow of his old pompousness. "I haven't wasted my time with a petty crime. The case will be a *cause célèbre*, of course. And it isn't as if we have a son able to inherit the estate. Poor George is finished. We both know it." He stood a moment surveying his wife's highly-coloured and tear-stained face dispassionately. "It's a great relief to tell you my true feelings at last. I trust you to see that Amelia's life isn't ruined by an unfortunate marriage."

"Papa!" cried Amelia in a heartbroken voice.

"My little girl—"

But Lady Arabella dismissed the one emotional moment with an authoritative movement of her hand.

"Let him go, Amelia. He is your father, but he is a monster."

Something made Fanny re-wind the watch she was holding and listen again to the tinkling tune. The shortish stout figure going out through the door into the hall was nothing without his watch, she realised. How strange. He had simply diminished away.

Chapter 26

So there it was at last, the voice of her father speaking. Fanny re-read the much-creased letter that had been concealed in Lady Arabella's pincushion.

"Dear Uncle Leonard,

How can I express my gratitude for your intention to leave me your property and capital. I fear my ownership will be of short duration for I am a dying man with perhaps one, perhaps two years to live, but if only you could know how you have eased my mind. Now I can die confident that my daughter Francesca is well provided for. She is only a baby who looks like her mother, but is a true Davenport in spirit. I am making my cousin Edgar, a man of the highest integrity, her guardian . . ."

It was quite impossible to sleep. At some time in the night, she wasn't sure how late, Fanny got up and tiptoed down the dark passages to Lady Arabella's rooms.

As she had guessed, a night light was burning in the bedroom. She tapped, and went in swiftly.

"Great-aunt Arabella? I thought you wouldn't be asleep!"

The old lady was propped up with pillows. She had been read-ing her large shabby Bible. She closed it, her finger holding the place she had been reading.

"Naturally I wouldn't. Sleep is for the innocent. What do you want?"

"You were never really my enemy, were you?"

"And what makes you think I am turning soft in my old age? Of course I was your enemy, until I realised I was wasting my time. Your will was stronger than mine. Which makes it formidable. I pity the man who marries you."

"I would like to think kindly of you," Fanny said earnestly. "I know you would have sacrificed me for George, but I can understand that because you loved him. And you did, in the end, give Nolly the pincushion so I would find Papa's letter. I want to thank you eternally for that." She looked very young, with her black hair tumbling over her shoulders, and tears on her lashes.

Lady Arabella said impatiently, "Pshaw! You and your extravagant emotion. You thank me eternally for something I should have done months ago. It could have saved lives. Do you realise that? I am a wicked old woman. But I'd do the same again." Her husky voice broke between a sob and a chuckle. "My son-in-law should have made more of a study of the human mind. He didn't even bother to discover that his great-uncle Leonard loved poetry and that his favourite poet was Chaucer. A well-worn volume of the Canterbury Tales was marked at the place where the old man had stopped reading with your father's letter. I thought such carelessness on your Uncle Edgar's part deserved a little punishment. I always did hate the pompous little man, anyway. Daring to marry my daughter! But he was George's father, and—I apoligise to you, Fanny—at that time that was far more important than demanding justice for you. Anyway," she said irritably, "you were to marry George and be mistress here, and it would all have come to the same thing."

"Uncle Edgar must always have wanted me to die," said Fanny sadly. "Do you remember the day I fell out of the boat? Perhaps he hoped I had inherited my father's delicate constitution, and would catch a chill and go into a decline. But I suppose he really thought it was tidier to let me come of age and make my will, almost as if he enjoyed the years of anticipation." She buried her face in her hands, shuddering. "It's all so horrible. How can a man's ambitions and ego turn his mind so? He would have killed, and killed again."

"They say it's easy after the first time," the old lady said. "I believe it even grows on one, like gambling, or drinking. And one doesn't look for a criminal where none is suspected, as your uncle pointed out. Besides, no one cared about the Chinese woman, no one was unduly concerned about that detestable fox Barlow. My death would have been an unfortunate accident caused by age and senility. Senility, ho!"

468

"And mine?" Fanny whispered.

For a moment the old lady's hand rested on her head.

"That was a habit of thought in your uncle's mind, a task that must one day be done. He would blame that wretched girl who once jilted him, and my daughter for her demands and her extravagances, caused, as he very well knew, by discontent in her emotional life. He would have retained a singularly innocent mind. But it didn't happen. Let us not talk of it. Here, sit beside me, and we'll read together."

Her stubby finger found the place. She began to read, "They are like chaff which the wind scattereth away . . . No sugar plums, tonight," she said. "George was always the one who liked them best." Her voice was full of desolation.

George, very flushed and unsteady, had come in late the previous evening, and gone straight to his room. In the morning he came downstairs dressed in the uniform of an officer of the 27th Lancers. He was shouting for his horse to be brought to the door. It seemed dangerous to oppose him, so the groom brought the magnificent animal, his father's last gift to him, to the door, and George mounted, and sat still in the saddle for a moment, very young and heroic and incredibly handsome. Then he shouted wildly, "I can smell the cannon smoke. Good-bye, all!" and with his superb horsemanship, he galloped madly away, the sun gleaming on his helmet, his white plumes streaming. When he came back hours later his horse was exhausted, and he was dazed and muttering something about the Cossacks and the deadly fire of the cannon.

"You realise, Louisa," Lady Arabella said with great gentleness, "that he will have to go away for a time, at least. We must find a suitable hospital. Come, George. Come Georgie, my lamb. Retreat has sounded."

Aunt Louisa was a ghost of herself, listening to everything her mother said, and agreeing mechanically. Yes, she would go and live in the Dower House on the Dalston estate, although it was small and dark and inconvenient. It was no place for a young girl just beginning life, but with the change in Amelia's fortunes she must be thankful for a place to which to retreat until some of the terrible scandal had blown over.

It was then that Amelia surprised everyone.

"No, Mamma. I'm not coming with you."

"And what, pray, are you planning to do? Live on Fanny's charity?"

"Aunt Louisa, please!" Fanny protested. "I have tried to tell you all morning how welcome—"

Amelia didn't let her finish. She lifted her round young chin, unexpectedly stubborn, and said that she had quite made up her mind, she was going to find a position as lady's maid with some nice family going to Australia.

"I know I can't sew very well," she said, "and I know almost nothing about starching and ironing. But Hannah is going to teach me, and I can learn quickly if I set my mind to it. I shall be quite a success."

Aunt Louisa was completely shocked.

"Australia! Are you mad? There's no need to go to the other side of the world. I know your father's case will be a terrible scandal, but people soon forget. There are plenty of young men who will admire you for yourself."

Her expression, overfond and distraught, did not deter Amelia.

"Yes, Mamma. I know one of those men already. But he is now in Australia, I believe, hoping to make his fortune in the gold-fields. I am going out to find him."

"Amelia!" Fanny exclaimed. "You can't mean the escaped prisoner! But you only talked to him for a moment."

Amelia's eyes were shining brilliantly. There was nothing of the plump immature girl left about her. She was a woman, with a proud confidence that at that moment made her beautiful.

"It wasn't just a passing thing. It was more. It was like—you might almost say like a moment in eternity. I told myself I was foolish and romantic. I tried to forget about him and fall in love with Adam. I thought I had. But I hadn't. I can't forget this man."

Fanny took her hand.

"I believe I see now what he saw. I believe you will find him. I pray that you do."

"I will," said Amelia.

"And anyway," Amelia had added after that conversation, "who is Adam Marsh?"

"I don't know," said Fanny. (But I know how his heart feels beating against my cheek . . .)

"Papa was right when he said he was interfering and inquisitive. Is he a fortune-hunter? Or is he a policeman in plain

470

clothes? Would you marry a policeman, Fanny?" Amelia asked, in her old inquisitive way.

"I would marry Adam whoever he was. If ever he asks me," she added under her breath.

For the first time the house oppressed Fanny. She dressed the children in their outdoor things and said they were all going for a walk. Marcus could bring his hoop if he wished, but Nolly was to pay attention to everything Fanny told her. She was to learn more about English birds.

She didn't miss the flicker of fear in Nolly's eyes, and went on calmly, "You are deplorably ignorant about them, my love. You scarcely know a robin from a crow. We'll take some crumbs to feed them."

"Put our hands on their beaks!" Nolly gasped. "Touch their feathers!"

"After weeks of patience you may perhaps entice one of them to eat out of your hand. You must remember that they're much more frightened of you than you are of them."

Nolly looked extremely sceptical.

"How can they be? They have beaks and claws."

But she allowed herself to be buttoned into her warm cape and gaiters and Fanny, half way through the task, thought how absurd this was. She was the mistress and doing the nursemaid's work.

"And I always will," she said aloud.

"Always will what? Cousin Fanny, why are you smiling?"

"I don't know. Perhaps I was thinking how happy I am to have you and Marcus."

Nolly made her usual attempt to scoff.

"Marcus doesn't care for being here. He would rather be in China. But I shall tolerate it—" Nolly's mouth pursed judiciously, "if I learn not to be afraid of birds."

It was a cold windless day, the sun shining from a clear colourless sky. The children raced across the garden, kicking up flurries of leaves fallen in yesterday's gale. Inevitably, their destination was the lake where there might be wild ducks and perhaps a swan.

The water was not dark and sinister today, but the colour of the sky, pale and translucent. The floor of the pavilion was littered with dead leaves. It looked as if it had not been visited for years. The summer tea parties had vanished as completely as the yellow flag irises and the water-lilies from the lake.

Fanny suggested a reward for the first person to see a robin, then forgot to look herself as she became lost in thought. She was so tired, so crushed by the weight of events, and yet so full of a sense of joy which surely she had no right to feel in the midst of tragedy.

"Cousin Fanny! I saw one. In that tree. He flew away. Cousin Fanny, Lizzie's coming down. Don't let her make us go back to the house yet." Nolly's face, healthily pink and happy, looked out from her blue bonnet. "You promised we could feed the birds."

"Miss Fanny!" That was Lizzie, breathless, scarcely knowing yet how to speak to the new mistress. "Mr Marsh has arrived with the old gentleman from London. Barker has put them in the library."

Fanny sprang up. "I will come at once." But in the next instant she saw Adam strolling across the autumn-yellowed grass. She waited, her heart beating too fast, until he came up.

He bowed and said good morning, and added that he hadn't the patience, like Mr Craike, to wait in the library.

Fanny was almost as breathless as Lizzie, but had the presence of mind to say, "Lizzie, ask Barker to be kind enough to pour Mr Craike a glass of Madeira. Mr Marsh and I will be up immediately."

"In fifteen minutes, Lizzie," Adam amended. "Miss Fanny and I have things to discuss."

"Yes, indeed," said Fanny. "Poor Uncle Edgar—poor George. And Amelia planning to go to Australia. Did you know?"

"And you?" said Adam softly. "Are you going to slap my face if I kiss you?"

Fanny strove for composure.

"Mr Marsh, naturally I can't keep those very valuable ear-rings. I realise the gift was a gesture—"

"You said you couldn't keep the Bactrian camel, either. That was mine. The ear-rings were my sister's."

"Your—*sister's!*"

Adam's smile was quizzical, a little amused.

"You shouldn't always have been accusing me of ulterior motives. The explanation is so simple. I merely wanted to observe, incognito, whether my brother-in-law had made a suitable choice of guardian for his children. When I saw you in London my

472

doubts were completely allayed. I knew that if you had the care of the children they would be happy. But I still wanted to make the acquaintance of Edgar Davenport. And when I received the letter from Ching Mei—"

"A letter from Ching Mei!" Fanny had to interrupt. "Nolly said she had written to you and I didn't believe her."

"The letter was written with Nolly's help. I had arranged it with Ching Mei in London. If anything troubled her she was to let me know. Naturally, your uncle taking possession of the children's fortune alarmed her very much."

"Of course," Fanny breathed, remembering the conversation in the Chinese language between Adam and Ching Mei.

"Anyway," he went on, "I came at once, intending to state my business immediately. But you will remember I chanced to meet you in the church. You were so different from the fashionable young lady I had seen in London. You were plainly, even poorly dressed. My curiosity, and, I must admit, my suspicions, were aroused. When I made the discovery that you, too, were a ward of Edgar Davenport I began to wonder. I knew about my niece and nephew's fortune for a great part of it was my sister's. Had you, too, perhaps had one? Meeting your uncle increased my suspicions. He was too hearty, too affable, too apparently generous, a façade, I suspected, that hid the real man. I decided the only way to remain on the scene and make investigations was to go on concealing my identity and cultivate the family, particularly the charming garrulous Amelia. Fortunately your uncle displayed no curiosity at all about the family of the girl his brother had married, or my game would have been up. He shouldn't have so underrated Oliver who was a nice fellow, and who made Anne Marie, whom he met when she travelled with my father on one of his trips to the East, very happy."

"Oh, how glad I am about this!" Fanny cried. "You will be able to talk to Nolly and Marcus about their mother. They will have someone to keep her alive for them."

"More than one person. My Aunt Martha is longing to have them with her at Heronshall. We will apply for their guardianship, Fanny, and bring them up with our own children."

Fanny caught her breath, the colour rising in her cheeks.

"We will live at Darkwater if you wish. It is very lovely. And plenty of lively children about will banish its ghosts, or make them happier ones. But I have a property just as beautiful in the

473

Western Highlands of Scotland. My father used to come back to it after his trips to the East."

"You have—decided all this?"

"Long ago. When I first saw you on the railway station in London. You knew."

"Yes, I knew," said Fanny, and forgot that she had ever doubted it.

"Cousin Fanny! Cousin Fanny!" called the children in their imperious voices.

All at once the windbells were chiming. Or was it the windbells, for no wind stirred. The sound had been remarkably like Ching Mei's high delightful tinkle of laughter.